"I sense agit ...
some out? ...

Arik leaned down and stared Limos in the eyes. "I don't hit girls." It was the wrong thing to say...which was why he said it. Half a second later, he found himself flat on his back, with her flip-flopped foot on his neck.

"I can see up your dress." It wasn't true, but the way her eyes went wide, and she started to sputter...totally worth it. With a yank, he tugged her leg out from under her and twisted so she came down on top of him. She looked so startled that she lay motionless on his chest, mouth open.

God, she was gorgeous. And that mouth...made to make a man beg for mercy. So he kissed her. For a brief, sweet moment, she kissed him back. And then, his world turned upside down. Limos reared back and slammed her fist into his cheek.

"What the hell" he shouted.

"You kissed me!" She backed away so fast she lost her flip-flops.

All around him, the ground began to rumble, and then there were giant, spiny arms punching up out of the dirt. His vision went dark...

"Larissa Ione pulls no punches…The love scenes are scorching hot and grab at your heart with their emotional intensity. Dark moments are written with just the right touch of hope that leaves the reader begging for a happy ending. I couldn't have loved *Passion Unleashed* more and hated for it to end. Raw, gritty, and tremendously passionate…It was awesome!" **—RomanceJunkies.com**

Desire Unchained

"4 Stars! Rising star Ione is back in this latest Demonica novel…Ione has a true gift for imbuing her characters with dark-edged passion…thrilling action and treacherous vengeance…a top-notch read." **—RT Book Reviews**

"A fabulous tale…The story line is fast-paced from the opening sequence…fans will relish a visit to the Ione realm." **—Midwest Book Review**

"Warning! Read at your own risk. Highly addictive." **—FreshFiction.com**

Pleasure Unbound

"Sizzling sensuality, dark wit, and wicked hot demons." **—Lara Adrian, *New York Times* bestselling author**

"What a ride! Dark, sexy, and very intriguing, the book gripped me from start to finish—totally recommended." **—Nalini Singh, *New York Times* bestselling author of *Mine to Possess***

IMMORTAL RIDER

LARISSA IONE

GC

GRAND CENTRAL
PUBLISHING

NEW YORK   BOSTON

Forever
Hachette Book Group
237 Park Avenue
New York, NY 10017
www.HachetteBookGroup.com

Printed in the United States of America

First Edition: December 2011

10 9 8 7 6 5 4

Forever is an imprint of Grand Central Publishing.
The Forever name and logo are trademarks of Hachette Book Group, Inc.

The publisher is not responsible for websites (or their content) that are not owned by the publisher.

ATTENTION CORPORATIONS AND ORGANIZATIONS:
Most HACHETTE BOOK GROUP books are available at quantity discounts with bulk purchase for educational, business, or sales promotional use. For information, please call or write:

Special Markets Department, Hachette Book Group
237 Park Avenue, New York, NY 10017
Telephone: 1-800-222-6747 Fax: 1-800-477-5925

For everyone in the romance community—readers, writers, and publishing professionals—who recently came together to help one of their own, and who continue to put together events that benefit individuals, communities, and even entire countries. You're an amazing group of people, and this Horseman is for you!

Acknowledgments

Huge thanks, as always, to the entire Grand Central Publishing team who worked so hard to get this book onto the shelves, with special thanks to Amy Pierpont and Lauren Plude for all their work and help.

Also, thanks to Cid Tyer for letting me have Rhys to torture a bit. I had a lot of fun!

And finally, a big thank you to Shawna Malone...now we just have to move you to Wisconsin!

Glossary

The Aegis—Society of human warriors dedicated to protecting the world from evil. See: Guardians, Regent, Sigil.

Agimortus—A trigger for the breaking of the Horsemen's Seals. An agimortus can be identified as a symbol engraved or branded upon the host person or object. Three kinds of agimorti have been identified, and may take the form of a person, an object, or an event.

Daemonica—The demon bible and basis for dozens of demon religions. Its prophecies regarding the Apocalypse, should they come to pass, will ensure that the Four Horsemen fight on the side of evil.

Fallen Angel—Believed to be evil by most humans, fallen angels can be grouped into two categories: True Fallen and Unfallen. Unfallen angels have been cast from Heaven and are earthbound, living a life in which they are neither truly good nor truly evil. In this state, they can, rarely, earn their way back into Heaven. Or they can choose to enter Sheoul, the demon realm, in order to complete their fall and become True Fallens, taking their places as demons at Satan's side.

Guardians—Warriors for The Aegis, trained in combat techniques, weapons, and magic. Upon induction into The Aegis, all Guardians are presented with an enchanted piece of jewelry bearing the Aegis shield, which, among other things, allows for night vision and the ability to see through demon invisibility enchantments.

Harrowgate—Vertical portals, invisible to humans, which demons use to travel between locations on Earth and Sheoul. A very few beings can summon their own personal Harrowgates.

Khote—An invisibility spell that allows the caster to move among humans without being seen or, usually, heard.

Marked Sentinel—A human charmed by angels and tasked with protecting a vital artifact. Sentinels are immortal and immune to harm. Only angels (fallen included) can injure or kill a Sentinel. Their existence is a closely guarded secret.

Quantamun—A state of superaccelerated existence on a plane that allows some supernatural beings to travel among humans. Humans, unaware of what moves within their world, appear frozen in time to those inside the quantamun. This differs from the *khote* in that the *khote* operates in real time and is a spell rather than a plane of existence.

Regent—Head(s) of local Aegis cells.

Sheoul—Demon realm. Located deep in the bowels of the earth, accessible only by Harrowgates.

Sheoul-gra—A holding tank for demon souls. The place where demon souls go until they can be reborn or kept in torturous limbo.

Sheoulic—Universal demon language spoken by all, though many species speak their own language.

Sigil—Board of twelve humans known as Elders, who serve as the supreme leaders of The Aegis. Based in Berlin, they oversee all Aegis cells worldwide.

Ter'taceo—Demons who can pass as human, either because their species is naturally human in appearance, or because they can shapeshift into human form.

Watchers—Individuals assigned to keep an eye on the Four Horsemen. As part of the agreement forged during the original negotiations between angels and demons that led to Ares, Reseph, Limos, and Thanatos being cursed to spearhead the Apocalypse, one Watcher is an angel, the other is a fallen angel. Neither Watcher may directly assist any Horseman's efforts to either start or stop Armageddon, but they can lend a hand behind the scenes. Doing so, however, may have them walking a fine line, that, to cross, could prove worse than fatal.

IMMORTAL RIDER

One

Arik Wagner had to hand it to the Four Horsemen of the Apocalypse; they threw one hell of a party.

Well, three of them did, anyway. The fourth, whose name had been Reseph before his Seal broke and he became known as Pestilence, had been lying low since his defeat at the hands of his siblings, Ares, Limos, and Thanatos, a month earlier. The asshole and his demon army was no doubt regrouping, but for now, everyone was breathing a sigh of relief.

Hence, the celebration, which was part celebration for the victory, and part engagement party for Ares and his fiancée, Cara. Everyone who'd survived the battle had been invited to Ares's Greek mansion. Ares had also extended an invitation to the Underworld General staff who had helped Cara when she'd been dying, so the place was crawling with demons.

There were even a couple of angels roaming around.

Reaver, who Arik had already decided was one big tool, was over by the chocolate fountain talking to a sparkly female angel named Gethel, who used to be the Horsemen's good Watcher before Reaver took the job. The Horsemen also had an evil Watcher named Harvester, but she hadn't been invited. Something about her being a world-class bitch who might eat the guests.

Thanatos, the fourth Horseman, bumped into Arik as he dove for a football someone had tossed from across the huge great room.

"Watch it, dickhead," Arik muttered.

"What's the matter, human?" Thanatos punched him in the shoulder with the ball hard enough to make Arik stumble backward. "Ping-Pong more your speed?"

Arik shot Kynan Morgan, an old Army buddy who was now one of the bigwigs in charge of The Aegis, an ancient demon-slaying organization, a *you-ready-to-go-or-what* look, and Ky, who was deep in conversation with Ares, held up his finger. He and Arik had intended to stay no more than ten minutes, since Ky wanted to get home to his wife, Gem, and their new baby. That was more than fine with Arik.

If Arik spent another minute inside with these supernatural, superior asshats, he was going to slit his own throat. Also, if Limos, the drop-dead-gorgeous female Horseman, caught him leering at her one more time, she'd likely slit his throat for him.

She might appear to be the definition of a sorority party girl, but under the skirts, nail polish, and flowers in her hair, she was every bit as dangerous as her brothers.

No one seemed to be paying any attention to him, so he strolled out of the house and into the cool November night air. He'd always liked Greece, had visited a couple of times on military assignments. The food was good, the weather perfect, and the people weren't assholes to Americans. Sure, the Greeks had a high concentration of demons living among them, but some of the oldest countries did. Demons, being extremely long-lived, if not immortal, had a tendency to stay in the places they knew well.

They really weren't all that adventurous. Pussies.

He parked himself on a stone bench overlooking the sea. He could feel the piggy eyes of Ares's Ramreel demon guards on him, but he ignored them and looked up into the heavens. The stars were bright tonight, their lights glittering in the pitch-black sky. He'd spoken to Cara for a few minutes out here when she'd had to usher a hellhound party crasher out of the house, and he'd been impressed with how easily she, as a human, had integrated into the supernatural world. Oh, she'd had trouble at first, describing some truly fucked-up events—Ares had screwed with her memories? Arik would kill someone for that—but she was happy now, all hellhound queen and engaged to a damned legend.

And speaking of legends, he smelled Limos before he heard her; the aroma of coconut drifted toward him on a breeze and made his blood pump a little faster. Coconuts had never turned him on before, but then, the scent had never been attached to a red-hot female with hair the color of the midnight sky, either.

"What are you doing?" Her velvety, feminine voice was so at odds with the warrior he knew she was, and he wondered how she sounded in bed. Did she hold on to her female side, or did she play rough, dominant, letting the fighter in her take over?

"Just needed some fresh air."

"Why?"

Because you were making me crazy. "Just did."

"Wanna fight?"

He blinked. "What?"

She came around in front of him. Her knees touched his, and her floral Hawaiian dress, an intense violet that matched her eyes, swirled around her shapely ankles, flapping at his boots. "I sense agitation in you. Want to let some out? A little hand-to-hand?"

Jesus. Okay, yeah, she might sense some tension in him, but it wasn't because he wanted to draw blood. He wanted to get naked, and the weird thing was, he imagined getting that way with her. She fascinated him with her contradictions, riled him up with her body, and earlier in the night, when he'd seen her helping Ares's servants clean a spill in the kitchen, he'd admired her. She'd gotten down on her hands and knees and scrubbed the floor, and she'd done it with a damned smile.

Of course, he'd smiled too, because the sight of her on her hands and knees? Instant hard-on.

Now, as Limos stood in front of him, things were hardening again at the idea that all he'd have to do would be to fist that dress, hike it up over her hips, and he'd be at eye level with her most private place. Would she let him go down on her? What would she taste like? Did that coconut scent permeate everything? Because he fucking loved coconut.

Somehow, he scrounged up enough self-control to put his hands on her waist and set her aside so he could stand. "I don't want to let anything out." *Except my dick.* She'd probably kill him if she knew what he was thinking.

He started for the house, because he was going to

drag Kynan out of there if he had to, but naturally, Limos would have none of that. These Horsemen seemed to have a huge sense of entitlement.

"Stop!" She grabbed his elbow and swung him around. "I'll let you throw the first punch," she cajoled, with a waggle of raven brows.

He leaned down and stared her in the eyes. "I don't hit girls."

It was the wrong thing to say. Half a second later, he found himself flat on his back, with her flip-flopped foot on his neck.

"See," she said brightly, "that is why I was offering to give you the first throw. At least this time I didn't break your ribs."

"Wow," he rasped. "Do you emasculate all the men, or am I special?"

Her sensual lips curved into an amused smile. "Oh, you're special, but I wouldn't take that as a compliment."

"I can see up your dress." It wasn't true, but he got a kick out of the way her eyes went wide and she started to sputter. He brought his hands up to grasp her ankle, his intention to lift it to give him some room to breathe, but her skin was so soft he ended up just lingering like that.

"What are you doing?" she gasped.

"Nothing." He smoothed his thumb up and down the side of her leg, in the sensitive place where the ankle met the calf. Her muscles were firm, her skin silky, and man, he wanted to slide his hands up higher. But he had her where he wanted her—off guard. Now to take it one step further...

"You," he purred, "are a HILF."

"A what?"

"Horseman I'd like to fuck."

With a yank, he tugged her leg out from under her, and at the same time, he twisted so she came down on top of him, breaking her fall. She looked so startled, so utterly disbelieving that he'd bested her, that she lay motionless on his chest, mouth open, staring at him.

God, she was gorgeous. And that mouth...made to make a man beg for mercy. So he kissed her. Didn't even realize he'd done it until his lips were on hers. He hadn't thought she could be any more shocked, but her eyebrows shot up so far it would have been comical if he hadn't been rocking his head up to put them into a more serious kiss. That was the thing about him—no half-measures. He might not have realized he was kissing her, but once he did? He was taking it as far as she'd let him go.

Command and conquer.

For a brief, sweet moment, she kissed him back. Her lips softened and her tongue met his, hesitantly, as though she wasn't sure what she was doing.

And then his world turned upside down.

Limos reared back, and with what he was pretty sure was all her strength, she slammed her fist into his cheek. Pain spiderwebbed across his face, along every bone, through every tooth. He'd been tasting her, and now he was tasting his own blood.

"What the hell?" he shouted...or at least, he tried to shout. His words were mushy, thanks to his mashed lips, cut tongue and, likely, badly fractured jaw and cheekbone. He heard something more like, "*Nut da bell.*"

"You kissed me!" Eyes wild, she backed away so fast she lost her flip-flops. "Do you know what you've done, you idiot? You're going to pay for kissing me."

Son-of-a—

All around him, the ground began to rumble, and a second later, giant, spiny arms punched up out of the dirt. Hands seized him, a dozen maybe. Agony wrenched through him as his limbs were twisted and pulled, and his skin was shredded.

Consciousness became a fluid thing, something he couldn't quite reach. His vision went dark, but his ears still worked, and before they shut down, he heard Limos's panicked voice, but what she said made no sense.

"Don't say my name, Arik! No matter what they do to you, don't speak my name!"

Limos was utterly frozen, terrified in a way she had never, ever been. And given that she was five thousand years old, that was saying something.

Her brothers and Ares's guests charged out of the house, weapons drawn, and then they skidded to halt.

"Jesus Christ," Kynan shouted. "Arik!"

"Limos, no." Thanatos tugged her against him, stopping her from going after the behemoths that had grabbed Arik and were dragging him down into the earth.

"He kissed me." She said the same thing over and over, her voice a high-pitched, terrified wail.

Wordlessly, Ares produced a small blade, and in one smooth motion, launched it. Limos's first instinct was to stop him, but the knife was already in the air, on a course for Arik's heart.

The whistle of an arrow cut the night, and Ares's dagger shattered. Pestilence, his ice-blue eyes glowing in the light of the moon, stood near the cliff, his bow in hand, a satisfied smile on his face. "You'll thank me later, sis."

Thanatos lunged, and a black, furry blur streaked past them both. Before Hal, Cara's hellhound protector, reached Pestilence, he opened a portable Harrowgate and stepped through it.

He was gone, and when Limos turned back to Arik, he was gone too. The only sign that he'd been there was a smear of blood in the sand.

"What the fuck just happened?" Kynan rounded on Ares. "Why did you try to kill him, you cocksucker?"

Limos couldn't speak. Funny how moments ago she'd been screaming incoherently, but now she couldn't dredge up a single word. Ares, for his part, stayed calm despite the fact that Kynan had called him a cocksucker and was now fisting his shirt and snarling in his face.

"He kissed Limos," Ares said, his voice rough as sandpaper. Maybe he wasn't as calm as she thought. "She isn't allowed to give her affections to a male in any way."

Kynan released Ares to turn his murderous glare on Limos. "Explain."

There were still no words. None. The night, which she'd always hated because it reminded her so much of Sheoul, closed in on her. How could Arik have done that? How dare he think it was okay to kiss *her*, one of the Four Horsemen of the Apocalypse?

"Goddammit," Kynan snapped. "Someone fucking answer me."

"We told you that Limos is to become Satan's bride," Thanatos said. "But not until her Seal breaks, she's captured in Sheoul, or until she does something to make him jealous."

"Okay," Kynan said, "so the big guy is jealous. Why is she still here but Arik is gone?"

"Because it's not that simple. The Dark Lord can't have her until the male who incited the jealousy utters her name while in agony."

Kynan swallowed loud enough for her to hear. "So he's still alive? Where?"

"Hell," Limos rasped. "Arik is in hell."

Two

One month later...

Arik didn't know how long he'd been in hell. Time was one never-ending, no-lube fuck when you were in the dark and in nonstop agony. And these bastard demons wouldn't let him die. He'd tried, but they just kept healing him.

At least right now it was quiet, a few stolen moments in which he could sleep. Sleep and dreams were his only pleasure...even the dreams that were about the female who had landed him in this hellhole in the first place.

Limos.

Closing his eyes, he settled back against the cold stone—bliss on his bruised, bare skin. With a little effort, he shut out the rumbling of his stomach and the incessant drip of water outside the cell that was intended to drive him crazy with want, since the demons rationed his water, and what little he got was usually stagnant and disgusting anyway.

He tried to think of his sister, Runa, and his nephews. Tried to force his thoughts toward his job with the U.S. Army's paranormal unit, the R-XR, as well as the forced-on-him involvement with the civilian demon-fighting organization, The Aegis. Tried to think about his escape plan...anything other than Limos, but his mind kept drifting to the beautiful ebony-haired, violet-eyed female. He hadn't liked her when he first met her, mainly because she'd kicked his ass, broken his ribs, and threatened to crush his organs into marmalade.

Marmalade...God, he was hungry.

So, no, he hadn't been overly fond of the third Horseman of the Apocalypse.

Still wasn't. Because of her, he'd been dragged to Sheoul, the demon realm deep in the earth, stripped naked, and tortured within an inch of his life. Repeatedly. And the weird thing was that all the demons who held him captive wanted was for him to say her name. Her freaking *name*.

What. The. Hell.

So far, he hadn't broken. Well, he'd *broken*, but the creepy-ass demons of unknown species kept a Seminus demon around to heal him so he wouldn't die and they could keep breaking his bones and peeling off his skin. They'd even tried sleep deprivation, starvation, and getting into his head to make him think he was somewhere much more pleasant so they could trick him into saying her name. He'd been subjected to every torture and violation known to man. And then some, 'cuz demons were creative as fuck.

But they wouldn't tell him *why* they wanted him to

speak her name, and though it would be so easy to let it slip, to finally free himself of the torment, he couldn't. Anything important to the evil bastards wasn't good for mankind. And Limos had been pretty adamant as he'd been dragged down here, his skin shredding like he was being scraped over a cheese grater. *Don't say my name, Arik! No matter what they do to you, don't speak my name!*

Right. What if her name caused a worldwide earthquake or put a fissure in the earth that released all demons from Sheoul? And the thing was, Arik wasn't sure how specific he had to be, so he hadn't called Limos by any name. Not Li, her nickname, or Famine, the name she'd go by if and when her Seal broke.

Fitting that her name would be Famine, cuz he was *famished.*

His stomach grumbled, and he threw his hand over his abs as he thought about Limos, hoping like hell her Seal was safe. Apparently, breaking her Seal involved finding some ancient, tiny bowl engraved with a set of scales. Once found, a Horseman had to drink from it. Drink... he'd give his right nut for a drink...

He swept his hand up and down his sunken-in belly, knowing his thirst and hunger were the least of his worries, because man, if her Seal broke, humans would truly understand the meaning of *hell on earth.* The Horsemen weren't evil—they were, in fact, half-angel, half-demon, and in a constant walk-the-line mode. But if their Seals broke ahead of the biblical prophecy timeline, they would turn evil and lead the way to Armageddon.

Arik had already gotten a taste of what that would be like: Before he'd gotten his ass handed to him in battle by his brothers and sister, the first Horseman of the Apocalypse, Pestilence, had caused death and destruction everywhere he went. Now Arik's captors indicated that Pestilence had regrouped, reassembled his forces, and was back to trying to facilitate the breaking of his siblings' Seals so the end of days could finally begin.

What an asshole.

A rock dug into Arik's butt, and he shifted, only to get poked by something else…the bone of some unfortunate previous cell inhabitant, probably. Still, he wasn't about to lie down. Spiny hellrats had a charming habit of eating your face while you were asleep. At least if he was sitting up he could punt them across the cell.

Thanks so much for this, Limos.

How the hell could a single kiss get him into this mess? It wasn't as if he'd forced himself on her. Yeah, he'd kissed her, and for one steamy, lingering heartbeat, she'd kissed him back. And then she'd flipped the hell out.

Though he wasn't sure why she'd freaked, he did know that Limos was responsible for every drop of his spilled blood. She'd said he'd pay for kissing her, and his captors confirmed it, relished telling him how "his lover's" lack of self-control had been his downfall, how her selfishness was at fault and it was because of her that he was being tortured.

They'd even given him an out; speak into a recorder and beg Limos to help him, and when she came to rescue his ass, they'd grab her and let him go.

"*Your worthless human life for hers. She'll take your place in chains. You'll have the satisfaction of knowing she's getting what she deserves. You must want revenge.*"

Man, those demons had read him like a damned gun owners manual. He wanted payback, but not like that. He

wouldn't allow a female, even one like Limos, to suffer at
the hands of these fucks.

So he'd refused the offer that was, no doubt, a lie anyway. Which had led to a sledgehammer to both ankles.
When he refused again, the sledgehammer had moved up
to his knees. His next refusal had earned him a broken
pelvis, but thankfully, he passed out and didn't have to
refuse anymore.

"You're a fool," his torturer, the one with the deceptively classy English accent, had told him later. *"You're
going to die down here, and it will be Limos's fault."*

Arik was fully aware of that fact. But the knowledge
didn't stop him from dreaming of him and her naked.
Sometimes they were on a beach, both covered in suntan
oil as he moved against her. Sometimes all he did was kiss
her hand as he looked into her exotic eyes. Other times, he
had her against the wall or was taking her from behind as
she clung to a palm tree. His favorite erotic dream was the
one where she was on her back in the ocean surf, and he
was kneeling between her legs, tonguing her wet heat and
tasting the salt water and her tropical cocktail essence.

She'd always smelled like coconuts and pineapple.

Man, he was starving.

And what was that saying? Right. *Revenge was a dish
best served cold…*

Limos was not in a good mood. She had, in fact, been in a
bad mood for weeks.

But she faked being happy really well, and right now,
she was working toward an Oscar nomination.

The Hawaiian sun beat down on her as she swung her

hips to the beat of Maroon 5's latest, her gaze fixed on a tall, dark male perched at the portable bar she set up for her beach parties. His eyes drilled into her hungrily as he sipped his margarita, and when he casually adjusted the erection in his black shorts, she knew she had him.

Slowly, provocatively, she moved toward him, putting extra sway in every step. Her bare feet sank in the warm sand, giving her legs a workout, and she knew the male was appreciating every flex of her toned muscles. The hot pink flowing miniskirt drew his attention, and his gaze darkened when a breeze flipped it up to reveal, very clearly, that she wasn't wearing panties. Her flat stomach, pierced with a gold ring, became the next object of his appreciative scrutiny, and she watched as his eyes roved upward to the barely-there bikini top that covered about as much as two Band-Aid strips.

On her shoulder blade, the set of scales that had been tattooed there when she was only a few hours old began to wobble as the right side, the evil side, and the left side, the one that measured the good half of her, warred.

When she was a few feet away, she smiled, gave him a *come-on-big-boy* look, and sauntered up the steps of her beach house. Of her two homes, this was the public one she used for parties that were frequented by humans— both locals and celebrities who flew in just for her big bashes. But this get-together was a small one, attended by only a couple dozen *ter'taceo*. She'd intentionally invited the demons, who could easily pass as humans, in order to lure this particular male. He was cautious, overly paranoid, and if she'd invited him directly, he wouldn't have come.

Instead, she'd chosen her guests with surgical precision—friends of his, demons with particular tastes who virtually guaranteed that he'd be lured by the promise of lurid, grotesque fun as night settled in.

He knew exactly who she was, but no way could he know what she wanted from him. No way could he know that Thanatos's intel had fingered him as one of Arik's torturers.

She slipped inside the house and mounted the stairs to the bedroom, smiling when she heard the door close softly behind her. At the top of the stairs, she untied her top and tossed it over her shoulder, leaving a seductive trail for him to follow.

Inside the bedroom, she circled a wicker chair angled so she could look out at the rolling surf and waited for "Rhys" to enter. His demon name, Xenycothylestiran-zacish, was... yeah. She used his human name.

He filled the doorway, sexual menace rushing at her like a deadly rogue wave. In the human world, he was a corporate raider of some kind. In the demon world, he was a master of torture, a hobby that leaked into his relationships with women, and Limos wondered how many missing prostitutes could be traced to him.

"What's your game, Horseman?" His deep, English-accented voice was the cherry on his sexy sundae, and she remembered how, centuries ago, she'd had a major crush on him. But he'd known she was betrothed to the Dark Lord, and he wasn't stupid enough to go near her. She wasn't that stupid either, and she never *had* been that stupid.

Until Arik.

Damned human. How dare he tempt her like that? How dare he kiss her and make her want him?

The kiss had doomed them both.

Now she was in a race against time to rescue him before he sealed the fate she'd been running from for thousands of years—marriage.

There was also that pesky Seal-breaking fate she had to deal with, but right now, she had to concentrate on the most immediate problem, which was finding Arik.

"I have no game," she purred, running a purple-lacquered nail over the back of the chair. "I'm sure you've heard that I succumbed to lust and gave my affections to a human."

Rhys's expression gave nothing away. "I heard."

"Well, that means that until he says my name while in the throes of agony, I can enjoy myself."

God, she hoped Arik could continue to withstand whatever torture the demons holding him were putting him through. A wash of admiration warmed her from the inside, because she didn't know if *she* could survive a month of torture, and Arik was a fragile human. She'd always sensed strength in him—it had been one of the things that had drawn her to him, besides his sense of humor—but she would never have guessed at the depth of that strength.

"And by enjoy, you mean..." Rhys trailed off as he prowled toward her, his bare chest, well-oiled and glistening, drawing her gaze.

Most females would lift their skirts right now. Limos had other plans, and Bones, her hell stallion who was currently decorating her right forearm as a tattoo-like glyph, writhed in anticipation.

"I mean that once Arik breaks, I'm going to be stuck bedding the same demon until the end of time. So play-time is now or never."

"Somehow," Rhys said casually, "I can't imagine that the Dark Lord will appreciate you coming to him less than intact."

She blinked innocently. "Intact? Of course I'm going to go to him a virgin." An ocean-scented breeze wafted through the room, caressing her skin, and she joined in, stroking her fingers over her nipple. "But I can do everything else. Don't you think he'd reward you well if I came to him knowing how to use my mouth?"

She nearly gagged at that thought, and not just because the idea of sucking the devil's dick horrified her. She'd never wanted to do that to any male. Women who claimed to like it had to be lying.

Rhys stepped closer. "I'm not so sure about that."

"Oh, come on," she cajoled. "It's just a little touching." Before he could protest, she gripped him by the shoulders, spun him, and planted him in the chair. Next, she straddled him so she was on his lap, facing him, her palms splayed on his smooth chest. "Touch me."

For a long, breathless moment, she thought he was going to dump her on her ass. His hands came down on her thighs and squeezed hard enough that a human woman would screech from the pain. But Limos wasn't human, and she didn't screech.

"If we do this," he said in a deadly, cold voice, "you do what I say. My rules. Understood?"

She made her eyes go all wide and frightened. "Y-yes." She even threw in a token tremble of her bottom lip for good measure. *Meryl Streep, you ain't got nothing on me.*

Rhys's smile was pure malevolence, something she'd been raised to appreciate during the twenty-eight years she'd spent in Sheoul, growing up under the thumb of a twisted, evil demon mother. If Limos were still that person, she'd be panting right now.

"Good." He took her right hand in his palm and trailed a finger over the black lines that formed the horse tattoo on her forearm. She could feel his touch in the corresponding parts of her body, and she hated it. Bones hated it too, had never like to be touched by anyone other than her, and he came to life on her skin, snapping his sharp teeth viciously. Rhys jerked his hand away, but not quickly enough. A tiny bead of blood formed on the tip of his finger. "Bastard."

"He's a little temperamental." That was an understatement. Of all her siblings' mounts, Bones was the most... unique.

Limos's first stallion, a normal warhorse like her brothers', had been killed, and her fiancé had sent Bones as a gift she couldn't refuse. Now she was stuck with the carnivorous hell stallion, and though he'd grown on her, she didn't call him out unless absolutely necessary. He was too hard to control, and he hated everyone including, sometimes, Limos. Well, he loved Ares's wife, Cara, but only because she'd saved his life.

Rhys's hands slid under her skirt, and both revulsion and anticipation rippled through her. She'd fantasized about Arik's hands doing the same thing. Her fantasies, as she pleasured herself nightly in her bed, *all* involved Arik.

They also involved the absence of her chastity belt—which was why her thoughts were pure fantasy.

Only one person could remove the polished pearl chain that circled her hips and fell between her legs, connected in the front and the back to the hip loop. In truth, it was beautiful, a priceless piece of jewelry that would make her feel sexy if not for its nasty little secret.

Rhys's hands drifted higher, and she feigned a moan as she arched so her breasts touched his chest and she could covertly slip her right hand around the back of the chair to the dagger she'd taped there.

"You are an eager little slut, aren't you?" he murmured.

"I have a lot to learn before I take my place at my husband's side." She nipped his earlobe, wishing it were Arik's. "Maybe you have friends who could join us?"

"When I'm through with you, perhaps."

Disgusting hellswine. "Hurry."

His hand came down hard on her ass. "What did I say? My rules."

Jesus, he hit hard. Her butt cheek stung like a son of a bitch, and didn't it figure that somehow, he'd missed touching her chastity pearls. "Sorry."

"Not yet, but you will be."

What a douche. She held her breath, fighting a shudder at his touch. She'd rather a snake crawled up her skirt.

He massaged her butt, his fingers biting deep into her flesh. She gripped the hilt of the dagger. The sound of his quickening breaths filled the room as he slid his palms around, his thumbs dipping between her thighs. There was a pause, as though he was trying to decide if he really wanted to go there.

Please, please go there. She rocked her hips, hoping he'd take it as a sign of desperate horniness rather than impatience.

"Whore," he whispered.

Dickweed, she thought.

He moved to cup her intimately, and finally, her chastity protection kicked in. Each of the pearls turned into a razor-sharp little spur, stabbing into her skin and most sensitive flesh. Excruciating agony ripped through her, but by some miracle, she didn't make a sound. Didn't need to. Rhys's screams would have drowned her out anyway.

Blood gushed—hers, but mostly his, as three of his fingers fell, severed, to the floor. Awesome. His species of demon was one that was damned hard to injure, weakening only if they lost a body part.

In a pained rush, she wrenched him to the floor, where she put the tip of her dagger under his eye. "Okay, asshole. Tell me what I want to know, or you lose more than your fingers."

"*Bitch*." Rage blackened his voice. "You cocksucking cum-slut!"

Limos shoved the blade into his eye. She had no patience when her privates hurt so bad. The spurs around her hips and between her legs had morphed back into pearls, but even as quickly as she regenerated, the injuries hadn't healed yet.

The demon screamed again, blood and ocular fluids squirting from his ruined socket. She shifted the knife to his other eye.

"My rules," she said, mocking him. "And my rules start with not calling me a cocksucking cum-slut or anything else disgusting and disrespectful." She squeezed her thighs, crushing his ribs. She'd done that to Arik once. Poor guy. "Feel me?"

"Yes," he gasped.

"Good. Because, hello, I'm a legend. I deserve a little reverence. Now, tell me where they're keeping Arik."

"I don't know."

"Tsk-tsk." She squeezed her legs harder, enjoying the crackle of breaking bones as he shouted out in pain. "I know you're one of his torturers. So let's try this again, and you'll answer, unless you've really had your heart set on getting a guide dog. Where is he?"

"As much as I fear your wrath, I fear your betrothed's more. If I so much as whisper a word, I won't make it more than a step beyond the hellmouth's gate before I'm torn to pieces."

"Take a look at the fingers on my floor. I'm already tearing you to pieces." She pricked the skin beneath his good eye, and a drop of blood welled up. "Where. Is. Arik?"

The demon laughed, and a chill shot up her spine. "If the human only knew how desperate you are to find him, he might have taken me up on my offer."

"And what offer was that?"

He sneered. "The human worm refused to make a trade. You for him. Even after I tenderized his lower body with a sledgehammer, he wouldn't deal."

Limos could hardly breathe through her rage. And her shock. Arik had been given an out, and he hadn't taken it? He'd protected her, someone she wasn't related to? Who would do that? And why?

"You couldn't have taken me, let alone held me."

"We'd have set a trap so the Dark Lord could have caught you, because yes, you're right. We couldn't have held you for torture. But the human didn't know that, and he still didn't deal. And that is why the human race will lose in the Apocalypse. They are sentimental. Weak. Pathetic."

"Weak?" she spat. "He didn't play ball with you after

you smashed his legs, and you call him weak?" She slashed the blade across his cheek, opening it up to his teeth. "*Where is he?*"

Rhys hissed, spraying blood. "It matters not, Horseman. Truly."

"And why is that?" she ground out.

"Because if he hasn't broken by now, he won't. The order has been handed down. He'll be executed tomorrow. He'll be dead in twenty-four hours." He grinned. "The honor will be mine."

"*Wrong answer, asshole.*" Limos slammed the dagger through his good eye, gave it a twist, and sent the blade straight into his brain. The demon jerked, his body spasming wildly. "That was for Arik."

She leaped to her feet, her mind working furiously.

Hellmouth's gate. Her breath caught as Rhys's casual mention pierced her fog of fury. Though very few humans knew about them, there were six hellmouths on Earth, passageways through which humans could enter Sheoul—usually dragged there by demons. Could Arik be near one of them?

God, she hoped so, because right now, it was all she had to go on. And she had to hurry, because if Rhys was right, Arik had only hours to live.

Three

Kynan Morgan freaking loved being immortal. Yeah, he bore a lot of weight on his shoulders because of it, weight in the form of the crystal pendant around his neck. But immortality was worth bearing that little piece of Heaven—literally, *Heaven*. Given the choice, he'd make the same decision to be charmed by angels in order to protect the pendant.

Today, as he surveyed the half-dozen injured demons lying on the floor of the underground Las Vegas pub where he and his new fellow Aegis Elder, Decker, had beaten them into submission, he was more grateful than ever for the charm. The gray-green reptilian bastards hadn't been able to lay a finger on him, which was great, seeing how their fingers were coated in a sticky acidic substance that bonded them to you like Superglue while they dissolved your flesh.

Decker was currently peeling himself out of his black

BDU pants, which were attached to one of the creature's hands. Just the hand...since Decker had amputated it from the demon's arm with his KA-BAR.

"Mother. Fuck." Decker got his pants caught on his combat boots and did some kind of crazy dance as he tried to extricate himself. "God...*damn*, these demons are nasty." He tossed the pants away and made a sound of disgust. The vampire bartender, one of the few people who'd remained in the pub when the fighting started, laughed, but shut up when Decker flashed a wooden stake at him.

"I'm just happy you're not a free-ball kind of guy." Kynan winced at Decker's Dale Earnhardt Jr. boxers. "Not that what you're wearing is much better."

Decker drew his Aegis sword from the sheath at his back, and hacked off one of the demons' heads. "*Some* of us aren't all charmed up the ying-yang."

Ying-yang did not sound right with a Texas twang, but Ky kept his mouth shut as Decker separated demon heads from necks, stopping with his blade poised over the heart of the last surviving demon. When the thing reached for his leg, Kynan used his single-handed modified Aegis crossbow to nail the demon in each palm, pinning its hands to the blood-soaked wood floor.

"Thanks, buddy," Decker said.

Decker had never called Kynan "buddy" before Arik went missing, and the reminder of why they were here pricked at Ky's temper. With a growl, he kneeled at the demon's side and held the tip of his double-ended, S-shaped stang to the creature's throat.

"Where is the human being kept?" he asked.

The demon rolled his lizardlike eyes up to meet Ky's gaze. "How...would I...know?"

"Because you and your scaly friends have been taking bets on how long it'll take him to break."

"Fuckers," the demon hissed. "We are...what do you call them...bookies? We hear things."

"You do more than *hear things*." Kynan used the tip of his blade to impale a demon tick the size of a damned quarter that was burrowing beneath one of the lizard-man's scales. "You've also been taking human form and insinuating yourself into human gambling operations."

The breakage of Pestilence's Seal had thrown off the delicate balance between good and evil that had, for so long, kept the worst of the demons at bay. Now scum like these demons, who had once been relegated to the depths of hell, were breaking loose and finding their way into the human realm, where they were wreaking havoc, either directly, by killing and maiming, or passively, by radiating evil like a dirty bomb. Humans whose souls were truly good were only mildly influenced by the hell-bombs, but evil humans and those who were on the fence became drunk with violence and possessed by evil thoughts; chaos was beginning to reign on the streets.

These particular demons had spread the gambling bug like one of Pestilence's viruses. Not only had organized crime tripled, but the stakes had increased. Nothing was off the table in the back rooms of even reputable estab-lishments. Money, drugs, children, human organs...all becoming disturbingly common as currency.

The lizardman was unrepentant. "Humans are stupidly blind. We can't be held responsible for their weaknesses."

Ky snarled. "Where. Is. Arik?"

The demon's nose, two black holes in his face, twitched. "We don't know where he's being held."

Kynan threw aside the stang and gripped the demon's throat in his bare hands. "Listen to me, you fucking Sleestak creep. You spill, or I'm going to turn you into a pair of boots and a belt. And then I'm going to hunt down every one of your family members and do the same thing. Got it?"

Decker casually lit a match and touched it to the end of a tiny capsule, a nasty little R-XR weapon that could be dropped on a demon, where it would immediately burn its way into flesh. The thing caused excruciating agony as it passed through the victim's body, its white-hot shell cauterizing as it traveled, preventing a total bleed out.

Fear flickered in the demon's yellow eyes. "I don't know," he said quickly. "Is the truth, slayer."

"Rumors, then. I know you've heard rumors."

"The...Iblis's torturing grounds are in the Doom region of Sheoul," the Sleestak said, using one of the many names for the big bad demon Christians called Satan. "But the human is said to have been handed over to experts."

Arik's torture had been contracted out? Fuckers. "And these experts are keeping the human where?"

"They have many chambers. All located near hell-mouths."

"Which one should we focus on?"

The demon said nothing. Ky squeezed his throat, and Decker crouched on his heels, holding the capsule over the lizardman's crotch. "Which. One."

"Erta Ale," it rasped. "The rumor is...Erta Ale."

"Isn't that an Ethiopian volcano?" Decker dropped the capsule on the floor and crushed it with his boot.

Ky nodded. "I'll search it. I need you back at R-XR

headquarters in D.C. You have to convince the R-XR to hurry up with the weapons they promised us."

The R-XR and Aegis had been working on weapons that could deliver doses of hellhound saliva into the Horsemen—specifically, Pestilence. But Ky wouldn't hesitate to use it on any Horseman who went bad.

"The R-XR is doing their best." Defensiveness crept into Decker's voice as he hacked off the lizardman's head with a little more force than was required.

"The R-XR is doing *what* they do best, which is being overly cautious." Kynan knew, because he'd been dragged into the secret Army unit, the Ranger-X Regiment, back when he was an Army medic who'd been attacked by a demon. The demon had nearly ripped out his throat, leaving him scarred and with a voice that made him sound like he was always chewing on gravel.

Decker's mouth tightened into a grim line. "The R-XR is proceeding with necessary caution, and you know it. Someone has to balance out The Aegis's tendency to act first and think later."

Decker was right, but Kynan's temper was on edge, just like the relationship between The Aegis and the R-XR. For years, they'd been allied, backing each other up in operations and sharing information, but when Pestilence's Seal broke, the relationship went south. The military preached caution and was still trying to cover up the growing threat, while The Aegis went in *weapons-hot* and was of the belief that it was time humans were let in on the existence of demons and the coming Apocalypse. The difference in approaches had caused a rift between the two organizations, and as a member of both, Decker was straddling the gap.

Kynan often wondered if Decker regretted signing on as an Elder three weeks ago. It was an unheard of move, bringing an outsider into The Aegis's top echelon, but they'd wanted to bring the military on board as fully as they could.

"I know that." Kynan stood. "But they need to do more to help us find Arik."

"I want Arik found as bad as you do." Decker wiped his blade clean on a dead demon's clothing, his movements jerky, edged with irritation. "But the military can't put all its resources into it. They...*we*...are busy trying to head off Pestilence's damned plagues and putting down the demonic outbreaks. So don't give me any bullshit about how we're sitting around and doing nothing."

Ky eyed Decker as he considered taking this little disagreement to the next level, but screw it. Their teams might be rivals, but they played on the same field. They needed to save their blood for demon battles.

"Come on," Ky said, slugging Deck in the shoulder. "Let's get you back to DC."

After that, it was off to see a Horseman about a volcano, and Ky had a feeling things were about to get hot. *Sheoul* hot.

⌒

"Want some water?"

Hell yeah, Arik wanted water. What kind of dumbass question was that? His throat was too raw and swollen to speak, so he merely nodded at Tavin, a blond Seminus demon Arik's torturers had hired to heal him.

Tavin frowned, and gripped Arik's shoulder with his right hand, which was marked all the way to his throat with tribal glyphs that all Seminus demons possessed. Apparently, they were a history of paternity, with the top symbol being personalized for each individual. Tavin's seemed to be some kind of worm. He must take all kinds of shit from Sems who had cool symbols, like weapons or hourglasses or lightning bolts.

Sucked to be Tavin.

Sucked more to be Arik, though.

The demon channeled his healing gift into Arik's body for the second time in the last ten minutes. The first time was to heal Arik's broken ankles, his lacerated spleen, and the evisceration that had left his intestines hanging out of his navel.

Arik really fucking hated demons.

He'd been pretty solid on that point even before he'd been tortured to the brink of insanity, but the word "hate" wasn't strong enough anymore. The English language needed a new word to describe how he felt about demons now.

Still, he supposed Tavin was okay for a demon. He wasn't overly friendly, but he gave Arik more water than his captors ever did, and he always brought a new pair of scrub pants—black, as Arik requested—to replace the ones the demons destroyed during their torture sessions. Tavin had even presented an argument to his captors; the clothing protected Arik's skin from infection that could kill him.

And, if Arik played his cards right, the pants would get him out of this hellhole.

Heat burned through Arik's body, a byproduct of the Seminus healing ability, which allowed the demons to either repair injuries, affect bodily function, or tweak the mind. After a few seconds, Tavin's energy had repaired damaged tissue and zapped Arik's throat back into working order. It was still sore—hell, his entire body was sore—but at least now the pain was bearable.

"Thanks." Arik rubbed his neck, mapping out the new scars. The demon had done an adequate job, and even the mental damage, the horrific memories, seemed to have faded. As always, after Tav was done with him, Arik felt whole again, not just physically, but mentally. "You've been patching my mind, haven't you?"

Tavin's expression was a whole lot of blank. "I have no idea what you're talking about."

"Bullshit. I should be a head case by now. Fuck, I'm so damaged after a torture session that I don't even know my own name. But when you're finished with me...I dunno. You're doing something." Arik narrowed his eyes. "And don't lie to me. I fucking hate liars, and I kinda think you're all right for a demon. Don't disappoint me."

There was a heartbeat of hesitation...two...three... and then the pathetic moan of some nearby creature seemed to break the lock on Tavin's silence.

"Seminus demons have only one of the three abilities." His brisk tone made it clear that the discussion was over as he handed Arik a clay cup containing a few table-spoons of muddy liquid. Tasted like piss and mold, which it probably was, but it was wet, and he'd learned to take everything he could get.

Well, not everything. Sometimes the demons tempted him with things like fluffy, moist slabs of cake; thick, juicy, char-grilled steaks; and frosty mugs of beer. But he'd learned to never, ever touch the offerings, no matter how much his mouth watered and his stomach ached. Doing so earned him hot pokers in places not meant to handle molten iron rods.

Tav's green eyes flashed with pity, and great, how pathetic were you when a *demon* pitied your sorry ass?

"Do you know why the demons want me to say the Horseman's name, Tav?"

"Nope." Bitterness dripped from Tavin's normally level voice. "I'm just the hired help."

"Why'd you take the job?"

Tavin took the cup from Arik and tucked it into his duffle of medical supplies. "No choice."

"There's always a choice."

"Not when you're an assassin locked into a contract."

"Assassin, huh?" Arik's rusty wheels started turning. "Don't suppose you know a couple of half-breed Sems named Sin and Lore? They're sort of extended family. They were assassins not long ago." Lore was now Underworld General's chief medical examiner, and Sin had taken a position in the demon hospital's infectious disease department, since her mutated Seminus gift had given her the unique ability to cause disease. Apparently, there was hope that she could also learn how to destroy it.

Tavin reached into his medical bag for a tube of ointment. "I used to work with them."

A sickly little flame of hope flared. "Can you get them a message?"

"Not until the demons who hired me no longer need me."

At which point, Arik would probably be dead. "Come on...the R-XR and Aegis will compensate you nicely if you do this." He couldn't believe he was trying to make a deal with a demon. But then, it wouldn't be the first time. At least in this case, his soul wasn't on the table.

Just his life.

"I can't risk it."

"If you're an assassin, you've got to be all sneaky and shit."

"I am. But the answer is still no." He smoothed a thin film of the greasy medicine over an abrasion on Arik's chest. Tavin's healing ability always tapped out before he could get to all the minor injuries. "Betraying this contract means an extremely long, painful death and possible eternal torment."

"Sort of like what I'm going through?" Arik muttered.

"Pretty much."

Arik glared. "Okay, so if you're an assassin, why are you healing me?"

"Your captors paid a shit-ton of money for my services, whether that be killing or healing."

"So you'd kill me if they asked you to?"

"Yep."

Nice. "Look, if you'll pass on a message—" Arik shut up at the sound of approaching footsteps.

Tavin stepped away as two ugly-ass motherfuckers stopped at the cell door. Six-inch claws wrapped around the steel bars. Arik's pulse leaped. He never knew if the demons were going to torture him, feed him, or merely taunt him.

"Human scum," the tallest one said, the tusks protruding from his lower jaw dripping saliva. "We're going to discuss your last meal."

Well, this couldn't be good. Arik rolled his shoulder in a nonchalant shrug, even though his heart was going ballistic.

"Last meal? How about surf-and-turf, medium-rare on the steak, fettuccine alfredo, and those amazing garlic cheese biscuits from Red Lobster? Could I get a Harp, too? Cold, though, not that room temperature crap they like in Ireland."

Two sets of humorless black eyes stared back at him. "Your choice is putrefied meat with maggots or fish skin."

"Awesome." Arik tapped his chin, appearing to consider his options. "Hmm...gross or really gross. Tough decision. I'll go with gross."

The shorter ugly-ass motherfucker clicked his claws in agitation. "Which is?"

"Fish skin. Yum." But hey, if it wasn't rotten, it would actually be the best thing he'd eaten down here, so things weren't all bad. And it sounded like they were actually going to kill him. He doubted it would be a quick death, but it couldn't be worse than anything they'd already done to him.

The beasts spoke to each other in a language Arik didn't understand, until about the tenth word, when his translation ability kicked in. They were discussing how much to tell him about how he'd die. They were also speculating about what would happen to his body afterward. Would they be allowed to eat him, or would his corpse be preserved and displayed somewhere? Maybe his body would be dumped outside of a hellmouth for his colleagues to find.

Right, okay, so Arik didn't like any of those options.

He watched the two demons lumber away and wondered if prayers could reach Heaven from here. "Whatcha think, Tav? Is my death going to be quick or slow?"

"Slow, definitely."

"Yeah, that's what I figured." Maybe this one time, Arik wouldn't have minded a little white lie. He ran his hand up and down his chest, wincing at the feel of his rib cage. He'd lost so much weight down here. He'd tried to keep some muscle by doing pushups and sit-ups when he could, but scrounging up the energy wasn't easy. "At least it'll be over soon, I guess."

"Don't look so relieved, human." Tavin stared at him, his eyes somber. "Death isn't a good thing."

"Spend a day in my shoes—you know, if I had them—and you'll change your mind."

The Sem heaved the duffel over his shoulder. "That's not what I mean. For you, it's not an escape."

Man, demons and their tendency to circle an issue. "Straight shoot it, Tav. What are you saying?"

"I'm saying that when a human dies here in Sheoul, his soul is trapped. You can't get out, and the most vile demons in existence will be able to torture you for all eternity. And trust me, what they've done to you so far is nothing compared to what they will do to your soul. You think you're in pain now? Just wait until you're dead. The soul is much more sensitive than the physical body."

More sensitive? Arik eyed the corner, his escape plan taking on a new, desperate note of urgency. Every time an opportunity had arisen, he'd carefully dug the thin, black elastic strings out of the waistband of his pants and stored them, scattered, in the crevices that defined the dark chamber. He didn't have nearly as many as he'd hoped, but it would have to do.

He waited for Tavin to leave, and then he sat down on the floor with his dozen little treasures and began to braid them together. This had to work.

Or he was worse than dead.

Four

It took Limos an hour to clean up the mess Rhys rudely left on her floor, then shower and change into pink board shorts and a lacy yellow blouse. Every single minute of that hour had been occupied by thoughts of what Arik had done for her, and she couldn't decide how she felt about it. Her emotions ran the spectrum from overwhelmingly awed that he would protect her that way, to confused about *why* he would protect her that way, to downright pissed that he thought he had to protect her.

Then there was the anger that she was baffled by any of this in the first place. It wasn't like her to obsess over someone else's actions, but here she was ... obsessing.

Muttering to herself, she hefted Arik's torturer in her arms and took a Harrowgate to Thanatos's Greenland residence. The temperature change between Hawaii and his godforsaken frozen wasteland was marked, and she shivered as she stepped out of the Harrowgate and onto the hard-packed ice near Than's keep's entrance.

And, for the record, Rhys weighed a ton.

Without a free hand, she kicked at the wood and iron door, and eventually one of Than's vampire servants, Artur, opened up. Since it was daytime, the vamp on duty was one of the old breed, the first vampires, who had never suffered an allergy to sunlight. They were rare, pretty much legend to most. How Than had found not just one, but ten, to serve him, she had no idea. He could be really tight-lipped sometimes.

Annoying.

As if you don't have secrets.

Oh, yes, she had lots and lots of secrets, made all the worse by the knowledge that something wicked inside her got a kick out of lying. The bigger the lie, the more potential it had to hurt or even destroy, the more powerful the high. Jolts of delicious, almost erotic adrenaline would cycle through her like a drug.

But she'd given up that drug hundreds of years ago, exchanging the need to lie with casual recklessness that gave her a similar high, but one that was far less addictive.

"Miss Limos?" Artur stared at her in that creepy way of his, and though she couldn't be certain, she'd long suspected that he'd been a cannibal before he became a vampire. There was just something . . . not right . . . about him.

She shoved the dead demon into the vamp's arms and strode inside the great room, her strappy sandals clicking on the floor. A fire blazed in the hearth, and Than sat in one of the cozy chairs next to it, his nose buried in a book. As their voluntary historian, he had a massive library, was always reading when he wasn't working out in his gym or haunting scenes of mass casualty.

His newest obsessions were seeking clues that might reveal the whereabouts of her *agimortus*, looking for a way to repair Reseph's Seal, and trying to find their father. Okay, sure, these weren't new obsessions, but now they were his *only* ones.

"Whatcha reading?"

Thanatos lifted his head, the twin blond braids at his temples banging against his cheeks. *Salt: A World History*.

"Wow. You know how to rock the literary."

Than cocked a pierced eyebrow. "Do you know how many wars were fought over salt?"

She gave him a *duh* look. "We were there, remember?" They'd profited from some of those wars, had started their fortunes from the salt trade, in fact.

"Yep. The good old days." Sarcasm dripped from his words.

"So why are you reading about it?"

"Because I met with Kynan half an hour ago to discuss their progress in locating your *agimortus*, and he mentioned that The Aegis had recently discovered a stash of Aegis texts inside an ancient barrel of salt. It occurred to me that before their subjugation by the Neethul, the Isfet were heavily involved in the salt trade."

The Isfet were the demons who had made—and hidden—the cup that bore her *agimortus*. Unfortunately, thanks to generations of births and deaths, as well as horrendous record-keeping, even they no longer knew where it was stowed.

"So you think you can find a clue in that book?"

Than shrugged. "Can't hurt. Maybe the author stumbled upon some information during his research." He put aside his book as Artur entered.

"What shall I do with the body, sir?"

"Who is it?" Than looked at Limos. "One of Arik's torturers?"

"Yep." She'd discussed the plan to nail Rhys with Ares and Than a couple of days ago, and though they'd wanted to help, she knew the cagey bastard well enough to know he'd smell a trap. "I need you to dispose of him."

Pale yellow eyes narrowing, Than sat forward in his chair, his black jeans creaking against the leather cushion. "You want to send a message to Arik's captors."

"Reading a book entirely about salt didn't make you any dumber." Than gave her a blank, unamused stare. "Yes," she sighed, "I want to send a message."

Thanatos would likely grouse, but he loved doing stuff like this. Causing trouble was what he did best. Well, Reseph had actually excelled at it, but his troublemaking antics had always been good-natured. Than just liked fucking with demons.

"It would be smarter to hide the body so no one will know what happened to him, and no one can tie his death to you," Than said, being all sensible. He must be spending a lot of time with Ares, whose thought processes operated like battle plans. "There's no sense drawing attention to yourself, Li."

"*Helloooo.* I'm a Horseman of the Apocalypse, and I'm betrothed to the most infamous, most powerful demon in existence. I couldn't draw more attention to myself if I wore Lady Gaga's meat dress to a PETA convention."

"But you don't need to keep poking the hornet's nest."

Thanatos gestured to Artur. "Take the body to the ice chamber." Once the vampire was gone, he turned his attention back to Limos. "What did the demon tell you before you killed him?"

She studied her multi-colored nails to conceal her concern. "That Arik is going to be executed." *And that Arik had refused to make a deal that might have freed him but would have doomed me.*

"When?"

Dammit, she'd chipped the orange paint off her pinky. "Soon."

"No doubt they'll kill him in Sheoul instead of aboveground. Damn." Than wanted Arik dead so Li would no longer have to worry about Arik speaking her name, but killing him in Sheoul was not the answer.

In fact, it would be worse for his soul to be tortured down there than his human body. Souls didn't pass out from pain. He'd break within days, and she'd be honeymooning in the Taj MaHell.

Though she had no doubt he could set records for holding out.

Once again admiration washed over her, this time accompanied by a fierce surge of desire that wasn't entirely sexual. Over the last month she'd fantasized about him, what it would be like to bed him, but also, what it would be like to just . . . be with him. To have that strength of character wrapping around her and making her feel secure. Yeah, she was an immortal Horseman, so mighty that she didn't need any male's physical protection. But, as she had seen with Ares and Cara, power didn't always come from muscles.

Li shifted her focus from her nails to her hair, wrapping a still-damp strand around her finger. "I did manage to get a little intel from Rhys. It's possible Arik is being stored near a hellmouth."

"Erta Ale," Than said. "Kynan mentioned it during our chat. He wants to search the area surrounding the volcano, but he won't be able to find the exact location of the entrance."

"Because he doesn't have enough evil in him." That was the thing about hellmouths—humans could enter without demonic assistance, but only if they were evil. "Guess that leaves me."

Than's already deep voice hit rock bottom. "I know you aren't thinking of sniffing around inside the hellmouth."

"Oh, I'm sniffing."

Thanatos burst out of his chair, veins bulging in his neck, visible even under the collar of his black turtleneck. "Dammit, Li, if you get caught, you'll be barefoot and pregnant with Satan's hellspawn before you can so much as scream. You can't—"

"You think I don't know the risks?" she interrupted. "I didn't escape just so I can get caught again."

Actually, she hadn't escaped at all, but that was something she could never say out loud. There was only one thing she feared more than marriage to the devil himself; losing her brothers. They'd taught her to love when, for countless years, she'd thought love meant enjoying others' suffering.

"Then I'm coming with you."

"Okay."

Than blinked. "Okay?"

"What, you expected me to argue? I'm not a complete idiot."

"That," he said, "you are not. Usually." His gaze

shifted over her shoulder, and she followed it, turning to see Ares striding across the room, his expression grim, tension oozing from every pore in his nearly seven-foot-tall body.

He was dressed for battle in his leather armor, his sword at his left hip. Trailing behind him was an ox of a hellhound. Limos hated the beasts, whose bites could incapacitate her and her brothers, leaving them paralyzed and vulnerable. Any weapon coated in their saliva could cause the same damage. Limos knew that firsthand. But Ares's wife, with her gift of animal whispering and healing, had charmed the damned things, and was bonded to every hellhound in existence. Thanks to the bond, she was now immortal, and all of the beasts held a powerful desire to protect her and Ares.

"Hey, bro," she said. "What's up? Where are Cara and Rath?"

Ares's black eyes heated at his wife's name, momentarily replacing the icy glint. "She's home, nursing a new-born hellhound pup. Pestilence killed its mother. Rath's napping."

Rath was their adopted kid. Literally . . . *kid*. He was a baby Ramreel, a goatlike demon whose father had also been murdered by Pestilence.

"What's going on?" Thanatos studied Ares as though trying to decide if he should armor up as well.

"Our brother has recovered from the blow we dealt him," Ares's voice, cold and hard, rang with anger. "A swarm of locusts is sweeping across New Zealand, the worst plague they've ever seen."

Limos frowned. "A plague could point to Pestilence's hand, but it's still a natural occurrence."

"Not when the locusts are eating animals and people too."

Eew. "I was hoping it would take him more time to regroup." There were a number of reasons for that, but foremost was the fact that when Pestilence wasn't causing chaos, Ares and Thanatos didn't fight. Ares wanted Pestilence dead, and Thanatos wanted to repair his Seal.

Unfortunately, Pestilence was in possession of the only weapon capable of killing him, and no one had found a way to repair his Seal. Hell, they didn't even know if it was possible. Thanatos was running on nothing more than a theory and hope.

"So was I," Ares said. "But tension in the Balkans is flaring up again, and so are battles in the Middle East. I just got back from a nasty one." Ares, as the Horseman who would be War when his Seal broke, was naturally drawn to battles, could sometimes be kept away from home for days, weeks, even months during the worst of the fighting. Fortunately, thanks to Cara's bond with the hellhounds, his Seal was safe—unless either Limos's or Thanatos's Seals broke.

"Dammit," Than breathed. "I'd been sensing an upswing in deaths, but nothing I could pinpoint."

"That's because the battles are scattered right now, mostly skirmishes, and the death rates are fairly low. Pestilence might be working his next attempt at an Apocalypse in gradual measures. Fly under our radar for a while. He's definitely up to something." Ares reached over and scratched the hellhound under the chin, and Limos didn't think she'd ever get used to that. "You guys make any headway in locating Arik?"

Limos nodded. "We were just heading out to Erta Ale to search. Wanna join us? There might be some fighting."

"Then hell, yeah. I'm there."

Limos touched her fingers to the crescent-shaped scar on the left side of her neck, and her Samurai-style armor snapped into place. Thanatos followed suit, his bone-plate armor clacking as it folded itself onto his body.

Time to ride.

Nothing.

They'd found freaking nothing but scorching lava, noxious gasses, and lung-choking ash near the Erta Ale hellmouth. Inside the entrance, they'd discovered the gnawed-on skeletons of half a dozen humans and tunnels that broke off into more tunnels. After a full day of combing the caverns, Ares and Thanatos had been compelled to another of Pestilence's wars, and Limos had to change her game plan.

She threw a Harrowgate to her place, intent on gathering a team of her servants to help her. As she stepped out onto the warm Hawaiian sand outside her home, another gate flashed, and that son of a bitch, Pestilence, burst from it on his white stallion.

"Hey, sis." In a clang of metal armor, he swung down from Conquest and called the horse to him. Conquest poofed into a wisp of smoke and slipped under his master's gauntlet to settle on his arm. "I have a job for you."

Her fingers flexed over the scabbard at her hip, the desire to run him through with her blade stronger than it had ever been. "If you think I'm going to do anything for you, you can go fuck yourself."

Pain flickered in his ice-blue eyes, startling the hell out of her. "I know I've been a bastard, Li. I can't help it." His shoulders slumped, and he looked down at the ground, his platinum hair concealing his face. "My dreams...man, my dreams mess with me. I remember how I was. I... miss that."

She took an involuntary step toward him. "Reseph?"

"I need help." With a jerky, uncoordinated movement, he grabbed his head as if it pained him, and his voice cracked. "Cure me...*please*." He inhaled a strangled breath. "Deliverance...under...my armor. Kill...me. I'm begging you."

"We'll help you, I swear," she said, reaching for him.

His hand snapped out, grasping her wrist so tightly she felt the grind of bones. "You sentimental fool." His head came up, a menacing crimson glow lighting his eyes. "Reseph is dead."

She hissed, anger and pain ripping her right down the middle. She had her sword out and was swinging it before Pestilence could release her. Blood sprayed as the blade hacked into his neck. He stumbled backward, slapping his palm over the gaping wound.

"That," he said, in a freakishly calm voice, "will cost you." He jerked his head as if working out a kink, and the laceration sealed up, a hell of a lot faster than the same wound would have responded before he'd gone evil. He'd gained strength when his Seal broke, his ability to draw on the power of Sheoul boosting all his abilities, but bloody hell, she hadn't thought he'd gotten *that* resilient. "Like I was saying, I have a job for you."

"I'm not doing anything for you."

He continued as if she hadn't spoken. "I found an ancient vault that once belonged to The Aegis, and I want you to tell them about it."

All her internal alarms went off, clanging loudly in her skull. "What's in this vault?"

"Harmless historical relics."

"Nope. Sorry. I'm not leading Aegi to a bunch of fake artifacts."

Pestilence blinked innocently. He could get away with that when he was Reseph. Now ... not so much.

"Fake?" He shrugged. "Nah. They're real. Most of them. And the vault truly is an Aegis hiding place." He opened a Harrowgate. "Come with me."

"How stupid do you think I am? We could come out in Satan's bedroom, for all I know." Shudder.

He rolled his eyes, as if her distrust was completely unwarranted. "Cast your own gate and link it to mine then."

"I have things to do."

Abruptly, Pestilence's demeanor took on a new cast, and he snarled. "If you don't want to regret confiding in me about your part in The Aegis's *loss* of Deliverance so long ago, you'll do this."

"Blackmail, brother? Wow, you really have sunk low."

"Says the girl who has been lying to her family about some really important shit."

Damn him. With a curse, she cast her own gate over the top of his. They would both enter the now-single gate, but she could back out if she didn't feel safe.

They went through, Pestilence first, and when she stepped out into a dusty cavern lit by hovering balls of mystical fire, it appeared he hadn't been lying. At least, not about all of it. They were definitely in some sort of manmade tunnel, and her built-in GPS told her they were somewhere in Egypt.

She shivered. She'd never liked Egypt, and the claustrophobic closeness of the walls tightened around her chest like a python.

"Where are we?"

"A forgotten crypt. Some formerly important dude is entombed in a chamber behind us." Pestilence knelt at the base of a chest-freezer-sized stone box, and although the lid probably weighed five hundred pounds, he lifted it as though it was made of paper. "Take a look."

Easing up to the box, she peeked inside, where a dozen pieces of ancient jewelry, coins, and clay figurines lay on top of a pile of dust. Very carefully, she picked up one of the figures. The clay rendition of a plump woman was cracked, the piece of cloth tied around its legs was brittle.

"Nice job with this," she murmured. "You missed your calling as a counterfeiter. What's its purpose?"

"That's none of your concern."

"You're such an asshole."

One blond eyebrow shot up. "After the things you've done, you have the gall to call *me* an asshole?"

"Just get to the point," she gritted out. "What do you want?"

"Bring an Aegi here. Tell them you discovered the vault in your search for your *agimortus*." Pestilence tossed something at her feet. Dogtags, she realized, when she bent to pick them up. Arik's dogtags, caked with blood. "You'll do it, or next time I bring you his eyes."

She clutched the metal chain and tags so hard her palm hurt. For some reason, this little piece of Arik made everything so real, so tangible. It was as if she could feel his pain in the blood smears. God, if she'd been stronger, if she'd resisted Arik and her attraction to him, she wouldn't be in this mess, and he wouldn't be in pain.

Shame sifted through her, but she couldn't afford to give in to it. Whatever Pestilence was up to was bigger than Arik's agony, and she couldn't let on that she felt anything for him.

"Do what you have to do to Arik," she said, her voice strong and sure, even if she didn't mean what she said, even if inside she was aching. "I won't help you."

"Then I hope you're prepared to face Ares and Thanatos after I tell them of *all* your deceptions." He bared his fangs. "And yes, I know. Our mother told me everything."

Limos's heart shot into her throat, but she still managed to stay outwardly calm. "Telling them won't benefit your cause." She stroked the words engraved into the dogtags, taking comfort in the feel of Arik's name under her thumb. "If anything, it'll hurt it. Any remaining feelings they have for you will turn to hate." She hoped. She was damned sure they'd hate *her*, anyway.

"I'm willing to take that risk. So, what will it be, sister? Tell the Guardians about this vault, or do I go to our brothers and tell them how you, and you alone, are responsible for the curse that turned us into Horsemen?"

Go, daughter. Go into the human realm and find your brothers. Let the rivers of blood flow. Their mother, Lilith, had spoken those words as Limos left Sheoul . . . freely. There'd been no battle, despite what Limos had claimed to her brothers. Limos had not escaped—she'd left with great pomp and circumstance, and with every intention of returning to take her place at her husband's side after she'd accomplished her task.

If Thanatos and Ares knew, they'd plunge Deliverance into her heart right after they did the same to Pestilence. Maybe before.

"Damn you," she growled. "I'll do it. But in return, you'll get Arik out of Sheoul."

"You're in no position to bargain." Pestilence smiled. "And if The Aegis even suspects that this might be a setup, I'll kill Arik *and* tell our brothers your secret."

She wished she could strangle him. He was right; she had no leverage. "You know what this lie is going to do to me."

Pestilence licked his lips, as if savoring the finest brandy. "That's the best part of this, sis. With every lie you tell, your addiction to it will strengthen, and with every lie, evil will grow within you, until you *want* to go to your husband."

"He's not my husband."

"*Yet*, Limos," he said. "Yet."

Five

Pestilence was in the most pissed-off, rip-heads-off-for-the-hell-of-it mood he'd ever been in by the time he arrived in the basement of the New Zealand mansion he'd commandeered after his locusts had eaten the inhabitants.

The meeting with Limos had not gone well. Yeah, he'd gotten her to do what he wanted. But he'd also fallen victim to weakness. The male he'd been before his Seal broke, Reseph, had somehow reared his idiot head, begging for help. Pestilence had played it well, had acted like he'd intentionally suckered Limos and played her for a fool.

But in truth…*he'd fucking begged her to cure or kill him.*

Roaring in fury, he shed his armor, palmed the dagger strapped to his chest, and plunged it into his own belly. Pain seared him, intense, fiery, and he crashed to his knees. His minions came running, but he waved them off. This was a reminder. A reminder that if he'd gone just twelve inches higher, sunk Deliverance into his heart, he'd be dead. *Dead.* He was holding the one weapon that could end him, and he had to keep it away from his siblings.

Reseph could not weaken him.

"What the fuck are you doing?"

Pestilence gnashed his teeth at the female's voice. Harvester. One of the Horsemen's two Watchers—one evil, one good, both angels. Harvester happened to be of the evil fallen angel variety.

"I'm playing with myself," he snapped. "What do you think I'm doing?"

She blinked, all mock innocence. "If you needed to be reminded how Deliverance can hurt you, I'd have been happy to offer a hand."

No doubt she would. She hated him as much as he hated her. "Why are you here?"

Harvester watched with amusement as he yanked the blade out of his gut. The injury sealed immediately, and the searing pain yielded to a dull ache.

"I received a curious assignment, and I wondered if it has anything to do with you."

"Dunno." He moved to a pot of water that was boiling over a fire and dipped Deliverance into it. *Clean weapons made clean kills*, Ares always said. Pestilence might think Ares was a blow-hard asshole, but only an idiot ignored his battle advice. "What's the assignment?"

"Top secret."

"I *am* the top," he pointed out, as he walked back to her.

"This goes above even your head."

Since Pestilence was at the top of the demonic food chain, that meant Harvester's orders could come from only a couple other demons, or Zachariel, the angel of the Apocalypse who had brought the Horseman curse down upon their heads in the first place.

"Are these orders for a Watcher assignment?"

"No." She eyed him as he shoved Deliverance into its sheath. "This task is all about Sheoulic interests."

Ah, then her orders could come only from someone inside Satan's tight inner circle, which included Lilith, Pestilence's succubus mother. Interesting. Smiling seductively, he trailed a finger over the smooth skin of her exposed shoulder. "You can't even give me a hint?"

She returned the smile, though hers was bitter. "It has to do with the forged scrolls, but that's all I can tell you."

She chewed her bottom lip, and as much as he hated her, he had to admit that the way her fang poked from between her lips was sexy. He loved that when angels fell, they lost their silly angel names and gained fangs and a taste for blood. He raked his gaze up and down Harvester's curvy body, because really, when it came down to it, fucking someone you hated could be even better than fucking someone you liked.

Harvester tucked her fang away. What a disappointment. "But I suppose it won't hurt to say that my assignment will help ensure that your plan is . . . unimpeded."

Thank the Dark Lord that at least one thing was going right. Now, if The Aegis fell for his ruse, he could put the other part of his plan into play. It wouldn't be easy to snatch one of Thanatos's vampires and replace it with a doppelganger, but he'd manage. He always managed. As Reseph, charm had gotten him what he wanted. As Pestilence, threats worked even better.

"*Your* plan, you mean." It stuck in his craw that Harvester had been the one to give him the idea for the "Aegis vault," and now he just had to hope it worked.

"Let's keep that between you and me," she said. "I don't want to be accused of 'helping.'"

"No doubt you don't." The last Watcher who had broken rules had suffered for decades before finally being destroyed.

Harvester sniffed. "Did Limos suspect anything?"

"I doubt it. She focused on the artifacts." Now he had to hope that the Guardian she took to the chamber would be astute enough to locate the hidden box where Pestilence had planted the true treasure he wanted The Aegis to find—the scrolls Harvester had referred to. The artifacts were decoys, placed so Limos would believe that the scrolls didn't have anything to do with Pestilence.

Harvester glanced around the basement, which had been remodeled into a demon playground, her gaze pausing on the Aegis Guardian in chains. "Where did you get him?"

"Snatched off the streets in Hungary. He was hunting a Croucher demon." The Guardian's moans were musical. Sensual. "You did know that I'm rewarding anyone who brings me an Aegi, dead or alive, yes?"

"Of course. The entire underworld knows you've put a bounty on Guardians. What kind of information are you trying to get out of the live ones?"

"The locations of their cell headquarters, as well as the location of The Aegis's main HQ. This one gave up the site of his cell near Budapest, and it's right now under siege by my minions." Pestilence sighed, practically able to hear the sounds of battle. "But he doesn't know where the regional hubs or global headquarters are."

"Their mission control is in Berlin," Harvester said.

"No shit." Pestilence gnashed his teeth. "But I don't know where, exactly. And none of these fucks will give it up."

"The exact location is likely kept from most of them."

Of course it was. The Aegis's head honchos wouldn't want to risk a low-ranking Guardian spilling his guts—literally, in this case—to an enemy who would use the information to stage an attack on their very nerve center. An attack would not only cripple the organization, but rumor had it that the bulk of their weapons, secrets, and artifacts were stored at headquarters, and that, to any demon, would be priceless beyond comprehension.

Pestilence gestured to the broken Aegi. "Want to see what you can get out of him?"

She brushed invisible lint off her black leggings. "I've got things to do."

"No, really." He dug his fingers into her shoulder so hard it had to hurt, but she didn't let on. "I'd love to see you operate."

"What part of, 'I've got things to do,' don't you understand?"

He narrowed his eyes at her. "You know, I've never seen you do anything but hang around and watch others get their hands wet. Maybe you're . . . squeamish?"

She snorted. "Hardly. I've done things you can't even imagine."

He doubted that. His imagination was truly awesome. "Then show me."

She stared at him, long and hard. Finally, she shrugged, chose a serrated blade from the selection of torture instruments hanging on the wall, and tested its edge. Blood welled along the cut on her thumb. She licked it, sealing the wound, and the sight, the scent, gave him instant wood.

"Have it your way," she said nonchalantly, and sauntered over to the Guardian, where she started her gruesome work.

He watched, his excitement growing with each of the human's screams. His plans were coming together. Soon, The Aegis itself would set the Apocalypse into motion, Limos would return to the evil bitch she was born to be, and Arik...he was going to die.

But not before Pestilence claimed his soul.

Fucking demons.

They were Arik's favorite two words, and he kept repeating them over and over. Well, they had always been favorites, but he kind of suspected that the time spent in this shithole had erased his vocabulary and left him only with *fucking* and *demons.*

Arik sat still as Tav finished healing him—again. It was the second time in twelve hours, which wasn't unusual, but Arik had hoped he'd have a reprieve from the torture since they'd decided to execute him.

Not so much.

He cast a glance at the door, where he'd looped his uber-thin braided string around a blackened bar between the wall and the lock. So far, so good. No one had noticed. Demons weren't the most observant creatures on the planet.

"So, Tav, whatcha got planned for later?"

Tavin peeled off his surgical gloves. "Sex."

Right. Seminus demon. Needed to have sex or die. "Groovy."

"And you?"

Escape. Arik shrugged. "I'll probably eat the bucket of fish skin and guts your friends bring me. After that, I'm pretty sure I have an appointment with the executioner. Why? You want to make a date?"

Tav shoved the gloves inside his medic duffel. "You're not my type. Sems can only come with a female."

"Huh. I'm not a Seminus demon, but I can only come with a female too."

Tavin laughed, something Arik had never seen him do. "I like you, human." He sobered, his smile turning sad. "I doubt I'll see you again."

Arik clapped the demon on the back. "You know, I appreciate gallows humor a lot more than sappy goodbyes."

Tav shouldered his bag and signaled the guard. "I hope you find peace, human." He lowered his voice just a little. "And remember that if you always go the right way, you never have to make a left-hand turn."

"Ah...okay. I don't have any baffling bits of wisdom for you, but hey, I make it a rule to never bet on white horses. Following that advice has never lost me any money."

"I'll remember that."

The door opened, and Arik strategically placed his hand over the handcrafted rope he'd wrapped around the vertical bar the door locked into. "See ya around, demon."

Tavin stepped out, and as the door swung shut, Arik dragged the strands of thread downward, grateful for the elastic stretch, so it formed a barrier between the lock mechanism on the door and the bolt catch on the bar. Now he just had to pray that the tiny bone he'd ground into a pick would be strong enough to work the lock from the outside as the rope put pressure on the slide from the inside. Stupid bastard demons didn't know Arik had learned their languages and listened in on their conversations to figure out that only bone would open the lock.

Score one for the human, assholes.

Tav offered a respectful wave, and once he and the guards disappeared, Arik went to work. Limping, because his ankles and right knee ached from the recent torture, he scrounged up the needlelike bone and moved to the door. Squeezing his hand between the bars, he inserted the bone shard into the lock and prayed this would work.

Carefully, he tugged on the rope, felt the give in the lock, and his heart leaped. As he dug around with the bone, he listened for clicks and felt for patterns in the mechanism. He increased the pressure on the rope, and gradually, the metal began to give, until the mechanism had retreated. He gently shouldered the door, and it creaked open, the ear-splitting—to Arik, anyway—noise putting his pulse into overdrive. If one of the demon bastards heard...

He stepped out of the cell. A sense of freedom lifted his heart, but at the same time, he had to fight a disturbing urge to return to the chamber. Adrenaline winged through him, making him sweat, making his skin tighten, and he actually eyed the inside of the cell with uncertainty.

Yeah, his hesitation was fucked up, and the logical side of his brain that remembered his military training reminded him that his reaction was common in people and animals that had been held captive. The horror of the prison could be far less scary than the horror on the out-side. The horror of the unknown.

But Arik had thought he was stronger than that.

Fuck it, he *was* stronger than that, and he took his first step down the dark passageway. Around him, he heard the incessant drip that had driven him crazy for weeks, but so far, no footsteps or voices. Silently, he padded on bare feet through the winding cavern, but when he came to a fork in the path, he paused. One way continued off into the darkness, becoming hazy the farther it went, and while the other path was just as inky, it seemed to have a slight incline. Since Arik needed to go up to get to the human realm, the choice was a no-brainer.

He started on the path, stopping now and then to listen for demons. There was the distinct scuffing noise of spiny hellrats as they scurried along the tunnels, but no other demon sounds. So far, so good.

Until the next fork.

Both tunnels were dark, shot through with stalactites and stalagmites, and seriously, what the fuck? How could the path go from being relatively smooth to a damned obstacle course?

He pondered the fork, played three rounds of eenie-meenie-miney-moe, and blew out a frustrated breath. Which way...

Remember that if you always go the right way, you never have to make a left-hand turn.

He blinked. Had Tavin given him a clue? That sneaky little Sem. Having no better option, Arik took the right path, carefully weaving his way around the stony projec-tions. When he came to the next set of tunnels—three of them, this time—he stayed right. The general curvature of the tunnel veered to the left, but again and again, when he came to choices, he hung rights. And oddly, he didn't encounter any demons.

He walked for what seemed like hours, until his feet bled and his gut cramped from thirst. The tunnels grew hotter and hotter, some thick with steam and smoke, and others so empty of oxygen that more than once he nearly passed out.

He left a trail of blood behind him as he walked, and shit, this sucked. Bad. He stumbled a few times, cut his hands, his knees, and his scrub pants were now little more than shredded rags. He fantasized about food and cold beer—and, to his annoyance, Limos—as he forged ahead, his eyes peeled, his senses, which had felt dulled for so long, now on high alert.

Then, from out of nowhere, his hopes and fantasies crashed in on him like he'd taken a hit from a Tomahawk missile.

"Hello, Arik."

The deep, ominous voice froze Arik to his very marrow. Pestilence had found him.

Six

Limos entered Underworld General's emergency room, which was busier than shit. A golden-haired nurse, Vladlena according to her nametag, slowed as she wheeled a gurney containing a bleeding patient past.

"Eidolon is in surgery." She pointed in the direction of the triage desk. "Shade is over there."

"I'm not here for—"

Vladlena took off without listening, but Shade had caught sight of Limos. Great. Shade had been a major pain in the ass lately. He was mated to Arik's sister, and though there didn't seem to be any love lost between Arik and Shade, the demon was not happy to see his mate worried about her brother. And naturally, since Arik's situation was Limos's fault—indirectly, since Arik kissed *her*, not the other way around—Shade had been making life hell for Limos.

Shade tossed the clipboard he'd been holding onto the reception desk and stalked over. "You have news?"

"Nothing new," she said. "I'm here to meet Kynan."

"I just got off the phone with him. He's on his way."

"Thanks."

"You can thank me by finding Arik." He strode away before she could respond. Jackass.

She plunged her hand in her pocket and played with Arik's dogtags as she observed the nonstop stream of patients coming through the ER. What was he doing right now? Was he screaming in agony? Was he huddled in the dark, cold and afraid? Was he thinking about her and cursing her name? She broke out in a sticky sweat that smelled like guilt. Putrid, thick, bitter guilt.

Desperate for a distraction, she grabbed Vladlena again. "Is it always so busy?"

"Lately," she sighed. "It's all the underworld turmoil. Those who want the Apocalypse to start are fighting those who don't, and then the warg wars have started up again, and a new plague is affecting feline shifters, so we're getting an influx of them."

Limos had no doubt that Pestilence was behind the shifter plague, his way of sending a message. Namely, that once the Apocalypse started, shifters had better side with him, or he'd take them all out with a touch of a finger.

Vladlena took off just as Kynan stepped out of the gate, his denim blue eyes instantly zeroing in on Limos. "What's this about?" he said by way of greeting.

"Nice to see you too," she muttered. "Come on. I have something to show you. Something you might find helpful." The lie stroked all her pleasure centers and made her a little dizzy.

Kynan cursed, but entered the Harrowgate with her. Since he had been charmed by angels, he had little to fear, but it didn't surprise her that when the gate opened inside the tomb, he hesitated.

"If this is a trap—"

"It's not." But yeah, she could understand his concern. She'd brought him to a sealed tomb, and if she opened a gate and got out without him, he would be trapped until his friends found him... which could be a long, long time. "See that stone box? It's an Aegis vault. I found it while I was searching for my *agimortus*."

A shot of adrenaline streamed into her veins, and for a moment, she had to breathe through the lovely jolt. It had been so long since she'd told such a big lie, so long since she'd gotten a forbidden thrill from it, that she'd forgotten how great it felt.

The weigh scales on her shoulder blade made a substantial tip in favor of evil, reminding her of the gravity of what she'd just done. The farther the scales tipped and the longer they remained weighted toward evil, the poorer choices she made, the less she cared about anyone but herself. Worse, she'd enjoy others' suffering. She'd start famines for fun, and all it would take was a touch. She could lay her finger on a single man, and it wouldn't matter how much food he ate—he'd slowly starve, and everyone he came into contact with would suffer the same fate. All the while, she'd laugh. She'd make Pestilence look like a Boy Scout.

Damn you, brother.

Kynan was silent as a cat as he crept up to the box and knelt next to it. Pestilence had left it open, the heavy lid askew. Kynan's assessing gaze traveled over the Aegis symbol on the lid, and then carefully, he picked up one of the coins inside, using his thumb to wipe off the dust.

"What is all that stuff?" she asked.

"I don't know. Some of these pieces could be enchanted, used in certain rituals...I'm not sure. We'll need to study them." He glanced over at her. "You're old...have you seen any of these before?"

Old? "I prefer to think of myself as worldly, and no. I've never seen them before." The lie slammed more pleasure into her body. Funny how the fib could give her physical gratification, but mental anguish. Some small part of her actually hoped Kynan didn't fall for this even as a tingly high fired along every nerve ending. "Do you guys find a lot of these forgotten Aegis chambers?"

Whatever Pestilence's plan was, it could hinge on the believability of her happening upon a lost Aegis treasure trove.

"Every once in a while," he said. "Records have been lost, so some of these places have been long forgotten. And in other cases, someone was given a task in haste, an object that needed to be hidden, and then, before the Guardian could reveal the location, they died. So yeah, there are a number of chambers we know exist but can't locate, and hiding places we never knew about that we stumble across. And with the Apocalypse coming at us, discoveries are popping up in record numbers."

"Because things once hidden want to be found when doomsday is nigh," she murmured, quoting an ancient Aegis prophet she'd met back in the days before Christianity.

"Exactly." Kynan traced his finger over one of the necklaces at the bottom of the vault. "As the end of days nears, secrets are revealed."

Secrets revealed. Limos did not like the sound of that. She closed her eyes, trying to black out her past, her guilt, and not doing a very good job. She'd deceived so many, from the very day she'd walked out of Sheoul to now. And as much as she wanted to warn Kynan about the objects she'd led him to, she couldn't. Too much was at stake. The artifacts were in The Aegis's hands now, and what they did with them wasn't her concern.

A scratching sound had her opening her eyes to see Kynan brushing sand away from the base of the stone box.

"What are you doing?"

He licked his lips, his expression one of intense concentration. "Sometimes these boxes have hidden compartments."

She squatted down. "Can I help?"

"I wouldn't. They're usually warded so that if anyone but a Guardian tries to open them, either the contents are destroyed, or the person trying to get in gets a nasty surprise."

He pressed on a carved symbol with his forefinger. There was a grinding noise, followed by a puff of sand that made them both cough. Kynan waved his hand to clear the brown cloud, and as the particles fell away, a drawer was revealed. Inside were three fragile-looking scrolls.

"Cool," she breathed.

She wondered if Pestilence had known about the drawer. Maybe this find would make up for whatever evil Pestilence was up to with the artifacts.

Kynan picked one up. "Seals are intact." His smile, as he looked up at her, was one that could make a woman drunk with want. "Thanks, Limos. Between the artifacts and the scrolls, this could prove to be one of our best finds in a long time."

Guilt soured her mouth. "Yeah. No problem. You ready to go?"

Kynan unfurled to his full height, which was well over six feet. "Yep. Just one minute."

He carefully filled his pockets with the treasures. "If you can take me to Berlin, I'd be grateful."

"Specific location?"

"Nope." His smile told her he didn't want to give away the location of The Aegis's headquarters, which she got.

She threw open a gate. "Let's go."

"Wait." He grabbed her arm, and she resisted the urge to throw him across the chamber for touching her. Not that she could. Trying to injure Kynan was useless. "Are you making any progress in locating Arik?"

"No," she said softly, "I haven't. I'm on my way back to the hellmouth, though."

Her cell beeped, and she checked it, expecting Than, but what she saw made her blood run both hot and cold. "Oh…God."

"What is it?"

The update flashing on her underworld app filled the chamber with an eerie glow. "The gambling network. It's buzzing." Pains stabbed her chest, and for a second she was pretty sure she was having a heart attack. "The odds of Arik dying tomorrow just tanked."

"That's good news."

"No," she whispered. "It's not." She looked up. "The rumor is that he escaped. Odds now are that he'll be dead in an hour."

"Hey, Pest." The light tone Arik went for didn't make it past his parched, raw throat.

"Did you really think you were going to escape?"

Arik swung around, hoping his wince at the painful twinge in his hip came across as a casual smile. "Nah. I broke out to get some exercise. How'd you find me, anyway?"

Pestilence, his big body encased in tarnished armor that oozed oily stuff at the joints, rubbed his chin as though deep in thought. As if the fucker had more than one brain cell. "Spiny hellrats are my spies. But for what it's worth, it was a noble attempt. Impressive, actually."

"I live for your admiration."

"I'm sure."

Arik's stomach rumbled, the sound magnified by the tunnel's acoustics, which was a little embarrassing. "What is it you want from me? 'Cuz I gotta tell ya, there's very little you can do that hasn't been done."

The Horseman smiled, exposing some serious fangage. "We're going to get close, you and I. Very, very close."

Arik swallowed. Tried to, anyway. His throat was too dry. But he definitely didn't like the sound of Pestilence's *close* thing. "Look, I'm sure you make all the lady demons cream their panties, but I'm just not that into you."

"You're into Horsemen, though, aren't you? You're here because you couldn't keep your hands off my sister." Pestilence shrugged. "I'm not judging. She's got that unattainable bad girl quality going on. Took balls for you to kiss her, what with you being a pathetic human and all."

Too exhausted to banter any more, Arik slumped against the wall of the cave. "Just do whatever you came to do. Take me back to the cell. Kill me. Whatever. I'm tired of the games."

Pestilence was in Arik's face in a heartbeat, his fingers wrapped around his throat. Arik didn't even have a chance to fight back before he was lifted into the air and slammed into the stone with such force that his teeth rattled.

"I would love to kill you right now, but I have other plans." Pestilence knocked Arik against the wall again, and the crack of breaking bones echoed like gunshots off the stone walls.

Pain set fire to every nerve ending. He dangled there, watching in horror as the fucker struck, sinking his huge-ass fangs into his throat. Arik punched, scratched, struggled as hard as he could, but nothing he did seemed to faze Pestilence.

Gradually, blood loss sapped his strength, until his struggles amounted to little more than spastic twitches. He became lightheaded, woozy, and eventually all the pains and aches melted away, leaving him blissfully numb.

Pestilence lifted his head, and though Arik's vision had gone dark, he felt the rasp of the dude's tongue sliding over the punctures. Crazily, Arik's only thought was how vampire-like the whole thing was.

Pestilence released him, and he dropped heavily to the ground, landing in a crumpled, motionless heap. Arik heard the clank of armor, and then something was against his mouth, and warm liquid was flowing over his tongue. At first, he was grateful for the wetness that relieved his parched tongue and throat, and he swallowed greedily.

Until he realized the wetness was blood.

Holy hell, he was drinking the Horseman's blood—

His body jackknifed as pain shot through him, and suddenly he was flopping around like a dying animal on the side of the road, his limbs out of control, his head banging on the stone floor. Pestilence wrestled him flat on the ground with his huge, armored body, forcing Arik to keep drinking, even though he wanted to vomit.

White spots floated in front of his eyes, and darkness surrounded him, sucking him into a spinning vortex of oblivion.

And then he was alone, lying on the ground. The narrow tunnel didn't look familiar, and the ceiling was so low that an average-sized man would have to duck to walk through it. Mixed with the stifling, searing heat was a cool breeze. Well, not *cool*, exactly. More like a slightly less blistering breeze.

And wait... what had happened? How had he gotten here? Why was he not in his cell?

Didn't matter. He needed to find the source of the breeze. He tried to get to his feet, but they wouldn't work. Nothing below the waist worked. He supposed he should be panicking, but mentally, he was as numb as his lower body.

The breeze beckoned him, and reaching deep for what little energy remained in his broken body, he dug his fingers into the black soil and dragged himself toward the fresh air. Heat blasted him, steam and smoke burned his eyes, and his fingernails tore. But little pinpricks of light appeared in the distance, giving him hope and the willpower to continue.

He pulled himself along, grunting with every inch of progress, until finally, dear God finally, he found himself at the precipice between hell and the earth.

And then he realized, as he stared into the gaping maw of a massive, bubbling volcano, that nothing had changed. He'd climbed out of hell, but this was no different. This was hell *on* earth.

The volcano's hellmouth looked the same to Limos as it had when she'd searched it earlier. Blackened, with steam rising toward it, though most of it was deflected by the air coming out of Sheoul.

Kynan had come with her, gated straight from the chamber in Egypt. All she could think of was the gambling odds she'd seen. The demons who monopolized the underworld—and, now, the *upper*world—gambling industry were eerily accurate, and the fact that they'd given Arik high odds of dying within an hour was beyond bad.

"Where's the entrance?" Kynan said, as he picked his way across a field of jagged rock.

She jerked her head at the shimmering bubble that spread across a gaping hole in the side of the mountain. "Right there. Let's go."

She started toward it, but a pained groan halted her in her tracks. Wheeling around, she zeroed in on a crack in the earth a few feet from the entrance to the tunnel. Was that a...hand? *Yes.* She bolted over stone as sharp as glass shards to where the hand became an arm, and then a torso and head became visible, and her heart went crazy.

Arik.

Dear...God. Mouth so dry she couldn't swallow, she fell to her knees next to him. She'd seen so much in her lifetime, but the sight of this man, who had been so powerful, so healthy...but who was now gaunt, his skin shredded, blistered from the heat and blackened from ash...the horror of it made her own skin shrink. On her arm, Bones writhed at the scent of Arik's blood.

"Arik," she whispered. "It's me, Limos."

Kynan came up behind her, and his muttered, "Christ," echoed through the crater. He went down on his heels and rested two fingers against Arik's throat as he leaned over to put his cheek near Arik's mouth. "He's breathing. Pulse is erratic. We have to get him to—"

Kynan leaped to his feet, startled by a swarm of demons that was charging from out of the hellmouth's entrance. He drew his stang and turned to her. "Go! Take Arik!"

Limos didn't argue. She threw a Harrowgate and gathered Arik in her arms, surprised by his weight. He was thin, but he'd retained some muscle and had somehow kept more weight on him than she'd expected.

An arrow sailed past her head as she stepped through the gate. It punched into a tree trunk outside her private Hawaiian villa, narrowly missing skewering her gardener. Keeping Arik tucked against her, she stepped into the sand. Her chef, housekeeper, and one of her three guards, all wolf shifters from a nearby pack, came running.

"I need help carrying him to my room." She nodded at her chef, Hekili. "Go to Underworld General and bring the doctor named Eidolon here. Quickly."

The others helped her get Arik settled on top of her frilly pink comforter. They brought her warm water and a washcloth, and while she waited for Eidolon, she wiped Arik down, making slow, gentle passes over his skin. What wasn't scraped raw or cut open was inflamed and discolored; his fingertips had been worn to the bone, and his neck had been savaged by a pair of huge fangs. There wasn't an inch of him that hadn't been injured.

"Oh, Arik," she murmured. "If you just hadn't kissed

me. If you hadn't made me want you . . ." One corner of his swollen mouth lifted in a ghost of a smile, and she jerked in surprise. "Can you hear me?"

His cracked lips ruffled in a bigger smile before they settled into a pained, pinched line again. On impulse, she leaned over and touched her mouth to his, lightly, hoping for a response.

Nothing. But then, what had she been hoping for? That he'd suddenly sit up, good as new? That her kiss would wake him from his torment? She'd always loved fairy tales, loved how princesses always got their princes, but this was no children's fable where he'd magically get better because of her touch. This was a horror story, and it was her fault he was hurt in the first place.

Sighing, she wiped away blood from a gash in his jaw. He'd been shaved recently, but she didn't ponder that for too long—demon jailers often shaved their prisoners to keep their skin exposed and sensitive to torture.

God, what he must have gone through. "I—" She cut herself off, unable to say it. *I'm sorry.* Growing up, she'd been forbidden to ever say those words. To ever feel sorry about any action. *Sorry* meant weakness. The one time she'd apologized, to a messenger bringing word from her fiancé, her mother had punished Limos by gouging the male's eyes out before throwing him to her slaves to defile.

No . . . sorry was not a word to be thrown around lightly, and she'd said it only once since. Last month, when Ares's servant, Torrent, had been killed, her brother's pain had overridden her upbringing, just as Arik's was threatening to do now.

Eidolon, dressed in scrubs, arrived, ending her dark ruminations, and wouldn't you know it, Shade was with him, looking all cocky in his black paramedic uniform. The brothers' resemblance was so strong that if not for Eidolon's short black hair and Shade's longer hair, they could be mistaken as twins. Kynan came in behind them, dripping with demon blood.

"You should have brought Arik to UG," Eidolon said, as he crossed to the bed.

The desire to make up some dramatic excuse niggled at her, because frankly, she could use a dose of euphoria right now, but she gritted her teeth and told the simple truth. "I didn't want anyone to know he's been found."

Eidolon grabbed a pair of shears from out of the red medic bag Shade placed at Arik's feet. "Who is anyone?"

"The demons he escaped from." She glanced at Ky. "I'm assuming you killed the ones who attacked us?"

"Yeah. Once you were gone, they tried to get back inside the hellmouth, but headless demons don't go far."

Shade helped Eidolon cut off Arik's shredded pants, and Limos practically shook with rage at the sight of swollen, bruised flesh and broken bones poking through skin. She would destroy the bastards who'd done this.

"You don't think anyone will guess Arik's with you?" Shade asked.

"No one knows where I live. Underworld General is sort of . . . famous. And I don't trust your staff."

Eidolon shot her a dark look before palming Arik's forehead, his *dermoire* glowing as he channeled his ability into the human. "He's in bad shape. Really bad." He frowned. "There's a lot of healed damage. Holy hell, he's had his ear drums punctured, every bone broken multiple times, his skull is a mass of fractures. His organs are caked with scar tissue."

"So someone healed him?" Limos was going to make Arik's captors experience everything he had. Without the healing. "What—or who—could have done that?"

Shade dug IV supplies out of his bag. "Spells could have been used. And there are some species of demons who have abilities similar to ours, though not nearly as powerful."

Eidolon's frown became a scowl, and then a growl. "I can't repair any of the old injuries, which means it was a Sem who healed him. Arik is going to be dealing with this damage for the rest of his life. I can fix a lot of things, but not another Sem's work."

"What do you mean?" Kynan moved next to her.

Eidolon palpated Arik's abdomen. "It's like someone setting a broken leg bone but not knowing what they're doing. The bone will heal, but it'll heal wrong, leaving the limb bent or twisted. Arik's healer did that with pretty much everything. Whoever did it was good enough to keep Arik alive, but he wasn't practiced."

"There's nothing you can do?" she asked, as Shade hung a bag of clear liquid from the bed post and then inserted a needle into the back of Arik's hand.

Eidolon shook his head. "Once something has been healed by another Seminus demon... it can't be undone."

Limos cursed. "What about the immediate injuries? The shit he's dealing with right now?"

"Those I can fix." Eidolon nodded at Shade. "Need your help, bro. He's got spinal fractures, a severed spinal cord, third-degree burns, bilateral compound tib-fib fractures, and multiple lacerations. If you can handle his pain, I'll get the healing started."

"Wait." At some point, she'd dug Arik's dogtags out of her pocket, and now she held them as if his life depended on her firm grip. "His back is broken? As in, he's paralyzed?"

"For now. We'll fix it."

The doctor sounded so confident, and she hoped to hell he could do what he claimed. Shade gripped Arik's wrist, and his *dermoire* started glowing like his brother's. She paced, worrying the dogtag chain and wearing down the hardwood floor. She tried not to look, but every time Arik moaned, she flinched, looked over, and ached at the sight of his pale, waxy skin and pain-pinched expression.

Twice she caught herself moving toward him, as if she could help, even if all she could do was hold his hand. Would he be comforted by her touch, or would she cause him more distress?

And why did she care? Sure, the scales on her shoulder blade were evenly balanced again, but this was still the first time she'd worried about how someone besides her brothers might react to her.

Frustrated by the direction of her thoughts, she concentrated on inane things, like planning her next nail color scheme. Would Arik like orange and lime?

Finally, Eidolon stepped back and wiped his sweat-dampened brow with the back of his hand.

"He'll need to rest, and when he wakes up, make sure he gets food and liquids." Eidolon pulled the bed sheet up to Arik's chest. "Call me if something isn't right."

Shade removed the tube and catheter from Arik's vein and tucked the empty IV bag and supplies into his duffle. "I'll let Runa know he's here. She'll want to see him."

"Of course. I'll contact you when he wakes."

"Limos." Kynan plunked a coin into her empty palm. "I got this off one of the demons I killed. Who is Sartael?"

Sartael? Well, surprise, surprise. She held the thin slice of metal up to the light and studied the winged-skull symbol that was Sartael's mark. "He's a fallen angel who presides over lost and hidden things. There are also some obscure rumors about him being our father."

Kynan cocked an eyebrow. "I thought your father was an angel named Yenrieth."

"Yes, but he hasn't been seen since Lilith got pregnant. Angels usually get a new name when they fall, and many say Yenrieth fell as punishment for impregnating a demon. According to some rumors, he became Sartael... who hasn't been seen since after Lilith gave birth."

"So why would a demon be carrying a coin with Sartael's mark?"

"Apparently," she mused, "he's back. He would have imbued this coin with location magic. It would lead the bearer to Arik."

"Is Arik still in danger of being found?"

"Now that he's no longer in Sheoul, he's safe from Sartael. Outside of Sheoul, Sartael's powers are limited to locating demons and demonic artifacts." She flipped the coin in her palm. "Arik will be safe with me."

Kynan's sharp gaze caught hers. "Ares tried to kill Arik before he was taken to Sheoul. How do I know he'll be okay with you?"

Limos tried not to take offense, but she still snapped, "Because I wouldn't have called for Eidolon if I wanted him dead."

"And what about your brothers?"

"They don't want him dead, either." That particular untruth came easily, probably because she wished it were true. "You have my word, Aegi. Arik will be safe."

Kynan gave a single nod and strode out with Shade and Eidolon. As the door closed, Arik groaned. The sound was a spear to the gut. She'd never been the type to offer comfort—she had no problem offering her opinion, but the desire to take care of another had never been part of her makeup.

She moved toward the bed, her steps tentative, as if she were approaching an injured bear and not an unconscious man.

"Arik?" Her voice was a froggy croak.

He groaned again, louder, his jaw clenched as though in unbearable pain. Maybe she should grab Eidolon—

His body tensed and trembled, and he tossed his head, the tendons in his neck straining as he opened his mouth in a silent scream.

Thoughts of grabbing the demon doctor went out the window, replaced by a sudden need to end Arik's suffering. Hastily, she climbed into bed with him and used her body to control his thrashing. As gently as she could, she rested her head on his shoulder and put her hand on his chest. His heart pounded into her palm and drummed in her ear. This was the closest she'd ever been to a man—intimately, at least, and was her pulse supposed to match his like that?

It made her body hum and felt oddly...right...when she hadn't even known there was something wrong.

Another moan dredged up from his chest, the sound of so much agony. He'd been physically healed, but mentally...she didn't even want to think about what kind of damage had been done. He jerked, his muscles spasming so violently that his arms flailed.

"Shh." Using a light touch, she stroked him, long,

soothing passes through his hair, over his jaw, and down his throat. He settled down, his breathing even, the rise and fall of his chest becoming steady. "That's it. Sleep."

His hand came up, startling her as his fingers circled her wrist. She watched, breathless, as he put her palm against his lips in what she swore was a kiss. Confused by his tenderness and overwhelmed by the feelings it stirred inside her, she went completely still. No one had ever been so... she didn't even know the word for it, that's how foreign what he'd done was to her.

All she knew was that her Horseman name, Famine, was fitting. She'd always been starving for something she couldn't name, because she hadn't experienced it. Now she had.

A man's touch. A man's affection.

Now she was hungrier than ever, and that could only be a bad thing.

Seven

Warmth. Softness. Comfort.

Arik moaned at the luxury. He opened his eyes, expecting to see the black starkness of his cell, but instead, a palm-frond fan spun in lazy circles from a pearly-white ceiling, and an ocean breeze and warm sunlight streamed through open windows.

Dreaming. He was dreaming again. Man, he loved to dream. For just a little while, he could find peace and a small measure of relief from the constant starvation and pain.

Closing his eyes, he rolled ... and bumped into a warm body. A warm female body. He didn't need to look to know who it was. Her tropical scent, like suntan lotion and rum, filled his nostrils.

He should shove Limos out of the bed and flat on her ass. But this was a dream, she was hot, and this was the best he'd felt since he'd been tossed into the cell.

In a heartbeat, he had her tucked beneath him, his

mouth on hers, and his hips cradled between her spread legs. She let out a squeal of surprise and indignation, but he silenced it with his tongue.

Ooh, and handy...he was naked. Usually in these dreams, he had to strip.

Or let Limos do the stripping for him.

Her hands came up to his shoulders, almost tentatively, which struck him as odd, since in all the dreams before this, she'd been aggressive, a demanding tigress who either took what she wanted or made him work for what *he* wanted.

Now she was all timid kitten, which had to be a game.

Her palms slid lightly down his back, and yeah, game. Limos didn't do light. She did in-your-face, scratch, bite, and kick, with a side of poison tongue.

Tongue...which was sliding against his, again, timidly, and damn, she was good at this sweet, innocent shit. Strangely, it was a turn-on, and he arched, putting his hard cock firmly against her heat as he smoothed one hand over her waist. His groan mingled with hers, and her touch grew firmer, her tongue action more confident. He played along, letting her learn his mouth at her own pace, even though his body demanded that he take her the way he always did in these dreams.

Limos licked his lips, stroked his teeth with the tip of her tongue as her fingers dug in the muscles at the small of his back. He wanted to tell her to grip him harder, to let her nails score his skin, but this was so different from the other dream sex, so real, and yet so unbelievably tender that he just let it happen.

"Oh, yeah," he whispered against her lips, his hips rolling despite his desire to take things slow.

He shifted so he could remove her shirt as he peppered her skin with kisses. She tasted like Heaven and hell, light and dark, sweet and spice. He licked and nuzzled her throat as he slid his palm up her flat belly to her chest. Again, this dream was different from the others in that her breasts weren't as large as before, were instead hand-fuls of firm flesh that fit his palms as if made for them. He flicked his thumb over a perky nipple and caressed the silky skin beneath it with trembling fingers. He felt like this was his first time with her, which was so fucking weird.

Limos's legs came up so her knees caught him at his waist, and she tilted her pelvis to meet his rocking motions, the friction between them building quicker than he'd anticipated. His shaft was so stiff it felt brittle, his balls so full of come he could explode, and when Limos's hands dropped to his ass and pulled him firmly against her, he knew it was only going to take a sensual touch or a naughty word, and it would be over.

A growl ripped from his throat, and Limos responded with a sexy purr of her own, dragging her mouth down his chin, to his neck, and gave him a stinging nip. So good... it was so damned good. For the first time since he'd mounted her, he opened his eyes, wanting to see her gor-geous body. The sight laid him out. Her bronzed skin was flawless over muscles that flexed in her arms and stomach as she writhed. Her breasts were two perfect swells that begged him to taste.

Unable to resist, he closed his lips over one, delighting in her throaty gasp of pleasure. Greedily, he sucked at her, drawing her warm flesh into his mouth and laving it with his tongue. He swore he tasted the sun and wind on her skin, and it was the flavor of freedom, of lazy days and hot summer nights, of sex on the beach.

Sweat broke out over his skin as he tried to hold it together, but the way she was undulating beneath him, so sexy, so perfect, sent him over the edge. In a rough surge, he lunged against her, taking her mouth again as he pumped his hips, drilling into her with an insane need that was as foreign to him as it was critical.

"Arik," she whispered. "We shouldn't...can't...oh, yes...right...there."

He didn't need her to tell him he had it right. Her reaction, the way she threw her head back, her mouth open, the soft, breathy sounds that escaped...yeah, he knew he was driving her crazy.

The orgasm boiled in his balls, ready to blow through his shaft. It hit him like a locomotive, slamming into him as she cried out in her own release. She was so hot, so wet around him...

Wait...he wasn't inside her. The thought punched through the haze as he shuddered through the last of his climax, as he felt the hot jets splash onto her belly and chest.

Arms quivering, he lifted his head and frowned down at her. Her violet eyes were sex-glazed, her cheeks flushed, lips swollen. She was everything every man dreamed of. Except, with horrifying clarity, he realized that this wasn't a dream.

Holy shit, this was a nightmare.

Limos's heart was still pounding, her body tingling from the first climax she'd ever had with a male. Damn, what she'd been missing. She could only imagine how it would be with the male actually inside her. Especially if that male was one delectable human with a body made to pleasure a woman.

God, how beautiful Arik had been when he came, his rugged features softened by both the late morning sun streaming through the windows and by ecstasy, his muscles locked up and defined with pulsing, bulging veins beneath glistening skin. Hot spurts of his semen had splashed on her belly, and though she would love to know what that felt like in her core, this truly was amazing. She'd made a man orgasm, and although she was one of the most powerful beings on the planet, what she'd done for Arik had given her more satisfaction than anything in her life.

She was intoxicated by what they'd done, her lips still tingling from his kisses, and she thought that had been the best part of the lovemaking. The affection she'd craved, that he'd shown her earlier when he'd kissed her palm, had flowed from the kiss like an electric current, energizing her and filling her belly with flutters.

Tentatively, she smoothed her fingers over his jaw. She wanted to express her regrets for what had happened to him. Wanted to tell him how amazing he was for surviving it.

All that came out was a croaked, "Arik."

As if his name was a trigger, Arik exploded into action, scrambling off her and off the bed. "Shut up." He stumbled backward, crashed into a dresser.

"It's okay, Arik." Limos sat up, swinging her legs over the side of the mattress. "You're safe."

"Safe?" he asked, incredulous. "Safe? I'm in hell, you stupid demon."

Okay, so she'd expected him to be angry about what

happened to him, but *stupid demon*? Awkwardly, she grabbed for her shirt. "Listen to me—"

"Who are you?"

She blinked. He didn't recognize her? He'd just done the humpty all over her, and he hadn't even known who was beneath him?

Humiliation seared her cheeks as she wiped his now-cold semen off her belly with a bed sheet and then jerked the shirt over her head. "It's me, Limos."

"Bullshit. Get out of my head." His eyes were wild, he was panting, and through the heady fragrance of sex, she could smell his anger and confusion. "Get out *now*."

She modulated her voice, trying to calm him. "Hey, what's going on?"

He looked at her like she was the crazy one here. "You can't trick me." With a swipe of his arm, he knocked the vase of fresh flowers off her night stand. The glass shattered against the wall, and water and broken flowers spilled across the hardwood floor. "This shit isn't real. I know I'm in my cell, and you're really some hideous demon pretending to be...her."

"Pretending to be me? Limos?"

"You can't get me to say her name, so put a lid on this damned charade now." He looked down at himself. "Jesus, I don't even get clothes in this acid trip?"

Shit. He really did think demons had gotten in his head and were making him see things that weren't real.

"Arik, try to remember." She eased to her feet, doing her best not to startle him. He was like a wild animal, cornered and injured, dangerously unpredictable. "You were imprisoned for a month. I don't know how you got out of your cell, but I found you at the Erta Ale hellmouth.

You were unconscious. I brought you here, to Hawaii, and Eidolon and Shade healed you."

"Shut up." He grabbed his head with both hands, as though trying to keep it from rolling off his shoulders. "For God's sake, *shut up*."

Limos exhaled slowly, unsure how to handle this. Clearly, her presence was agitating him.

"I'm going to get you something to wear and eat, okay? Why don't you clean up. Get comfortable. There are new toothbrushes and toothpastes and soaps in the bathroom." She gestured to the patio door. "You can go out on the patio, but there will be guards below. You're not a prisoner, but until you're better, I can't allow you to leave."

He glared. "How does not being allowed to leave *not* make me a prisoner?"

"Because I said so."

Oh, *that* was mature. Dammit, Arik had a way of calling her out and throwing her off balance. She needed to regroup. Fast.

Heart racing like she'd run a marathon, she practically hurled herself out of the bedroom and down the hall to the kitchen, where she sent a quick text to Thanatos to bring some clothes. Then she settled in to doing the only thing she could think of to help Arik; feed him. She slapped together a sandwich piled high with sliced turkey, cut a wedge of banana cream pie, and grabbed a bottle of water from the fridge.

The sound of footsteps froze her to the floor before she'd taken three steps back to the counter.

Reseph.

She'd know the cadence of his saunter anywhere. Except he wasn't Reseph anymore, and though ninety-nine percent of the time she was well aware of that fact, sometimes she slipped, her mind taking her back to memories of him doing something familiar, like bopping through her house looking to party, or pestering her into going to a movie with him.

"Hey, sis," he drawled, as he set up shop in the doorway, his big, armored body blocking the way to Arik's room. "Aren't you going to thank me for saving your pathetic human pet?"

"He *escaped*, you liar."

"He got out of his cell," Pestilence countered, "but I got him to the hellmouth entrance before demons got him. Granted, I left him in worse condition than I found him, but there's always a trade-off, isn't there?"

"You," she snarled. "You're the reason he was so battered."

He shrugged, one of the spiked metal shoulder plates carving a deep groove into the white paint on the doorjamb. "I didn't do anything his captors hadn't done to him. Or would have done to him if you hadn't gotten to him before Sartael's team did."

"You're despicable."

Pestilence clutched his chest dramatically. "You wound me."

Oh, she'd like to wound him, all right. "What do you want? I did what you asked, so get the hell out of my house."

Her brother fingered the engraved bow-and-arrow symbol on the back of his gauntlet. The right touch would pop a real weapon into his hand, and Limos hoped he didn't suddenly decide to put an arrow between her eyes.

"I came to give you a heads-up," he said, halting the finger play.

She stared. "Really."

"Yup." The amused glint in his eyes grew sinister, and his lips peeled back from fangs as long as her pinky. "I fed from your boy. He's smooth going down. When your Seal breaks, you can see for yourself."

Fury that he'd stuck those fangs into Arik was a gasoline fire in her veins. Her brother had committed violence against Arik, had hurt and used him, but there was an envious element to her anger, as well. Pestilence had been intimate with Arik...granted, the intimacy was sick and twisted, but there was definitely a forced closeness to feeding, to the penetration, and she had no doubt her brother had gotten off on what he'd done.

Even though she wanted to hurl one of the knives from the butcher block at Pestilence's head, she didn't give her brother the satisfaction.

"My Seal isn't going to break," she said calmly.

"It will." Pestilence pushed off the doorframe. "That's the only reason I haven't killed the human yet. I want you to be the one who does it. I want to watch when you drink him to death."

"Why would it matter to you if he's dead?"

"Because," he said, his voice as dark as the black stuff leaking from the joints of his armor, "he fed from me too. Which means that when he dies, his soul is mine. And I have plans for it."

Horror clamped down hard on Limos's throat, squeezing so viciously she couldn't breathe, and she fought the urge to launch herself at him.

When she could speak again, her voice was a raw rasp. "Why? Why would you do that?"

But before the question was even fully out of her

mouth, she knew. Every soul Pestilence took made him stronger, but this went far beyond that.

"Yeah," Pestilence drawled. "You know why. You always had more brains than boobs." He flashed his fangs. "Your husband will give me anything I want in trade for Arik's soul."

Her calm evaporated. She snatched up a butcher knife and hurled it with all her strength.

Pestilence took a graceful sidestep, and the blade punched into the wall, the handle vibrating harmlessly. Casting a smile over his shoulder, he took the corner, disappearing from her sight.

That asshole. That goddamned son of a bitch!

Closing her eyes, she planted her fists on the counter and stood there until her blood pressure wasn't in danger of blowing out her eardrums. But even as the thud faded away, she once again heard the sound of footsteps. At least this time, it was Thanatos who stepped into the kitchen, wearing his usual black pants and a long black coat that buckled from the high collar to the waist. She'd bet he had on a black turtleneck under it. Instead of his favorite thick-soled Goth boots, he wore combat boots.

"You look like hell." He tossed a pair of sweat pants and a T-shirt onto the table. "And why is there a knife in the wall?"

"Pestilence was just here, and that knife was meant for the back of his skull."

Thanatos tensed, his yellow eyes darkening to a golden amber. All around him, shadows gathered. "What did he want?"

"Mostly to taunt me."

God, she hated this. Hated that her brother had gone

evil. Hated that he had so much power over her. Hated that he now owned Arik in a way she never would. Not that she wanted to own his soul, but she definitely didn't want Pestilence having it. Arik was . . . what? Hers? Impossible, even if he didn't hate her.

Thanatos had gone still, as if considering what their brother might have done to taunt her. She expected him to ask, so she was surprised when he said, "How's the human doing?"

"I'm not sure. He doesn't remember escaping."

"Did you mess with his memories?"

She and her brothers could erase memories— depending on the situation and individual, they usually couldn't go back more than a couple of hours or so, but often, that was all that was needed.

"I haven't done anything to his mind. He thinks he's still in Sheoul." She blew out a frustrated breath. "I'm a little worried." A little? She was freaked.

"Yeah, well, remember how screwed up you were after you got away from The Aegis?"

How could she forget? Those bastards had paralyzed her with hellhound spit and kept her in a dungeon while they poked and prodded, and threw in a little torture for fun. Reseph had rescued her, and she'd spent two full days trying to get her bearings.

"He just needs some time."

Thanatos shifted his weight. "Speaking of that . . ."

"Don't say it," she growled. "Killing him so he won't get grabbed by demons isn't an option. Our asshole brother did some sort of blood exchange with him, and now if he dies, his soul belongs to Pestilence."

"Fuck," Than breathed. "That's not cool."

"You think?" She loaded the food and water on a tray. "What I don't get is why he's waiting. Why not kill Arik now?"

"No idea. Maybe tethering a soul is like turning a vampire? It has to 'take'?"

"I don't know about that, but I do have some good news." She dug Sartael's coin out of her shorts pocket. "Look who's surfaced." She flipped the coin at Than, who snatched it easily out of the air.

"Well, well," he murmured as he studied the coin. "The angel of hidden things came out to play for the Apocalypse." He looked up. "How did you get this?"

"I killed a demon who was using it to track Arik," she said, enjoying the flush of heat that tingled over her skin. She could have told Than the truth, that Kynan had killed the demon, but her brother would have wondered why she'd been with Ky in the first place. "I thought Sartael was dead."

"There have always been rumors that instead of death, he was imprisoned by Satan. Some say he was turned into a hellrat and kept as a pet."

"So why let him out now?"

"Maybe your fiancé was desperate to find Arik after he escaped?"

"It's possible, but it seems pretty extreme to bring Sartael back after so long just to find one human." She eyed the knife in the wall. "Pestilence," she spat. "He mentioned Sartael when he was here. I'd bet your left nut that Pestilence arranged for Sartael's release so he could help him find my *agimortus*."

Thanatos bounced the coin in his palm. "I'd appreciate it if you didn't use my balls as wagers, but yeah, that makes sense."

"Can we use that coin to find Sartael?"

"I might have something in my library about it. Reaver might know something as well. I'll summon him."

Awesome. It was about time they had a concrete plan. She grabbed the tray and clothes, and allowed Than to walk her to the bedroom. Ever protective, he stepped in front of her to open the door and scan the room before he let her enter. Arik was sitting in a corner, still naked, his forehead propped on his knees.

He looked up as they entered, his gorgeous hazels seething.

"Hey," she said softly. "I brought some clothes." She tossed them on the bed. "And food."

She eased forward, stopping when his lips peeled back in a silent snarl. Behind her, Than was a black menace, which wasn't going to make things with Arik go any easier.

Go, she mouthed, and when her brother didn't budge, she nudged him with her elbow. After shooting her a look that conveyed his displeasure, Than stalked outside and slammed the door closed.

Very slowly, she set the tray on the floor and backed away from Arik. Going by the stark hunger in his expression, she expected him to leap on the food. Instead, he shrank back even more.

"You think I'm stupid?" His voice was an angry rumble. "You think I'll try to eat that? Where is my bucket of eyes and guts?"

Eyes and guts? The realization made bile bubble up in her throat. They'd fed him nasty shit, and probably taunted him with real food, punishing him when he tried to eat it. She'd never wantèd to commit mass murder more than she did right now.

"No eyes and guts today. Special treat."

"Fuck off. I want my usual. And don't tell me you're out of maggot-ridden rotting meat, because you seem to have an abundance of that."

"Tell you what," she said lightly. "You can have the nasty stuff after you eat this." She backed toward the door, hoping he'd eat after she was gone, but suspecting he wouldn't.

Turned out, she was right.

She covertly watched through the sliding glass door that led from the back deck to the bedroom, as he stared at the food with a desperate longing in his eyes. Finally, when it was clear that Arik wouldn't touch the food, she found Hekili taking inventory in the pantry.

"I need something…disgusting-looking," she said. "Something that's edible, healthy, but won't look like it's real food." She paused, considering the whole torture chamber scenario. "And put it on a paper plate or a cheap pie tin."

"I can get just the thing." Smiling, Hekili wiped his hands on the towel draped over the shoulder of his chef jacket. "Haggis."

Yeah, that would do it. "Perfect."

Eight

Harvester hated taking orders from anyone, but the instructions she'd recently received couldn't be ignored. She didn't understand them, but she knew that if she screwed up, she would be in big trouble. And if she succeeded, she could be in even bigger trouble.

What she was about to do could put her life in danger the moment she exited Sheoul and entered the human realm, where the forces of Heaven could snuff her like a cigarette. Complete with the crush of a galaxy-sized boot.

She glanced around her residence, which, though richly decorated in artwork from around the various regions of Sheoul, was as cold and unappealing as the blackened forest all around the house. Her werewolf slave, Whine, was the only thing that gave her home life, though today he was dragging ass. She'd taken a little too much blood from him last night, and though he would never complain about being tired, she saw it in the way he moved—slower and with far less grace than usual.

But she couldn't afford to feel bad, and she certainly couldn't afford to show him any compassion. In this place, kindness killed.

"Stop dawdling," she snapped. "I need the guest chamber prepared immediately." She didn't wait for Whine to nod. She flashed straight to the one person who could help her carry out her mission, the most powerful Orphmage in the underworld.

The Neethul, Gormesh, occupied a crystal tower on the craggy banks of the river Acheron. Guards circled the tower, which was clear as glass right now, but could change color and opacity at Gormesh's whim. He was in his lab, walking between rows of test subjects. Unwilling test subjects, if the way they were strapped to tables and locked in cages was any indication.

The guards didn't mess with her, and she passed through the front doors with no problem. The moment the doors closed, the palace walls turned smoky, and in moments, the sorcerer appeared at the top of the grand staircase.

"Harvester." His voice was as smoky as the walls. "It's been centuries."

Which hadn't been long enough. She cut to the chase. "I need something that will paralyze an angel."

Gormesh whistled, long and low. "Angels aren't easily immobilized. You know that."

"Of course I know that," she gritted out. She might have left Heaven thousands of years ago, but every memory of her time as a pure angel was as sharp as one of the Orphmage's scalpels.

"Why not simply trap your angel with a containment spell and cut off his wings?"

"Because this particular angel won't be easily led into a trap, and I don't have the time to set up something elaborate." She started up the stairs, holding the sorcerer with her gaze. "My orders are coming from the very top, so any help you can provide will be most...appreciated."

"The very top, you say?" his elflike ears twitched. "Come with me. This will cost you, but we'll figure something out."

Great. The fucker didn't come cheap for the simplest things. This? This was going to cost her more than she could afford.

But the payoff would be spectacular. Reaver wouldn't know what hit him.

Reaver smiled down at the pile of dead demons in the dirt at his feet. Of all his duties, his favorite was killing demons. As a battle angel of the Power order of angels, it was what he'd been bred for, and he was good at it. Sure, back when he'd been stripped of his wings and cast out of Heaven, he'd worked as a doctor at Underworld General Hospital, where he'd healed demons. But he'd been selective about who he saved, because the truth was that not all demons were evil, just as not all humans were good.

There was balance everywhere, a yin-yang thing going on since the beginning of time, and for the most part, it had worked.

Until Pestilence's Seal had broken, and now the balance between good and evil was rapidly shifting...and not in the favor of good. Evil was spilling out of Sheoul and was infecting humans everywhere, including here, in this remote Polish village where people had turned on each other, not knowing that their actions had been influenced by the demons Reaver had just killed.

Gethel, the angel who had been the Horsemen's good Watcher before Reaver had taken the assignment a little over a year ago, emerged from inside one of the houses where a family had been slaughtered.

"All souls have crossed over," she said, as she glided toward him. "But far too many crossed to the wrong side."

That was the problem with the kind of evil they were dealing with now. Too many humans who wouldn't normally fall to darkness were allowing evil into their bodies and minds. In the battle for souls, Heaven had always had the advantage, but even that was starting to change.

Gethel eyed the dead demons, her lip curling in distaste. "Your power is impressive, Reaver. I can see why you were chosen as my replacement." Smiling, she spread her wings—white, shot through with gold—and performed a pre-flight check as she folded and unfolded them again. "Give Limos my best. I do miss her. And Reseph." Her smile turned sad. "He was the one I thought might retain some humanity even after his Seal broke."

"I did too." Reaver lifted his hand in the stick-in-the-ass formal manner his fellow angels were so fond of. "Fare well, Gethel."

She lifted off so fast that even Reaver would have missed it if he'd blinked. Around him, the dead demons disintegrated, as they always did in the human realm—unless they were shapeshifters or weres, or a species such as Seminus demons, who appeared to be human.

Basically, if they couldn't pass as human, they decomposed in a matter of seconds.

His scalp prickled, a split-second of warning before Harvester materialized.

"Hello, you sexy beast," she said, the sarcasm in her voice setting his teeth on edge. She stood before him, her shiny hair and wings as black as her soul.

"What do you want? I have things to do." Namely, he had to respond to the summoning that had become a fizzy tug on his insides in the last few minutes.

Thanatos was calling him, and Reaver wondered what was up. The Horsemen didn't screw around with a summons, though sometimes Reaver wished they would. Would it really hurt them to summon him for, say, a barbecue? Or for one of Limos's beach parties? Angels had to eat too.

"I merely longed to gaze upon your angelic handsomeness." Harvester batted her eyelashes, and Reaver snorted.

"I think it's more likely you came to smash me under a mountain again." He gestured to the countryside. "You have an entire mountain range to work with."

"Tsk-tsk. You don't trust me at all, do you?"

"I probably didn't trust you even when we were in Heaven together." *Probably*, because he didn't remember. His memory, as well as all evidence of his very existence, had been wiped for some reason, and he couldn't recall anything that had taken place before the event that caused his fall a quarter-century ago. Even when he'd been given his wings back, his memory hadn't returned, and no angel he knew of, fallen or otherwise, could remember him either.

Harvester shrugged, a slow roll of one curvy bare shoulder. Geez, she was dressed like a stripper in a black leather bustier and miniskirt, fishnet nylons, and six-inch stilettos. Reaver might be all holy and good now, but one of the dangers of being on Earth—especially now that evil was permeating everything—was that angels felt everything humans did, including lust, and Reaver had always had a thing for scantily dressed, naughty girls.

He narrowed his eyes. Was Harvester aware of his dirty little secret?

"I wasn't always untrustworthy," she said, sounding a little stung despite her casual attitude. "I did enjoy serving." Her smile flashed fangtips. "But I enjoy ruling more."

"Are you here to chat, or are you here about something important?"

"It's definitely important."

"About the Horsemen?" That would be the only reason she'd seek him out. It was the only thing they had in common.

"In a way. You know the human, Arik, escaped from Sheoul."

No, he didn't know that. Must have been what Thanatos was summoning him about. "I'd heard."

She bent over to pick up what looked like a ring on the ground, exposing a thin scrap of black underwear that didn't cover nearly enough, and Reaver bit down on the inside of his cheek as he averted his gaze.

"How pretty," Harvester murmured, as she straightened. "I'm sure it's a priceless treasure. Now, what about Arik?"

"He's with Limos." She handed Reaver the silver ring, and he was too distracted by the fallen angel's breasts, which had nearly popped out of the bustier while she'd been bent over, to wonder why she'd hand him anything. "Pestilence has claimed his soul."

Reaver drew a quick, sharp breath. "He what?"

"Yep. Pestilence made sure that when Arik dies, his soul is sent straight to him. He's developing talents like that faster than any of us could have foreseen."

Damn, but the evil Horseman was growing powerful. Before Reseph's Seal broke, only Thanatos had any control over souls. Now Pestilence could not only absorb them from humans while they were still alive, turning them into obedient minions and adding to his own strength, but he was capable of claiming souls in a way only a handful of the most powerful demons could.

"This isn't good," Reaver muttered.

"It's not good for *you*," she corrected. "It's very good for my team." Smiling, she sauntered up to him and placed her hand on his chest. Her voice went low and husky. "You know what else is good for my team? You. In my custody."

An alarm clanked inside his head, an impending sense of doom coming down on him like a shroud, but before he could identify the source, his body went rigid, so solid he might have been encased in ice.

Harvester had trapped him. Somehow, she'd immobilized him. His heart couldn't even beat in panic, but he felt her finger jam into his chest, felt his body tip over so he was on his back, staring up at the gray afternoon sky. A minute later, his vision blurred, but he made out faces above him. Voices around him. He felt hands grab him roughly, and then there was a flash, and suddenly, the massive pain spreading through his chest told him where he was.

Sheoul.

Harvester had flashed him into hell. This was a huge violation of the Watcher covenant. Clearly, Harvester didn't care.

"Take him into the guest room."

He wanted to fight, to scream, anything at all, but he couldn't move a muscle. He could only feel. Sucked that all his other senses had dulled, but that one remained perfectly intact.

Reaver was manhandled as he was carried, and then he was thrown face-down onto what he assumed was a table, and chains wrapped around his wrists and ankles.

He was held fast, unable to move, barely able to think.

"Now, Whine." Harvester's eyes gleamed with anticipation as her werewolf minion came forward with a serrated blade—an old bone saw. He'd worked with them at Underworld General, and he knew damned good and well what they looked like.

And as other minions closed in on him, ripped open his shirt and dug into his back to stretch out his wings, he realized he'd soon know what they felt like, too.

Pestilence couldn't decide if he was in a good mood, or a bad one. That happened a lot lately. Usually he just fucked and killed something, which was always a supercharged Prozac. But today had been a roller coaster of ups and downs, ending with what had happened when he'd watched Harvester take Reaver from the dying village.

He'd seen the fallen angel flirt with Reaver, showing off her tits and ass, and Pestilence had been...jealous.

Why, Pestilence had no idea. He hated Harvester. He wanted to cause her as much misery as he could, which was why he'd tethered Arik's soul to him—he was going to kill the human and take his soul to the Dark Lord, where he'd use Arik as a bargaining chip. A bargaining chip to get Harvester as his mate.

Yes, he hated her. But she was one of the most powerful females—next to his mother—in all of Sheoul. Having her on his side to rule after the Apocalypse, when he and his siblings would be at war with each other for dominance and control of the earth and of souls, would be advantageous.

It would also be fun, because he'd love forcing her into his bed every night. He would get off on her screams, her tears, her pleas for mercy.

A shiver of delight went through him, followed immediately by a burst of raw rage. His plan had hit a snag. A big one, which he'd learned when he visited Limos, intent on killing Arik in front of her. The moment he'd stepped inside her house, he'd encountered a problem.

He couldn't sense Arik's soul, which meant that the human's soul belonged to someone else.

Some fucker had already staked a claim on it, and now Pestilence had to find that someone else before Arik was killed.

It figured that just as everything was coming together, one thread had begun to unravel.

But that was okay. He'd work it out. He always did. And now that Lucifer had brought Sartael out of whatever prison he'd been in, finding Limos's *agimortus* could be only days away.

Pestilence climbed out of the hellhound blood-filled stone pit where he'd bathed to feed his armor, leaving behind the dead bodies of the Amish family he'd enjoyed until they'd died. Time to get to work. He'd finally perfected the plague he'd been working on for weeks, and the human race had a nasty surprise waiting for them.

Nine

For the last hour at least, Arik had stood, back to the wall, eyeing the sandwich and pie. His mouth watered, but his mind was in turmoil. If he ate the food, he'd suffer in ways no man had ever suffered. Well, no man except Arik, because he'd already been through it. A couple of times.

You're a slow fucking learner, boy. The voice of his father pounded through his head, and what the fuck? He'd been done with the abusive son of a bitch since the day he'd passed away in the hospital, nothing but an empty shell, mentally and physically. It had been surreal to look at the hands that had pounded Arik, Runa, and their mother into bloody pulps and to see how fragile they were, the skin paper thin and bruised by IV catheters and blood draws.

Not once had Arik felt sorry for his old man's premature death, but now that he'd gotten an eyeful of Sheoul firsthand, he almost regretted cursing his father to hell. Almost, because some people deserved to be there. *Here.* Arik was still in hell, and he needed to remember that.

He inhaled, taking in the fragrant sweetness of the pie, because the demons wouldn't beat him for breathing. He knew, had tested them time and time again by getting as close to the forbidden food as possible and taking deep, full lungfuls of air, as if maybe he could absorb some calories that way.

So. Fucking. Hungry.

He swore, long and loud, and then turned his attention to the clothes. The black sweat pants were too long and the waist too big—who the hell wore these things?—but the drawstring tightened enough that he didn't have to worry about them falling off. The T-shirt, black, with *Guinness* written across it, fit better, though it was loose around the shoulders.

The door opened, and he stiffened, waited for this dream to fade and reveal that he was back in his cell.

Instead, the Limos-demon entered and put a plate and plastic bottle on the floor. As hungry as he was, he couldn't look away from her to the food. They'd gotten her image perfect, right down to the jewel-colored eyes, the satin black hair, the tan curves that could make a guy weep.

He'd come all over that fabulous body.

The demons must have gotten a serious laugh over that, but Arik just wanted to puke. Bastards.

He waited until the female removed the other food and backed out of the room to creep forward. He eyed the stained paper plate, unable to identify the pile of stuff on it. Looked like it had been scraped out of some animal's intestines. Probably had.

Crouching, he sniffed at it. Didn't smell putrefied. In fact, it smelled almost familiar. He sniffed again, and blinked in surprise. Dog food? They were giving him dog food now? Well, hell, it was an improvement over unidentifiable, rotten organs and week-dead animals. He looked at the plastic fork in confusion. They'd never given him utensils, which could potentially be used as weapons.

What game were they playing with him?

Whatever. He was starving. He scooped up a bite, and moaned at the taste. It was awesome. The best thing he'd eaten in weeks, and it actually tasted like food. Some sort of sausage, maybe. Man, people were feeding dogs well these days.

He inhaled the food, licked the plate, and then downed the water. He'd already gulped water straight from the bathroom faucet, so he wasn't thirsty, but the clear, icy liquid tasted like heaven in a bottle.

There was a tap at the door, and he stood, wondering what was coming next. Usually after eating he got to rest for a little while before the torture started, but sometimes the demons thought it was fun to see how much pain it took to make him throw up the food.

The demon pretending to be Limos entered the room. "I brought you more clothes." She tossed a U.S. Army duffle with his name stenciled on it, onto the bed.

"Where did you get that?"

"Kynan—"

Without thinking, he was on her, slamming her against the door, his fingers wrapped around her throat. "How do you know about Kynan?"

She clawed at his grasp, her strength enough to keep her from choking. "Arik, listen," She sucked air. Hard.

"This is real. I know Kynan because he helped us. When Ares's Seal was in danger of breaking. You helped too."

How long was this mind-fuck going to continue? He released her and stepped back, knowing he'd earned a big, fat beating for daring to touch one of his keepers. God, he was going crazy waiting for it. Being tortured was so much easier than the suspense. These bastards had a new tack, and it was working.

So...fine. He'd play their game. They were obviously working hard to convince him that this bullshit was real, so he'd give them a taste of who he was when he wasn't being held in a filthy dungeon. He'd take charge of this situation and teach them real fast that he was in control of what was in his head.

"So." He kicked the paper plate into the corner. "I'm really in Hawaii, and you're really who you say you are. The Horseman who got me tossed into hell."

A black brow arched, just a little. "So you believe me?"

"I'm willing to give it a shot."

"You can say my name now."

Like hell he could. "That's not going to happen. I'm not taking any chances. So tell me why, exactly, my captors wanted me to say it."

She dragged her hand through her hair, and even though she wasn't the real thing, his fingers flexed, wanting to do the same. "Did they tell you why you were taken to Sheoul?"

Only about a million times. "They said it was because of you. Because you lost control somehow and were selfish."

Surprise flickered in her gaze, and her lips parted on an indignant sound. "Hardly. You went there because you kissed me, and that was forbidden." Her chin came up as if she suddenly remembered she was supposed to have a superiority complex.

"A kiss? A fucking *kiss* got me tortured to within the last inch of sanity? Maybe you could have laid out the rules for messing around with you? You know, before I did that?"

She sniffed. "You should have known better."

This demon had Limos's mannerisms and attitude down pat. "So why do—did—they want me to speak your name?"

"Because I'm engaged," she said nonchalantly, as she studied her nails. "But my fiancé can't claim me unless I'm captured in Sheoul, my Seal breaks, or the male I give my affections to utters my name while in agony."

"Oh, *now* you tell me you're engaged?" he said between gritted teeth.

She let out a long-suffering sigh, as if his questions were a bother. "I didn't think it was important. Seeing how I hadn't planned to do anything more intimate than kick your ass."

Steam turned his body into a pressure cooker. "You little liar. You kissed me back. You wanted it."

"I did not." As if she'd just shot up with a speedball, her pupils dilated, swallowing the purple, and then went to pinpoints before returning to normal.

"Don't fucking lie to me. I've kissed enough women in my life to know, so stop the bullshit."

A low, pumping growl rumbled in her chest. "How many women have you kissed?"

"Why?"

"*How many?*"

Oh, now this was rich; she was jealous. She had no right to be fucking jealous. Not when she was engaged to another man. The steam scoured his veins, because even though the logical part of him didn't think any of this was real, his body and emotions weren't as sure.

"You want the truth? Because you won't get lies from me. So be very careful what you ask for."

She crossed her arms over her chest and stared. When it was clear she didn't really want an answer, he went back to the original subject.

"So let me get this straight. I say your name, and you walk down the aisle with loverboy. That's it? I was hung from hooks and roasted over coals just so you didn't have to reserve a church?"

He was so going to say her name. He'd shout it from the rooftop. With a blowhorn.

"It's not that simple." Calm again, she caught a lock of hair and twirled it around her finger, and Arik wished she'd stop with the ADHD routine. "I mean, yeah, you saved me from bedding down with the big boy, but it's about more than that—"

"Wait." He held up his hand. "Who, exactly, is your fiancé?"

"Um… well… that would be Satan."

Arik's entire center of gravity wobbled, and he threw out a hand to catch himself on the dresser. "*The* Satan? As in, cast out of Heaven, ultimate evil, fallen angel? Lucifer?"

She rolled her eyes. "Actually, Satan and Lucifer aren't the same. A simple mistranslation led to that belief— you'd be surprised how often mistranslations and biased interpretations have screwed with history and religion. Ask me about the Wars of the Roses or the Seven Deadly

Sins sometime. Anyway, Lucifer *is* a fallen angel, but he's Satan's right-hand man."

"Thanks for the history lesson," he muttered. Jesus. How the hell had he gotten himself into this mess? *You were thinking with the wrong head, that's how.* Yeah, well, Decker was always saying that his dick was going to get him into trouble someday.

This went beyond *trouble* and right into FUBAR territory. Especially when a horrifying thought came to him.

"Earlier," he croaked. "In bed...did things just get worse for me?"

Limos turned bright red. "Ah...yeah...that. No. The damage is done. It doesn't matter what I—*we* do now."

"There is no we." And why had he even asked that question, if this was just one big *Star Trek* holodeck scenario?

He turned around, put his hand on the glass pane. The view was gorgeous, but a gilded cage was still a cage. Weird, though, how the last time the demons had tried to trick him like this, the world had been fuzzy, dreamlike. Details had been off. Everything here was crisp and sharp, accurate down to the way Limos smelled like coconuts.

Clearly, a far more competent magician was spinning this trick.

"Arik." Limos's hand came down on his back, and though his first instinct was to get away from her, he couldn't.

"Arik?" she repeated.

"What?"

"I wish none of this had happened." There was an underlying tremor in her voice, and he almost believed her. Almost.

"Wow. If that was an apology, it's lame. Are you really sorry?"

"Yes."

For some reason, her answer pissed him off. "Sorry" was for when you forgot to take out the trash when it was your turn. "Sorry" was for when you bought the wrong kind of wine to go with dinner. "Sorry" did *not* work when you lost your temper and beat the shit out of your wife and kids. "Sorry" wasn't enough when you blew your paycheck on booze instead of on food for your family. And "sorry" sure as hell didn't cut it when you got someone sent to hell to have their skin peeled off.

He wheeled around, snaring her wrist as he backed her against the glass. "You do not get to be sorry. If this isn't real, you're just fucking with me. If it is, your sorry isn't good enough."

"What can I do to prove it to you?"

"For starters, you can admit that I didn't force any kiss on you. You can admit you wanted it. You wanted *me*."

Her violet eyes grew liquid. And that was how he knew this was bullshit. The real Limos would kick his ass and tell him to go fuck himself. But this one looked as if he'd just plunged a stake into her heart.

"I can't," she whispered. "If I do, this was all my fault."

"Newsflash, My Little Pony, it was." Releasing her, he stalked away, and then realized he had nowhere to go. He stopped in the middle of the room, but didn't turn back to her. "Why don't you just kill me? Am I really worth that much to you?"

"Yeah." Her voice was a tortured rasp. "Yeah, you are."

The next sound was that of the door closing.

Ten

~

Limos stood outside the bedroom door, her heart pounding, her entire body shaking. She'd thought Arik was making progress, but now it was clear that he still didn't believe he was free of his prison, and she had no idea how to help him. She'd even tried summoning Reaver for help earlier, and when that failed, she'd called out to Harvester. Neither angel came.

Closing her eyes, she let her head fall back against the wall, remembering how disoriented she'd been after Reseph rescued her from Aegis hell. He'd taken her to Ares's island, and when she couldn't stand, couldn't speak or even understand where she was, he'd walked out into the surf and sat down, fully clothed, in the waves. The shock had brought her around, and the whole time, he'd just held her. Reseph had been her anchor, the brother who loved her more than anything.

Maybe Arik's anchor was his sister.

She made a quick call, and within minutes, the door-bell rang.

"Thanks for coming." Limos ushered Shade and Runa inside, mentally comparing Arik and his sister, but the only resemblance Limos could see was in their muscular builds, which wasn't a surprise. Kynan had said the caramel-haired woman was a werewolf, and Limos had never met a warg that didn't look like it could win body-building contests.

Shade's arm came protectively around Runa's shoulders, and though Limos had never needed anyone's protection, she experienced the oddest twinge of envy that Runa had a mate who kept her safe.

"How's he doing?" Runa's hands clenched together until Shade gently took them in his.

"Physically he's fine," Limos assured them. "But I'm having a hard time getting him to eat."

Shade scowled. "Why's that?"

"I think the demons tormented him with food." She hesitated, because this wasn't the kind of thing you wanted to know had been done to a loved one. "I'm assuming they put it out and then punished him when he tried to eat it."

Horror flashed in Runa's stunning champagne eyes. "Can I see him now?"

With a nod, Limos led them to the bedroom, but before she opened the door, she voiced her concerns. "I said that physically he's fine. But mentally...he's confused. He still believes he's in Sheoul. He thinks demons are in his head and controlling what he's seeing and who he's talking to. I'm hoping you can convince him he's free."

They entered, and Arik, who had been standing at the patio door and gazing out at the ocean, swung around.

He'd changed into a pair of black BDU pants and a black T-shirt that probably fit a little looser than it used to, but still emphasized his broad shoulders and thickly muscled arms. A neutral mask slipped over his expression, but his eyes sparked with anger when he saw his sister.

"Arik." Runa started toward him, but Shade grabbed her arm and pulled her back.

"Don't." Tension rolled off the big demon in waves that scorched Limos's skin. "I don't trust him."

"You've never trusted him." Runa shook off her mate's hold and moved toward her brother, who stiffened as she got closer. "Arik? It's okay."

"Yeah? Why don't you tell me who the fuck you are? *Okay?*"

Her step faltered, but she kept moving forward. "It's me," she said softly. "Runa."

"You do not get to say her name." His mask of calm shattered into a million pieces, and in an instant, his face contorted with fury, and he let out a murderous, animal growl. "You are not my sister."

He struck, slamming his fist into Runa's cheek and then driving a spin-kick into her gut. She flew across the room and landed in a heap on the floor.

And then the shit hit the fan.

As Limos darted toward Runa, Shade morphed into a massive black werewolf, his roar of rage joining Arik's as they came together in a storm of fists, claws, and teeth.

"No!" Limos entered the fray, desperate to separate them before Shade killed Arik, and then there was another furry blur, as Runa, now a toffee-colored werewolf, took Shade to the ground, her mouth around his throat. What the hell? Werewolves were bound by the moon, unable to change at will. Mature Seminus demons could shapeshift, but what in God's name was Runa?

It was a question for later. Right now, she had to subdue Arik, who was diving for Shade and Runa, his intentions as clear as a neon sign that flashed KILL.

Limos caught him around the waist and wrestled him onto the bed. A fist caught her in the side of the head, and his knee drove so viciously into her stomach that she grunted, but she managed to pin him. He was strong, much stronger than she would have guessed, and when he bucked, she had to put effort into staying on top of him and avoid being thrown. Maybe the blood exchange with Pestilence had given him an injection of Superman.

A big, tattooed hand came down on Arik's shoulder, and Shade's *dermoire* lit up with a bright glow. Almost instantly, Arik calmed, his eyelids drooping and his expression going slack. Within seconds, he was out like a light.

"What the fuck happened?" Shade snapped, as he stepped back. Runa was dabbing blood from her mouth with the back of one hand and holding her ribs with the other.

"I told you," Limos said. "He thinks he's in hell."

Shade swung around to his mate and enveloped her in his arms. "I'm sorry, baby," he murmured. "He was hurting you—"

"I know." Runa's gaze met Limos's as she pushed off of Arik. "Can we go outside?"

They all filed out the door, and as soon as it closed, Limos slumped against it. "Shit," she breathed, more shaken than she'd cared to admit. "I hoped seeing you would snap him into reality."

"This is going to kill him." Runa's voice was shattered,

her expression just as cracked. "When it dawns on him what he's done…" Runa licked the blood from her lips. Shade reached for her, but she pushed his hand away. "He swore he would never hurt me. Or any woman. Not after what our father did." Shade kissed the top of her head and stroked her hair, but instead of soothing her, it seemed to have the opposite effect, and she flinched. "I'm going to just…get some air." She took off like the house was on fire, leaving Limos with Shade.

"What's going on, demon?" Limos crossed her arms over her chest. "What does she mean about their father?"

"He was an abusive monster." The expression on Shade's face was as harsh as his voice. "He liked to beat women and children. It was bad. Real bad."

Limos's jaw tightened. "Arik and Runa?"

"Yeah. I don't know much about what happened to Arik, but Runa said he tried to protect her and their mother. So either he's turned out like his old man, in which case I'll kill him for hitting Runa—" Shade slammed a frustrated fist against the door, as if sending a warning to Arik "—or he's not going to like himself much when he comes around, and I'll let him live."

"You won't touch him. My brother tethered his soul. Arik can't be allowed to die." She wouldn't let it happen anyway, and she'd kill Shade if he tried, simple as that.

"Your brother is an asshole."

She stiffened. Yes, Pestilence was an asshole, but he was her brother, and this demon didn't know what kind of man he'd once been.

"Watch your tongue, Sem."

Shade glanced in the direction Runa had gone before turning back to Limos. "Look, I had a brother like that once. He lived to torment us, and we had to destroy him." He eyed her speculatively. "Are you and your brothers close? You'll need to bond yourselves together stronger than ever to stop Pestilence. Don't hesitate, and don't let sentiments get in your way of what needs to be done. We made that mistake, and a lot of people died because of it."

"It won't be easy. Reseph was the most decent of all of us. He wasn't always evil." She didn't know why she was defending Pestilence, except that no matter how much she hated him now, she'd loved Reseph for thousands of years, and she just couldn't let go of that.

"Then what is your guilt about?"

She blinked. "What?"

Shade moved closer. "I can sense darkness...guilt... in females. You, Horseman, are drowning in it."

She felt a tremor of unease that went all the way to her soul. "You don't know what you're talking about."

"I know I've never encountered anything as intense as what you're giving off. I know I would have had to go through hell in order to coax it out of you." His voice was a disturbing, dark rumble, and what did he mean by *coax* it out of her? "But, thank gods, it's not my problem." He started off after Runa. "Keep us updated."

Shade's order should have raised her hackles, but what he'd said about both her and Arik shook her to her marrow. What did Shade know about her guilt? Could he read minds? Okay, she could seriously go into a panic about this, but now wasn't the time. She had to focus on Arik, because yes, she was being crushed under the weight of her guilt, but right now, the human was her first concern.

If he realized what he'd done to Runa, how would that affect his recovery? Her brothers had never once struck her in anger—even though she deserved it...more than they knew. But she could only imagine how they'd punish themselves if they ever hurt her.

And the idea that Arik had been abused as a child... God, she'd always been numb to such horrors, or, more accurately, she'd never allowed herself to become sensitized to it. But picturing Arik bruised and bleeding under the fists of his own father tweaked a nerve somewhere deep inside her.

She'd been raised like a princess, encouraged to be petty and cruel, while at the same time, never knowing how it felt to be beaten or betrayed. She'd always thought she'd been treated like royalty because her mother loved her and other demons revered her...but what if her treatment had been about making sure she'd never feel empathy, since she hadn't experienced pain?

The very idea made her ill, but again, this wasn't about her. She'd never suffered, especially not at the hands of her own father. Hell, she'd never even met her father.

For a moment she wondered if Arik's father was alive, and then realized that Shade would never have allowed the man to live, and yet another stirring of jealousy went through her at what Runa had that Limos never would.

Shaking off the useless self-pity, she entered Arik's room again. He was still out cold, sprawled on the bed as if he were sleeping off a wild bender. Right now, it didn't seem as if he'd ever come out of the hell that he was living with inside his skull.

She sank down on the bed beside him and offered what little comfort she could, smoothing his shirt and brushing his hair off his forehead. She'd done the same for her brothers when they'd been injured in battle, hoping they'd find peace in her touch. Sure, they regenerated quickly, but if the injuries were bad enough, they suffered in misery for hours, even days while they waited.

This sucked. She felt so helpless. No matter what she did, things continued to get worse for Arik. Though... wait...maybe she could help. If he never remembered hurting Runa...

Yes. Smiling, because she could finally do something for him, she thumbed open his eyelids and stared into his glassy eyes. Very carefully, she reached into Arik's mind with hers and snipped the pesky memory of striking his sister away. Unlike Ares, she couldn't restore the missing memory, but she wouldn't need to.

Runa's visit was something he was better off never remembering.

Eleven

Kynan sat in the conference room at The Aegis's Berlin headquarters, his head spinning. His mind was still trying to wrap itself around the information revealed in one of the three scrolls he'd brought to his fellow Elders with the other treasures in the vault Limos had taken him to.

The little artifacts had, so far, turned up nothing, but one of their historians was still researching their origins and could yet discover something useful. Similarly, two of the scrolls had been accounts of battles with demons—interesting, but ultimately, not great archaeological finds.

But the one scroll...Jesus. If what it said was true, it could alter the course of human history.

"So." Valeriu, an elder who was distantly related to Kynan by marriage, lifted his glasses and rubbed his bloodshot eyes. They'd been studying the scroll nonstop, searching for related texts in their libraries, trying to hash out some of the most cryptic phrases. "We think this could be the key to stopping the Apocalypse. But do we want to risk an Aegi's life on a hunch?"

Malik, who had fought demons for thirty years throughout the Middle East before being promoted to the Sigil, shook his head. "I do not like it. We have asked Guardians to do things we knew might end in their deaths, and they understand that danger comes with the territory. But this..."

Lance, a Canadian who lost his fashion sense somewhere in the 80s, spun a coffee stir stick on the table. "The Guardian would be a volunteer. She'll know there's no guarantee of success."

Yeah, and that was assuming they'd *get* a volunteer for this secret plan. What they were going to reveal to the Guardian waiting outside the room was going to knock her on her ass.

Fuck. Ky didn't like any of this. Life had been much less complicated when he was nothing but a soldier on the Aegis's front lines. He'd been in charge of a large cell of Guardians, but mainly, he fought demons. Kill or be killed. Simple shit.

Now he was manipulating fate and lives, and none of it sat well with him.

Valeriu leaned back in his chair and stared at the painting depicting a battle between angels and demons. "We have to have faith that this will work."

"Faith?" Decker, who was usually easygoing, sat in his chair, stiff as a board, his hand skimming back and forth over his blond high-and-tight. "Faith is for people who want to believe in something they can't prove. I could have faith that I'm invisible, but that wouldn't make it true." He shook his head. "You people are making me nervous. You're dealing with magic and prophecy and shit none of us understand."

"And you think the military could do any better?" Malik asked.

"I didn't say that." Decker's Southern accent grew more pronounced as he grew more agitated. "But you have no safeguards in place. Until you—*we*—do, you shouldn't put a plan in motion."

Decker had a point. The military's paranormal unit dealt in the same things The Aegis did, but because it was the military, the R-XR had strict procedures to follow, a chain of command that didn't allow for deviation, a firm distrust of magic, and safeguards on top of safeguards. The Aegis relied on what the military feared—magic— and had a tendency to act more spontaneously.

Which could be a good thing…or could be very, very bad.

Right now, the R-XR was preaching caution in every move, insisting that now was not the time to be rash. The Aegis took the opposite tack—with Armageddon on the horizon, there was no time for slow and careful.

"All I'm saying," Decker said, "is that maybe we should concentrate on finding out what Thanatos's Seal is instead of this cockamamie backup plan."

"He won't tell us." Lance shook his head. "So unless you can translate his weird prophecy, we don't have a lot to go on."

Ky ran his fingers over the page in the *Daemonica*, the demon bible, that outlined the four prophecies for the Horsemen—the four prophecies that would turn them to evil. The Aegis now understood three of the four. Thanatos's was the wildcard, and all the Horseman would say was that his Seal was in no danger of breaking.

*Behold! Innocence is Death's curse, his hunger his
burden, a blade his Deliverance. The Doom Star cometh
if the cry fails.*

What. The. Hell.

"We don't have a choice," Val said. "It's now or never.
Humans are dying by the hundreds of thousands. The
R-XR itself has calculated that if Pestilence continues
the way he has, in a year, half the world's population will
be dead. Our plan is a Hail Mary move for sure, but it's
all we have."

"For the record," Decker said, "I don't support it."

For the record, neither did Kynan. But Reaver was MIA
and not available for advice, and The Aegis was going to
move ahead on this, with or without Kynan's approval. Ky
might as well be there to make sure no one got hurt.

Lance snorted. "Funny hearing a military guy being so
squeamish."

The light blue in Decker's eyes turned icy, and before
tempers went out of control, Val cleared his throat imperi-
ously. "Bring in Regan."

Kynan refilled his coffee mug while the only female
Elder was called into the meeting. She entered, her dark
braid hanging over her shoulder, the ends frayed, and he
knew she'd been toying with it while she waited outside
the conference room. She took a seat, her model good-
looks in no way taking away from her natural warrior
aura. She was a fighter through and through, literally born
into The Aegis.

"Okay," she said, in her smoky voice. "What is this
about?"

Malik cast her a grim look. "First, you must keep this
secret, even from the other Elders."

Regan frowned. "I don't understand."

"What we're about to tell you can't get out," Val said. "Of course we trust all our Elders, but the fewer people who know our plans, the less chance of being discovered. Once the first part of the plan has been carried out, we'll let the other Elders in on what's going on."

Lance gestured at the scroll with his coffee stir stick. "This document was discovered in an ancient Aegis vault. We believe that it may hold the key to stopping Pestilence."

"And what do I have to do with any of this?" Regan asked.

Everyone exchanged glances. Just when Kynan thought no one was going to speak, Malik chimed in, his voice as grave as the look he was giving her. "Kynan and Arik have been our middlemen for dealing with the Horsemen. But, obviously, Arik can no longer function in that capacity."

"So you want me to play Horsemen jockey."

Val choked on his coffee, and Kynan came close to doing the same on his own tongue. "That," Val wheezed, "is incredibly accurate."

Regan huffed. "Spit it out, people. What are you saying?"

"We need you to be more than just a middleman. We'll arrange for you to stay with one of them."

"Who?"

"Thanatos," Kynan said.

Lance jumped in before Ky could soften the coming blow. "And we want you to seduce him."

Regan sucked in a harsh breath, and her normally bronze skin turned pale. "You . . . what?"

"You need to get him into bed."

She shoved to her feet. "What the hell is that scroll? Some sort of Aegis romance novel? Underworld erotica? Screw you all."

"I told you she wouldn't do it," Lance said. "She hates men."

"Just because I shot you down doesn't mean I hate men, you asshole."

Lance's face turned red. "You turn down everyone." He glanced around the table. "Have any of you ever seen her with a guy?"

No, Kynan hadn't, but he didn't give a shit about her love life or lack of it. "Calm down, both of you."

"I just don't understand why it's so important that I climb into bed with…with…a *Horseman*." She practically shuddered out the last word.

"Because," Val said quietly, "that's the only way you'll get pregnant with his child."

Pregnant. Her colleagues wanted her to get pregnant with Death's kid.

Regan's first instinct was to start yelling. Or to maybe storm out of the room. But twenty-five years in The Aegis had given her more discipline than that, and she tamped down her angry instincts the way she'd been taught since the day she'd come to the demon-hunting organization as a newborn infant still covered in her mother's birth blood.

"My answer is no, but tell me why you think Thanatos needs a roll in the hay, and why you think I'm the one who should give it to him." Jesus. Sleeping with a fucking Horseman?

Val sat back in his leather chair, a signal that a lecture was about to begin. "According to the scroll, after the Antonine Plague that killed upwards of five million in the ancient Roman Empire and was blamed on Pestilence, one of the first Aegi prophets, Marcus Longinus, recognized that if Pestilence was that dangerous before his Seal broke, he'd be a million times worse after."

Malik nodded. "We know that The Aegis's focus has long been on Pestilence. But until now, we didn't know that any concrete plans had been made in the event that the Horsemen's Seals started breaking."

"Why would the focus be on Pestilence?" Regan asked, tucking her fingers into her jeans pockets to tamp down her tendency to talk with her hands, which made her appear excitable and stupid.

"Because the *Daemonica* told us that his Seal would be the first to break," Kynan said. "The dagger, Deliverance, was forged to kill the Horsemen. But Pestilence has the dagger, which means that none of the others can use it to kill him. That's where our buddy Marcus Longinus comes in."

"He secluded himself in a meditation cave and wrote down his visions," Val said.

Lance snorted. "Of course, we now know that meditation caves were filled with natural gasses that caused hallucinations, so Marcus could be full of shit."

Regan hated to agree with Lance about anything, but that was exactly her fear. In ancient times, everything was thought to be an act of God—or the gods, depending on the time and the religion. So some dude all hopped up on cave air could see all kinds of crap and think the visions were sent by a deity.

"Okay, so what 'shit' did Marcus dream up?"

Val pushed his glasses up on his nose. "He had a vision that the only hope for the world, should the *Daemonica*'s prophecy come to pass and all the Horsemen turn evil, would be a secret child conceived by the joining of an Aegis warrior and a Horseman. That child will be the savior of mankind."

"Ah...couldn't any of the Horsemen do, then? And any Guardian? Why can't this stupid vision involve Limos and Arik?" She smiled at Lance. "Or maybe *you* should man up and do the deed. Or maybe you hate women?"

"I love women as much as you probably do," he shot back, and she rolled her eyes at his lame barb.

She wasn't a lesbian. She was just...well, she didn't take chances with sex. For her, an orgasm was a few seconds in which her carefully maintained control was lost...and when you had supernatural abilities like hers, you didn't want to lose control of them.

"We believe the Horseman in question is Thanatos," Malik said. "We have a couple of clues. The words 'From Death will come Life' are engraved on Deliverance's hilt and are written here, on the scroll."

"So you think that literally, from Death—Thanatos—will come life...in the form of a baby." Regan could really use a stiff drink right now. You know, before she got knocked up and couldn't drink anymore. Jesus. "And does the scroll explain how a female Guardian is supposed to get close enough to seduce him?"

"No," Val said, "but Pestilence has put a price on Aegi heads. The remaining Horsemen are more willing than ever to help us, since we're on the front lines with them. They obviously have a lot of knowledge, things we're missing, especially their histories since The Aegis broke with them hundreds of years ago. We'll tell them that we need the gaps filled in, and we want to send a historian— you—to work with them."

"How can you be sure they won't want this Aegi to work with Ares or Limos?"

"It's not a matter of want," Kynan said. "It's a matter of practicality. Ares and Cara are busy being newlyweds and training an island full of hellhounds. Limos has her hands full with Arik. Thanatos, on the other hand, is alone, and he has the best library. He's really the only option."

"Huh. Well, good luck finding some sucker who wants to sleep with him, because it isn't going to be me."

"Regan." Val looked down at his hands, which he'd folded in his lap. "We can't force you to do this. But I'm going to ask you to think hard about it. You are one of our greatest assets, and we don't ask you to do this lightly. We ask because, with your abilities, you truly are the only one who *can* do it."

The reminder of what she was sobered her up, real fast. Only the Elders knew about her psychic gifts, and sometimes she suspected that Val knew even more than she did about the extent of them. He'd been the one to argue for her life when she'd been born to a Guardian mother who abandoned her because of what her father was. He'd been the one who had sworn he'd be the one to put her down if her powers grew out of control.

He was the one who had killed her father.

She schooled her expression, refusing to let anyone here see her discomfort. Because yeah, it did bother her that everyone except Kynan was looking at her like she was a bomb ready to blow. Like her, they'd put her abilities in some locked box in their memories, but were now recalling exactly what it was she could do. And what she'd been forbidden to do on the penalty of death.

"I don't understand what you're saying, Val."

"One of Thanatos's defenses is armor that stores souls," Kynan said. "When he's pissed or when he releases them, they kill."

"Your ability could protect you from them," Val said. "You're the only Guardian we could even consider putting in his path."

She clenched her fists. "For twenty-five years, you've trained me not to use my ability. The Aegis *kills* people like me. And now you're asking me to embrace it?" She crossed her arms over her chest. "That scroll. Where did you find it?"

Kynan reached for it. "In an Aegis vault Limos took me to."

"Did it occur to you that it could be a trick? Fake? The world's first paranormal romance?"

Ky's mouth quirked in one corner as he passed it to her. "That's why we need you to verify its authenticity."

Shit. Of her two abilities, this was the one she was allowed to use, but she didn't like to, especially not in front of anyone. "You know I can't tell how old it is or anything. I can only tell you what whoever wrote it was feeling."

"We know."

Inhaling on a curse, she unrolled this idiotic thing that supposedly said she should screw Thanatos, and ran her fingers over the ink. Instantly, her body was flooded with emotion and images. Images of hell burst in her brain, horrific scenes of torture and pain and . . . she jerked her hand away.

"Yeah," she croaked. "Whoever penned The Biblical Horseman's Secret Aegis Baby was sincere. They believe the child is important. And they were also a very tortured individual." She cleared her throat. "How, exactly, will this baby save all of humanity?"

When everyone averted their gazes, alarm bells rang. Finally, Val looked up. "That's the catch. We don't know. Apparently, there's a twin scroll that will explain it. We have faith that by the time the baby is born, we'll have found it."

"Oh, that's just great," she drawled. "Maybe I should jump off a cliff and have faith that by the time I hit bottom, I'll have grown wings?"

"So?" Lance prompted, as if she hadn't spoken. "You going to ride a wild pony?"

God, she hated him. Ignoring the asshole, she turned to Kynan. "What does Thanatos look like?" Visions of a bony old dude who looked like the Crypt Keeper's twin brother popped into her head.

Kynan shrugged. "If you don't mind tats and piercings, he's attractive, I guess."

"You guess?"

"Sorry, I happen to be into women, so Thanatos doesn't do it for me. But it's probably fair to say that if I were gay, I'd do him."

"That's so helpful," she said, dryly. "So what are you going to do with this kid? I mean, what happens after it's born? I'm not exactly mother material."

"Gem and I will raise it," Kynan said softly.

"And your wife is cool with that?"

"It isn't like we don't already have a child who is part demon. And I do have a huge family full of demons, angels, vampires, and werewolves to help out and keep the child safe. We'll love it like our own, I promise you that."

Shit. She couldn't believe she was actually considering this. But The Aegis was her family. They'd raised her when no one else would—or could. She owed them, and if this was how she could make her contribution to save the world, then she couldn't say no. Besides, she couldn't subject another female Guardian to this risk.

Right now, no Aegi outside the Sigil understood the magnitude of what was happening in the world, and very few knew of the existence of the Four Horsemen. Bringing an outsider up to speed would take time. Hell, finding the right woman would take time.

"Make the arrangements." She'd never been one to run away from anything, but right now she needed some fresh air and a moment alone, so she yanked open the door. "And that includes plans for my funeral, because if this doesn't work, I want a really nice one."

Twelve

~

Arik woke, groggy, fuzzy-headed, but for the first time in forever his belly wasn't twisted inside out and eating his own spine in hunger. He opened his eyes, and realized he was still in the demon-induced fantasyland. Maybe it wasn't so bad here after all. At least he got food, showers, and a soft bed.

And a toothbrush. Who would have thought such a simple item could make a person happy? As he brushed his teeth, he practically moaned with orgasmic appreciation at the taste of the minty toothpaste and the stroke of soft bristles. Oral sex, that's what this was.

Okay, not quite. Limos popped into his head, and all those fantasies of having her spread-eagled and arching against his mouth trumped the toothbrush sex, for sure.

Cursing himself for an idiot, he spit, rinsed, and stepped into the bedroom just as Limos, her tan body covered in a skimpy yellow swimsuit and a sheer wraparound that hung low on her hips, tapped on the glass patio door outside the room. He didn't move to let her in, but the door wasn't locked, so she slid it open.

"Hey, sleepyhead."

"Sleepyhead?"

"More like comahead, really. You've been sleeping for twenty-four hours." She crooked her finger at him. "Come outside. I've got a day of sensory therapy planned. I'm going to overload you with normal, familiar sensations to prove all of this isn't a trick and bring you back to reality."

Reality. He wasn't sure what that was anymore.

He eyed Limos warily but appreciatively, following the gold chain around her neck down to the quarter-sized Seal that rested between her breasts. Her flat, muscular stomach gave way to slim hips and long legs that tapered from powerful thighs to curvy, hard calves and dainty feet. Her toes were painted pink, and she had gold rings on her middle toes. He'd like to suck them right off.

Fucking moron. He was losing his mind. This wasn't real, and even if it was...what? Shit, he'd be so happy he wouldn't care what she'd done or he'd done to get him ferried off to Sheoul, so yeah...he'd suck on her toes.

The warm breeze wrapped around him, tempting him, but when he didn't immediately walk outside, Limos turned away. She stood there, hands on the rail, her hair whipping around her shoulders as she looked out at the ocean.

"Come on, Arik." Her voice was soft, cajoling, and hey, what would it hurt to go out there?

For some reason, his stomach fluttered. *Stop being a pussy.* He stepped outside, was immediately drenched in warm sunlight and tropical scents. Twenty feet below, sand stretched along a beach lined with lush forest as far as he could see. Seagulls flew overhead, dotting the azure sky and then dipping into the dappled ocean waves.

"See?" she said, as she gave him a blinding smile. "It's gorgeous out here."

She was gorgeous. "I guess."

She turned to him and lifted her hand to his cheek, and though he wanted to jerk away, he didn't. In fact, he kind of leaned into the soft warmth of her palm.

"Feel it. Feel how real it all is. The sun, the breeze, my touch."

"*Feeling* has never been the issue."

She dropped her hand. "Okay, let's play a game. Let's pretend you've been working for The Aegis and R-XR all this time, and you took a break and came here to see me."

"You mean, pretend I kissed you outside Ares's place and I *didn't* get dragged to Sheoul?"

Something flashed in her eyes, and if he didn't know better, he'd think it was regret. "Yes. Where would we be right now?"

He wasn't sure what to say. He'd spent hours upon hours thinking about how he was going to take his revenge on her, but in all honesty, he'd also wondered what would have happened if she hadn't freaked and he hadn't been grabbed to star in his own episode of *Survivor: Sheoul.*

"I don't know," he said. "If you weren't engaged . . . you know, if you were available, would you have let the kiss go on?"

Her chin came up, and he knew she was going to pull the *I didn't let it happen in the first place* bullshit. Nope, that Frisbee wasn't going to fly again, and he moved close, so close she backed up, bumping into the railing. It was funny how she was a bad-ass warrior, but when faced with a male's attention, she became nothing but a female who had to deal with her basest desires.

"Don't," he said. "Don't deny it again. There are no gray areas here. Just black and white. You either wanted the kiss or you didn't, and you will never convince me you didn't. And here's the thing about that kiss. If I hadn't been dragged to hell, I wouldn't have stopped. I'd have had you stripped and under me in a heartbeat, and I'd have had my mouth in places that would have shocked you. That's all I thought about when I was in that hellhole, and I've got it mapped out in my head down to how long it would take me to lick you until you screamed my name. I might not know if any of this"—he made a sweeping gesture with his arm—"is real, but *that* would have been. That's the truth."

Crimson splotches colored her cheeks and she got that damned superior gleam in her eye again, as if she was trying to regain some control over him, this situation, and her own feelings. "I've let some things slide, but you can't speak that way to me. I'm a—"

"Easy there, Trigger." He grabbed her by the arms, tugged her against him, and slanted his mouth over hers. Mainly, he wanted to shut her up, but he also wanted to prove her wrong, show her that for all her protests, she'd wanted that kiss outside Ares's mansion. She might be a Biblical legend, and he a mere human, but when their bodies touched, they were man and woman, and neither had any tactical advantage. Her entire body went taut, but then her tongue met his, and it was game over. He'd won. He'd made his point.

"There," he said, a little breathlessly. "You wanted me to feel. I felt. But I'm still not convinced this is real."

He might not be sure, but his dick was, and he casually adjusted his erection.

Limos pulled back from him, and though her eyes were lust-glazed, her lips wet from his kiss, she was alert, and the horse tat on her arm was writhing. "It is real." She sounded as breathless as he was, to his satisfaction. "Come with me. I'm not done proving it."

The mouthwatering scent of flame-broiled beef hung in the air as Limos led Arik to the dining room. Though he hadn't argued, he moved slowly, warily, like a cat in dog territory.

Hekili had placed two plates at the round table, as well as two ice-cold bottles of lager from her favorite Hawaiian microbrewery. She normally drank "girly" drinks, as Ares liked to say, but every once in a while she liked a beer with her burgers.

"Sit." Limos gestured to the seat that offered a view of the beach, and Arik took it, his body so rigid she was amazed his joints worked.

Limos stood across the table as Arik sat in his chair, staring at the burger, which was slathered with Hekili's private recipe barbecue sauce and a thick slice of pineapple. "Arik, please. Eat it."

He just stared.

God, this had to work. The idea had been Ares's, his experience with what was now called post-traumatic stress disorder beyond vast. He'd come by with Than to discuss Sartael's coin and Reaver's no-show to Than's summoning, and Ares had taken one look at Arik's comatose body and nodded decisively.

"Stimulate him."

"Ah…excuse me?"

Ares rolled his eyes. "Not like that. Overload him with all the senses. Shock his system out of the 2-D world inside his head."

Ares had promised to talk to Cara to see if they could get some hellhounds here to help guard the house, and then he and Than had left moments later, drawn to some catastrophe Pestilence had caused. Her own insides were quivering with the need to gate herself to a rapidly spreading famine in China, but she was going to wait until the last possible second. So here she was, trying to ply Arik with a damned burger.

"Arik, listen to me." She sank down in the seat opposite him and took a swig of her lager. "I know you're having a hard time with this. But I promise you won't be punished if you eat. All the food we've been giving you has been real. Well, some people might not consider haggis real food, but it really wasn't dog chow."

He lifted his gaze, which had darkened. "Bullshit."

"I'm telling you the truth." *Truth.* It struck her that even though Pestilence had re-ignited her desire to lie, it wasn't coming second-nature the way it used to, and she was finding it easier to resist. Back when she'd lived in Sheoul, and for a good thousand years after she'd come to the human realm, lies were the only things that came out of her mouth. Maybe this relapse wouldn't be so bad.

At least, it wouldn't be bad as long as no one learned about the things she *had* lied about.

Arik's gaze dropped back to his plate, his voice haunted. "You tricked me."

Yes, she had, and she didn't feel bad about it at all.

"You had to eat. And I wasn't going to give you...what did you call it...eyes and guts?"

For a long time, he did nothing. Then, slowly, he reached for the burger. His hands shook, and he cursed, put them back in his lap. Another five minutes passed, and he tried again. Just as his finger touched the bread, a bird chirped, and he reared back, hands up to defend himself, as though he expected a blow.

Limos's heart cracked wide open. How odd that her brothers, who had started out as tender, gentle babies, had grown hard as they got older, but Limos was the opposite. She'd been raised by demons who expected her to live and breathe cruelty. She'd been harder than a diamond and incapable of tenderness or love when she arrived in the human realm. But she'd gradually learned to feel, and where her brothers had erected walls, hers had been breaking down.

Arik had the potential to take down the last of them, and the thought both terrified her and thrilled her. She couldn't afford to be vulnerable to her feelings, and yet, belonging in a relationship was all she'd ever wanted.

Of course, the relationship she'd wanted so long ago was a far cry from what she wanted now.

When no one came out of the woodwork to beat Arik, he picked up the burger. His throat worked hard even before he raised it to his mouth. He took a bite, but his eyes were wild. Again, when no one popped out of thin air to torture him, he relaxed slightly and chewed. Then he took another bite. And another. He gobbled the burger like a starving dog, and when he was done, he drained the lager.

Very carefully, he set down the bottle. "This is real, isn't it," he whispered.

"Yes," she whispered back.

He bowed his head, and his entire body began to tremble so hard the chair rattled on the floor. "How? How did I get out?"

"You escaped." She wanted to go to him, to hug him tight, but he was in a fragile place right now, and she didn't want to do anything that might send him fleeing back into his mental nightmare. "Kynan and I found you at the Erta Ale hellmouth."

He looked up, and she was relieved to see that there was no suspicion in his expression. "How did you know to look there?"

She grinned. "Kynan interrogated some bookies, and I tortured one of your torturers."

"Nice." One corner of his mouth tipped up, and wow, it was great to see him smile.

She gave him a sly wink in return, becoming aware of an exhilarating buzz, a sensation inside her that rivaled what she experienced when she told a lie. Was this what people in love called butterflies?

Not that she was in love. As much as she liked to dream about having a normal, happy relationship, it just wasn't in the cards for her.

"It was good times all around." She gestured to his empty plate. "Want another?"

He shook his head. "I'm not used to eating much anymore. I'm pretty full." He gazed out the window, but where he went, she couldn't follow. "Who all knows I'm here?" His head swiveled around to her. "My sister must be going crazy—"

"No." Her fingers tightened around the sweating beer bottle. "Eidolon and Shade came here to heal you, so your sister knows you're okay. Kynan too."

"So Kynan really did get those clothes for me?"

"Yes."

He pinched the bridge of his nose with his thumb and forefinger. "Fuck. Everything is so jumbled up."

She reached for him. "Arik—"

He leaped out of the chair. "I need a minute, okay? Give me a minute alone." He took off, weaving almost drunkenly toward the bedroom.

It wasn't until she heard the crash that she knew something was terribly wrong.

Thirteen

Pestilence had upped his game, and his chessboard was made of human flesh, his chess pieces crafted from bone.

Thanatos and Ares had been compelled by violence and death to gate themselves to New Zealand, their brother's newest playground. The plague of flesh-eating locusts had turned much of the country into a wasteland, and when New Zealand defense forces had gone in to try to contain the crow-sized insects, they'd been attacked by demons—demons who had, until now, been confined to Sheoul.

As Than and Ares slogged through gore and fought battle after battle, they'd made a disturbing discovery: Pestilence had saturated the southern half of New Zealand with so much blood, evil, and destruction that he'd been able to claim it in the name of Sheoul. It was now demon territory, and a major victory on Pestilence's game board.

His next move, which Than had discovered when he'd hopped over to Australia to investigate a disturbing sense of death that wasn't quite...death...was something right out of a horror flick.

Pestilence had unleashed an unthinkable plague, one that was turning humans into honest-to-fuck zombies. Thanatos liked *The Walking Dead* as much as anyone, but the real thing was nothing like fiction. This plague was Reseph's sense of humor turned twisted in the being who was now Pestilence, and no doubt, the evil son of a bitch was having a good laugh.

Thanatos cursed and slammed his fist into the punching bag in his gym, where he was desperately trying to work off the residual high that coked-out his body when he was immersed in a lot of death. He needed to level out, needed to regain his ability to concentrate, because after leaving Australia, he'd unearthed information that might prove to be a huge break in his quest to repair Reseph's Seal. But if he couldn't get out of this killing mood, he wouldn't be able to follow up on that lead with a clear head.

Atrius, one of his daywalker vamps, interrupted him with a soft tap on the doorframe. "Master, you have a visitor."

Than pulled his last punch. "Could you be more specific?"

"It's an Aegi."

Kynan, then. "Let him in."

"Ah...it's not a him. It's a her."

Than wheeled around. "Did you verify that she's a Guardian?" Pestilence had been sending succubi on a regular basis to tempt him—there was, in fact, one of said succubi chained naked in the great room, awaiting his interrogation. He definitely wouldn't put it past his brother to resort to trying to trick Than into believing a succubus was an Aegis slayer.

"Of course. She wears the Aegis symbol on a ring, and she gave me this to present to you." Atrius held out a cell phone.

Thanatos took it, cycled to the address book, and sure enough, the name Dean Winchester was listed among the hundreds of other names in the book. Right after Arik had been taken, The Aegis and Horsemen had come up with a way, a code of sorts, to ensure that no false Aegi could ever again gain entrance into a Horsemen stronghold or trick them as one had when he'd walked into Ares's house and handed him a poisoned weapon.

The Dean Winchester thing had been Limos's idea. She loved her supernatural TV shows.

Than snatched a towel off the treadmill bar. "Show her in."

He wiped the sweat off his brow and face, then drained a bottle of water. As he lobbed the empty vessel into the garbage, a woman entered. And...damn. The Guardian was striking, made even more beautiful by what others might consider flaws. Long, thick lashes framed nondescript hazel eyes that were a little too far apart, and her slightly crooked nose had clearly been broken at least once. A scar puckered the bronze skin at her temple and again at her chin.

But her injuries only made her that much more attractive to Than, who could appreciate a woman who had survived combat.

She wore a crimson turtleneck that molded tightly over

full breasts and emphasized a slim waist. An embroidered candy cane sat above her left breast, reminding him that for the humans who celebrated it, it was Christmas time. Low-slung jeans hugged wide hips and slim thighs, and on her feet were leather boots that came up to mid-calf and that no doubt concealed a handful of weapons.

"You done checking me out?" she asked in a husky, smoky voice, and he took his time dragging his gaze up.

"Not checking you out," he drawled. "Sizing you up."

"For?"

"A hole in the ground." He stalked toward her, but she didn't give way. Nice. "It was stupid to come to me unannounced, slayer."

"I tried tweeting you, but looks like you Horsemen-types are afraid of social media."

Funny. A comedian Guardian had come to visit. "What do you want?"

"What? They didn't teach manners in your day? I don't get tea or anything? Maybe you want to chain me up like the naked chick in the other room?" She licked her lips, which he just noticed were full, maybe too full, and his erotic imagination took off. And since imagination was all he had when it came to all things erotic, he could spin out some amazing fantasies.

"Answer me," he barked, and she didn't even jump. Impressive.

"Can we talk somewhere else? Maybe after you put some clothes on?"

He grinned. "Does my bare chest tempt you?"

"Hardly. But your tattoos are distracting."

He got told that a lot. Probably because many of them were depictions of death and destruction, scenes taken right out of his head by a demon tattoo artist. Her talent allowed her to layer the tattoos so older ink wasn't obliterated by new, creating a 3-D effect people often found disconcerting.

Thanatos called for Atrius, who appeared immediately. "Take her to the great hall. Put the succubus in my bedroom and give the Guardian tea. I'll be right there."

Atrius took the female, and though Than shouldn't have looked . . . he did. He watched the sway of her perfect ass as she walked away, and then he had to wait for his erection to subside and his fangs to stop throbbing to join her. He really didn't give a hellrat's ass if she got an eyeful of boner, but he'd kept his canines under wraps since the day they'd dropped and demanded blood.

He considered showering, but fuck it. She'd interrupted his workout, so she could put up with his sweaty, smelly self. He did throw on a sweatshirt, though.

She was waiting for him by the fire, hands behind her back as she studied the portrait over the mantel. "You like looking at yourself, huh?"

That voice. Damn, he could listen to that voice all day. "It was a gift," he said, but didn't elaborate.

His vampires had commissioned the painting a couple of hundred years ago, and he hadn't wanted to insult them by not displaying it. Granted, he'd originally placed it someplace a lot less noticeable, but someone kept moving it here. It had become something of a game now, and every couple of years, he'd move it and see how long it would take them to notice it was gone, find it, and return it.

She turned to him just as Atrius arrived with a pot of tea and a single cup and set them on the narrow oak table against the back of the couch. "I was kidding about the tea," she said, but she poured it anyway.

"I didn't want you to think I'm a terrible host. Now, tell me why you're here."

As if he hadn't spoken, she blew across the steamy surface of her tea. "Mm. Smells good."

Of course it did. He only bought the best. "Where is Kynan?"

"Dunno." She regarded him over the rim of her cup. "It's not my day to watch him."

Infuriating human. "Why isn't he here? We've been dealing with *him*."

"You've been dealing with him because he's the only one of us who can travel through Harrowgates. He's the one who brought me here, actually. And can I just state for the record that I hate being knocked out for the journey? Gave me one hell of a headache."

"I'm not going to ask you again. Why are you here?"

A slow, secret smile curved that sensual mouth, and she gestured to a suitcase near the entrance. "Because," she said silkily, "I'm moving in."

⌒

Regan had never been as terrified in her life as she was right now.

The disbelief on Thanatos's face had veered sharply to fury, and now there were shadows flitting at his feet. The shadows they'd discussed back at Aegis headquarters... souls of the demons, animals, and humans Than had killed. Shadows he could release to do more killing.

Deep inside, her forbidden ability stirred.

"You are what?" His voice was as cold as the snowstorm she'd battled to get here. Kynan had gotten her through the Harrowgate, but she'd had to ride the rest of

the way on one of the several corralled snowmachines
Thanatos kept near the gate and at the keep, which would
be her getaway vehicle if her scheme went as planned.

Or, more importantly, if it didn't.

She inhaled, seeking the calm outer shell she'd had in
place since she arrived. She took another sip of tea, which
really was wonderful. And she didn't normally like the stuff.

"I'm moving in. The Elders discussed it, and we
decided that one of us should hang out with you full time.
I drew the short straw."

He practically sputtered, his face turning red. "You
discussed it? *The Aegis* discussed it without talking to
us first?" He spat out a dozen curses. "You people have
always been too full of yourselves. This wasn't discussed
with any of us. So get out."

"Look," she said calmly, even though inside she was
quivering, "this isn't about us being full of ourselves. It's
about repairing the bad blood between The Aegis and the
Horsemen. So just show me to my room, and I'll get out
of your way for a while. Give you some time to get used
to the idea."

She thought his eyes were going to pop out of their
sockets. But what stunning eyes they were. They'd been
pale yellow when she'd first seen him, and now, in anger,
they'd deepened to a burnished gold. She hadn't been prepared for them, nor for his sheer size or looks. Oh, she'd
known about the souls he kept, and about his tattoos and
piercings. But she hadn't expected the souls to be so eerie,
the tats to be so remarkable, or for him to be so handsome. Hell, despite what Kynan had said, she'd still figured on him being some bony, withered dude wrapped up
in a Grim Reaper robe.

Thanatos was as far removed from that image as possible, and even though he might terrify her down to her marrow, she couldn't help but admire him. *Remember that when he's slaughtering you. It's important that the guy strangling the life out of you is drop-dead gorgeous.*

She was such a moron.

The shadows around Thanatos swirled faster, faces forming in the inky billows, and her ability, which could rip a soul right out of a body, writhed inside her like a living thing. It wanted to be used. It wanted to free the souls from Than's armor the way it "freed" souls from humans and demons.

"Why is this so important to The Aegis?" Than asked.

"I told you." She gripped her cup tight. "If we want to combat the coming Apocalypse, we need to do more than work together. We need to learn everything we can about you and fill in the blanks."

"Why you?" He looked her up and down, and the shadows went crazier.

She was so glad she'd bucked Val's advice to dress provocatively and instead went for casual and covered up, but now she had to see if her decision to play hard-to-get, which was her normal state and easy to do, would be more effective with Thanatos than flirty sex kitten.

"I told you. I drew the short straw."

"The short straw. I'm flattered." His sarcasm echoed off the stone walls and the lofty ceiling, and the one tattoo that was different than the others, one of a horse on his right forearm, moved. She blinked, watching in amazement as the horse threw its head. Hadn't Kynan said that their horses lived on their bodies?

Fascinated, she drifted closer to the big warrior. Her heart rate rocketed and her stomach became alive with butterflies, but she couldn't stop her feet from moving or her gaze from locking on the horse. Thanatos barked out something in a language she didn't know, and the shadows that had been circling him dove at his legs, seeming to absorb into his body.

"It's remarkable," she murmured, reaching out to touch his skin, but Thanatos hissed and jumped backward, startling her into leaping back herself.

"Go back to your colleagues and tell them to send someone else." His voice was a nasty rasp. "Send a male."

She puffed up like a pissy hen, as her last foster mom would have said. "Listen up, Horseman. I know you were born back when women were thought of as little more than brood mares and slaves, but it's the twenty-first century, and we can do anything a man does. I'm as good as any male Aegi, so get over your chauvinist pig self."

"I have a sister who can give any male a run for his money, and I can't imagine her as either a slave or a brood mare, so my issue isn't with your competence." He stalked her, and instinct told her to retreat. But she ignored her first impulse and stood her ground, even when he bumped up against her so they were chest to chest and she could smell his smoky scent. "My issue is that I prefer to surround myself with males."

"Well," she said tightly, "you're out of luck, because there are no male Guardians available right now. So you're just going to have to suck it up and deal with me."

Thanatos's eyes glowed with a fierce light she'd be willing to bet people saw just before he ripped off their heads. "You can walk out of my house on your own, whole and healthy, or I will throw you out, a lot less healthy, in pieces. Your choice."

Think fast... think fast... Regan looked over his shoulder at the entrance to what looked like a huge library. Perfect. She hated to do this, but the *in pieces* thing didn't sound pleasant.

"You're looking for Limos's *agimortus*, right?" she said quickly. "And a way to mend your brother's Seal. I can help. I have a special ability that can be useful."

His eyes narrowed. "What special ability?"

"I can interpret ink on skin. That includes parchment."

"I can interpret ink on parchment too," Than said dryly. "It's called reading."

She brushed past him, ignoring the zing of awareness that shot through her body when they touched, and stalked to his library, where she looked around at the piles of parchments and scrolls and bazillions of books, some modern, but most ancient. Quickly, because Thanatos was coming at her like a locomotive, steam practically coming out of his ears, she grabbed a book with a cover that appeared to have been made from... oh, ick... human skin.

Whatever. She laid it on the desk, flipped it open, and put her fingers to the ink... blood?... on one of the pages. The language was unknown to her, but the emotions that seared her fingertips were not.

Jealousy, as thick as gelatin, rolled through her. "The author," she murmured, "is... upset. Jealous." Flashes of violence flickered like a grainy movie through her brain. "It's a female, I think. She wants to kill... horribly... another female. The other female is beautiful, black hair, violet eyes. Whoever wrote this was thinking of a naked male. With wings." She inhaled a shaky breath. "Angel?"

Thanatos's fingers circled her wrist and pulled her away from the book. "You can do this with the documents pertaining to my sister's *agimortus*?"

Regan nodded, the visions in her head still vivid. "Who were those people?"

"The author was a succubus named Estha. The violet-eyed female is Lilith, my mother. The male is either Azagoth or Sartael, before they fell, and one of two rumored to be our father."

"Azagoth? The Grim Reaper could be your father?"

Thanatos didn't say anything else, instead standing there and watching her speculatively. "You could be of use, but I'll come to you. No female stays here."

She had the upper hand right now, and she was going to use it. "That won't work. I need access to your library. You need my help, and The Aegis needs yours. I'm not leaving, female or not." Smiling, she sauntered out of the library and shouldered her duffle. "Now, please show me to my room."

With a snarl, he stalked away, and though a vampire showed up a moment later to lead her deep into the freezing keep, she didn't feel victorious at all. On the contrary, she was pissed as hell.

The Horseman she'd been sent to seduce... was gay.

Fourteen

⸺

Arik lost it. It was fucking great news that he was no longer in Sheoul, but now he was a big head case. Chunks of his memory were gone, and what was there seemed fuzzy, dreamlike, and he couldn't tell memory from dream. Christ, he hated that, had always prided himself on having a damned good memory, especially after intensive military training that helped him recall minute details following encounters with demons. Now he wondered how much of his life he'd lost, and if any of it would come back.

In his freaked-out state, he'd gone to his room—Limos's room, he guessed—but claustrophobia had wrapped around him tighter than a bulletproof vest, and he'd gone for the sliding glass door—only to find that it had been locked. From the outside.

Panic set in, and he'd smashed a chair through the glass, leaped over the railing, and whacked the male

who'd been standing guard below. Arik ran, barefoot, into
the jungle behind the house. He didn't know how far he'd
gone when he heard Limos calling to him, but he didn't
stop until his lungs were burning for oxygen, his skin was
damp with sweat, and the path was blocked by a waterfall
that split the jungle in half.

Panting, he bent over and braced his hands on his
knees as Limos came up behind him.

"I'm impressed." Her voice was soft as her hand came
down on his shoulder, and now that he knew she was real,
her touch felt better than ever. "You managed to knock
out Kaholo, and he's his pack's martial arts instructor."

"I've been fighting demons since I was a kid, first in
my own house, and then for the military. I'm not a total
slouch." God, he couldn't believe he'd just brought up the
kid thing, and if Limos possessed a single female gene,
she'd latch onto that like a tick on a hound.

"I don't think you're a slouch." Her hand fell off him as
he straightened and turned to face her. "You managed to
knock me off my feet once, if I remember right."

A glint of amusement flashed in her eyes, and he
snorted at the memory of gripping her ankle and tugging
her feet out from under her so she landed on top of him.

"There are some serious holes in my memory, some
doubts about what's been real and what hasn't, but I do
remember that." He inhaled a shaky breath. "Was the
stuff you told me about your...fiancé...real?" Limos's
gaze skittered away. "Horseman?"

Her eyes shifted back to him and narrowed. "Say my
name."

"Answer my question."

"Say. My. Name."

Frustration spiking, he bent down, getting right in her face, nose to nose. "*Answer the fucking question.*"

Clearly, they were at an impasse, and he was not going to back down. If two dozen ugly-ass demons with meat hooks, sledgehammers, and skinning knives couldn't make him say Limos's name, she didn't stand a chance.

She must have realized that, but not wanting to concede defeat, she flipped her hair over her shoulder and stalked to the edge of the crystal pool at the base of the waterfall, where she looked down at her fingers. "Dammit. Broke a nail."

"Jesus." He threw up his hands in frustration. "Can you ever focus on one subject or take anything seriously?"

"I take my nails very seriously." She huffed. "When you've lived as long as I have, you learn to enjoy the little things. Speaking of which, I have something of yours. I don't know how important they are to you, but I've kept them with me."

She held out his dogtags, the silver chain dangling from her closed fist. He took them, another small connection with reality, and when he looped the chain around his neck, he almost felt whole again. Now he needed his weapons and Army ring, and he'd be good to go. Unfortunately, his captors had taken his ring, so there was no getting it back.

"Thank you." His voice was humiliatingly hoarse.

Limos had guarded the dogtags, which he could replace for a few bucks, as if they were a treasure. And she'd treated him equally as well, he realized. She could have dumped him off at Underworld General or handed him over to the R-XR or The Aegis, but instead, she'd nursed him back to health herself. She'd done what she had to in order to get him to eat. She'd engaged all his senses to bring him back to reality.

Arik had no doubt that if she'd left him with the military or The Aegis, he'd be strapped to a bed, attached to IV lines, and doctors would be poking, prodding, and digging into his brain. Hell, they could have made him *worse*.

"You still don't believe this is real, do you?" She looked down at the water swirling around her feet and bubbling around the smooth pebbles.

Reaching out, he hooked his finger beneath her chin and lifted her face to his, needing the sensation of touching her warm skin to make absolutely, one-hundred percent sure that he would be telling the truth. "I believe it. Nothing in that hellhole was as warm as you."

She swallowed. "Then why won't you say my name?"

"I can't take the chance that anyone will hear it. You said it has to be uttered while I'm in misery, but I won't risk it."

"Why? After everything you've gone through because of me, why don't you want to say my name and watch me get what I deserve?" Her words were bitter, her voice hard, and he wondered what kind of life she'd had to make her think he'd do something like that.

"I won't tell you I didn't think about it," he admitted. "When I was in Sheoul, all I could think of was revenge. But I know you didn't mean for what happened to happen, so no, I can't do that to you."

She reached up to play with her Seal pendant. "And why, when you were dreaming of revenge, did you turn the demons down when they offered you a deal . . . my torture for yours?"

Ah, damn, he wished she didn't know about that. He didn't need anyone knowing what he'd endured down there. Torture, it turned out, was a deeply personal, albeit, horrible, experience that he'd rather not share.

"I couldn't take the deal because I couldn't have lived with myself." A sudden, gory image of Limos being brutalized at the hands, claws, and tools of those demons flashed in his head, and he had to tamp down a growl. "I know what those fuckers were capable of, and I would never wish that on you."

Her throat worked on a swallow. "What *do* you wish on me?"

"Me," he said with brutal honesty. "Fool that I am, I wish *me* on you. Like, *on* you. When I said in the bedroom that I'd have had you under me in a heartbeat, I meant it."

She blinked. Opened her mouth. "But h—" He didn't give her a chance to say anything. He grabbed her shoulders and hauled her against him. She let out a little gasp, but she didn't refuse him anything as he took her mouth the way he'd fantasized about every time he closed his eyes.

Water splashed around them, tiny droplets of mist blanketing their faces as their tongues met. Limos's lips were soft, her body hard, her fingernails sharp as she dug them into his biceps. But, like before, when she slid her hands up to his shoulders, her touch was tentative, halting.

He wasn't so reserved.

He dropped his hands to her thighs and then dragged them up and under her wrap, but she grasped his wrists and stopped him.

"Why," he murmured against her mouth. "Why are you so skittish?"

"Because I've never done this."

He whipped his head back. "Bullshit."

"It's true."

"You're saying you're a virgin? You're five thousand years old and you've never had sex?"

"How could I?" A bird fluttered past, and he wasn't surprised when Limos's attention went with it. He waited impatiently for her to turn back to him. "I was betrothed when I was a child. You experienced what happened when I kissed you."

God, he hadn't even thought of that. Of course she wouldn't have been able to be with anyone if her fiancé took jealousy to a galactic extreme.

"Why me?" he asked, dying to know why, after all that time, she had finally given up a kiss. "Why did you give in to me that night?"

Her entire body began to tremble, and he held her tighter. Then, as if a switch had been thrown, she stopped shaking. "Because I'd been drinking."

Instant bullshit flag. He'd been watching her all night, and yeah, he'd seen her suck down some nasty-looking blue drink and later, a slushy pink one, but no, she hadn't been drunk.

"You're lying." He palmed the back of her neck and massaged, urging her to come clean.

"I'm not."

"That's a lie too. There's nothing I hate more than lying, Horseman." Leaning in, he kissed her throat to soften his words, though nothing would ever soften how he felt about lying. He'd fallen for far too many of his father's lies, had seen his mom and sister deeply wounded by those same lies. "Tell me why you finally gave in."

A soft cry escaped her, almost as if telling him the truth pained her, and for a terrible second, he was afraid she'd say that she'd done it on a whim. To satisfy her curiosity. That he could have been anyone and that he'd been the chump who'd rolled the crappy dice.

"Because in all those centuries, you're the first male I've wanted that badly."

Masculine pride puffed him up at her answer. "That's really cool to hear, but why me?"

Her lips, swollen from his kiss and dewy from the waterfall's mist, turned up in a dazzling smile. "Do you remember the first time we met, at Than's place? And you were all in awe of us?"

"Awe is a strong word," he muttered, and she laughed. She was beautiful when she did that.

"You amused me. Not many people do that. And you took having your ribs broken really, really well."

"So you were attracted to me because I have a high tolerance for pain?"

"Well, that's hot, but you also made me laugh, and you give me butterflies," she added brightly before sobering. "You also…you looked at me like I was…I don't know…"

"Wicked sexy?" he offered, and that smile hit him again.

"That, but more. Like I was a puzzle. I liked it. Males usually look at me like I'm good for one thing. Which is funny, because that's the only thing I'm not good for." She sighed. "And then at Ares's party, I saw you watching me. And I saw you coax Rath out from behind the cement planter where he was hiding from all the strangers in the house. It was sweet."

He shrugged. "He was just a baby, and he was scared half to death. Poor Cara was going crazy looking for him."

"See? It just...I dunno. It made me want to be near you."

"So you asked me to spar?"

"It's all I could do. That's as close as I could get to any male. But then you got all arrogant and called me a HILF, and as outraged as I was, I was flattered and turned on, and then you tugged me down on top of you and kissed me...and I'm babbling." She scowled at him. "I never babble."

It was probably some sort of mortal offense to think of a Horseman as cute, but she was. She might be able to kick his ass to the moon and back, but she was also the most feminine woman he'd ever met. Everything about her appealed to the male in him...the protective side that wanted to cage her in his arms and make sure nothing hurt her, and the carnal side that wanted to push her up against the wet boulder behind her and make her scream his name. Even if all they did was more of what they'd done in her bed, he would coax sweet noises from her lips.

"I like it when you babble," he said. "It's cute."

"*Cute?*"

Yep, as expected, a mortal offense. He loved it when she had that spitting-mad cat thing going on. He didn't bother with banter, because frankly, his blood had already started to heat from just thinking about the boulder scenario. How would she react if he grabbed her right now and...fuck it. He'd find out for himself.

Stepping into her, he caught her around the waist and pushed her up against the smooth rock surface and parked himself between her legs.

"Arik," she gasped, and he went impossibly hard at the sexed-up sound of his name coming from her perfect mouth.

"Shh..." He pressed a series of kisses to her neck, tasting the fresh water and the sun on her skin.

"But I need to—"

He closed his hand over her breast, and she sucked air. "I know what you need," he said against her throat, and when she opened her mouth to talk again, he bit down, some weird, driving need to possess and dominate taking over his entire body.

She melted against him, and with her capitulation, his inner animal howled in victory. Her hands gripped his ass and dug in as she arched, allowing him unlimited access to her breasts and putting her sex against the ridge of his cock through the fabric of their clothes. They'd been in this position before, on her bed...but he'd been out of it. This was much better. Much more real.

"Do you like this?" He rocked his erection into her, groaning at the hot friction tempered by the cool breeze around them.

"N-no," she breathed, rolling her hips to increase the sensation.

He licked her neck. "Liar. Remember what I said about that?"

His fingers found the bikini ties around her neck, and in a few nimble twists of his fingers, he had the knot untied, and the top fell off, landing on the ground beside them. He bent to taste her rosy nipples as Limos's hands slipped under the waistband of his pants to grip his ass. Her nails scored his skin, and he wished she'd do it harder. Or slide those soft palms around front.

As if she could read his thoughts, she sank her nails deep, and then dragged them around to his hips. A low sound erupted from his throat when her thumbs smoothed the sensitive skin of his pelvis on either side of his shaft, and he held his breath, waiting for her to touch him where he needed it so badly.

When her hands stopped moving, he thought he might die of anticipation. For a long, agonizing moment, she didn't move. Okay, she was afraid. Maybe he was moving too fast. He could do slow, no matter what his body was telling him.

"I'm scaring you," he whispered.

"I'm . . . a Horseman," she whispered back.

He pressed a lingering kiss into the coconut-scented skin between her breasts. "You're a woman. A gorgeous woman who has experienced everything except this, and you aren't sure what to do. You're not used to that feeling."

"I hate that." Her voice was a low, pleasured moan. "I hate how you call me out on things, like you know me better than you do."

He smiled. "You love it, and you know it. Keeps you on your toes." He dragged his tongue leisurely under the swell of one breast, and then gave the same treatment to the other. Limos practically purred, but her hand remained tamely frozen. He repeated the action, this time pausing to suck first one nipple deep into his mouth, and then the other. Another moan, but no movement.

He wasn't experienced with virgins, but he knew how to loosen up a woman, and he kept up the tongue action, licking and suckling her sensitive skin, her sweet gasps mingling with the calls of the jungle birds and the soothing splash of the water around them. She didn't seem to notice when he unbuttoned her skirt and unwrapped it, leaving her in a yellow bikini bottom.

Jesus, she was exquisite. A one-two punch of deadly and sexy that made his instincts whack out with the need to rip the bottoms off and take her. But he had too much respect for women and too much military training to let his base desires rule, and he tugged her against him and bent to put his mouth to her ear.

"I've dreamed about this," he growled. "I dreamed of all the things I'd do to you. But in none of my fantasies were you a virgin." He nipped her earlobe, and she gasped sweetly. "I would have killed anyone who made my sister regret her first time, so yeah ... you call the shots here."

All of a sudden, she tore out of his arms and scrambled away from him, backing up on a grassy bank, panting and eyeing him as if he'd sprouted horns. "I can't."

Confused as hell, he eased up to her, slowly, because with every step he took, she breathed harder and looked like she was going to bolt. "I won't make you do anything you don't want to do."

She wrapped her arms around herself, covering her breasts. "It's not that. I want to. You don't know how badly I want to."

"Then what?" He cursed as the answer popped into his head. "Your fiancé."

He'd never been one to poach, but this was different. It wasn't poaching when the male in question was the evilest scumbag to ever exist. Then again, that was about the best reason *not* to poach there ever was.

"Sort of." She swallowed audibly, her throat muscles working hard as her hands went to her bikini. Almost mechanically, she shoved the bottoms down and stepped out of them.

Holy shit. The sight took his breath. Her tan skin was perfect, unmarked. Her hips were slim, slightly flared, and the place between her muscular thighs was bare.

And around her hips was the most amazing piece of jewelry, a delicate gold and pearl chain that fit like string thong underwear. How he'd love to run his tongue over every pearl, following the chain to the one pearl that mattered. After he made her come with his mouth, he'd move the chain aside and enter her... God, he could practically feel those smooth little jewels caressing his shaft as he pumped into her.

"You're gorgeous," he managed, noticed he'd moved closer.

"Don't touch," she said, stepped back and bumped into a tree. "This—" she hooked her thumbs under the chain at each hip—"is a chastity belt. Only my husband can remove it."

He frowned. "How is it a chastity belt?"

"If any male touches it with bare skin, it turns into something like razor wire. It severs toes, fingers... cocks."

Well, if that didn't just shrivel him up and make his balls crawl up inside his body. "What about you?"

"It hurts." She shrugged like it was no big deal, but given how the thing was placed... yeah, no wonder she didn't want males to get close.

He reached for her, careful to keep his lower body away from that beautifully deceptive bit of jewelry, but she lashed out, shoving him away.

"Don't! Don't you get it? *You can't touch me.*"

"Dammit, Horseman, I didn't get tossed into Sheoul for nothing. We'll find a way to work around this."

Her eyes nearly bugged out of her head. "Are you saying I owe you? You want me to work off all your torture?"

"What? No. Jesus, you're cynical. I'm saying that I'm a stubborn son of a bitch, and I'm not going to let those skin-peeling, razor-slicing, ass-raping bastards win. I wanted you then, and I want you now. You saved my life and you nursed me back to health. I can't be angry anymore."

"Don't," she rasped. "Don't make me better than I am."

What the hell did that mean? He was about to ask, when twin flashes lit up the area. Instinctively, he wheeled in front of Limos as two huge, armored males popped out of summoned Harrowgates. Ares and Thanatos looked at him, looked at Limos, and sized up the situation in less time than it took an M-16 bullet to strike a target at thirty yards.

In all the time Arik was in the torture chamber, he suspected he'd die.

This time, he *knew* he was dead.

Fifteen

Ares and Thanatos moved before Limos could blink. In a coordinated swoop, Thanatos grabbed Arik while Ares blocked her. She couldn't see beyond Ares's broad shoulders, but she heard growls, grunts, and then a splash.

"Dammit!" Swiping her fingers over her throat, she armored up, covering her nakedness, and slammed Ares out of the way. He grabbed her, but she kneed him hard enough in the groin for him to loosen his grip. She used the split second advantage to lunge for Thanatos, who held a struggling, splashing Arik under water.

"Stop it!" she screamed. "You're killing him."

Than's eyes glowed with golden death. "Yes."

Shit. Once Than went into killing mode, he was nearly unstoppable. There was no time to reason with him, so she tackled him, grabbing him around the waist and knocking him off balance. It was enough for Arik to get his head above water for a deep, choked breath, but then

Thanatos was back at his task, brushing off Limos as if she were no more than a pesky fly.

Ares came at her, and she was done being nice. In an instant, she drew her sword and swung it in a broad arc. Her aim was perfect, and the reverberation from the impact of metal meeting the flesh and bone in Than's neck jolted her arms. Blood sprayed, coating the sword, turning the water around them red. Thanatos yelped, releasing Arik to slap his hands over the gushing wound.

She ignored his curses and Ares's shouts of "What the hell, Limos?" and hauled Arik up from the water. He surfaced, gasping for air, relief and fury alternating in his expression.

"You jackasses!" she snapped, and then found herself holding Arik back from trying to take a piece out of Than as her brother fought to keep from bleeding out. Oh, her strike wouldn't kill Than even if he did bleed out, but it would take a good day for him to regenerate. "Arik can't be allowed to die. You know that!"

Ares snarled, his hand poised over his sword, his furious gaze fixed on Arik. "What was he doing to you?"

"Nothing I didn't want." Ares's hand dropped to the hilt, and Limos, who never panicked . . . panicked.

"Didn't Than tell you?" She turned to Than, who still looked murderous. "You *know* we can't kill him, you fool."

"Why not?" Ares asked.

"Yeah," Arik rasped. "Why not? Not that I'm complaining."

Than settled down as logic finally wrestled his death haze into compliance. "Pestilence fouled him."

Well, that was a groaner. Thanatos had never had a knack for diplomacy or tact.

"What?" Arik climbed onto the shore, where he sat, arms across his raised knees. "What do you mean, Pestilence *fouled* me?"

Limos braced herself for his reaction. "He drank your blood," she said. "And he made you drink his."

"I don't remember any of that. How do you know?"

"He told me. After I found you."

"Okay, that's gross and I want to puke, maybe right after I cut his fucking head off, but what does this have to do with not killing me?"

Thanatos peeled his hand away from his throat, which had partially healed and was oozing now instead of spurting. "Pestilence bound your soul to him."

Arik leaped to his feet. "He *what*?"

"When you die," Limos explained, "your soul will belong to him." Hopefully, it would be a long time before that happened. She just wished she could figure out why Pestilence was holding off. Reseph had never been the patient kind, and turning evil had only made him even more of an instant-gratification sort of guy.

"Son of a—" He broke off to peg her with a hard stare. "Why didn't you tell me this earlier?"

"When should I have told you?" She huffed, her temper suddenly caustic, the result, she was sure, of a bitter blend of sexual frustration, her brothers' overprotective idiocy, and Arik's suspicious tone. "Maybe when you were already hating me for getting you thrown into Sheoul? Or how about when you didn't believe anything I said was real? Or while you were eating something decent for the first time?" She snapped her fingers. "Oh, I know, telling you my evil brother owns your soul would have been awesome sexy talk while you were trying to get into my bikini."

There was another low, menacing growl from Than, which she ignored.

She gathered her bikini and wraparound. "It was for your own good."

She could feel Arik's anger practically blistering her skin, but it faded quickly, and he offered her a respectful nod of apology or, perhaps, acknowledgment that what she'd said made sense. In her experience, few men were so quick to admit mistakes, but he definitely didn't seem the type to be ruled by irrational or defensive anger. She shot him a small smile of thanks before turning to Thanatos.

"Why are you here?"

"Because Reaver still hasn't shown up. I've tried to summon both him and Harvester several times. And now The Aegis is playing some kind of game with us." Thanatos's hands fisted at his sides. "I want to know if our Watchers know anything about it."

"What kind of game?"

"They sent an Elder to live with me."

Talk about an unwanted house guest. "You're kidding."

Than splashed water over his throat and then shook droplets out of his hair like a great cat. "Do I look like I'm kidding? Because you know what a practical joker I am."

A pall fell over them for a second, because Reseph had been a huge lover of practical jokes, and their lives had become decidedly less fun since he turned ghastbat-shit insane.

She cleared her throat to break the tension. "Who did they send?"

Ares flicked his finger over the crescent-shaped scar on

his neck, and his armor melted away. "It always seems so wrong to wear armor on a tropical island," he muttered. "They sent a female named Regan."

"Regan?" Arik snorted. "Good luck with her. Why don't you just say no?"

"Because it's a good idea," Ares said. "We've been out of touch with The Aegis for a long time. This is our chance to catch up on what they've learned over the centuries. And she may be able to help us find Limos's *agimortus* with her gift."

"That's good news." Arik said, wiping beads of water from his brow. "We know it's a small cup, but we don't have its history. Maybe you can shed some light on that?"

"The Aegis and R-XR knows what it needs to know," Than said.

Arik rolled his eyes. "You arrogant asses. Your stale grudge against The Aegis is blinding you."

"Human," Than barked, "you don't talk to us like that."

Arik's eyes went heavy-lidded, his body relaxed and Limos tensed. Reseph used to do the same thing, and that was when he was the deadliest.

"Fuck off, Horseman."

Limos leaped between Arik and Thanatos, heading off the inevitable. "Lock it down, both of you. Arik's right." She glanced at Ares, seeking his support, and he didn't disappoint. When it came to strategy, he generally didn't let emotion cloud his thoughts.

"I agree," he said. "I was reluctant at first, but it's time we put some trust in The Aegis again. We may have made temporary inroads in our fight against Pestilence, but we've been fooling ourselves if we think we can defeat him without the full cooperation of the humans."

Than's souls swirled at his feet as his emotions boiled, and before they got out of hand, Limos took his hand in hers. "Brother, stop. You know we've got to do this."

It was strange the way Thanatos had always been the quietest of them, and yet, he truly was the most volatile. Reseph's emotions had been on his sleeve, Ares's a little more under control, and Limos's somewhere in between. But Than…he was an underground spring of emotion that only an idiot would tap.

"We've already been working with them," Than said.

"Yes," Ares agreed, "but we've played it close to the vest. At this point, we have little to lose by sharing whatever information we have."

There was a tense silence as Thanatos met each of their gazes. "Do what you think is best," he finally said, but he shot Ares and Limos looks that said clearly, *But my privacy is my own.*

It wasn't as if Thanatos's secrets would be important to The Aegis in the long run anyway. His *agimortus* didn't need to be found or guarded. Thanatos could protect it by himself.

Now that the sharing thing had been settled, she turned back to Arik. "So, back to my *agimortus*. Legend has it that it's about the size of a sake cup, made of ivory or bone, and engraved with a set of scales. It was made by an enslaved demon race, the Isfets, who used it as a unit of measure. One Isfet used the cup to secure his freedom and a life in the human realm, but the cost was his sister's life. He had to drink her blood from the cup, which granted him immortality and human form. When his clan found him, they took him back to Sheoul and hid the cup so he could no longer keep it with him…thus, losing his immortality. Over time, the demons died and the cup was forgotten. There are hundreds of theories about where the cup is hidden, but we've checked them all out."

She paused, waiting for Arik to ask more questions, but he was motionless, not even looking at her. "Arik?"

Arik's gaze was fixed on the forest. "There's something out there."

"I don't see anything." Ares might not see anything, but he armored up nonetheless.

"I don't either." Arik's stance widened, his shoulders squaring, and a chill shot up Limos's spine at the battle-ready posture. When he made a protective gesture for her to get behind him, she actually obeyed. As if she couldn't take care of herself. Oddly, she got warm fuzzies from the idea that he was trying to protect her. "I feel it."

"What do you feel?" she asked.

"Evil," Arik whispered. "I feel . . . evil."

Hellfire throbbed through Arik's veins, a searing, screaming warning that evil was within striking distance. The foreign sensation drilled into him, and he moved forward with an almost desperate need to destroy whatever was threatening him and Limos.

Thanatos and Ares were on their own. Which was an idiotic thought, since Limos was fully capable of taking care of herself as well.

Behind him, he heard the unmistakable clatter of armor snapping into place, followed by the hiss of steel clearing leather housings.

Oh, good, and here Arik was with no weapon.

The bushes rustled, and even as Arik opened his mouth

to let out a warning, mastiff-sized, four-legged demons burst out of the foliage. *Khnives.*

Limos shouted something about Pestilence's spies and buried her blade in one of the *khnives'* chests.

Arik wheeled out of the way of the first one, its snapping teeth grazing his arm. Rolling, he grabbed a thick tree branch and nailed the second *khnive* in the throat, sending the skinless, opossum-like creature slamming into a tree trunk.

"Human!" Ares tossed a dagger, and Arik caught it, spinning in time to jam the blade into a beast's brain with an upward stroke under its jaw.

Waves of evil buffeted him like a windstorm, growing more powerful as dozens of the demons came at them. The things had long, sharp claws and razor teeth between powerful jaws, but where their deadly abilities lay was in their numbers. Within seconds, Arik and the Horsemen were overwhelmed.

All around them, blood dripped off leaves, streamed down tree trunks, and turned the crystal pool red. Than had unleashed his souls, and the godawful shrieks of the attacking shadows joined the chorus of screams and growls from the dying demons.

Three demons leaped simultaneously, but as Arik slashed at one, another hit him from the side, knocking the blade from his hand and slamming him to the ground. Limos shouted, bringing her sword down in an arc that sheared off the thing's head. The other two came at Arik's throat. Snarling, because fuck if he got out of Sheoul to die at the teeth and claws of demons considered by even other demons to be lowlife scourge, he grabbed one around the throat and squeezed.

The thing stiffened and fell dead.

Arik blinked in shock, but who the hell cared why

the thing died so easily? He went for the other, with the same result. Another came at him, and this time he didn't bother with grabbing its throat. He punched the fucker in the face, and it dropped. Time after time, he took the demons out, going through them like a lawnmower.

Eventually, he was standing waist-deep in demons, staring at the carnage around him, and the Horsemen were staring at him. At least the weird sensation of being watched by evil was gone.

"What the hell was that, human?" Ares asked.

"I have no idea." He lifted his head, his newfound spidey-senses tingling again, but this time without the intensity. "Over there."

Thanatos moved like a snake, faster than Arik could track as he disappeared into the brush. There was a squeak, a thud, and he emerged, carrying a rat by its tail. "This?"

"Yeah. That was it." Arik scrubbed his hand over his face, confused as shit. "What the hell?"

Limos winced. "Crap. The blood exchange. Like vampires."

"Ah." Ares nodded. "Makes sense."

"To you," Arik muttered. "You want to include me in your cryptic conversation?"

Limos sheathed her sword. "*Khnives* are summoned demons. Spies. A lot of demons can summon one or two, but only a handful of beings could have summoned this many *khnives*, and Pestilence is one of them. Even as Reseph he could command disease carriers and use them to gather intelligence or spread disease...or he could destroy them at will. The blood exchange gave you his abilities. To what extent..." She shrugged. "Time will tell."

"I'm still not following. You mentioned vampires."

"Vampires often transmit their special abilities to

those they turn," Thanatos explained. "But since you didn't technically turn, I suspect there's something unique about you. What are you not telling us? Do you have a demon dangling from your family tree?"

As tempting as it was to tell Thanatos to fuck off, Arik wanted to know what was up as well. "No demons in my DNA, but I was bitten by one a few years ago." He figured he'd leave out the part about how the demon that bit him had been sent by the demon he'd made a bad deal with back when he was a teenager, desperate to end his father's reign of terror. "The infection from the bite nearly killed me, but Shade saved my life. There was a...side-effect." He glanced over at Limos, who was watching him curiously. "I can learn demon languages after hearing just a few words."

"You Aegi are full of surprises," Ares murmured.

Arik had found that statement to be true enough. "So why did Pestilence send his spies to attack? I mean, if he wants me dead, can't he do it himself? If he'd come with a few of his minions, I could have been toast by now."

"You're right." Limos frowned. "It doesn't make sense."

"Maybe it was your charming fiancé?" Arik asked, but she shook her head.

"That doesn't make sense either. I doubt he knows that Pestilence owns your soul. Satan would want you dragged to Sheoul to die, so he could have your soul. He'd lose it if you died here."

"So what you're saying then, is that there's a new player in town."

Ares nudged one of the *khnive* bodies with his foot. "A new player who wants you dead."

Thanatos whistled. "Sucks to be you, human."

Man, there were days you just shouldn't get out of bed.

Sixteen

No more creepy demons attacked Arik and Limos on their way back to the house, and when Arik saw Kynan standing on the huge wraparound deck at the front of Limos's house, he rethought the not-getting-out-of-bed thing. Limos disappeared to give them a moment as he folded Kynan into a bear hug and practically lifted him off the deck. Ky gave him a few manly pats on the back, and they broke apart, Arik grinning like an idiot.

"Man," he breathed. "It's so great to see you."

"Ditto. You gave us a scare." Kynan clapped him on the shoulder. "You look good. Shade and E did you right."

"Speaking of Shade—"

"He and Runa are on their way," Kynan interrupted.

"Good." Arik sank down on one of the bar stools that cozied up to the bamboo mini-bar. The east decking was set up with tables, the bar, and a hot tub, and Arik wondered how much partying Limos did here. "Runa's probably been a little worried."

"A little?" Kynan snorted. "I think the only thing keeping her together has been all the time she spends in Underworld General's daycare."

Arik had forgotten that UG had a daycare run by Runa and a couple other in-laws of his, Serena and Idess. That was some weird shit. A hospital run by demons, with a nursery run by a werewolf, a vampire, and an ex-angel. There was a book or TV show in there somewhere.

Arik propped one heel on the stool rung and leaned back, letting the sun hit his bare skin. "I'll bet the hospital has been busy."

"Everything has been busy. It's bad, man." Kynan dragged his hand through his hair. "The Aegis is overextended, and we've lost nearly ten percent of our Guardians in assassinations and battles with demons. We even lost an Elder. Decker took his place."

Arik's eyes shot wide. "You made Decker an Elder? He isn't even an Aegi."

"He is now."

Arik rubbed the back of his neck, stunned at this new turn of events. "Wow. The Aegis has a really intensive selection process, doesn't it?'

"Ha-ha." Kynan shook his head. "We had a few candidates shortlisted, but we decided to take someone from the R-XR."

"Why? You already had us, well, him, as a consult."

"Yeah, but as an Elder, we can share more sensitive information with him, and when he's sworn to keep something secret, he has to."

"You mean, keep something secret from the R-XR."

Arik hated all the secrecy crap. How the hell were they supposed to solve the end-of-the-world puzzle when the players wouldn't share their pieces?

Ky shrugged. "So...now that you're back..." he trailed off. "You *are* back, right?"

Arik looked up at a seagull soaring overhead and wondered how to respond. This was something he didn't know how to answer. His mind was still scrambled, Pestilence held the deed to his soul, he could alert to spies like a bird dog, a gob of people were trying to kill him, and then there was the...whatever it was...going on with Limos.

"Look," Ky said, interrupting Arik's musings, "if you need time off, a vacation...therapy...it's understandable. Hell, it's required. But the world situation isn't getting any better. The Apocalypse took a break, but it's knocking at our door again. We need you, man."

"Trust me, I want to kick some demon ass. But I'm not sure leaving right now is a good idea."

"What, you want to stay here?"

Fucking idiot that he was, yeah, he wanted to stay. Because hey, nothing like self-torture to make one's life complete. "My soul is in danger. If I die, I become Pestilence's soul-bitch. Long story, but if he decides he wants me dead, I'm probably safest here. Our best defense against an evil Horseman is another Horseman."

"*Fuuuuuuuuck.*" Kynan scrubbed his face. "I could use a double shot of whiskey right now."

"I'm sure Flicka keeps hard liquor behind the bar."

"Flicka?"

"I don't want to say her name."

"So you're calling her horse names?" Ky cocked a dark eyebrow. "I can't wait to see how she reacts to Mr. Ed."

The slatted-wood double doors that opened to the deck from the living room swung wide, and Arik leaped to his feet as Runa stepped out, Shade at her side.

"Sis!" As Arik moved toward her, Shade put his big body in the way, menace all but leaking from his pores. What the hell was that about?

Runa, seemingly unconcerned by her mate's reaction, went around him and threw herself into Arik's arms.

"Thank God," she whispered. "Thank God you're okay."

"Yeah." His throat closed up a little. "Yeah. I'm okay."

She pulled back so he could see her face. "You know it's me, right?"

"Ah, yeah." What the hell?

"You on the up-and-up?" Shade asked. "Because you pull any shit like you did last time, and I *will* gut you. Runa won't stop me this time."

"Shade!" Runa scolded. "He's fine."

"Overprotective, much?" Arik glared. "And what the fuck are you talking about?"

"Hey, everyone, why don't we give Arik some time to rest?" Limos, changed into a bright blue sundress, hurried outside, her smile so fake and unsteady that it was obvious she was trying to keep Shade and Runa from answering Arik's question.

"No deal, Secretariat. I don't need any rest." He swiveled around to Shade, knowing the demon would give it to him straight. People who didn't give a shit about you were always the most honest. "Answer me."

"Arik, this isn't necessary." Limos took Arik's arm to lead him away, but he didn't budge, and Shade didn't seem inclined to listen to her either.

"Let me refresh your memory." Shadows writhed in Shade's dark eyes, and he poked Arik in the chest with one finger. "We were here yesterday. You beat the shit out of Runa. Broke her cheekbone, smashed her nose, and fractured three ribs."

The ground shifted beneath Arik's feet. "That's not possible. I would never—"

"It's okay, Arik," Runa said. "You were out of your mind. You didn't know what was real."

"No way." He shook his head, as if he could shake loose his memories. "I can remember my locker combination from boot camp, so I would have fucking remembered laying my hands on my own sister." Just saying those words made his stomach turn inside out.

"There are a lot of things you can't recall." Limos moved toward him, and something inside him got all shivery in anticipation of her touch. She had a healing effect on him, as evidenced by the way she'd brought him out of the hellish existence inside his own head.

But right now, he didn't want to be healed. He wanted to remember.

He wheeled around, slapping his palms down on the deck rail. Runa joined him, her caramel-honey hair blowing in the breeze.

"Arik, everything is fine. I shifted and healed most of it, and Eidolon healed the rest. No damage was done."

It was nice of her to try to console him, but he knew better. She'd suffered so much as a child, and being beaten had to have brought back memories best left buried. And wait...buried...when he'd been at the engagement party for Cara and Ares, Cara had told him about how Ares had used his special skill on her when they'd first met.

"He erased my memories so I wouldn't freak out," she'd said. *"Which, of course, I did the moment he unlocked them."*

"Son of a bitch." He spun around to Limos. "You erased my memories, didn't you?"

"No." She said it so easily, so convincingly that he wanted to believe her, but something was off. A flare in her eyes, or a twitch of muscle, or maybe it was just the same hinky sense of unease he'd felt whenever his father told him something Arik wanted desperately to believe.

I'll be there for your ball game, I promise. This Christmas, we really will have presents. I swear I'll quit drinking.

Yeah, Arik's bullshit meter was pegged at the max.

"You want to try that again, Horseman?" *Please, please tell me the truth.* If she said no again, he'd take it. He'd believe it, just like he'd believed his dad all those years ago. But when she just stood there, his heart sank. "You did it, didn't you? What else am I missing in my head?"

Her mouth opened. Closed. Son of a bitch. Of everything that had been done to him over the last month, this was what felt like the biggest violation.

He turned to Kynan. "I was wrong. I don't want to stay here. Let's go."

It had been three days since Arik had gone. The house felt empty, which was weird, because Limos had never thought of her house as being empty. But then, maybe that was why she had the other, public villa on the other side of the island, where she always had a party going on.

She didn't like empty.

She also didn't like Sheoul, with its claustrophobic atmosphere, sinister vibes, and hazy light, but here she was, riding Bones along a path in the Horun region, sandwiched between Ares and Than as they followed a lead on Sartael.

Thanatos had managed to squeeze some information out of Orelia, his demon tattoo artist, and if her intel was to be believed, the Dark Lord's right-hand man was leading Sartael around by the nose and using him as a bloodhound. With the end of days on the horizon, Satan and Lucifer were in a scramble to locate ancient objects of magic and power that could be used in the final battle. Apparently, they'd just procured a mystical dagger rumored to have belonged to Charlemagne, and they were now on the hunt for the Spear of Destiny.

Limos and her brothers were here to stop them—and convince Sartael to help them find her *agimortus*.

All of them were on edge as they went from one underworld city to the next, and it didn't help that the hellhound accompanying them, Gore, kept nipping at Bones's heels. Bones was not happy at all, and it took every drop of concentration she had to keep him from attacking the canine.

"I hate this place," she muttered.

Thanatos scowled at her. "Then you shouldn't have come," he said, and Ares nodded in agreement.

She didn't argue, because they were right. But with Arik gone, she'd fallen back into her old self-destructive mode, the one that drove her to take risks, to start fights, to go all out in an all-encompassing effort to grab the high that only pain—and lying—could bring about.

Except that wasn't true, was it? Only after Arik was gone had she realized that being with him gave her a similar high. Similar, but better, because it was a pure, feel-good sensation that didn't make her hate herself.

I've got to get Arik back. Her brothers turned to stare at her. Oops, she'd spoken out loud. "What? I don't trust The Aegis or R-XR to keep him safe."

Always the warrior, Ares returned his sharp gaze to the landscape as he spoke. "Have you contacted Kynan?"

"He won't tell me where Arik is." She patted Bones's ebony neck, unsurprised when he growled in irritation. "And since he's charmed, I can't torture it out of him."

"It's probably not a good idea to torture the people we're supposed to be working with," Ares said wryly.

"It's a good idea," she protested. "As long as I don't get caught."

"I'm cool with kicking Guardian ass," Thanatos chimed in.

It was often hard to tell when Than was being serious, but in this case, he was a little too enthusiastic about the prospect of bloodying up a Guardian, and she wondered if his resident Guardian was the reason for his attitude.

"I have to do something." She shooed Gore away as he crept up on Bones again. "Too many people want Arik dead, including whatever asshole sent the *khnives*."

"I'm curious about the *khnives* too." The deep, resonant voice from behind them made all their mounts whirl and the hellhound snarl.

"Lucifer," she hissed, and before the demon's name was even fully out of her mouth, Ares had thrown open a Harrowgate and Than had launched a dagger. The blade caught the tall, black-haired fallen angel in the shoulder, but he just laughed, his pure crimson eyes glowing like laser beams.

"Your husband is looking for you, Limos. It's time for you to go to him."

Gore went low, belly to the ground, lips peeled away from razor sharp teeth and ears flattened against his skull, but wisely, he didn't make a move. Lucifer could snuff him with no more than a snap of his fingers.

"She's not going anywhere." Ares crowded Battle against Bones in preparation to bulldoze them into the Harrowgate.

"Where is Sartael?" she asked.

"Funny you should ask. He just completed an assignment for me." Lucifer snapped his fingers, and a winged man dropped from the sky, landing in a crouch next to him.

The male raised to his full, seven-foot height, his dried-blood-red leathery wings rising high above his bald head.

"What?" he snarled, and Limos got the distinct impression that he was less than happy to be dealing with Lucifer.

"Meet the Horsemen," Lucifer said, his voice all silk and slime. "Pay extra attention to the female, since your next assignment will be to locate her *agimortus*."

Limos snorted to cover up the fact that her heart had stopped. "Yeah, good luck with that, Sarty. You can't find what hasn't been hidden or lost, and I've already found it."

Oh, that lie felt good. The orgasmic jolt was mild; she didn't get much of a physiological kick out of lying to scumbags. It was just awesome to screw with Lucifer in general.

"You're rusty, Limos. The Prince of Lies will want his Princess of Lies to have skills befitting the title." Lucifer smiled, his blackened lips cracking. "Speaking of which,

I have an offer for you. Go to the Dark Lord, and I will call off my minions."

Bones pawed at the ground, wanting a piece of the demon, and Limos was right there with him. "A, you could use some ChapStick. B, what minions?"

"The ones who are awaiting my signal to bring Arik to me, now that Sartael has found him."

She smiled. "Now who's lying? Sartael's power in the human realm is limited to finding demons and demonic artifacts."

"Silly, stupid girl," Lucifer drawled. "Arik's soul belongs to a demon. Therefore, he's a demonic artifact." Limos's *oh-shit* meter topped out, then blew the lid off at Lucifer's next words. "And I'm going to deliver him straight to your husband." Lucifer's boneless gait brought him even closer, and she forced Bones to dig his hooves into the earth to keep Ares from shoving them through the gate. "You should have been his a long time ago, Limos. You have played very loose with the terms of your contract, and he is not . . . pleased."

Her heart ricocheted around her chest as if seeking a way out. If her brothers knew how loose, they'd toss her to Lucifer themselves.

"And your mother . . ." Lucifer affected a sad expression. "She's so disappointed in you. She raised you to be more responsible."

Thanatos eased Styx closer to Bones. "How irresponsible of Li to not want to enter into an arranged marriage with the most evil being to have ever existed."

"Limos is the envy of every female in the underworld. She knew what he was when she agreed to be his mate," Lucifer pointed out.

That was true. Oh, God, was that ever true. She'd been promised to him as an infant, but had willingly stood before him to pledge her intentions later, as a teen who was fully aware of what she was doing.

But she'd changed her mind, and it was all crashing down on her now, and she wondered when she'd be crushed under the weight of the fallout.

"She didn't agree." Ares's voice dripped with disdain. "This was forced on her as a child, against her will."

Oh, fuck. She tensed up so hard that Bones groaned at the pressure of her thighs against his ribs. Lucifer's head swiveled around slowly, creepily. The sinister smile on his face was something right out of a horror movie.

"Is that what she told you?" Throwing his head back, Lucifer laughed.

In a sudden, blind burst of panic, she cast a Harrowgate next to Lucifer, using it as a weapon. It sliced into him like a giant blade, severing his left arm, shaving his shoulder from his torso.

The sound he made, one of pain, fury, and hatred, blasted her ears with such force that her eardrums burst. Pain exploded in her head, and a chorus of yelps and shouts said it was torture on her brothers and the hellhound, too. The ground rumbled, and Lucifer morphed into a dinosaur-sized monster, a black, scaly thing with grotesquely misshapen limbs and exaggerated teeth and genitals. It raked the hound with its claws, ripping gaping wounds the length of Gore's body.

Before she could react, Ares and Battle rammed her through his gate.

Limos and Bones came out in Ares's courtyard. And they weren't alone. Bones spun as Sartael burst out of her

Harrowgate. He leaped for her, and though Bones caught him in the ankle with his teeth, the fallen angel managed to knock her out of the saddle. They hit the ground and rolled, throwing punches and slashing with weapons.

His hand came around her throat, and he slammed her head hard into a rock. Bones screamed in fury, and his hooves filled her vision. Wet, cracking noises became one with Sartael's shriek of pain as Bones's feet went right through his back and out his chest, pinning him in the sand.

Limos scrambled out from under him, grateful that the hell stallion's hooves had missed her. As her burst eardrums knit back together, she crouched next to the fallen angel.

"Following me was stupid, Sarty." She patted his bald head. "Because now that I have you, I'm going to make you tell me where Arik is, and then you're going to help me find my *agimortus*."

He laughed...well, sort of coughed, since his mouth was full of blood. "I'm going to take you to your husband. And I'm going to strip your human's skin off his body while he watches the Dark Lord fuck you until you tear in half."

"You are disgusting." She looked up at Bones. "Make him hurt a little."

Bones bared his razor-sharp teeth and took a bite out of the angel's shoulder. Flesh ripped away with a curious zipping noise. Sartael screamed in agony.

"Now, you piece of shit," she purred. "Agree to help me, or next time Bones goes for something more tender. He's always loved Rocky Mountain Oysters. I guess we'll call them angel oysters, yes?"

"I'm going to see you fry," he ground out. "I'm going to tell your brothers how you stood before the Dark Lord and begged him to take you as his bride. How you promised to bring your brothers to him as wedding gifts. How you stood motionless, your thighs dripping with your lust, as the chastity belt was placed around your waist."

Her throat went as dry as the sand under her feet. "You weren't there. You don't know." Except his details were spot on.

"I was the hellrat chained to Lucifer's wrist during the ceremony. I spent almost five thousand years as a rodent—punishment for letting another angel fuck your mother before I could. *I* was supposed to be your father, you whore. I was supposed to be *the princess's* father." He smiled grimly. "Now I will be the princess's bedmate when her husband is through with her."

Cara called out, and Limos looked up to see her running toward them. In the same instant, flashes of light penetrated the evening shadows as two Harrowgates opened up several feet in front of her. Limos's past was closing in on her, choking her, coming at her like a plane in a spiral death dive.

Crying out, she brought her sword down across Sartael's throat, silencing him, and his ugly truths, forever.

Than stepped through one gate, dragging Gore with him. The hellhound could barely stand, was gushing blood like a waterfall. Ares exited through his own gate, leading a limping Battle.

Cara ran straight to the animals, and even as they collapsed onto the ground, she laid one hand on each. From all around, dozens of hellhounds moved in, silent as shadows, and fell upon the dead angel. Quickly, before Bones started a fight, Limos called him to her, and he dissolved into smoke before winding around her arm.

Cara's healing gift slammed into the animals, and in minutes, their wounds had sealed.

"What the hell happened back there?" Than barked at Limos. "And why did you kill Sartael? He was our best shot at finding your *agimortus*!"

"I know." That, at least, wasn't a lie. "He threatened Arik. I freaked." Another truth.

"You freaked?" Thanatos's words dripped with skepticism. "You never freak. Not like that."

Ares helped Battle to his feet as Cara finished with the hound. "And why does Lucifer think you participated in your betrothal willingly?"

"Because he's an idiot." Yet another truth. Before her brothers could question her further, she changed the subject. "We've got to get to Arik. Now. Lucifer wouldn't lie about knowing where he is."

Ares fed Battle a sugar cube. "Yeah, well, *we* don't know where he is."

"I'll bet Runa does," she said, throwing a gate. "And I'm going to make sure she knows exactly what's going on with her brother."

Because if there was one thing Limos knew something about, it was how far one sibling would go to protect another.

Or betray one.

Seventeen

In hindsight, Arik figured he should have had Kynan take him to his apartment. Instead, he'd asked Ky to take him to R-XR headquarters, which had been a colossal mistake. They'd immediately rushed him to medical for a full exam and every kind of test known to both human and demon science. Then he'd been isolated for questioning and another battery of tests, this time to assess his mental health.

He should have known he'd be held prisoner—he'd helped draw up the SOPs for any military member who had been captured and held by demons.

The questions were endless, repetitive and, sometimes, ludicrous. *Are you sure you didn't give up any sensitive information?* Yes. *Did any demon possess you?* No. *Were you impregnated?* Jesus, he hoped not. *Did you grow attached to any demon?* No.

As long as Limos didn't count, damn her.

When the interrogators moved past his time in Sheoul and started on his time with Limos, Arik became a lot more selective in what he told them. No way in hell was he going to share how he'd been in a constant state of lust around her, or how he'd been so afraid to eat food that he'd only eaten when he thought she was bringing him dog food. Or how he still refused to say her name.

Or how she'd fucked with his memory.

He also left out the part where Pestilence drank him like a milkshake, forced Arik to drink him in return, and gave him the curious side-effect of being able to sense spies and kill them with a touch.

The R-XR would have him splayed open on a dissection table for that one.

The upside to all the questioning and tests was that it kept his mind off what he'd done to Runa. Shade's words kept clanging in his head, a brutal thump against the inside of his skull that he deserved. He'd sworn to protect Runa. He'd sworn to never become the monster their father had been. And what had he done? Become the monster who used to haunt her dreams until Shade took them all away. Now Arik wondered if he'd reversed all Shade's progress.

It didn't matter that he'd attacked Runa while he was out of his mind. Their father had often delivered his most brutal beatings while out of his ever-loving mind, three sheets to the wind. It wasn't an excuse, and Arik wasn't going to make excuses for himself, either.

Man, he needed a vacation, but that particular line of thinking always took him to a tropical beach that looked suspiciously like Hawaii, complete with a certain raven-haired Horseman. Not that he was taking a trip anytime soon; he'd been released from the R-XR medical facility and put into one of the Fort McNair dorms, and though he was free to come and go within the facilities, he still wasn't cleared to leave the base.

Which sucked. He was a soldier, and the human race was at war. He needed to do something. Needed to fight for his team, which was Team Human, not Team Horsemen. Sure, they were on the same side, but definitely not on the same team.

Except it had felt great to fight next to Limos against the *khnives*, hadn't it. She'd had his back, and their moves had been in sync in a way he hadn't experienced with anyone but Decker.

He caught himself rubbing his chest, as if trying to soothe his aching heart, and what the hell? Had demon Alcatraz turned him into a lovesick puppy? Annoying.

A pounding on his dorm door jolted him out of his pathetic musings, and then Ky and Decker strode in before he even had a chance to tell them to come in. He forgave them because he really needed to get his mind off Runa and Limos. And because they brought beer.

Decker pulled a bottle of Bud out of the six-pack and tossed it to Arik. "You can take the redneck out of the country..." Arik said.

"...but you can't take the Bud away from the redneck," Kynan finished, and Decker shot them both the bird.

"The way I see it," Decker drawled, "you can drink warm water from the tap, or you can drink an ice cold Budweiser." He held up the six-pack, minus one, dangled it in front of Kynan.

"Yeah, yeah. Give me the damned beer. But don't think I'll spontaneously start watching NASCAR or something."

"I'm telling ya, you'd love the short-track racing," Decker muttered, tossing him a beer.

"Only if the drivers are demons," Kynan said.

Decker shrugged. "There's been speculation about the Busch brothers. They ain't right. And Jimmy Johnson. He wins too much for it to be natural."

Rolling his eyes, Kynan took a seat in one of two chairs, and Arik took the other. Like old times, Decker threw himself on the bed and sprawled out like he lived there. Their friendship had been an easy one...sure, there had been moments of tension, but didn't every relationship have them? It hadn't even occurred to Arik that he'd need more in the way of relationships, not when he had good friends and a tight military community around him.

So yeah, everything felt the same. Natural. And yet... there was the sense that something was missing.

You miss Limos, idiot.

Fuck, he was screwed.

"So," Decker said. "You look pretty good for being in hell's belly for a month."

Arik downed half his beer. "I don't recommend it as a vacation spot."

"You okay?" Kynan asked, his voice low, gaze serious.

Arik was tired of that question. There'd been way too much doom and gloom and *are you okay*.

"Couldn't be better."

"Runa wants to see you. Said you aren't returning her calls."

"Been busy." Busy avoiding her.

Ky got the hint and didn't push the issue. Decker didn't either, took a swig of beer and changed directions, bless his little ole redneck heart. "So...what possessed you to kiss a Horseman and earn yourself a ride on the long black train?"

Man, sometimes Decker needed a translator. "Long black train?"

Kynan beaned Decker with his bottle cap. "It's from one of Decker's country songs he forces me to listen to. Something about a train to hell."

"Yeah, well, there's no train. Just big, thorny arms." Arik shut down that memory and downed the rest of his beer.

"Well?" Decker tossed him another cold one. "Why'd you do it? I didn't think you swung that way."

"I kissed the *female* Horseman, you idiot. I'm not gay."

"Duh. I know you're not gay." Decker propped himself up on an elbow. "I was talking about supernaturals. I didn't think you walked on that side of the tracks."

Kynan snorted. "Train metaphors aside, if you saw Limos, you'd walk there too, Deck."

Arik sighed. "You two meatheads here for a reason?"

"You have something better to do?" Kynan asked.

"No, but you didn't come here to bring me beer and sit around taking up space. So you're either here to gauge my mental fitness, or you're here to bring me up to speed on Aegis and R-XR shit. Which is it?"

"Both," Decker admitted, falling into pro mode. He came across as a big, slow hick at times, but Arik wasn't entirely convinced it wasn't an act. The guy was sharp as a stang blade at times.

Arik sat forward in his chair. "What's up?"

Kynan kicked his booted feet up on the desk. "When you were with Limos, did she give you any information about her *agimortus*?"

Arik filled them in on the stuff about the Isfet demons, which was all new to Kynan. "Damn," he breathed. "All we've had to go on are the lines in the *Daemonica*. *A Horseman, should he drink from the Cup of Deception and Lies, will loose Famine to ravage the earth.* Did she give you anything about Thanatos?"

"They've been tight-lipped about him," Arik muttered. "The world is screwed. Unless you brilliant minds have come up with some sort of plan while I've been at Disney-land." Kynan and Decker exchanged glances, and Arik got a bad feeling in the base of his gut. "What? What are you guys not telling me?"

"Did Limos give you any insight into Thanatos and his...ah..." Kynan trailed off as if looking for the right word, which was strange, because the guy rarely beat around the bush.

Decker rolled his eyes. "What do you know about his sex life?"

Arik froze with his beer an inch from his lips. "His sex life?"

"Yeah. You know, what's he into? Men? Kinky shit? Dangerous shit? Or is he like you and all vanilla?" Decker delivered the last bit with a teasing smirk.

As if he was one to talk. The dude had dated the same sweet, missionary-only girl since high school until last year when he couldn't take lying to her about his job any-more, and broke up with her. It had come down to keep lying or leave the R-XR. Decker had chosen his career, and Arik couldn't blame him. Now was not a good time to lay down weapons, for sure.

"Do I look like I'm the guy's confessor? How the hell should I know what he's into? And why are you asking?" Arik eyed the two males, who were squirming like schoolboys who'd been caught with their hands down their pants.

"Because we sent Regan to seduce him."

Arik choked on his beer. "Regan?" he wheezed. "She's got the feminine wiles of a rabid cactus."

Decker frowned. "I don't think cacti can contract rabies."

Kynan shot Decker an are-you-kidding-me look before turning back to Arik. "Listen, this has to be kept between us. It doesn't leave this room. Only a handful of Elders know."

Still floored, Arik sighed. "Okay, I give. Thanatos said you'd sent her, but he thinks it's because The Aegis wants to fill in historical blanks or something. Why did you send her to sleep with the guy?"

"Because we need her to get pregnant," Kynan said.

Arik blinked. Hard. "I . . . don't think I heard you right."

"Yeah, you did," Decker said, his voice going all sorrowful Eeyore. "Fucking sucks, too, cuz I think she might have been sweet on me."

Kynan drained his beer, and then he explained the situation, which amounted to prophecy, blah, blah, immortal child saving the world, blah, blah, from Death comes life, blah, blah, and a whole lot of buzzing in Arik's ears because most of what Kynan was saying didn't compute.

Regan the ice queen was sacrificing herself to bed a Horseman, while Arik couldn't bed the one he wanted to.

He was about to ask Decker to toss him another beer when Kynan's cell rang, and at the same time, Decker's went off. Outside, klaxons blared in shrill alarm.

Decker peeled the curtain away from the window.

"We're under attack. Fuck. How the hell could demons get on base? It's warded."

"Son of a—" The sound of gunfire joined shouts and screams, but the soldiers would have no way of knowing that bullets were useless against most demons.

The highest ranking officers on base were in the know about demons, but for the most part, the soldiers here *weren't* aware of the existence of underworld creatures. All the soldiers were doing was angering the demons with their piddly little bullets.

Arik tore open the door as the demon horde swarmed toward the dorms.

"We are so fucked," Decker muttered, even as he reached under his jacket for a stang. Kynan did the same, tossing one to Arik.

"You guys ready?" Ky said.

Arik tested the gold end of the S-shaped blade, drawing blood on his thumb. "Let's send these fuckers back to hell, where they belong."

Limos, Ares, and Thanatos gated themselves right into hell on earth. Literally.

Thousands of demons swarmed Arik's military base, ripping through the soldiers as if they were made of tissue paper. Gunfire and screams filled the air, and the cloying scent of blood and bowels churned in Limos's nostrils. Guiding Bones with her knees, she cut down demons as she searched for Arik, while Ares's great sword cleaved bodies in half. Thanatos's long-handled scythe sliced heads from shoulders.

Bones, who viewed every battle as an all-you-can-eat

buffet, bit the head off some smallish thorny creature and chomped down on it like a normal horse would eat an apple.

"There!" Thanatos pointed toward a huge, boxy building where Kynan, Arik, and a blond male were slashing at their attackers with stangs and daggers. The fighting was bloody, dirty, and Arik, in his black BDUs, was death on legs. His movements were purposeful, economical, and with a few spins, slashes, and kicks, he'd laid out six huge demons like they were scarecrows. The boy could *fight*.

So. Hot.

Then the tide changed. A duo of fallen angels flashed into the fight from nowhere and tag-teamed Arik, one slamming him to the ground while the other zapped him with some sort of power that had him convulsing, blood shooting from his nose.

Limos had had it up to her chin with fucking fallen angels. She hadn't made Sartael suffer enough, but she'd make up for that now.

With a roar, Limos charged, kicking Bones into a dead run. They bowled over demons and humans alike, and she didn't care. No one hurt her male.

Her male. There was no use in denying it any longer. She'd viewed Arik as hers since the first kiss. He'd been right, and he'd called her on it; she'd wanted that kiss. She'd wanted *him*. And Limos had always considered what she wanted to be hers.

Bones smashed into one of the fallen angels, crushing him beneath his hooves as he tore at its wings with his teeth. Limos was a whirl of blades as she leaped from the stallion's back and made the remaining fallen angel bleed from two dozen wounds before he even knew what hit him.

Gunfire rang out at close range, and Bones screamed, rearing up and splashing blood from a baseball-sized hole in his side. It healed almost instantly, but she knew it hurt like hot hell. A bullet pinged off her armor, and dammit, the stupid humans couldn't tell friend from foe. Arik came to his feet, his eyes blazing with fury. At first, Limos thought the anger was directed at her, but when he charged at a soldier whose M-16 was trained on her... well, she melted a little.

Another set of fallen angels interrupted her mushy appreciation at Arik's defense of her, one hitting Kynan so hard against the side of the building that when he crumpled to the ground, his arm was skewed in an unnatural angle, the end of the broken bone jutting out of his skin.

"Arik!" she yelled. "We have to go!"

He wheeled around, his fists tangled in the soldier's shirt. "I'm not leaving."

She ran to him, followed by Bones, who struck out at demons that tried to attack her flank. "The demons are here because of you. If we go, they'll go. It's the humans' only chance."

Arik only hesitated for a second before cursing and shoving the stunned soldier away. "Let's do it."

Limos opened a gate, grabbed Arik's hand and Bones's reins, and darted through the portal. Their feet hit the warm, white sand on Ares's Greek island, a hundred yards from where she'd killed Sartael. She so did not want to be reminded of that incident, and she prayed Ares and Thanatos would let it go.

"Son of a bitch," Arik snapped. "How did the demons get on base? It's warded."

"Not from underneath," she said. "And not from the kind of power Lucifer wields. Once the demons came up from below, they disabled the wards, which is how we and the fallen angels got in."

"Lucifer?"

She nodded. "He told me he'd found you and was going to grab you. Those demons had to be his, and trust me, your people have never come up against anything like him before. And the fact that he can extend his power into the human realm means that the barrier between realms has been compromised. It won't be long until it falls and every demon in Sheoul will escape."

"I thought the Seals had to break for that to happen."

She dug a piece of elk jerky out of Bones's saddle-bags and fed it to him. "The more powerful Pestilence becomes, and the more human earth he claims in the name of Sheoul, the weaker the barrier becomes."

"That's fantastic." Arik carefully tucked his stang in his pants pocket. "So why are we here?"

"Cara sent hellhounds to my island to root out anything that could potentially be a threat or a spy hoping to learn where you are. I need to check with her to make sure it's clear before I take you back there." She sighed. "I just hope the helldogs don't eat any humans."

Arik gave her that stare that said "dumbass" without words. "Yeah. That would be a bonus."

She held out her arm. "Bones, to me." The stallion, his jaws still working on the jerky, dissolved into smoke and settled into her skin without protest.

"Then what?" Arik asked, as he wiped away a stream of blood on his temple. "You gonna take me back to your house and lie to me some more?"

She started toward the front door. "I'm sure you're a pillar of truth, Arik."

"I've never stolen someone's memories and lied about it." Arik fell into step beside her, his combat boots making heavy thuds on the pavers.

"Oh, right. So holier than thou. You're saying you've never lied? Do you tell everyone you meet who you are and who you work for?"

"That's different. My job is beyond top secret."

"And what do you tell the women you meet? Do you have to lie to them about your job? About who you are? Do you fuck them with all those lies between you?" When he stiffened, she snorted. "That's what I thought." And worse, she was so freaking jealous about it.

"There's a huge difference between lying to hurt someone and omitting information to protect someone."

"You keep telling yourself that, Pinocchio."

Arik wiped blood from his nose. "How did you find me, anyway?"

"Runa told me when I explained you were in danger. She also said you haven't returned any of her calls."

"Tattletale," he muttered.

Cara, looking freshly showered with her hair wet and clad in her usual flannel pajamas, met them at the door. "The hounds have cleared your island. There was one... mishap, but other than that, you should be good to go. Six hounds will be outside your house at all times." She bit her lip. "If they want in, though, I wouldn't argue. You should probably put a sheet over your couch. Dog hair."

Great. Just great. Limos had never even had a normal dog as a pet, and now she had a pack of hellhounds to deal with.

A Harrowgate opened, and Ares stepped out, his armor dripping blood and gore. Arik jogged over to him. "How's the base? The soldiers? Ky and Decker?"

"Kynan is on his way to UG. Decker's helping to triage the injured. There were a lot of casualties. Enough that Than is hung up there."

"Damn," Arik breathed. "I need to help—"

"You can't." Ares's voice was intense but level, a sign of respect from one warrior to another. "You'll only lead the demons back to them."

"So when can I go back?"

"Don't you get it, Arik?" Limos asked softly. "Lucifer is after you. My brother owns your soul. You will forever be a liability to your own race. You belong with us now."

The last time Reaver had experienced the loss of his wings had been when he'd fallen. The removal had been painless—physically, anyway. There were two levels of punishment for angels, and an angel drop-kicked out of Heaven to the earthly realm felt his wings shrivel and disintegrate on the way down. These angels, the Unfallen, could earn their way back into Heaven, as Reaver had.

It was a very different story for the second level of punishment. An angel who was cast from Heaven to go straight to Sheoul had his wings torn off by other angels. The unlucky bastard was then dragged to a hellmouth or Harrowgate and tossed inside, where, like Harvester, he would be called a True Fallen, and he'd eventually grow new wings—leathery batlike things with claws.

An angel's wings were the main source of his power, which was why an Unfallen who existed in the state

Reaver had been in for decades couldn't draw on the power of either Heaven or hell. And now that Reaver's wings had been cut off with an incredibly dull bone saw, he felt as powerless as he had back when he walked the earth, toeing the fine line between good and evil.

He sat on a cold floor wearing only his slacks, blood still trickling down his back at the places where his wings used to be, his feet secured with chains to hoops embedded in the stone. He'd discovered that the chain holding him had been constructed from the bones in his own wings. Some sort of evil magic had been used to soften and mold them, and when they were locked around his leg, they sank into his flesh and fused with his ankle bones. His own body was holding him prisoner, and putting strain on the chain caused agony so intense that he'd passed out from the pain.

Ingenious. Twisted and sick, but ingenious.

He looked up as Harvester appeared in the doorway, a sheer black robe draping her sleek body. In her hand was a bottle of what he thought might be red wine. "Good. You're awake."

"Good," Reaver mimicked. "You're still a bitch."

She sauntered into the room. "I think someone woke up on the wrong side of his chains."

Closing his eyes, he leaned back against the wall, which hurt like hell, but he wouldn't give Harvester the satisfaction of knowing that. "Why are you doing this?"

"Because I've always wanted a pet angel."

He snorted. "Who helped you, Harvester?" He opened his eyes. "Obviously, you had help, because you couldn't have taken me by yourself."

"Taken you?" She tapped her chin thoughtfully. "Now,

that's something I might have to consider. I'll bet you're great in bed."

He fought a wave of revulsion. "I am. But you'll never know."

"Oh, I could know if I wanted to. I saw the way you looked at me. Do you know how easily distracted you were? All I had to do was show a little ass, and you were panting all over yourself."

"I was disgusted, and I looked away."

"You were turned on, which is why you looked away, and it was exactly what I was counting on. It allowed me to activate the spell I used to incapacitate you. It was in the ring I gave you." She sighed dramatically. "Males are so easy. Doesn't matter if you're demon, human, or angel. Show you guys a little snatch, and you go brain-dead. And you? You think I haven't noticed the way you look at females who dress like porn stars? You think I didn't ask around about the type of females you fucked when you were fallen?"

He clenched his fists, wishing her neck was between them. "Jealous?"

She laughed. "Hardly. Apparently, you stayed away from humans, but no shifter, were, fallen angel, or succubus was safe if she was wearing a short skirt and thigh-high stockings." In a fluid, sensual movement, she straddled his legs, causing her robe to part and reveal way too much thigh. "And apparently, you're a real fan of a good blow job."

He gave a casual shrug, which wasn't the smartest thing he'd ever done, because it caused his wing wound to rub on the wall. "What guy isn't?"

"I suppose that's true." She sank down to perch on his

legs, and involuntarily, his gaze dropped. Instantly, he raised it again to focus on her face, but it was too late— he'd gotten an eyeful of deep cleavage and a tantalizing glimpse of the shadowy feminine place between her thighs. "Don't even think about trying to overpower me, or I'll yank those chains so hard your femurs will slide out of your skin."

"You *will* pay for this." he gritted out.

Smiling wickedly, she traced her tongue around the rim of the bottle, the action no doubt calculated to make him imagine her tongue swirling around something much more personal.

"Do you know how I fell?" She dipped her tongue into the bottle and made a show of flicking it free of the rim. "As a Throne, I was a dealer of justice to humans." She reached out, used a long nail to nick the skin above his clavicle. "For centuries I only killed murderers and those with evil in their hearts. With each death, the thrill I got from doing it grew. But one day, I accidentally killed an innocent. The thrill turned to flat-out electrifying power. I wanted more. So I started killing for the sheer fun of it." Leaning forward, she licked the drop of blood that had welled in the tiny cut on his chest. "And when I discovered that dragging humans to Sheoul to kill them allowed me to enjoy the screams of their souls over and over..." She groaned in pleasure. "Oh, the rush is better than an orgasm."

"Why are you telling me this? What do you want with me?"

"I'm telling you because you need to know how far I'll go to take the power I want. Which is why you're here." She cocked her head thoughtfully. "Well, part of it. I have orders to keep you occupied. And I also need to borrow some strength from you."

She put the bottle to his lips. "Drink it."

Clenching his teeth, he shook his head.

"It's not poison. It's wine."

He shook his head again.

"Don't be so stubborn." She called out to Whine, and the big male was there in an instant. "Open his mouth."

Whine wrenched Reaver's head to the side and jerked hard on his lower jaw while palming his forehead and tugging back. Snarling, Reaver slammed his palm into Harvester's chest while he rocked his head back, catching the big warg in the mouth. Harvester flew backward and blood splattered on the floor, but Reaver didn't have a chance to enjoy his victory because Whine's meaty fist caught him in the jaw so hard Reaver heard bone crack and felt his jaw dislocate.

Harvester cursed...and made good on her earlier threat. With a nasty growl, she yanked on the chains, and his bones seemed to separate from his flesh. Agony blinded him and snatched the breath right out of his lungs. Something slammed into his mouth, and warm, thick fluid flowed over his tongue. Blood?

"There, it's working." Harvester was a dim blur in front of him. "Neethul marrow wine. You'll love it."

Alarm wrapped around his chest, as restricting and painful as the chains that held him. He'd tried marrow wine once, back during his days as a fallen angel, and after the first sip, he'd plunged immediately into addiction. For months he'd drowned himself in drink, until eventually, some demon had found him holed up in an abandoned barn and had contacted Underworld General for help. Shade and his sister, Skulk, had been the ones to treat him and take him to the hospital, where Eidolon had gotten him clean.

Had it not been for the good Samaritan demon and the staff at UG, he could have ended up in a very bad place. Incapacitated Unfallens were often dragged to Sheoul against their will, completing their fall and turning them irreversibly evil.

"Whine," Harvester said, and was her voice fuzzy, or was that him? "Drain him. Have the blood delivered to the Orphmage."

Oh, damn. His blood...what were they going to do with his blood? The question became a non-issue in the next moment as the familiar burn worked its way into his belly and then spread like hellfire. He arched, a wave of pleasure wrenching through his body and relieving the pain. Heat washed through him in erotic waves, and behind the fly of his slacks, his shaft pulsed and his testicles throbbed.

An incredible series of spasms shot into the base of his spine, and then hot liquid ripples rode up the length of his penis and blew past the head as the full-body orgasm took him over and over, an endless wave of pleasure he knew would leave him as helpless and weak as a newborn when it was over.

Somewhere in the back of his mind he knew he was in big trouble. But right now, he just couldn't care.

Eighteen

⌒

Thanatos was one grumpy-ass Horseman. He'd asked
Regan to feel up a ragged document for him, but he hadn't
explained why, and when all she could tell him was that
whoever scribbled the writing on it believed they were
translating a message from the Dark Lord, he'd nodded
and shoved her out of the library. Since then, he'd avoided
her unless he needed her assistance or she requested his
help to translate something from his collection. Made it
hard for a girl to seduce a guy.

She had, at least, determined that he wasn't gay, if the
constant female traffic was any indication. They came
at all hours, in various states of dress, but the vampires
always turned them away. She supposed that could mean
Thanatos didn't like women, but if that were the case,
she'd have thought females would have gotten that news
a long time ago. And if that were the case, where were the
males?

There weren't any. So basically, she was pretty sure he wasn't gay. He was just an asshole who didn't like anyone.

She had her work cut out for her, for sure.

She wasn't sure where he spent his time, but it wasn't at his freezing ice palace. His vampires handled her needs, from food to fresh towels, which had made her uncomfortable at first. She'd been raised to kill the bloodsuckers, not have them wait on her hand and foot. But the weirdest thing was that some of them could walk in the daylight. When she'd questioned them, they'd been silent on the subject. Interesting.

She'd spent most of her time either working out in Thanatos's amazing gym or going through his library, which rivaled some of the Aegis libraries at the larger regional headquarters. Sure, her primary purpose was to sleep with the Horseman, but she'd also come to make use of his library and his knowledge . . . both of which were extensive.

She'd also offered some insight into documents he'd already pored over. So far, her help hadn't provided any groundbreaking discoveries, but she'd been able to assist him in determining which documents had been written with a false hand.

The thing she found most curious was how, while he was obsessed with both finding a way to restore Reseph's Seal and locating Limos's *agimortus*, he seemed to be just as focused on finding his father. The difference was that when it came to the subject of the angel who sired him, he tended to guard his words, as if his personal quest was somehow wrong or selfish.

Or as if he was protecting himself from disappointment.

His search shook something loose inside her, because

as much as she hated to admit it, she had a tender, raw
spot when it came to fathers. Maybe it was stupid of her,
but she'd spent a little extra time going over Than's material that related to his history, wanting to help him.

Of course, helping wasn't a hardship when it meant she
got to spend hours in his library, which was stacked from
floor to ceiling with books she'd never known existed.

Demon cookbooks. Fiction ranging from children's'
books to romance and horror novels...all written by
demons. And, for the record, demon erotica was freaking gross. She also found books about the Four Horsemen
written by humans, demons, and even an angel. Many
of the works were fiction—Thanatos seemed to collect
everything that had anything to do with the Horsemen,
from video games, TV shows and movies, to books—
but several dozen were non-fiction. Lots of "first-hand
accounts" and speculation.

The one that made her blush to her roots, though, was
the book written by a succubus who claimed to have had
intimate relations with all of the brothers.

The book read like a cross between an urban fantasy
novel and a *Penthouse Forum* letter, and Regan found
herself curled up on the oversized leather chair next to the
cozy fireplace in Thanatos's library, flipping pages as fast
as she could. God, she didn't even need the fire, not with
the way her blood was running molten in her veins.

The succubus, whose name was Pilani, claimed to
know some truly intimate details about the three brothers, had first spent some time with Ares after meeting
him in an underworld pub called the Four Horsemen.
She described his power, his furious and extremely rough
lovemaking, and Regan squirmed. She'd only had sex

once, and it wasn't anything like what Pilani described with Ares. Fast, hard, lots of weapons.

Regan definitely hadn't had *that* many orgasms or been *that* exhausted afterward. No, there'd been the one orgasm, during which she'd felt her power stir, as if it had wanted to snatch her boyfriend's soul right out of his body. Regan had broken up with him that night and hadn't risked sex again.

Pilani had moved on to Reseph, who she claimed was playful and gentle when the mood called for it, tireless, adventurous, and risky at other times. And, apparently, he really liked...Regan's jaw fell open, and she turned the page, skipping past Reseph's reported willingness to try *anything.*

Mouth dry and practically panting, Regan flipped ahead to Pilani's experiences with Thanatos.

I approached him where he sat in the dark corner of the Four Horsemen, his eyes glowing as he watched me. I'd had his brothers, several times. In fact, Reseph watched with amusement from his own corner, where he was encouraging a Trillah female to feel him up even as other females gathered 'round him to join in what would surely turn into one of his notorious orgies.

I'd offer myself to him, of course, if Thanatos turned me down. I'd never found anyone who admitted to fucking the tattooed warrior, though I'd seen a few females disappear into the back room with him.

"Death," I purred, and he growled the way he always did when someone called him by that name. The Horsemen were sensitive about their names, for some reason... all but Limos, who didn't mind being called Famine.

"Go away."

*He put his ale to his lips. Lips I wanted to know inti-
mately. I wanted to be the first of all the groupies, the
Megiddo Mount-Me's, to have scored a trifecta. Hell, if I
managed to get Thanatos, maybe I'd try a little girl-on-girl
with Limos and secure my place in Horsemen lore.*

*Naturally, I ignored him and took a seat next to him,
making sure my skirt hiked up to show tantalizing hints
of everything. He noticed, and the front of his breeches
swelled. Shifting, I lifted my leg over his and palmed his
cock.*

*"Let me suck it," I murmured, and his eyes darkened.
I had him. I knew it. And when he swept me up and carried me to the back room, where I'd been with both Ares
and Reseph, I came the first time before he even set me
down. The second time was when he—*

"You enjoying yourself?"

At the deep rumble of Thanatos's voice, Regan
screamed and dropped the book. Her cheeks burned and
her throat felt like she'd been breathing smoke.

"I—I...it was research." Oh, God, she was babbling
like a teenage girl caught doodling the name of her secret
crush in her notebook. Or like a grown woman caught
reading erotica.

Erotica about the very man standing in the room, leaning casually against the doorframe, one ankle crossed
over the other, an amused smile tilting his mouth.

And whoa, she'd thought he was handsome before, but
that smile put him at a number that was off the charts.

"Research, huh?" He moved close, his gaze never
wavering from hers even as he leaned over to pick the
book up off the floor where it had fallen. "My library is
full of books that would probably be a lot more useful."

"But not nearly as interesting," she said, shooting for light and breezy, but failing miserably. She sounded breathless and desperate. Horny.

He opened the book to what appeared to be the very spot where she'd left off. One pale eyebrow lifted as he read, and then the other, and then...was that a touch of pink on his cheeks? Yes, yes it was.

Good. Maybe he was as embarrassed as she was.

"His fingers found my swollen pearl, wet with my honey," he read, and okay, so maybe he wasn't embarrassed. "He pushed one inside me, and I moaned as my body exploded with pleasure."

Regan cleared her throat. "I see you can read. Impressive. Can we stop now?"

"You don't want to know what happens next?"

"I assume she earned some sort of honor for banging all three of you and now has a commemorative tramp stamp on the small of her back or at the base of her tail or whatever."

Thanatos stared at her for a moment, and then he threw back his head and laughed, and dear Lord, she had just revised her definition of melt-my-panties-hot.

"She does not have a tramp stamp," he said, when he'd finished laughing, but the smile remained. "At least, I don't think she does. Haven't seen her in centuries. She gave birth to a few dozen little hellspawns and went her own way." He closed the book. "And no, none of the demonlings are ours."

"Demonlings?"

"It's what Reseph calls them." The smile fell from his lips, replaced by the familiar scowl. "Used to call them. I'm guessing now he calls them dinner."

It was surprising to see his reaction to his brother's transformation—up until now, she'd seen little from Thanatos but anger. Well, there was the little blip of amusement, but it was gone so fast she sort of wondered if she'd imagined it. Except that her heightened body temperature and racing heart were pretty clear evidence that he'd affected her in more than the angry way.

"Were you close to him?" she asked.

"He's my brother." He peeled off his coat and shoved up the sleeves of his black turtleneck.

"That's not an answer."

His gaze glittered like canary diamonds in the sun. "We shared a womb. We shared battle, pain, loss, and drink. *He is my brother.*"

So...that was a yes to her question. The intensity rolling off him shocked her. Not that she'd expected anything less of the Horseman who would be Death, but she hadn't been prepared for the depth of his feelings for his siblings. Somehow that humanized him in her eyes...and at the same time, shamed her. She'd never loved anyone. Not like that.

She rubbed her arms, though she was anything but cold. "So even now, after what he's become—"

"What he's become is his own personal nightmare," he interrupted. "We'll find a way to change him back."

"You've got to have some idea how." Yeah, she was one to talk, since The Aegis still had no idea how Death's child could save the world. Her stomach churned a little at that thought, because she'd been concentrating so hard on how to get Thanatos into bed that she hadn't thought much about the consequences.

"I do have an idea. I've finally made a breakthrough."

He took a thick book off a top shelf and splayed it open on his desk. As he flipped pages, she realized it was a scrapbook, filled with notes, pictures, clippings from newspapers, even, and from what she could tell, most of it had to do with Pestilence. "I believe this is a clue." He drew out the parchment he'd had her inspect the other day. "I've translated the text, and it basically says that disease is cured by death."

"Well . . . yeah. Death sort of cures everything."

He shook his head. "A few days ago, I found this in a demon temple dedicated to Pestilence's worship. It was on an altar that wasn't there the last time I checked, and it was wrapped around exact metal and wooden replicas of Deliverance and a scythe . . . my symbol."

"Pestilence has a temple dedicated to him?"

"We all do." He said it like a normal person would confirm that of course they had milk in the fridge. Like, who didn't? He traced his finger over a photo taped to the next page. "Beneath the replicas was this writing carved into the stone altar. It's a warning that Deliverance, if wielded by me at a precise moment, will restore Pestilence to his weakness, which, in evil demon terms, means he'll become Reseph again."

"So that's it? You stab him and he's better?"

He paused, his gaze focused on the parchment. "We forged Deliverance so that stabbing him in the heart will kill him. Or any of us. But if this new information is to be believed, a perfectly timed jab of the blade will return him to Reseph. We just need to find out what that 'precise moment' is." He tapped the writing with his forefinger. "At least the first part of the mystery is solved." On his arm, the horse tattoo kicked. He looked down and ran his finger over the shoulder, and the lines seemed to settle down. So weird.

But he'd just given her the opening she needed to get her hands on him. "Can I touch it?"

His head snapped back. "What?"

"The horse. Can I touch it?"

"Why?"

Because in the Horsemen erotica it says you feel everything the horse feels in corresponding parts of your body. Oh, yes, she could use this to arouse him, to make him crave more of her touch.

"It's fascinating," she said truthfully. She might have ulterior motives, but she was also curious as hell. "Your other tattoos are multicolored and metallic. This one... it's like a henna tattoo. Just lines, but it moves."

"Because it's alive," he said. "Surely you're aware that our horses are part of us."

"Yes, and that's what's so interesting." She stepped closer. "May I?"

He looked at her like she'd asked if she could chop his head off, but finally, he gave a curt, sharp nod and held out his arm. It was odd how the other tattoos were layered on top of each other, which should have caused a jumbled mess, but somehow they were distinct, multi-dimensional. But the horse lay flat on his skin with no other tattoos beneath or on top.

She took Thanatos's hand, palm up, in hers, and his entire body tensed. Hers did too, as the inked bones on his wrist took on lives of their own, and in her head, she got their story—how they'd gotten there, and oh, wow... this Horseman was holding on to some serious pain.

She saw the female demon who was responsible for

putting the tats on his skin. Regan wasn't sure how it worked, but this demon took memories and feelings out of her customers' heads and put them on their bodies. But why? These tattooed bones told her so much...the death he'd caused in one day. Demons...a demon war. He'd fought on the side of humans, had taken dead demons to a pit to be rendered down to their bones.

Her stomach rolled, and quickly, she shut off her unwelcome gift.

"You okay, Aegi? You're turning green."

"Yeah." She cleared her throat of the raspiness. "Just overwhelmed. You know, being here with a legend." Oh, gag, she sounded like a teeny-bopper mooning over Justin Bieber. But hey, flattery got you everywhere, right?

He made an indecipherable grunting noise, and she went back to what she was doing, which was trying to seduce the guy. Or, at least, learn the key to seducing him.

Tentatively, she touched the tip of her finger to the horse's long neck. Even though she'd shut off her gift, faint stirrings of confusion, annoyance, and anger filtered in, but she couldn't tell if it was coming from the horse or from Thanatos.

She traced the lines, working her way over the animal's ears, jaw, nose, then down the front of his throat. When she slowly drew her finger along its chest, Thanatos inhaled harshly, and his pulse picked up, hammering into her thumb. He liked this, so she lingered, stroked. In the silence marked only by the crackle of the fire, she eased her fingertip along the beast's belly and then up, over its back and down around the curve of its rump.

Again, she stroked, feeling the textures in Thanatos's skin, the hard, pulsing veins that shot through the

"Can I make a suggestion?" he asked.

She shrugged. "Sure."

A wicked, crooked smile lifted his lips as he reached for the Horsemen erotica. "This. In case you need to stay warm."

In case you need to stay warm? What kind of crap was that? Than was an idiot. He didn't need to be playing with fire, and Regan was a damned inferno.

What he needed was to get the hell away from her. He spun around, but she stopped him with no more than a word.

"Wait."

He stared at the doorway, because hell if he was turning back to look at her. "What?"

"How does it end?" Her voice was soft as a whisper, just like her touch. "The story, I mean."

"I told you. She has a bunch of kids, and—"

"No. Your part of it. After you were done with her. When you came back out into the tavern, and Reseph was with all those females. Did you share stories?"

"You mean, do I kiss and tell? Is that what you want to know?"

"Sort of."

He had no idea what got into him, but in an instant, he was in front of her, one hand gripping the back of her head, the other at her waist as he tugged her to him. Then his lips were on hers, and his head was spinning, his blood was thundering through his ears, and her eager mouth was open to him. Their tongues met in a hot, wet tangle, and his erection was a throbbing rod of need against her soft belly.

He pulled away, enjoying the way her eyes had glazed over. "Do I kiss and tell? Guess you'll have to find out for yourself."

This time he stalked out of there, and this time, he intended to stay away. If five thousand years had taught him anything, it was that he could tease himself to the point of insanity and still come away without getting his dick wet.

There'd been a time when he'd taken himself to the edge, had drowned himself in females just to see how far he could go without plunging deep inside them. But he'd been young and dumb then. He'd enjoyed kissing, working females up, and for the first hundred years, he'd played games that had been... cruel. He'd used his status as a Horseman to bring a female home, and then he'd kiss and tease, and never once allow them the ultimate pleasure. It had been a way to torture them both. The females were always demons, and in a way, he figured he was torturing them for their part in his curse.

The males he just killed outright.

He stalked to his room, which he kept cold as the air outside. He stripped, relishing the blast of freezing temperatures. His skin shrank, but naturally, his cock wouldn't care if he dipped it in liquid nitrogen. It wanted relief.

It wanted Regan.

Stupid bastard.

He fell onto his bed, hissing at the icy covers against his fevered skin. He sprawled out, staring at the rafters high above. His thoughts drifted back to the Guardian, and his erection jerked. He was strung tight, wound completely around the axle, and though he knew he could control himself around the female when things were calm, the periods of calm were growing few and far between.

Even Limos was coming unraveled. The human male had thrown her off balance. That had to be the reason she was suddenly a bundle of nerves. She could be impulsive and flighty, yes, but raw panic and fear? Never. But she'd been terrified during the confrontation with Lucifer, and he'd seen the same terror in her eyes after she'd destroyed Sartael. Was her fear for Arik? Had she fallen for him? God, he hoped not. That would be a doomed relationship, for sure. The human wanted her—Thanatos could see it in his eyes, and a male like that wasn't going to settle for heavy-petting.

Then again, that was what Than had to settle for. His lips tingled in remembrance of Regan's kiss, and he palmed his cock, so worked up that his hips bucked at the touch, punching up into the ring of his fist. He wasn't going to last long at all.

He didn't want to imagine himself with Regan, but she was there in his mind anyway, naked, on her hands and knees as he pumped into her from behind. Her tight, wet heat gripped him, and he groaned. He squeezed his shaft, building sensation, and then he dropped his palm to his sac, wondering what it would feel like to slap against her swollen flesh.

Slowly, he slid his hand back up, now imagining that he'd flipped her and was driving into her in the way a male made a female his—face to face, mouths fused, hands clasped. He knew he shouldn't think that way, because there were some fantasies that were too hazardous to even consider. When he dreamed of having his own female, depression darkened his mood and dangerous ideas popped into his head.

Sometimes, at his lowest points, he thought he should

just fuck a woman and get it over with. His Seal was going to break eventually, so why put off the inevitable? He wanted sex, dammit. But there was the problem; if he was going to break his Seal and bring down all of mankind, he wasn't going to screw some random female. He wanted one to love. Which created the next problem: how could he possibly make love to a woman he cared about, knowing that as soon as it was over, he'd turn evil and she would probably be the first to die by his hand?

Yep, it was a nasty circle, a catch-22 he'd never get out of.

Viciously, he jerked his thoughts in another direction, flipped the imaginary Regan over again, and plowed into her as he pinned her against a wall. She was whimpering in pleasure as he hammered into her, and yeah, that was better. Keep it impersonal.

His cock kicked in his palm, reminding him that this was as impersonal as it got. Him, alone in bed, with only his hand as his date. Awesome.

Fuck.

He snarled, pumped his fist from root to tip, pausing to smooth the drop of precum around the smooth head. The sensitivity multiplied, and he pretended his thumb was Regan's tongue.

That did it. His climax brought his hips off the bed and made a strangled groan rip from his throat. Hot jets of liquid shot onto his stomach and chest as his balls clenched. The pleasure was intense but fleeting, as empty as his bed. And as he stood and cleaned himself off with the shirt he'd thrown to the floor, it occurred to him that there was a beautiful woman in the room next to his, one who was probably reading about his sexual exploits and maybe touching herself the way he just had.

The difference was that the empty bed thing was, for her, only temporary. Eventually, she'd go back to her human life, to her human job, her human house. And if she wanted, she'd find a human male to fill her bed.

And fill her.

Thanatos snarled, spun, and put his fist through the wall.

Nineteen

You will forever be a liability to your own race. You belong with us now.

Arik hadn't bothered to argue with Limos or Ares. She'd gated him back to her house, left him to shower, and he'd numbed out under the hot spray, his mind drawing a blank on all the reasons they were wrong.

All he'd wanted for his entire life was to fight for what was right. He'd started by defending his sister and mother. He'd moved on to join the military to fight for his country. Eventually, when the R-XR had tapped him, he fought for the entire human race. The idea that he was now a liability, a threat, even, left him dazed. The situation wasn't acceptable, and somehow, he had to fix it.

He threw on the jeans and a white T-shirt that were in the duffle that was still in Limos's bedroom, and then in a bizarre move, Hekili had called him to the kitchen, thrust a beer and a towel into Arik's hands and motioned toward the water. As Arik started down the steps to the beach, Hekili stopped him.

"She is in one of her...moods. Help her before she hurts herself."

Arik had no idea what the warg was talking about, and he didn't have a chance to ask because Hekili took off like his kitchen was on fire.

He found Limos fifty yards away, acting as if she didn't have a care in the world.

She was, in fact, dancing on the beach like a lunatic. A sexy, gorgeous lunatic in a hot pink bikini. With a white flower in her hair. No one looking at her would know that the ultra-feminine woman doing the hula could kick ass like the newest model Terminator.

What the hell had Hekili been talking about? The only way she was going to hurt herself would be if she threw her hip out of joint from dancing like that.

Arik laid out the towel and sank down in the sand, back against a palm tree, his fingers gripping the cold beer so tight he figured it was close to shatter threshold. How could she dance without spilling her margarita?

When she spotted him, she stilled, her too-gorgeous-to-be-real eyes drilling into him. In a slow, deliberate motion, she brought her margarita glass to her lips. Her tongue came out and swiped the rim, licking off a line of salt before she locked her lips onto the glass and sipped. In Arik's hand, the beer bottle shook.

Limos walked toward him, her hips swaying, her toned muscles flexing. She was beautiful, so fucking beautiful. He stood, figuring she was ready to head back to the house. He'd welcome the air-conditioning to cool off his suddenly overheated skin.

"I think I'm going to throw a party at my other house," she said, stopping in front of him.

"The Apocalypse is knocking at the door, and you want to throw a damned party?" No wonder she had never found her *agimortus*. She'd spent her life drinking, dancing, and painting her nails.

"I like keeping myself busy."

"Yeah, well, here's an idea. Instead of acting like a sorority butterfly, you could keep yourself busy by searching for your *agimortus*."

She sipped her drink and started swaying to a silent beat. "I lost my chance. Killed the bastard who might have been able to find it. So...whatevs."

This. Was. Bizarre. "You lost your chance, and that calls for what...a celebration?"

She shrugged, her tan shoulder glistening in the splashes of sun that streamed between the palm fronds. "Not a celebration. A distraction."

A warm breeze stirred her hair, and he resisted the urge to brush it away from her face. "Now isn't the time to lose focus, Horseman."

"Horseman." She said the word as if it were something bitter she was testing on her tongue. "Yes, I'm that. That, and Satan's fiancé." Her lips turned up in an impish smile. "And I'm feeling the need to slip into Sheoul to taunt him. To dare him to catch me."

"What?" Arik wondered what she'd do if he grabbed her and shook some sense into her. "Tell me you aren't serious."

"Oh, I'm serious." She spun in a graceful circle, head back, hair flying, as if she were on a dance floor. "He'll get me, you know. No matter what, he'll get me."

Something dumbly primal turned his brain to mush and his vision red, and he grabbed her by the upper arms. "I'm not going to let that happen."

Surprise in her expression faded to sadness. "You can't stop it. And you can't stop me from meeting my fate. It's coming. I saw a preview of it today."

"What are you talking about?"

She reached up and traced the outline of his dogtag chain under his T-shirt. "The barriers between the demon world and human world are so thin now. It's only a matter of time before I won't need to go to Sheoul for Satan to grab me. He'll be able to do it here. The invasion at your base was just the beginning." She moved closer, and his heart beat faster. "Then there's Sartael." She peered up at him, and God, he'd never seen anything so sad in his life as the look in her eyes. "He was the best hope I've had of finding my *agimortus* in thousands of years. And I killed him."

"I'm sure you did what you had to do."

Her sudden burst of laughter startled him. "Yeah," she said. "I did." Throwing back her head, she downed the rest of her drink and hurled the glass into the sand. "Just like I did what I had to do when I erased your memory."

He stiffened, the raw anger from what she'd done coming back at him with as much force as if she'd slapped him. And he knew from experience that she could hit hard.

"What's the matter, Arik?" She pressed up against him in a bold, unexpected surge. "You still mad at me? That's fine. I deserve it. I deserve every drop of hate you have to spare. It was my fault you went to Sheoul. I did want you to kiss me, and I wasn't strong enough to stop it." She dragged her hand down his chest and stopped with her fingers on his waistband. "Oh, I'm powerful enough to slaughter a legion of fallen angels, but I didn't have it in me to turn you away. And the memory thing? I thought I was helping you, but you know, maybe I did it because it's what *I* would have wanted. Because I'm not strong enough to own up to hurting my brothers. So I assumed you wouldn't be either. But you are, aren't you?"

Arik's heart was pounding against his ribcage, and his thoughts were a messy knot. He had no idea what the thing with her brothers was about, and Limos's behavior was confusing the shit out of him. Worse, he sensed there was a whole lot of pain behind her actions that he couldn't do anything about. How did he fix something he didn't understand?

"Look, it wasn't so much the fact that you messed with my memories that pissed me off as it was the fact that you didn't tell me, and then you lied about it."

"Lies," she murmured, as she trailed her fingertip along his waistband, letting it dip underneath as if testing the waters. "My entire existence is built on them. They're catching up with me."

Squeezing her shoulders, he gave her a little shake. "Horseman!" he barked, trying to snap her out of whatever this mysterious mood was. "Tell me what's wrong."

"I don't think I have time to tell you what's wrong." Leaving one hand on his waist, she brought the other up to his neck and dragged his head down so his lips were so close to hers he could almost taste the salt and lime on them. "There are things I want before I'm taken, Arik," she whispered. "I know you hate me, but please...give me this."

She kissed him. Hard. Her tongue met his with an aggression he hadn't anticipated. Before this, she'd been timid, accepting of his actions, but whatever was driving her now was also starting to affect him. Because she was wrong about him hating her. Very, very wrong. Oh, he wanted to hate her, but at this point, he needed to be with her more than he needed to hold onto his anger.

Fisting her silky hair, he hauled her against him, and when his hips met hers, he groaned at the intimate contact. He'd been naked with women, skin on skin, but nothing had rocked him like this.

And then, in a shocking move, Limos dropped to her knees on the towel and clawed at his fly almost desperately, as if getting his pants open was the key to saving the world or some shit.

"L—" Cutting himself off before her name spilled from his lips, he grabbed her hands. A wild, animal sound came from her throat as she swatted him away and dove back to her task, this time managing to unsnap all the buttons in a single yank.

He was hard, and his cock sprang free, but before she could go any further, he tackled her, taking her to the ground, half-on, half-off the towel.

"Let me!" she shouted, once again reaching low for him, but he seized her by the wrists and pinned them to her belly.

"*Stop*." He used his weight to control her, though he knew that if she wanted to, she could throw him like a two-thousand pound rodeo bull. "Sweetheart, stop. You don't want this."

"I do." She snarled up at him, and for a long moment, they locked gazes and simply concentrated on breathing.

In the distance, thunder rolled, as if the heavens were echoing her mood.

Gradually, he eased up and loosened his grip, hoping the fight had gone out of her. But when she pulled her wrists free and wrapped her arms around his neck and locked her legs around his waist, he knew she'd merely changed tactics. Angry sex: scratched. Tender sex: at the starting gate.

Arik: fucked.

Limos stared up at Arik, unable to believe he was trying to stop her. After all the pain she'd put him through, she was offering to make him feel good. Offering to let him use her to take back some of what she'd done to him.

Offering to let him punish her.

Did he not understand that she was on the verge of losing everything? That it wouldn't be long before her secrets were unearthed and her brothers tossed her to her fiancé themselves. Or her fiancé would come for her, but either way, it was only a matter of time. She had to give Arik what she could now, before it was too late. And if she was hurt in the process, so be it. It was what she deserved.

"Arik, please."

He reared back, and she let him untangle himself from her. "Why?" He went up on his knees and gently took her hand to pull her up too. "Tell me why."

The urge to lie was so great it made her tremble, but he deserved better than that. Okay, so...honesty. The very thought of such deep-down sincerity made her stomach cramp and the scales on her shoulder blade wobble wildly. "I owe you."

His lips formed a grim, hard line. "And you think giving me an orgasm is how you pay that debt?"

"Why not?"

"You know what? Fuck you." He shoved to his feet. "You don't get to work off your guilt on my dick."

She leaped up and seized his forearm. "Then hit me."

"Excuse me?"

Frustration and unspent lust turned to sudden poison in her veins and on her tongue. "Hit me," she spat. "Do to me what the demons did to you. Take your revenge on me. Now." He stared at her like she'd sprouted horns, which was fitting. All the demonic vileness in her was surfacing as the weight of centuries of lies and pain bore down on her and the tattooed scales dipped in favor of evil. "Are you deaf? Break my bones, Arik. *Make me bleed.*" She shoved him hard enough to make him stumble backward. "Or is it only your sister you like to beat?"

It was a low blow that slammed the scales into such a deep imbalance that she felt like she might tip over from the amount of malevolence growing like a cancer in her evil half. Somewhere inside, her angel half was crying out in anguish.

"Stop it." Arik paled, his skin taking on a waxy sheen. "What is wrong with you?"

"It's what I deserve." It was what she craved. Need oozed through her, a need to go crazy with fun and danger and pain. "Dammit, Arik, you are so stubborn." She cast a Harrowgate, but before she could step into it, he snagged her arm.

"Where are you going?"

His hand on her skin was like a balm, smoothing out her raw edges, and some of the oily anger inside eased. Her scales even shifted a little. "Sheoul. I...need to."

"You need to—" He sucked in a harsh breath. "Jesus. You punish yourself. That's what this is all about, isn't it?"

Yeah, it was. When she was afraid, stressed, or when people suffered from famine, she wanted to hurt herself with recklessness and risks. She got utterly stupid and self-destructive, but she didn't like that Arik had determined that. She hated the way he saw through her.

"It's part of my curse," she said flatly.

"Being self-destructive? Losing focus? Being a total ass?"

His hand was still on her arm, his thumb rubbing circles on her skin. She might hate how easily he saw through her and called her out on her shit, but she loved the way he could bring her down with his touch, his voice, his very presence.

"Yes," she sighed. God, she despised herself sometimes. She despised the demon half of her that tapped into a well of evil so deep it would never run dry. "You're right. I'm an ass. I didn't mean what I said about your sister." Her scales leveled out, and she gulped a breath as if she'd been drowning.

"What about when you said you owe me?"

She closed her eyes and chased away the desire to lie, but not because her nature was demanding a lie, but because the truth meant exposing a part of her she wasn't used to showing off.

"I do owe you, but that's not the only reason I want to...to...get you naked." Her cheeks heated, and she wondered how much she was blushing.

"So what's the other reason?"

"Remember when I asked you how many women you'd kissed?" She opened her eyes. "Answer me now."

"Why?"

"Because I want to know."

He narrowed his gaze on her. "No, you don't."

"See," she said quietly. "You don't want to tell me because it would hurt me, right?" When he didn't answer, she nodded. "But if I really, really wanted to know, you'd tell me the truth."

Muscles in his jaw twitched, and finally he ground out, "Yes." Lightning streaked across the sky, and it seemed to take forever for the thunder to follow.

"You're a good person, Arik. Being honest comes easily to you. Protecting those around you does too. I like that. I like that when the *khnives* attacked, your first instinct was to shove me behind you. You make me feel... vulnerable."

One dark eyebrow lifted. "Isn't feeling vulnerable a bad thing?"

She shrugged. "Ares would say yes. But I like that *you* make me feel that way." Her hand trembled a little as she pressed her palm against his chest, needing to feel the life pounding in his heartbeat. "You make me feel like a woman. Like I'm not a big, bad warrior who has to stay strong all the time. I like how your strength lets me relax so I can be the person I want to be instead of the one I'm expected to be. That probably doesn't make sense—"

In a quick movement, he gripped her biceps, hooked the back of her knees with a sweep of his leg, and took her down to the towel. She landed half on top of him, and she didn't hesitate for a second. She kissed him hard, and he met her aggression tongue for tongue, nibble for nibble, lick for lick.

She lifted herself to crawl more fully on top of him. His

hands stroked her back, her hair, her arms, wisely keeping his fingers away from her lower body. Her bikini covered the chastity belt, but no one in their right mind would take any chances, and Arik was definitely not a dummy.

"I want to touch you," she murmured against his lips.

His tongue made a sensual sweep over her bottom lip. "You sure?"

In answer, she dragged her hand down his rippled abs to where his pants splayed open and his cock jutted upward. He hissed and arched into her touch as she closed her fingers around the thick shaft. The textures fascinated her... silky skin over steely flesh, ridges and bumps that gave way to the velvety smooth head. And when his hips began to roll into her grip, her own pelvis rocked, rubbing her center against his thigh.

With a groan, he gripped her hand and stopped her. "Can you touch yourself? With your chastity belt, are you allowed?"

Heat flooded her cheeks. "Uh-huh."

A naughty smile curved his lips. "I so want to see that."

She pushed herself up off his chest. "You want to... watch?" God, she didn't think she could do that.

"I can't touch, so... yeah." He dropped his gaze to her bikini bottom. "Take it off."

"But—"

"Do it." He sat up and whipped off his own T-shirt. "*Now*, Horsewoman."

His voice, a resonant, husky command, had her shivering in appreciation. She'd never taken orders well, but something about Arik's erotically charged directive made her want to obey. As he peeled off his pants, she knelt next to him and reached behind her to undo her top.

Arik's eyes smoldered behind heavy lids. He lay back on the towel, propping one arm behind his head while his other hand palmed his cock. As she removed the top, his hand began to pump long, slow strokes along the length of the dusky brown shaft. She'd never thought that a man touching himself could be so sexy, but she could watch this all day.

His body, magnificent to begin with, hardened, all the muscles bunching, the tendons in his neck standing out starkly as he threw back his head, eyes slitted and focused on her. Pleasure was etched on his face, his mouth open slightly, and lower, his fist pumped faster.

Heat built in Limos's veins, and wetness bloomed between her thighs. She licked her lips, found herself drifting closer. She could replace his hand with hers. Then kiss her way down his chest, his stomach…oh, damn, was she actually thinking she'd like to put her mouth… there?

Yes, yes she was.

The plum-colored head glistened, its color deepening, and the desire to run her tongue over the tip intensified. As if he heard that thought, his entire body undulated, his hips surging, bringing to mind how the motion had been similar when he'd been on top of her, rocking, riding her hard.

"The bottoms," he said roughly. She'd hesitated, her fingers on the waistband. "Now."

She hooked her thumbs inside the fabric and pushed down, noting the way his strokes increased in speed. Again, she paused, just before the fabric cleared her center. "I wish you could do this."

His gaze, which had been locked on the bikini, flipped

up to hers. "I do too. I want to touch you, taste you, so bad."

Oh, she wanted that too, and she felt herself go utterly wet at the very idea of him doing those things. Quickly, because it was a waste of time to fantasize, she shoved the bikini bottoms down and crawled toward Arik, intent upon putting her mouth on him. But even as she brushed her lips across the swollen cap, he hooked her thigh with his arm and dragged her toward him.

"What are you doing?"

He waggled his brows. "Sixty-nine."

"Wait, what?" She dug her knees into the sand, refusing to budge. "You can't."

His grin was wicked. "No, but you can touch yourself, and I can watch."

He tugged hard, and in a heartbeat, she was kneeling over him, straddling his head.

"Fuuuck," he breathed. His voice was husky, slightly strangled. The power she had over him was remarkable and entirely unexpected. "You're so beautiful." She might have melted right there, if he hadn't taken one of her hands and brought it up between her legs so her fingers were at her core. "Make yourself come."

She was pretty sure her face was the color of a ripe apple, but she did what he asked, slipped her fingers between her folds and stroked. The smooth pearls rubbed alongside her hand, and if she closed her eyes, she could pretend it was Arik touching her. Licking her. And when he blew a hot breath over her, she felt the first stirrings of a climax.

Flooded with desperate need, she lowered herself on one elbow and took his shaft into her mouth. His body arched beneath her, and a desperate, low groan rumbled his chest. "I'm not…not going to…last."

She dipped one finger inside her and dragged it up to the little knot of nerves that was screaming for release. "Me either."

Sucking him deep, she swirled her tongue around the top of his cock while she swirled her finger over her clit in the same rhythm, and in no more than a dozen heartbeats, she was on the edge, her hips pumping, her breath coming in furious gasps around his shaft.

"Now," he moaned. "Now."

Yes, now. The orgasm exploded through her, a scalding, white-hot strike of lightning that intensified at the feel of his breath on her core. In her mouth, his shaft swelled, and warm fluid spurted onto her tongue and down her throat. He tasted salty and tangy, and suddenly, the act that had grossed her out for her entire life became something she wanted to do again and again.

But only to Arik.

His body jerked, his pelvis rocking as his climax waned and hers ebbed. She continued to stroke herself until her flesh became too sensitive, and instinctively, she read Arik's sensitivity in his gasps and twitches. Gently, she licked up his shaft to clean him off, and then, while he lay there recovering, Limos scrambled to throw on her bikini so her chastity pearls wouldn't come into contact with his skin.

When she finished, she lay down next to him, resting her head on his shoulder.

"Another first," she murmured.

"What, a modified sixty-nine? 'Cuz I gotta say, that was a first for me too."

"No, this. Snuggling up to someone. The only males I've ever even hugged have been my brothers and Reaver."

His hand came up to stroke her hair. "I can't even imagine," he said quietly. "We humans get lonely so quickly . . . hell, I know a lot of people who are so needy that they can't go more than a couple of months, or even weeks, without a man or woman to be with."

"What about you?"

"I've always been too busy to worry about it."

"You can't tell me you've never had a relationship."

He shrugged. "I got laid a lot in high school, but it was more about getting away from my shit at home. Joined the military the day I turned eighteen, and I dated a little, but nothing serious. And then I joined the R-XR, and that pretty much ended any chance of a serious relationship unless I wanted to date someone I worked with."

"How long have you been with the R-XR?"

"Ten years. I was twenty, on leave in Japan. My buddy and I got lured into this underground bar by two really hot chicks. Turned out they were vampires. I barely got out with my life, my buddy was killed, and when I woke up in the military hospital babbling about vampires, I thought for sure I was going to end up in a rubber room. But I was sedated, and the next time I woke up, it was at the R-XR facility in DC."

"So in all the time you've been with the R-XR, you've been . . . single?"

"Yeah. Can't tell anyone what I do, you know?"

"You can't expect me to believe that you've been celibate all that time."

His rumbling laughter echoed pleasantly through her. "No, but trust me, it's nothing I want to talk about. One

night stands here and there." Limos had the intense urge
to find every one of his partners and turn them into hellhound snacks. "What about you? I know you couldn't be
with anyone, and you said I was the first you wanted to be
with, but weren't you ever a little tempted?"

"No." *Lie.*

She'd been tempted by the Dark Lord himself. Though
the verbal betrothal had taken place when she was only
an infant, when the time came to negotiate the written
contract, she'd walked into his chamber, as regal as any
queen, her sights set on landing the king of all demons.
Lust had taken her by storm the moment she'd laid eyes
on him, and fear had only heightened her desire. A mystical aura surrounded him, and anyone who stepped
into it became drunk with his unimaginable power and
supercharged sensuality, and Limos had proved to be no
different.

Females and males alike succumbed, unable to resist
his draw any more than the moon could resist the Earth's
gravitational pull. In her heightened emotional state, she'd
been jealous of the naked females engaging in orgies all
around him, had been homicidal as they touched him.
She'd even had to stand by and watch Lilith give herself
to him.

But Limos had gone untouched. It hadn't even been his
hands that fastened the chastity belt around her waist. At
the time, she'd been furious. Now she was very, very glad.

Problem was, it had taken far too long to get to the
glad point. For hundreds of years after she and her brothers had been cursed as Horsemen, she'd plotted to start
the Apocalypse and take her brothers to her husband as
her wedding gift. She'd been a demon in every sense of

the word, living up to her upbringing, lying to everyone she met, including her brothers. She'd schemed, plotted, stabbed them in the back at every turn.

And they'd embraced her.

They hadn't known that every word out of her mouth was a lie, that for centuries, she was behind all the horrible things that happened to them, from the deaths of their servants, to attacks by demons.

But eventually, they'd worn her down with their affection and their constant support and protection. And then one day she'd found Thanatos standing over the body of a slave who had died saving his wife from their master's lust.

"Are you sad for that human?" she'd asked, her question almost a taunt.

"No." Thanatos's voice was hollow. *"I'm sad that we will never know what it's like to love like he did, or have someone love us like that."*

"We have each other." Another taunt. She was a bitch. And she liked it.

"And I'm grateful beyond measure." His yellow gaze lifted, and burned right through her. *"But it's not the same. Who would die for you when the time came, Limos?"*

Something in that conversation had stuck with her, and later, she'd gone back to the scene, unsure why. She'd grabbed the slave owner's wife and threatened the woman to see what he would do if given the choice of saving her life or his. He'd chosen his. He could get another wife.

In that moment, she'd realized that the marriage she'd chosen would offer the same results. She would be the queen of the underworld . . . and a brood mare that could be replaced.

Screw that. She'd killed the man and gotten a whole new outlook on life.

Arik's warm palm massaged her neck muscles, which had grown tight at the memories she despised. His other fingers stroked her right arm, tracing the lines that formed Bones.

"Can he feel that?"

"Mmm-hmm." Right now Arik was caressing the beast's leg, and her thigh tingled in response. "He likes it. I think you might be one of the few people he won't try to eat."

"Good. Cuz that would suck." Bones stomped his foot, letting Arik know he'd had enough, and Arik took the hint, settling his hand over hers. "You grew up in Sheoul, right? Raised by Lilith?"

Ugh. Not a subject she wanted to discuss. "Yes."

"I'm guessing it wasn't pleasant?"

"It was horrible," she murmured, and the fib spread through her with a familiar warmth. "But I escaped, and here I am. Now, let's talk about you, because that's much more interesting."

And because if he was talking, she wouldn't have to worry about lying.

Twenty

Arik did not want to talk about himself. Limos was much more interesting, but when she rubbed her palm in a slow circle over his chest, he fell into a lulling sort of trance and forgot why he didn't want to talk.

Limos cleared her throat. "Can I ask you something?"

If that wasn't a prelude to a question that was going to be hard to answer, he didn't know what was. "You can ask, but I can't guarantee I'll answer or that you'll like what I say."

She nodded, cleared her throat again. "Runa said you wouldn't like yourself if you knew what you'd done to her, and Shade said your father was abusive, that you used to protect Runa and your mother."

"So?" He knew he was being defensive, but this was one of the very few subjects he didn't like to talk about.

"So...tell me."

He eyed her sideways. "That's not a question."

"You sound like Ares," she grumbled. "Okay, let's try this. Where are your parents?"

"Dead."

"Did you kill them?" She asked with such matter-of-fact innocence, as if killing your parents was a normal thing to do. What different worlds they'd grown up in.

"Suicide and cancer took them."

Limos resumed the circling of her palm over his chest. The sensation was amazingly intimate. "How did you protect your mother and sister? I mean, you were a child, right?"

Seriously, he did not want to talk about this. But Limos worked him like a master interrogator, except she got him to talk with pleasure instead of pain. As her fingers traced a tingly path from one nipple to the other, he cracked like a thin-shelled egg.

"I ran interference," he said, gruffly. "When my old man was beating on one of them, I pissed him off so much that he turned on me." Oh, but that wasn't all. By the time he hit his teens, he'd learned to bargain. *I'll get booze for you, if you stop hitting mom. I'll score you some weed if you'll lay off Runa. I'll fetch that prostitute off Third and Division if you'll stop making mom scream at night.*

Eventually, he'd learned the art of threats, too. *If you make mom or Runa bleed again, I'll go to the cops.* And finally, after three days of no food in the house because their dad had spent all the money on booze, Arik had hit rock bottom too. *Go to AA and clean up right now, or I swear, I'll make you feel everything you've done to us.*

That had led to a physical altercation between the two of them that had ended in Arik's broken arm and his father's missing teeth. And nothing changed. Not until Arik went to the "weird guy" in school, the one who always wore black, sketched skulls and pentagrams on his notebook covers, and said he worshipped the devil.

Runa always believed that it was their mother who had given their father the ultimatum that made him get sober and become a model father, but no, it was Arik and the weird guy, who summoned a demon and made a deal that Arik had regretted with every fiber of his being.

"How did you get out of that situation?" Limos asked.

For a long moment, he lay there, listening to the sounds of the thunderstorm puttering out and a hellhound howling nearby. Who would ever have thought that the eerie sound of a hellhound would be a comfort? But that was the world he was in now, one that had changed radically in the last couple of years, and even more in the last few days. Especially for him.

"This is one of those questions you won't answer, isn't it?" Limos sighed. Limos, who had become the biggest part of his new world. And hell, since her brother had claimed his soul, he supposed it couldn't hurt to tell her it wasn't the first time that had happened.

"How did I get out of the situation? I sold my soul to a demon who promised to make my father go sober and straight."

Limos shot straight up, her raven hair falling forward to cover her breasts, which was a shame. "*You did what?*"

"Yeah, it was stupid. But I was desperate. Convinced that the next time my old man got violent, he'd kill Runa or my mom." He reached up to play with a strand of her silky hair. "It worked. He got sober and stopped beating the shit out of us and cheating on mom, but then he got lung cancer, and our mom committed suicide, so I sold my soul for nothing I guess."

"How long?" Limos rasped.

"How long what? Until he died?"

"How long until the demon collects?"

"He already tried. Remember when I said I was bitten by a demon? That was his calling card. I was supposed to die, but Shade saved me."

"What kind of demon?" She gripped his leg so fiercely he knew he'd have bruises by morning. "What species did you sell your soul to?"

"Charnel Apostle. Why?"

Limos jumped to her feet, startling him. "Get dressed." She snatched her bikini top out of the sand. "Hurry. We have to find this demon."

He tugged on his pants. "He failed to kill me. The contract is broken."

"No," she said, her voice laden with impatience, "it isn't. Charnel Apostles never allow for out clauses." She cursed in a few different demon languages. "Gah. That's why Pestilence hasn't killed you. I wondered about that, but now it makes sense."

"Not to me." He slipped on his shirt and helped her tie her bikini strings in the back while she lifted her hair. "Interesting tat." He frowned at the set of scales, which he'd swear had been weighted differently the last time he saw it.

"We don't have time for tats," she said, spinning around to him. "My brother tethered your soul, but someone else has a claim on it. In order to get it for himself, he has to buy it from the other demon. Or, more likely, kill the dude. We have to get to that demon first."

"How?"

She fiddled with her navel ring as she spoke, her words

spilling like a dam had broken. "I've seen Gethel perform rituals to bargain for souls before. We need an angel. And some blood from everyone who participated in the summoning of the demon who took your soul."

Arik shook his head. "That's impossible. The guy who did it died in prison a few years ago. But that's good news, right? It means Pestilence can't find the demon, either."

Limos's creative curses blistered his ears. "No. Pestilence will be able to sense the holder of the soul he's trying to claim. We're screwed."

"In more ways than one, I think." He gestured down the beach at Thanatos jogging toward them. Thankfully, they were dressed, but the guy wasn't an idiot, and if he had a single brotherly instinct, he'd...yep...the Horseman's eyes narrowed as he approached, and Arik readied himself for Death Match: Part Two.

Fortunately, though Than gave Arik a look that spelled out L-A-T-E-R, he didn't pull a big brother.

"Human." Thanatos's voice was as dark as his expression. "You said you can learn any demon language."

"Yeah. Why."

Thanatos held out a slip of parchment. "Can you read them?"

"What's this about?" Limos asked, as Arik took the page and studied the strange scribblings.

"I have Regan going over everything I've found about your *agimortus*. She said that this piece of Isfet writing felt angry, but I don't know what it says. I was hoping your boy here could translate."

Arik shook his head. "Sorry. I can't read demon languages. Just speak them."

"Dammit," Than snarled. He glanced down at the

messy towel and churned up sand, and those damned shadows started swirling around his feet.

Not good. With the Horseman's focus off the *agimortus*, it was locking in on Arik and Limos. Think fast… "Why don't you just ask an Isfet? Or do they not exist anymore?"

"They exist," Limos said, "but no one but the Isfet know their language. That's why most of what we think we know about my *agimortus* is legend and not fact."

Arik slapped the parchment into Limos's palm. "Then let's go find an Isfet, because you've got yourself an interpreter."

Arik's soul might still be the rope in a tug-o-war, and Limos might still be engaged to Mr. 666, but if they could secure her *agimortus*, it would be a huge win for the good guys. And as long as Thanatos could keep his Seal from breaking, having Limos's Seal safe would mean that everyone could shift their focuses from her to stopping Pestilence.

This could be the much-needed break the R-XR and The Aegis had been looking for. Arik grinned.

Pestilence could suck it.

Limos and Arik waited for Ares and Thanatos at the Temple of Limos, which was the only temple constructed for the Horsemen that wasn't inside Sheoul. Limos's temple existed inside a bubble of sorts, where the demon and human realms met and where both humans and demons could walk, but neither could pass into the other's realm. This bubble was deep inside an ancient Incan cave that Limos doubted had seen a human in hundreds of years.

From the looks of the temple, it hadn't seen demons either.

She looked around at the dust and crumbling stone altars. "This is really insulting."

Arik kneeled next to a time-bleached skeleton chained to the wall. "Why are all these skeletons here?"

"They were sacrifices to me."

Her boots clacked on the floor as she moved to one of the altars, where a bunch of colored stones had been laid out in the pattern of a set of scales. Under her armor, her own scales, the tattoo, remained balanced, which was a relief. It tended to tip to evil when she was in one of the bubbles or inside Sheoul.

Grimacing, Arik stood. "Nice."

She watched him wander around the temple, studying its marble walls, every inch of which was engraved with symbols or writing. When he stopped in front of a carving of her and her brothers standing before kneeling humans and demons, he traced his finger over her image, and she swore she felt his touch on her skin.

"You and your brothers are close, but what's supposed to happen if all of your Seals break?"

"I think, after the Apocalypse is over and evil has won, we're supposed to be at war with each other." The very idea made her sick.

"I can't imagine going to war with Runa," he said, dropping his hand from the carving.

She smiled. "We have that in common."

Their love for their siblings had made them both go to extremes. She kept harmful secrets from her brothers, and Arik had sold his soul for his sister. Limos was still reeling from that revelation, but in a small way, it was actually good news. It meant that Pestilence didn't own Arik's soul—yet. As soon as they were done here, she was going to grill Arik for every drop of information she could get about this demon. They had to find him before Pestilence did.

Arik moved on to a wall that was covered in huge blocks of lettering. "What does all of this say? Looks like a couple different languages."

She nodded. "Some is in Latin, but most is in Sheoulic." She ran her finger over a block of black lettering in the gray stone. "This is the legend of our origins." She pointed to another section. "That's a wedding program of sorts."

A curious, dark anger rolled off his body, but she instinctively knew it wasn't directed at her. "What's it say?"

"A bunch of crap from my contract, mostly." Assuming he knew Sheoulic, she read the words aloud. "The daughter of Lilith shall be married by the blood of an angel no more, and the pearls of virtue shall then be broken by her husband."

His expression turned both thoughtful and angry, and she swore she heard him growl. Inexplicably, she was a little... turned on... by his reaction to the wedding plans. He twined his fingers in hers and tugged her a little closer, and she let out a happy sigh as Ares and Than entered, a tall, green-skinned Isfet walking between them.

Ares remained at the door as Than led the Isfet inside. "I don't think he knows why he's here. We couldn't really communicate."

"How'd you get him to come with you?" Arik asked.

Than shrugged. "We kidnapped him."

Kidnapping was so something Reseph would have done, and she couldn't help but smile. "You *will* return

him without the Neethul learning of this, right?" The
Neethul kept the Isfet as slaves, and they were experts in
the art of cruel punishment. No doubt the Isfet would be
blamed for his own kidnapping.

"Of course," Ares said.

Than grinned. "And if any Neethul find out, we'll
make sure they can't repeat it to anyone else." Now *that*
was one hundred percent Thanatos. He glanced over at
Arik. "Ball's in your court, human."

Arik, who had changed into black BDUs and was
loaded down with weapons Kynan had brought to Limos's
house before they left, turned his attention to the Isfet.
"Greetings," he said, in perfect Sheoulic. "We would like
to ask you some questions."

The Isfet, who Limos assumed was a male, though
she wasn't sure why, blinked his big, round eyes. "This
demon you ask?"

Right. She'd forgotten how bad their Sheoulic was.

Arik sank down on one of the benches, and she got
the impression he was trying to look non-threatening.
Though with his chest harness and gun belt, she didn't
think it worked. It did add an extra layer of sexy to him,
though.

"Can you speak to me in your language?"

The Isfet nodded, his long, spindly fingers curling
around his walking staff. "Is I know?"

"Criminy." Arik scrubbed his hand over his face as he
looked at Limos. "No wonder you've had a hard time talking to them."

The demon's skin changed color like a chameleon's,
turning sparkly silver, and he said something in the
Isfet language. Arik frowned, but made a gesture for the

demon to continue. After a few minutes, Arik blew out a long breath.

"This language is freaky. I've never had to listen this long to learn one. Just when I think I might have it... wait." Arik spoke a few words Limos didn't understand. The Isfet jerked, his tiny mouth falling open. Arik spoke again, and with an animated flapping of his arms, the Isfet spoke about a million words a minute.

Arik turned to Limos. "Have you been searching chambers of...ice?"

"Yes." She moved closer to him. "Some of the rumors we followed up on spoke of ice caves, both in Sheoul and in the human realm."

Arik took her hand again and pulled her down next to him. "What about the boiling glass?"

Limos sighed. "We assume that could be lava, so we've looked in volcanic chambers as well."

"And towers," Arik mused. "They speak of towers."

Arik turned back to the Isfet, and they engaged in another conversation. "Okay," he said. "The location wasn't lost to legend. It was lost to translation. You know they can barely understand or speak Sheoulic...they only know a few words, enough to sell their product."

"Why couldn't they learn Sheoulic?" Than asked.

Arik shifted to address them all. "It's like communicating with dogs. They can read our body language, and they can understand a few words, can read the tones of our voices. But they can't understand conversations, and that can't be taught. It's a species thing."

"So you're saying that the Isfet are like dogs?"

"Yes. They're like no other demon. Hell, they might not even be demons."

Limos glanced over at the Isfet. "What else would they be?"

"No idea." Arik shrugged, making his shirt stretch tight over his broad shoulders. Yum. "Aliens, maybe?"

"Aliens." Thanatos's voice was flat, disbelieving.

"Your skepticism is funny, coming from one of the Four fucking Horsemen of the Apocalypse."

She supposed Arik had a point, but still, in all her time, she'd not come across a single alien. She didn't think so, anyway. "Okay, so whatever they are, you understand them, now, right?"

"Sort of. He said the cup is in a chamber of...I can't figure out the right word."

The Isfet shuffled over to the altar and tapped one of the stones.

"A crystal," Arik breathed. "That's it. It makes sense. It's in a chamber of crystals."

"Not ice?"

"No. That's how it was translated into Sheoulic, so that's how you understood it. And it was flooded with hot water."

"Boiling glass," she murmured. "What about the towers?"

He spoke with the Isfet, and then turned to Limos. "Not towers. Columns. Huge columns of crystal inside a big cave. And he said that since I know their language, I'll know the signs inside. Unfortunately, he doesn't know where the cave is."

"Google." Everyone turned to look at Ares, who shrugged. "Cara likes to say that you can Google anything. Can't hurt."

"So we Google for caves of crystal?" Arik grinned. "Let's get Googling."

Twenty-one

⌒

They found the cave in half an hour.

Google searches for crystal caves turned up a bazillion results, but after refining the searches, one stood out; a giant crystal cave discovered in Mexico...once filled with scorching water. Miners had pumped out the water, but volcanic vents kept the cave so hot that it could kill unprotected humans within minutes.

According to one of the Internet articles, scientists theorized that over the course of the million years it took for the crystals to form, water levels inside the cavern had varied from full to empty. Limos's *agimortus* could easily have been placed inside during one of the low-water periods.

Arik had called Kynan to aid in the search, but Kynan had been dealing with an attack on an Aegis stronghold outside of Frankfurt that had left twenty Guardians dead, so he'd sent his vampire-demon buddy in his place. The demon, Wraith, was some sort of expert treasure hunter, and Kynan swore he'd be as useful as he'd been a couple of months ago at the big battle they'd had with Pestilence.

Kynan had better be right, because Limos had never met a more annoying Seminus demon in her life.

Currently, Wraith was exiting the mining facility and sauntering toward Limos, her brothers, and Arik. He'd arrived before they had, so he'd gone in to check things out and grab Arik an orange "ice suit," which apparently kept chilled air blowing on the inside via a miniature air-conditioning unit. He handed it to Arik.

"Here, dude. You get to play astronaut. Oh, and I took care of the humans who were inside."

"Took care of?" Arik asked.

"Don't get your panties in a twist," Wraith said, shoving his hands in his jeans pockets. "They're still alive. Just...tired."

Limos helped Arik get the bulky suit on. "From what?"

Wraith flicked his tongue over a fang. "Anemia."

Thanatos laughed. "I like this guy more every time I see him."

"Good," Limos said, as she helped connect the respirator and air delivery system that sat on Arik's back like a big box. "He can be *your* cave buddy."

Wraith and Thanatos bantered all the way to the entrance, followed by Ares, and Limos and Arik brought up the rear. Just before they entered through the massive steel doors, Arik stopped her.

"Hey." He tucked his mask under one arm and cupped her cheek with his hand. "I don't know what we'll find in there, but I want you to know I have your back."

Dipping his head, he kissed her. His warm lips were so

velvety, and it never failed to surprise her that a male as powerful and hard-bodied as he was possessed such softness and was capable of such tenderness. She loved the contradiction, loved how it made her feel even more.

"Ahem."

The sound of a throat clearing broke off the kiss, and Limos turned to see Ares holding the door open and giving Arik the evil eye. Fortunately, Than and Wraith had already entered. Wraith would probably have gotten off on making fun of them, and Than might have tried to drown Arik again. Never mind that there was no water around. She'd seen Than drown a man in his own blood before.

Cheeks stinging with heat, she gave Arik a shy smile and entered the facility, where it became clear that Wraith had definitely *taken care* of the humans who were supposed to be monitoring the scientific equipment. They all lay unconscious in the white, tunnel-like antechamber. The heat was already oppressive, and as Ares swung open the heavy door that led to the crystal cave, the temperature went from dry desert to sauna.

Arik donned the suit's protective face mask, while the rest of them put on the helmets with attached lights hanging on the antechamber wall. Anticipation tripped through Limos as they armored up and entered the cave that resembled a big, hollowed out snowball.

The giant crystals formed vertical and horizontal towers hundreds of feet in length and some as wide as a two-lane city street. At the very bottom, razor-sharp crystals rose up like a bed of nails. One slip, and it would be pincushion-city.

She stayed close to Arik as he eased along the crystal

that formed a bridge between several points of crystal clusters. Stretching, he ran his gloved fingers over a rough crystal. "I'll be damned. Symbols."

Ares was behind them, his eyes searching every nook and cranny. "What do they say?"

"They're more like directions." Arik pointed down. "That way."

Thanatos leaped off the crystal to another that jutted out of the side of the cave, and Wraith joined him, coming down much more lightly. But then, the demon wasn't wearing clunky bone armor.

"Heights." Arik peered over the edge. "Figures."

"What's the matter, human?" Than looked up, a taunting smirk on his face. Her brother really had the oddest sense of humor sometimes. "Too mortal to jump down here?"

"Nah," Arik called out. "It's just that your fat asses are taking up the whole ledge."

Thanatos laughed and jumped to the next lower crystal, and before Limos could stop him, Arik launched himself, coming down next to Wraith and nearly knocking the demon off. Wraith cuffed him in the head and jumped to a ledge near Than.

Limos just tried to not have a heart attack. Arik was fearless. Or maybe insane.

She kind of liked it. "Well? Do you see another symbol?"

"Not yet." Arik ran his hands over the crystals, and the rest of them joined him in the search.

She was beginning to lose hope when Wraith called out. "Yo, Horsepeople. I found a symbol." He was crouching next to two huge crystals that formed an X, peering into the inch of space between them.

"How the hell did you find that?" Arik said, as he eased up to the demon. "It's hidden."

Wraith shrugged. "I'm good at finding shit."

"Damn," Arik breathed. "Glad Ky sent you. We'd never have found that."

Wraith shoved lightly to his feet. "What? You aren't glad I'm here for my sparkling company?"

That was something Reseph would have said, and Limos found herself smiling in remembrance. Man, she missed her brother.

Arik lowered himself to his hands and knees to peer between the crystals. After a moment, he stretched out on his belly and reached down, his arm disappearing under the crystal he was lying on. Suddenly, Arik came to his feet, a tiny white cup dangling from a leather thong in his fist. "Got it!"

Limos damn near screeched with joy. Her brothers whooped, Wraith muttered something about being hungry, and she was about to jump down to Arik...

When all hell broke loose. One minute, Limos was celebrating finding her *agimortus*, and in the next, Pestilence was crouching on a ledge above them, a silent snarl peeling back his lips and making his fangs glint.

"How'd he find us?" Arik dove across one of the gaps in the crystals, but Pestilence was beside him in a flash.

As Arik skidded across the smooth surface, he flung the *agimortus* up to Ares. The act cost him, and before Arik could escape, Pestilence seized him by the throat.

"Let him go!" Limos ran toward them as Arik punched and kicked, but when her brother squeezed his throat harder, Arik's struggles weakened.

"Stay there, little sis," Pestilence said, and everyone froze. "I'll trade him for the cup."

If he'd asked for anything else, she'd agree, but the cup was so off limits. *Stall.* "How did you find us?"

"Ah. That. Did you know your boy sold his soul to a Charnel Apostle?"

Arik slammed his boot into Pestilence's shin. "She knows, you horse's ass."

Pestilence ripped the mask away from Arik's suit, and Arik gasped at the sudden heat and thick air. "I found him, killed him, and your soul defaulted to me. I can now sense you wherever you are."

"Let him go, Reseph," she said quietly.

"Don't think you can appeal to Reseph," Pestilence snarled. "He's gone. Get used to it." He clamped down on Arik's throat again, and Arik's face turned crimson. "Give me the damned cup."

She couldn't. But she couldn't let Arik die, either. Every bone in her body screamed at what was running through her mind, but she quelled the noises and stepped forward.

"Take me instead." The crystal walls closed in, suffocating her the way Sheoul's confines would do forever after this. "You can take me to my husband and get whatever reward you've been seeking."

Arik, Than, and Ares all shouted "No," simultaneously, but she ignored them. This was her worst nightmare—well, second worst, the first being to have her Seal break, but to save Arik, she'd do it.

Pestilence's eyes glinted with icy evil. "I think we've made a deal."

Than leaped for her, but she spun out of his way. "Don't," she whispered. "I have to do this." She moved toward Pestilence with leaden feet. "I also want Arik's soul returned to him, so that when he dies, you don't get possession."

"Agreed."

"Don't, baby," Arik rasped. "Don't do this."

"If I don't, he'll kill you, and you'll spend eternity being tortured. I can't let that happen." She kept her eyes rooted on Pestilence as she stepped within arms' reach. "Release him."

Pestilence shoved Arik off the ledge, and only Wraith's catlike reflexes saved him from falling to his death on the crystal shards below.

"*Bastard!*" Limos slammed her fist into her brother's jaw.

Pestilence's head snapped back, and she struck again, this time swiping her fingers over his armor-scar. Instantly, his armor melted away, leaving him in worn camo pants. Sticking out of the leg pocket was Deliverance, in all its shiny, horse-headed glory.

As Pestilence reached up to re-armor, one of Arik's knives impaled his wrist in a well-executed throw. Blood splattered Limos in the face, blinding her in one eye as she rammed her shoulder into Pestilence's gut and seized Deliverance. The dagger felt cold in her hand. Heavy.

Without thinking, she plunged the blade into her brother's heart.

The cavern went silent. Horror and disbelief flashed in Pestilence's eyes. His hands shook as he grasped Limos's hand, which was still wrapped around the hilt of the dagger. Blood flowed over her fingers and gushed from his mouth, where it dripped off his chin.

Pounding footsteps rang out as her brothers, Wraith, and Arik rushed toward her.

"Oh, fuck." Than's voice was choked. "Li, what have you done?"

No words would form. Pestilence crumpled to his knees on the crystal bridge, and she went with him. The moment her knees hit the rock, searing grief hit too. *No... no... this wasn't happening!* Thanatos was supposed to restore his Seal, and oh, God, what *had* she done?

"Limos," Pestilence gurgled through the blood, and then he was Reseph again. Limos knew it, could see it in the way the ice of his eyes melted into tears. "I've missed... you."

Her throat constricted so violently she could barely breathe. "Forgive me."

His entire body shuddered. "I-I'm... sorry."

"No," she rasped. "Don't be. None of this was your fault."

His head fell forward, and his hair spilled into his face. "You don't... understand," he whispered. "I'm sorry... to... to... disappoint you." His grip tightened on hers with so much force that she gasped. "You must be so disappointed that Deliverance didn't kill me."

His head came up, his eyes glowing red, and he yanked the dagger out of his chest as if it were nothing but a sliver.

Holy mother of—

Another of Arik's knives hit Pestilence's hand. Deliverance fell out of his grip, the blade spinning. Limos snatched the dagger out of the air and scrambled to her feet, nearly bowling over her brothers. Pestilence moved in a blur, armoring up. Within a heartbeat he had a sword in his hand and was swinging it at her head. Than shoved her out of the way, and she heard the distinct sound of metal crunching into bone. Thanatos stumbled and hit the crystal, Pestilence's blade lodged in his skull.

Ares attacked Pestilence with a vengeance, and suddenly, the cave came alive with snarls, as a horde of demons seemed to crawl up through the crystals below. Wraith leaped into the fray while Arik produced another throwing knife from his boot and took out one of the scaly beasts as it skittered up a crystal.

"Go!" Ares tossed her the cup. "Get out of here!"

She wanted to stay and fight, but Arik was still in danger, and she had to protect her *agimortus*. Cursing in frustration, she threw a gate. The portal shimmered like a sparkly curtain, waiting...and she didn't even realize she was hesitating until Arik tackled her, forcing them both through the gate to land in the sand outside her house.

Yes, they had Deliverance and her *agimortus*, but somehow, none of what had happened in that chamber felt like a win.

Twenty-two

Arik's heart was jackhammering so hard and so fast that his ribs hurt. Or maybe the ribcage pain was from Pestilence's killer right jab. Or it could be from Deliverance's hilt jamming into his chest.

Carefully, he eased off of Limos and started to help her to her feet, but when he looked into her moonlit eyes and saw the horror pooled in them, he sat down beside her.

Her bloody hands clutched Deliverance in a white-knuckled grip, and her pale face was streaked with tears.

"I tried to kill Reseph." Her thin voice was barely audible over the crash of the waves on the beach.

"Hey." He pried the dagger out of her hands and stabbed it into the sand. "You did what you had to do."

"You don't understand. I wanted him dead, Arik." Her eyes were wild, her nostrils flaring as she fisted his collar in some sort of crazed desperation. "*I want my brother dead.*"

Arik stroked her hands, using his touch and his voice to soothe her. "That's because he's not your brother. Not anymore, and you know that."

Limos looked at the dagger he'd jabbed in the sand. "You're doing it again."

"Doing what?"

"Calling me out on things even *I* don't know."

"You know." He drew her against him and cradled her head against his chest. "You just lie to yourself."

"Of course I do," she said quietly. "I do it to everyone else, so why not to myself?" She closed her eyes and took a deep, shuddering breath, then jerked in alarm as a gate opened a yard away.

Ares stepped out, bloodied, one eye swollen shut, one arm dangling uselessly at his side. "We're all okay," he said, before Arik or Limos could ask. "Wraith took Than to Underworld General." He glanced at Arik, as if needing to explain. "He'll heal on his own, but the damage was extensive, and we can't let him be weakened for long." He sank down on his haunches next to her and put his hand over hers. "You did what you had to do."

She nodded. "But why isn't Pestilence dead?"

"I don't know, but this failure is catastrophic. Deliverance was our only way to stop him. And it gets worse."

"How can it possibly get worse?" Arik asked, and then realized he really didn't want to know.

Ares wiped a trickle of blood off his cheek. "Chaos showed up and took a bite out of Pestilence."

"Don't tell me he's immune to hellhound poison," Limos ground out. "Do *not* tell me that."

"No, not immune, but damned near. He went still for all of five seconds. He's growing stronger, Limos, and I'd be willing to bet that it won't be long until even a hellhound bite won't affect him at all." He cursed in Sheoulic, and Arik understood every one of the nasty words. "Where the fuck are Reaver and Harvester? We need them now more than ever before, and they've gone MIA."

"This is all my fault," she murmured. "My fault. Maybe I didn't get the dagger in the right spot. Maybe—"

Arik squeezed her hand. "You nailed him dead center in the heart. You couldn't have had better aim. This is not your fault."

"Arik is right." Ares took the dagger and made it disappear into his armor. "I'm going to go to UG." He nodded at Arik. "Take care of her."

"Yeah," he said. "I will."

Once Ares was gone, Limos slipped the leather thong attached to the cup around her neck and over the top of her Seal pendant. Arik gathered her in his arms and carried her into the house, surprised she didn't fight him. Neither did she resist when he stripped her and put her into a hot shower. He left his clothes on, not wanting to accidently cut off any protruding body parts if he came into contact with the deceptively beautiful pearls, and when he was done washing her, he tucked her into bed.

"Join me?" she asked, and yes, he planned to, after he took his own shower.

He washed quickly, and when he got out, he found Limos out on the deck, dressed in a pink, fluffy robe, looking out at the dark ocean. He tugged on a pair of shorts and joined her.

"What are you doing?" he asked.

"Thinking."

"About what?"

She looked up at the starry sky, a faraway glimmer in her eyes. "About you."

"What about me?"

"I owe you everything, Arik. Without you, we never would have found my *agimortus*." She suddenly flew into his arms, her body so tight with tension it broke his heart. Seeing her so vulnerable fired up his protective instincts like nothing else could.

This woman had been willing to go to hell for him. Literally. She was prepared to give up everything to join her husband and spend eternity in misery, just to save Arik's soul.

"No," he croaked. "I owe you. What you were willing to do for me...that was the most unselfish act in history, I think."

She laughed bitterly. "You have no idea how selfish I am."

"You'll never convince me."

For a long time they stood like that, the warm night breeze blowing around them. It was strange to think that it was December, nearly Christmas. He was so used to snow at this time of the year. The thought gave him visions of log cabins, snapping fires, a decorated tree, and Limos, naked on the floor in front of it. Only in this fantasy, instead of the chastity pearls, she was wearing a big red ribbon.

He had to find a way to make it happen. There had to be a way to break her contract and that damned gold chain. Because after everything that had gone down since he'd gotten out of hell, and especially after tonight in the crystal chamber, he wasn't going to give her up.

"Arik?" Propping her forehead against his chest,

Limos slid her hands up and down his back. "Remember how I said it was my fault that Deliverance didn't kill Pestilence?"

"It *wasn't* your fault."

She pulled away a little and looked up at him. The silver moonlight reflected in her eyes, turning them into frosted purple glass. They were remarkable. *She* was remarkable.

"I need to tell you something. Something I can't even tell my brothers, but maybe you can help. The R-XR or The Aegis...I don't know. Because I do think I'm the reason the dagger didn't work on Pestilence."

Arik hated that she blamed herself, and though what he really wanted to do was take her into the bedroom and make her forget everything but how her body responded to him, he sensed that she needed to get something out in the open.

"Go on."

"Remember how The Aegis lost Deliverance a few hundred years ago?"

He scowled, wondering where this was leading. "Yeah...and they don't even know how they lost it."

"That's because they didn't lose it. I stole it."

Limos waited for Arik to get angry. Freak out. Give her a disapproving look. *Something.* Instead, he merely watched her. With unflappable patience. "I'm guessing there's an explanation."

"Yes," she replied, "but it's one you won't like."

"Try me."

Somehow, his calm, nonjudgmental reaction was worse than if he'd flown off the handle. At least then she wouldn't have to worry about him getting mad. As it was, the longer he showed faith in her, the worse it was going to be when she let him down.

She could stop now, make up some cover story, but what if she was right and Deliverance didn't work because of what she'd done so long ago? Arik might be able to help. God, she hoped so.

"Remember how you pointed out that I turn self-destructive sometimes?" That still rankled. It might be true, but she didn't like being so transparent to anyone. Not even Arik. "Well, around the time the Templars were falling into disfavor, the world was in turmoil. The various crusades had left the Middle East in crisis, and in Europe, crops were failing thanks to what scientists now say was a climate change. By 1300, the people were starting to starve." She shivered despite the warm temperature, remembering how dark that time had been for everyone, including herself.

"I fell into a self-destructive depression, and all I wanted was for the Apocalypse to start. There was talk of it among humans, the first major fears about it since Christianity had taken root. Since then, every generation thinks they're ushering in the end of days, but this was really the first time there was a mass consensus, you know?" No, of course he didn't. He hadn't been there. It was weird talking to someone so . . . young. "So anyway, I was all gung-ho for it to happen and get over with."

"So you stole the dagger?"

"Yep. Took it from the Templars. The *Daemonica* said that Reseph's Seal would break first, so I figured that if I had Deliverance, I wouldn't have to worry about Ares or Than trying to kill Pestilence. So I kept it until 1317, when

The Aegis, blaming me for the Great Famine, performed a spell that summoned me."

Arik frowned. "Wait...if they...we...can summon you, why did Kynan have to use Reaver to contact you guys a couple of months ago?"

She turned away and gripped the railing so hard that her fingernails left dents in the wood. "Because I destroyed the knowledge of summoning after that." She glanced over at Arik, but his expression was still carefully neutral. "See, they captured me by freezing me with hell-hound venom, and I had Deliverance on me. They took it, and they spent a week or so torturing me for information. Eventually Reseph found me. He never got angry often, but when he did, very little could stop him. He killed every Guardian in the keep where they'd held me. When he finished, I had to admit that I'd stolen Deliverance, and now that The Aegis had it back, I was worried the account of it would show up in their records."

She'd lied to Reseph about why she'd taken the dagger, though. She'd told him she hadn't trusted The Aegis to keep it safe, and Reseph, being so trusting, had believed she'd taken its security into her own hands.

"So what did you do?"

"We searched out every Aegi who knew of my connection to it, and we...took care of their memories."

He stiffened, because yeah, sore subject. "I see."

"It took some time, but with Reseph's ability to go back farther into someone's memories than any of us, we took care of almost everyone involved. The problem was that the person who ultimately got the dagger went into hiding with it. Now we know that he altered its use so it could be used to kill Ares's *agimortus* in order to save him."

"Why just Ares's?"

"He's the only one of us with an *agimortus* that is an actual person."

He nodded. "Okay, so what does this have to do with Pestilence not dying when you stabbed him?"

An ocean-scented breeze washed over her face, and she took a moment to enjoy the whisper of wind caressing her face and teasing her hair. She'd spent a relatively small amount of time living in Sheoul, but the dark, claustrophobic experience had been carved into her very soul, and every day she spent out in the open like this was a gift, and she treated it as such.

Finally, she turned back to Arik. "I think the side-effect was that it rendered it useless to kill a Horseman. There's just no other explanation for why it didn't affect Pestilence at all."

Limos could practically see Arik's wheels spinning as he considered everything she'd told him. His powerful body was so beautiful in the moonlight, and though she ached to touch him, she sensed that he was in military mode, his mind working on a solution.

"Where did the engraving on the hilt come from?" Arik asked. "Was it always there, or was that added later?"

From death comes life.

"When we originally forged Deliverance, the Guardian who helped enchant it had a vision. Those words appeared to her, and she insisted that they be carved into the handle. That's why Than believes that Pestilence can be turned back. He thinks that he can do something to make it happen, because Deliverance is specifically mentioned in Than's prophecy."

He cocked his head to the side, studying her for so long she began to fidget. "What?" she finally asked. "Do I have food on my face or something?"

He chuckled, and then sobered. "I'm just glad you told me."

"You don't hate me?"

The two feet of space between them closed in an instant, and he dipped his head, brushing his lips lightly over hers. "There's your answer," he said, stunning the hell out of her. "I think you should have told your brothers, but I get it. I've kept things from Runa."

"Like?"

He exhaled slowly. "Like the fact that I sold my soul to a Charnel Apostle in order to save her life." He squeezed his eyes shut, but doing so didn't hide his pain from her. "She's dealt with so much, and she carried horrible guilt with her until Shade took it." He opened his eyes. "I can't tell her about that either. She'd blame herself."

"How does Shade take guilt away?" Because she could really use a dose of that magic.

"Trust me, you don't want to know." He grimaced. "There are things I do *not* want to think about my sister doing."

"Oh. Sex." Okay, so she didn't want any of that. Not with Shade. But if Arik wanted to sex her out of her guilt, that would be another story.

"Sort of."

Sort of? There was no such thing as TMI for her, but Arik obviously didn't want to go certain places when it came to his sister.

"About Runa..." Now, *this* was a place she didn't want to go, but for the first time in her life, she felt like she could.

Like she could talk about something she'd done without the fear that she'd be hated. Arik's reaction to the truth about her past—granted, he still didn't know the worst of it—had given her a new confidence, and a new desire to come clean, if only to him. "There are no words in Sheoulic for 'I'm sorry,'" she began. "So I grew up without them. Once, when I tried to find the right words, the person I wanted to use them on was punished. I've had a hard time saying them since, so please believe me when I say I'm sorry I messed with your memories. I had no right to do it."

"No, you didn't." His voice was hard, but not unkind. "But I get why you did it. You wanted to protect me, just like you did when you offered to give yourself up to Satan." His big chest expanded on a deep inhale as he reached out and caressed her cheek. "Just promise you won't do it again."

She smiled, even though none of this was funny. "Which one?"

"Either. That bastard can't have you." Growling, he dropped his hand, and it clenched into a fist, as if he was preparing to go a few rounds with her fiancé. "Nothing is iron-clad. There's got to be a way out of your contract."

She snorted. "Sure there is. You can take my virginity."

Oh, she wasn't serious, but just thinking about it made her ache for it. Made her desperate to have Arik on top of her, making love to her the way a male should. To have him between her legs like that, his muscles flexing, his skin glistening with sweat... God, she could only imagine the places he'd take her.

"There's one hell of a catch in that particular out-clause." He frowned. "Wait, how did you say your chastity belt can be removed?"

"It can't. Not by anyone but my husband."

He considered that. "The spell infused in the belt and contract... were those the exact words used? Did it say 'husband,' or Satan?"

"Husband." She drew in a harsh breath. "But Harvester drew up the contract. She wouldn't have left a loophole like that." Limos paced the length of the deck, her bare feet making no sound, even if her mind was clacking like an old typewriter as she tried to untangle her marriage contract and Deliverance's failure. The only thing she was sure about was that she needed help. "I need to talk to Reaver."

"Do your Watchers disappear often?"

"Sometimes. But when we really need them, they've always shown up. Ares and Than haven't had any luck, but I'll give it a shot." She stopped at the far end of the deck and closed her eyes, calling out to Reaver in her mind.

Reaver, our Heavenly Watcher, I require your presence. She repeated the official words of summoning, and then added, *Like, now. We're in trouble, Reavie-Weavie.*

Arik's hands came down on her shoulders, and she allowed herself to lean into him. He slipped his arms around her waist and held her like that as they gazed out over the moonlit ocean. His strength surrounded her, easing her, giving her comfort—and a connection—she'd never had before.

He might be a human, but she'd never met even an immortal with such bravery and resilience. Everything about him fortified her, made her stronger. It was as if she were a sturdy building, capable of standing on her own, but he was her buttress, supporting her outer walls and keeping them steady.

"You are a beautiful couple." The female voice startled them both, and they whirled around, Arik tucking Limos behind him.

An angel stood on the deck, her white robes glowing as if warding off the night.

"Gethel." Limos eased next to Arik, who remained in a stiff, battle-ready stance. She took Arik's hand and squeezed. "It's okay. She was our Watcher before Reaver."

"Reaver is why I'm here," Gethel said. "I heard your summons, but I fear he won't show."

"Where is he?"

She shook her head. "I know not. He and Harvester have both become invisible to our eyes."

Oh, this was bad. If even other angels didn't know where Reaver was, this was trouble. "Are they in danger?"

"I can only speculate, but I would say yes."

"Who would...or *could*...have taken them? And why?"

"Pestilence?" Arik asked, but Gethel shook her head.

"For a Horseman to kill or imprison the Watchers would be the gravest of violations." She glanced at Limos. "Why were you summoning Reaver?"

Her instinct was to lie. Instead, she forced herself to speak the truth. "I stabbed Pestilence with Deliverance and he didn't die. Do you know why?"

Gethel's eyes flashed. "Yes. And so do you."

Nausea swirled in Limos's stomach. "So it *was* my fault." Arik's arm came around her, once more bracing her when she needed it. "Why didn't you say something? You could have warned us."

"I didn't know until you confessed your sin to Arik." She flapped her wings in that way she always had when she was irritated. "You know I love you, Limos, but you brought this on yourself."

"Hey." Arik's voice cracked like a whip. "She regrets what she did, and it took a lot of courage to own up to it, so lay off, angel."

Lightning streaked overhead. "You are either brave or foolish, human."

Arik's fingers dug possessively into her shoulder, not hurting, but marking. Claiming. "Yeah, well, what does wanting to marry a Horseman make me?"

Limos whipped her head around to stare at Arik. "You...you're serious."

His stare was intense, smoldering. "I told you I won't let him have you. You said it yourself—the Sheoulic in your contract says husband, not Satan."

"That's because the being you know as Satan has many names," Gethel said. "By naming only one, it could have been argued that the contract wasn't valid according to some religions."

"So..." Limos licked her lips, which were as dry as her mouth. "So if Arik marries me, becomes my husband, he could break my chastity belt?"

"In theory," Gethel said, "he could take your maiden-head and remove you from Satan's grasp."

Limos's heart burned with the desire for Arik's plan to work, and not just because she'd finally be free of Satan. Arik was offering up her dream on a sexy platter—a marriage, children, sex. Oh, Lord...*sex*!

And something else, something so priceless she could barely contain her excitement; he'd be giving her someone she could confide in. Someone she *wanted* to tell the truth to. After they were married, she'd never lie to him again.

"Don't turn me down, Horseman," he said, and it was funny how he still refused to say her name. "This might not be the most conventional marriage ever, but if it works, I won't have demons after my ass to torture your name out of me, and it'll save you from being Satan's ball and chain."

She noticed that he didn't bring up love as being part of it, and though it shouldn't sting, it did. But that was okay. Even if he never learned to love her, she loved him enough to make up for it.

"Yes," she said, her breath trembling in her throat. "My answer is yes."

On her shoulder, her one side of her tattoo dipped deeper than it ever had.

In favor of good.

Twenty-three

Reaver was still fighting. Harvester watched him from the doorway, amazed at his resilience. He sat against the wall, tossing and catching a rubber ball Whine had given him. Reaver hadn't said a word since she'd forced the marrow wine down his throat. He'd simply played with the ball, focusing so intently on it that she expected it to burst into flames.

He was incredibly alert, his agility in no way diminished by his captivity, mutilation, or intoxication. She couldn't help but wonder what was going to happen when he was free again. Would he continue to keep that leashed power inside, or would he let loose and destroy everything in his path?

Harvester had no doubt she'd be the first one he came after, and though she could hold her own, she didn't want to expend energy fighting him when there was an Apocalypse around the corner.

Whine approached, his footsteps a mere whisper. "You have a visitor." Whine's voice was gruff. He didn't like strangers, though Reaver seemed to have grown on him. "He said you're expecting him."

The Orphmage. She brushed past Whine and met Gormesh in her living room.

He looked up from studying the Neethul sculpture on her wall. "You're late with your first payment."

"I have it right here." She reached for a clay bottle on the shelves next to her. "Angel blood. So fresh it's still warm."

Gormesh made the flask disappear into the folds of his robes. "I want to see the angel." He started toward the hall, but Harvester blocked his way.

"That wasn't part of the agreement."

"You agreed to give me the angel's blood." The pointy tips of the Orphmage's ears poked out from his waist-length white hair, and now they twitched in agitation. "You didn't specify how it was to be taken. I will bleed him myself."

"What is in the jug is more than enough."

"But it's far more potent when taken directly from the source."

Even more so if it was taken while the subject was screaming in pain, which Gormesh no doubt intended to make happen. "No."

He hissed, all pretense of civility gone. "You *will* grant me access."

"You *will* kiss my ass." She sensed Whine easing up behind her, could practically feel the tension rolling off him. His protectiveness didn't come from a place of affection, but rather from self-preservation. He was bound to her, and if she died, his slave contract would default to her killer.

The Orphmage was as cruel a master as he was a scientist.

Gormesh stiffened, baring his teeth. "You have just made an enemy you didn't need, Fallen."

"I'll add you to the list," she said. "Now leave."

"You still owe me."

"And I have a year to pay. So get the fuck out."

His eyes went flat, and for a moment, she thought he was going to attack. When he spun around and stormed out of the house, she sagged with relief. In a battle, she had the advantage, but as a mage, he had some nasty tricks up his sleeve, and winning wouldn't be easy...or without a lot of pain.

"Whine," she said softly, "fetch me some marrow wine."

"For the angel?"

"No, for me." Tomorrow she'd go back to dealing with Reaver. Tonight she was forgetting him.

⁓

Death. Destruction. It tugged at Thanatos with sharp, hooklike claws.

Eidolon had healed him, but Than had been delirious with pain, and it had taken Wraith, Ares, and a vampire named Con to hold him down. In his delirium, he'd released his souls, and had it not been for an ex-angel named Idess who could communicate with them, the casualties might have been staggering.

The second Than was healed, he'd gotten the hell out of Underworld General, the demon side of him clamoring for a deadly rampage. Instead, he'd gone home.

Where Regan was.

The Guardian had been running around his keep in tight leggings and cropped sweatshirts, her flat, rippled stomach, tight ass, and multitude of sexy battle scars driving him nuts. She'd taken over his library, her neat stacks of notes invading his space. And she flipped the fuck out if he moved them.

So at least once per day, he knocked a page or two off their stacks.

Her frustrated curses amused him.

Right now, though, he was not amused.

As he strode into the great room, Artur met him, his expression uncharacteristically strained. "Milord. It was the Aegi."

"*What* was the Aegi?"

"The dead succubus. You said to allow them in..." The vampire was practically wringing his hands, and yes, Than had said succubi were to be admitted. Pestilence kept sending them to seduce him, so Than wasn't about to pass up the opportunity to interrogate them about his movements, his intentions, his locations...and then kill them himself.

But no one else was allowed to kill in his house. Not when death made him crazy. His home was his sanctuary.

"Where is she?" He swiped his fingers over his throat and got rid of his armor, leaving him in nylon jogging pants and a T-shirt.

"The gym, sir."

He stalked to the gym, violence still scratching at the surface of his mind. Going to see Regan wasn't the smartest idea right now, but his brain was still operating on a primal level, and logical thought hadn't caught up.

Regan was on the floor mat, going through a martial

arts routine and kicking the stuffing out of one of the training dummies. Her tan skin, marked by scars on her arms, stomach, and back, glistened with a fine sheen of sweat. The scent of blood was thick in the air, another lash to his self-control.

"Are you injured?" He was at the mat before the question was fully formed.

She leaped, spun, and instead of nailing the dummy in the head, she hit him in the chest, knocking him into the treadmill. "Does that answer your question?"

With a roar, he came at her, and though she danced out of the way with more grace than he'd anticipated, he managed to catch her arm and flip her. Again she surprised him, landing on her feet and then hopping immediately into another spin kick. But this time he was ready, and he laid her out with a sweeping kick of his own that caught her behind the knee. She hit the mat hard, and when his instinct screamed at him to kill her while she was down, he gnashed his teeth and stood his ground, allowing her to roll and pop to her feet.

"Nice to see you too, Horseman." She wiped sweat from her brow with the back of her hand...a hand sporting bloodied knuckles. "Are we sparring, or are you really trying to kill me?"

"Now," he growled, "would normally be the time when I warn you to get away from me and lock yourself in a room. But I want to know what happened with the succubus."

"Bitch freaked out when she saw me. Said it was her job to get you in bed. No idea what the fuck she was talking about, but she attacked me, and I defended myself. Sorry, did I kill your lover?"

He ignored that. "Is fighting her how you hurt yourself?"

"This?" She held up her hand. "Yeah." She then did the worst thing she could have done, short of stripping naked. She put her bleeding knuckles in her mouth.

Than's fangs shot out of his gums, saliva surged over his tongue, and his skin broke out with sweat. Shit. He stumbled backward.

"Get. Out." His voice, warped with dark need, didn't sound like his.

"Thanatos, what's wrong?" She approached him, her scent clouding the air. Blood and woman, both tantalizing aromas, had his desires warring with each other. At least the driving need to kill had taken a back seat to lust and hunger.

He shook his head, unable to speak, lest she see his fangs. They were his secret shame, foul tools he'd carelessly used during the years after his curse when he'd gone on a rampage. When he'd emerged from that dark time, he'd learned that he'd sort of . . . fathered a race, and it was something he wasn't exactly proud of.

Since then, as long as he kept himself well fed on the vampires he kept here at his home, there were no problems. But lately he'd been distracted, and between the violence around the world and Regan driving him nuts, he hadn't fed properly.

"Thanatos?"

He turned away so he could speak. "Now would be a good time to go."

"Or?"

Closing his eyes, he inhaled, and his mouth watered. She smelled like battle and death, sunlight and honey, and his groin stirred. "Or—"

He didn't remember moving. Had no idea how he found himself smashed against Regan, pinning her to the wall as he fused his mouth to hers. She was taut beneath him, her participation in the kiss dubious, but mixed with the scent of her fury was arousal, as pure and sharp as his.

"Did you finish the book?" He palmed her breast through the sports bra. "Did you like what you read?"

Her hand dropped to cup him through his sweats, and he guessed that was a yes. Stinging, hot desire lashed at him, and his hips did an involuntary roll into her palm. This was stupid, was far more dangerous than any of the games he'd played in the past. With her, his control was limited, and in this state of mind, it was a brittle string ready to snap.

No penetration. Just remember . . . no penetration.

Fumbling with the drawstring on his sweats, she pushed her tongue into his mouth as she deepened the kiss, turning it into one of dominance. She was still fighting, this Aegi warrior, and when she bit his lip hard enough to draw blood, he was ready to throw down with her.

He dropped his hand to her waist and slid his fingers beneath the elastic band of her sweat pants to cup her ass and bring her up against him. Her moan joined his at the feel of his hard cock pressing against her core. She still managed to tunnel her hand into his pants, and at the first brush of her fingers on the tip of his cock, he nearly exploded.

Her warm hand closed around his shaft and began to stroke. The friction instantly made him mindless, as if her touch was magic, reducing him to a spellbound lump of clay. Normally he'd resist, unwilling to give up any control. Female demons had tried to seduce him for thousands of years, and some of them possessed seductive gifts or tricks, requiring him to be alert at all times.

But unlike the demons who'd tried to bed him, Regan hadn't come to him for that, and it felt good to let himself go, even if just a little bit.

Bringing his hand around to her abdomen, he kicked her feet apart to spread her legs as he trailed his mouth over her jaw. She made a sexy, rumbling noise in her throat, and he latched his mouth onto the skin there, letting his fangs scrape lightly. He wouldn't bite. Couldn't. He hadn't bitten a human in over a hundred years, a female one in over five hundred, and he wasn't about to fall off that wagon again.

Shoving those thoughts away, he slipped a finger inside her and groaned at the silky wetness. She arched into him and squeezed his hard shaft, and he nearly lost it. Her firm strokes were heaven, and within seconds, he was rocking into her grip.

His own hand was coated in her juices, and she was rocking too, and she gasped when he slipped another finger inside her tight opening. Damn, she'd feel good around his cock, and he imagined that they were horizontal on a mattress instead of against a wall engaging in heavy petting.

The fabric of her underwear and sweats hindered his hand, and with a growl, he ripped the satin panties away, leaving the slightly looser sweats still hanging from her hips. He could deal, he supposed. Especially because she was panting now, riding his hand, and he was right there with her, walking the fine line between pleasure and frustration. All it would take to push him over the edge would be her thumb over the head...ah, yes. She'd read his mind. The light stroke ignited him, and at the same time, her cries rang out and the scent of her lust clouded his brain. The climax crashed over him, and he rode the waves as he worked her, and when she peaked again, so did he.

Balls pulsing, he pumped his hips, releasing another hot flow. So...good. So...damned...good...

Outside, the wind howled against the window, bringing him back into focus as his climax waned. His legs were rubbery, and he thought that maybe the only thing holding him up was the wall and her arm around his waist.

Their labored breaths were the only sound in the room until she nipped his earlobe and whispered, "Let's move to the bedroom to finish this."

Finish? His cock sprang to life again, taking her words to heart. A thread of admiration for her stamina crept up on him, but at the same time, so did bitterness she didn't deserve, but that she was going to bear the brunt of nevertheless.

He pushed away from her and tugged up his pants. "We *are* finished," he said gruffly.

Confusion flashed in her eyes as she awkwardly adjusted her sweats and wiped her hand on a towel. "I don't understand."

"Let me make it easy for you." He got up in her face so he'd be nice and clear. "This was a mistake. It won't happen again. I'm not available, Regan. We'll work together, but know that I'm counting the days until you're out of my home and out of my life."

He steeled himself against the hurt on her face, spun on his heel, and stalked out of the gym.

Twenty-four

Ares took the wedding news a lot better than Thanatos did. Ares merely looked contemplative as he lounged on his sofa with Cara and a sheltie-sized, newborn hellhound pup next to him, a baby Ramreel hopping around their feet playing climb-the-mountain on the hellhound lying on the floor. Arik had seen a lot of strange stuff in his life, but the domestic scene that involved baby goat demons and hellhounds was fucked up with a capital F.

Also unsettling was the way Thanatos's shadows flickered around him as he stared at Arik and Limos after they'd spilled the news. Arik had hoped the guy would still be at Underworld General so they could talk to the more level-headed Ares alone, but no such luck. Thanatos was healed of Pestilence's attempt at a lobotomy and was as asshole-ish as ever.

"Married." Than's fists clenched and unclenched, and Arik was pretty sure he was envisioning Arik's neck in them. "Limos, you do realize that by breaking your contract with Satan, you could piss off the one being in the underworld who can imprison you? Possibly even destroy you?"

"He won't do that," she said, taking Arik's hand as they sat on the couch across from Ares and Cara. "There's nothing Satan has ever wanted more than to see hell on earth, and destroying me would screw up a lot of apocalyptic prophecies. Prophecies that favor us as his champions during Armageddon."

"It's a good plan," Ares said, and Arik held his breath in anticipation for Than's reaction. On the way over here, Limos said that generally, if Ares saw the value of a strategy, Than fell into step.

Fortunately, she was right, and the shadows surrounding Than melted out of sight. Still, his voice was gruff when he spoke. "How will you do this? Your contract states that 'the daughter of Lilith shall be married by the blood of an angel no more.' What does that mean?"

Limos, in a short, flirty orange and purple sundress, leaned back against Arik, getting all cozy, and damn, it felt good. Felt *right*. "I asked Gethel about that. She said it's part of angel mating ceremonies. An 'angel no more' will bind us with his or her blood. Can I have a margarita?"

Ares gave an exasperated sigh. "I'm out of margarita mix. And I'm assuming an 'angel no more' is a fallen angel?" He flung his arm around Cara, who snuggled against his chest. "Where are you going to find one of those? No True Fallen would risk pissing off Satan by marrying his fiancé off to someone else, and Pestilence killed all the Unfallen a couple of months ago."

Limos palmed Arik's denim-clad thigh, and naturally, Thanatos zeroed in on that, his pale eyes flaring gold. She was going to get him drowned again. "Arik's got that one covered."

All eyes shifted to Arik. "The contract says *angel no more*," he began. "What if it doesn't mean a fallen angel? What if it's exactly what it says?"

"What, like someone who used to be an angel?" Than's voice was thick with skepticism. "I've never heard of anyone being demoted without falling."

Ha. Smug bastard. Arik had one up on Mr. Five Thousand-Year-Old Horseman. "I have. One of my in-laws, Idess. You might have met her at the hospital. She was Memitim, some sort of guardian angel, and she gave up her wings to be with Sin's twin brother, Lore."

"Interesting," Ares murmured. "This could work. It certainly can't hurt."

Arik didn't bring up just how badly it *could* hurt. If the marriage ceremony didn't break Limos's contract and Arik tried to remove her chastity belt, it could hurt a whole lot. But if it did work...he nearly groaned out loud at the visual in his head. He'd never really thought he'd get married, not when his job didn't allow for much dating, and not when his only marriage model—his parents'— had turned him off the idea.

But he'd also come around a little after seeing how happy his sister was with Shade. And Kynan didn't seem to be suffering in his marriage, either.

This marriage to Limos might not be happening the way he'd have chosen it, but she'd become as much an important part of his life as Runa, and marrying her was about more than saving her from a fate worse than death and saving him from demons who wanted to torture him. This was about giving himself over to someone without reservation, something he'd never been able to do.

He'd always had to hold things back from women—his past, his job, even his temper. The result was short relationships in which he didn't allow himself to grow attached. But Limos knew everything about him, she could definitely hold her own against him, and he'd absolutely grown attached.

"What about Pestilence?" Than asked. "Other demons might lay off you if Satan no longer needs you to speak Limos's name, but our brother owns your soul. He'll want you dead more than ever, if for no reason other than to see Limos suffer."

"It's a risk I'm willing to take." Arik met Than's cool gaze with a steady one of his own. Arik wasn't backing down from this. "I've committed to your sister and given my word. I'll deal with Pestilence when the time comes."

Than stared for a long moment, and then, finally, he nodded, and Arik felt like he'd passed some sort of test. "So where are we having this shindig?"

"Greece is nice this time of year," Cara said, stroking her hand over the squirming ball of black fur next to her.

Limos kicked up her bare legs across Arik's knees. "It is. But Than's place is bigger, and I want a huge wedding."

The little goat demon slipped under Thanatos's ankle-length coat and tried to climb his leg. Smiling, he scooped up it up and tickled it under the chin. "I would have taken you for a shotgun kind of girl."

"Funny, Than," Limos muttered. "You're always pointing out what a girl I am, and yeah, I want it all. A dress, a cake, and a ceremony. But we kind of have to do it fast, since everyone wants Arik dead. And also," she said, "it's Christmas time, and Than's place is a winter wonderland."

Arik raised an eyebrow. "You guys celebrate Christmas?"

"Not as a religious holiday." Somehow, Limos had practically crawled into Arik's lap without him noticing, and now she twisted around and wrapped her arms around his neck. "But yes. Presents and parties and pretty decorations . . . I love it." *He* loved how well she fit against him. "Reseph loved it, too. It was his favorite human holiday."

"Nah," Ares said. "He liked Halloween more. He lived to scare the shit out of people."

Than shook his head. "New Year's Eve. He planned out his party strategy months ahead of time so he could hit a big city in every time zone and get dozens of New Year's Eves in one night."

The Horsemen tossed around stories of Reseph's antics, and for a few relaxed minutes, Arik got an idea of how it must have been for them before their brother's Seal broke. And for the first time, he saw how much they had lost.

Eventually, an awkward silence fell, and Hal, the hell-hound on the floor, whimpered as if feeling the strain. Finally, Ares cleared his throat and brought them back on track. "I don't even know how to go about planning a big wedding," he grumbled. "We did the simple beach thing with just Than and Limos."

Cara grinned. "Limos and I will handle it. You come with me, and we'll get you ready." She patted Ares on the chest. "Gather your Underworld General buddies, and I guarantee their mates will help out."

"They aren't my buddies," he sighed, but Cara ignored him.

She grabbed Limos's arm and pulled her to her feet. "Come on, Li. We'll have a wedding by the end of the day."

Twenty-five

"Arik, are you crazy?"

Arik smiled at his sister as she looked around Than's place, where servants from all the Horseman households were scrambling to set things up for what promised to be a huge party.

"Maybe," he said, and hell, it might be true. What was definitely true was the tension between Runa and him, the unspoken crap about how he'd been avoiding her calls.

"I just don't get it." Runa rubbed her arms through her cream Angora sweater. "Limos sent you to hell, and now you want to marry her?"

"She didn't *send* me to hell. It was sort of a misunderstanding."

Runa gave him a look that she usually reserved for when one of her triplets was misbehaving. "A misunderstanding is when your mate missed recording your favorite TV show because he was listening to a football game instead of you." She glared over at Shade, who gave her a sheepish grin as he shoved trestle table benches around. "A misunderstanding is not when someone lands you in hell for a month."

"That's behind us," he said. "This marriage is the only way to save her." And, if it worked, himself.

"So this is a marriage of convenience? You don't love her?" Runa sounded almost relieved, and he so wasn't sure how to answer that.

He *had* fallen for Limos, but he couldn't say it out loud. Not yet. When he said it, it would be to Limos. He might not have thought he'd ever get married, but now that he'd made the decision, he'd take it seriously, and his wife would be his partner in every way. *She* would be the first person to hear the important things, like how he felt about her.

"She saved my life," he hedged. "She was prepared to make a huge sacrifice for me, and now I can do the same for her. I want this, Runa."

His sister took a deep, long breath before turning her gaze on him. "Okay, then." She folded herself into his arms and squeezed him tight. "I'm happy for you."

Hugging her back, he kissed the top of her head. "I figure marriage hasn't hurt you, so there's hope for me, I guess."

She pulled back to look up at him. "Wow. That's the first time you actually sound like you approve of me and Shade."

He snorted. "I still don't like the bastard, but I'm not stupid. He's good for you, and there's no one I trust more to keep you safe."

"What about you?" Runa's voice went low and serious.

"Are you safe? Will this marriage put you in any kind of danger? If her Seal breaks—"

"If her Seal breaks, we're *all* in a lot of trouble." He smiled, hoping to reassure her. "Limos found her *agimortus*, and she's keeping it on her until we can secure it somewhere it'll be safe forever."

That, of course, was an issue of contention between the Horsemen, the R-XR, and The Aegis. They'd all done a brief teleconference an hour ago to discuss the best course of action, and naturally, everyone thought they were the best people to safeguard Limos's little cup.

"What about Pestilence?" she asked. "He *is* her brother, so what if he decides he wants to hurt her through you?"

"Stop," he said softly. "Everything will be okay."

He prayed he sounded more confident than he was. Runa didn't know Arik had been soul-sucked by the asshole, and if he had his way, she never would. She was strong enough to handle it; he'd never doubt her strength. But if she knew, she'd never stop worrying, and after all she'd been through, she deserved a life free of the ugliness in his.

"What about you? Are *you* okay?"

She didn't need to expand on that. She was asking if his time in hell had affected him. "I'm okay." At her skeptical look, he rolled his eyes. "Seriously. I know I should be a drooling mess on the floor, but I think the Seminus demon who patched me up might also have patched my mind, too." A vampire walked by, his arms loaded with a case of Dom Perignon. Damn, these Horsemen didn't screw around, did they? "Hey, ah . . ."

"Don't." Runa stepped back. "Don't ruin this with talk about our past."

He hadn't planned to, exactly, but this was related, and

he swallowed against the sudden dryness in his throat. "I just wanted to say that I was sorry for avoiding you lately. What I did to you—"

"Wasn't your fault. Stop it, okay? And don't ask for my forgiveness, because there's nothing to forgive."

"Are you sure?" He glanced around the room, the way he had a hundred times since arriving, to make sure he kept track of everyone who came in and out. You could take the soldier out of the battle, but the wariness always remained. And in this case, the battle was still going on. "Did your nightmares return?"

She'd been plagued by nightmares about both their childhood and the part she'd played in their mother's death, and regret had eaten her alive for years. Until Shade had released her from all of it.

Guilt flashed in her eyes, giving him the answer he dreaded. "Only for a night. Shade ended it." Her lips curved into a secret smile. "Trust me, it wasn't horrible."

Arik held up his hand. "Okay, that's enough. I definitely don't want to get into TMI territory."

"Ew. Neither do I." She looked over at Shade, who was clomping his way toward them, looking like the Terminator in his black leather jacket, sunglasses, and big boots that cracked like gunshots on the floor. "I'm going to have him take me to Limos so we can do the girl thing to get her ready. I'll be back for the ceremony, okay?"

He hugged her again. "Thank you for everything."

"No," she said softly. "Thank you. Until Shade, you were the only person who never let me down, and the only person who was ever completely honest with me. You trusted me with your secrets, and you didn't doubt my strength when even I did. Without you, I never would

have learned to trust any man. So really, it's because of
you that I'm happy."

Shade came up next to Runa and offered his hand to
Arik, who took it, and that was the first time they'd ever
shaken hands.

"Good luck, man," Shade said. "That's one hell of a
family you're marrying into." Shade's voice went low.
"Just never forget how much your mate's brothers mean to
her. Because I can tell you from experience that she'll put
you on the floor if you forget."

Smiling, Runa hooked her arm around Shade's waist.
"Love you, bro."

"Love you too," Arik croaked.

Runa took off with Shade, leaving Arik drowning in
a stew of conflict that was entirely of his own making.
Because of him, Runa had learned that not all men were
lying, cheating, abusive scumbags. Great. Awesome. Give
him a goddamned medal.

But he *had* lied to her, and suddenly, no matter how
much he told himself that the things he'd kept from her,
his "omissions—*not lies*—" had been for her own good,
he wasn't sure he was convinced anymore.

Limos really liked Cara. She had since meeting the
human, but after spending the day with her, she realized
how truly special the female was.

They'd done a speed-shopping trip in New York City,
where Limos had bought a wedding gown, shoes, jewelry,
and makeup. All the while, Cara had been texting and
phoning more people than Limos could keep up with, but
she heard the names Sin, Tayla, Kar, Runa, Serena, Gem,

and Idess bandied around. Then, by the time they went back to Ares's place to get Limos ready, Runa and Idess were there, and Cara took off with Ares to handle something at Than's place.

It was the first time meeting Idess, and Limos was struck by the statuesque brunette and how nice she was. Not that Limos expected her to be a bitch or anything, but angels who lost their wings tended to be a bit bitter.

Speaking of bitter, Harvester still hadn't turned up. Neither had Reaver. Limos couldn't let their disappearances ruin tonight, but she wished Reaver could be there for her. He hadn't been their Watcher for long, but she'd connected with him instantly. He wasn't like other angels, with their stuffy, formal, stick-up-the-ass-ness. Reaver was actually...fun. His time as an Unfallen seemed to have given him a stick-up-the-ass-ectomy.

"So you're truly okay with performing the marriage ceremony?" Li asked the ex-angel as they stood in Cara's bedroom. "You could be risking a lot."

Idess tested the heat for the flat-iron she intended to use on Limos's hair. "From the sounds of it, *not* doing it would risk even more. The world can't afford for you to be paired up with the greatest evil to have ever existed." She shrugged. "And besides, Arik is Runa's brother, and I'd do anything for family. I owe the Sem brothers a lot."

"Idess also has a very powerful father who few would tangle with." Runa twirled Limos around to fasten the buttons on the back of the wedding dress.

Limos looked up from admiring the exquisite beadwork on the front of the floor-length gown. "Who?"

Idess grinned as she took a piece of Limos's hair and pulled it through the flat iron. "Azagoth."

"The Grim Reaper?" Limos hoped her voice didn't sound as strangled as she thought it did. "He's your father?"

"Yep."

Limos and Idess could be half-sisters. Now was probably not the time to mention that, and truthfully, until Pestilence was no longer a threat—if he was *ever* no longer a threat—it was best to keep anyone he could hurt out of his realm of knowledge. If he learned he had another sibling, Limos wouldn't put it past him to torture Idess for fun.

"Okay," Limos said, needing a change of subject. "So you're cool with this." Her stomach fluttered as Runa came around to slip Limos's white satin high heels on her feet. "And you, Runa?"

"Arik deserves to be happy." Five words, but Runa said it all. She might not approve, exactly, but she'd accept this was what her brother wanted.

"He does deserve that. I've not met many males like him," Limos said quietly. "Arik...he makes me want to be a better person." Telling Arik the truth made her feel better than telling any lie ever had. "That's so sappy, isn't it?"

"It's your wedding day. Sap is expected." Runa's smile reminded Limos of Arik. Their coloring was different, but they had the same mouth, the same shaped eyes, and the same precise, deliberate movements.

"Can I ask you something?" Limos said, and Runa shrugged. "Not to be rude, but... what *are* you?"

One of Runa's eyebrows arched. "You're thinking about my warg shift in the middle of the day?" When Limos nodded, Runa continued. "I was bitten by a werewolf and left to die. Arik found me, took me to the R-XR, and they experimented on me with a potential cure. It didn't work, but I now have the ability to shift at will instead of only on full moons. Now, enough of monster talk." She took a small jewelry box off the bed and opened it to reveal a pair of stunning blue topaz earrings. "Something borrowed and blue."

Idess handed Limos a white garter. "Something new. And hold on for something old." She dug into a small satin bag and pulled out a delicate bracelet made of tiny carved ivory beads. "This is from Wraith's mate, Serena. She's a treasure hunter, and she found this in an honest-to-God pirate chest. Legend has it that it was worn by Eleanor of Aquitaine at her wedding to her first husband, King Louis the seventh."

"Ah...you do know that the marriage ended badly, right?" Limos asked.

Idess shrugged. "Well, she didn't wear it for her second marriage, and that one didn't turn out so well, either."

"Good point." Limos slipped on the bracelet, the garter, and put in the earrings. When she was done, she looked in the mirror for the first time since the other females had messed with her hair and makeup.

She nearly fainted.

"Are you okay?" Runa asked.

Limos's eyes stung. "I...I'm..."

"Beautiful," Idess finished.

"Yes." Limos's voice was little more than a whisper.

Human girls all over the world dreamed about their wedding day, spent years going over it in their heads. But Limos had spent *centuries* fantasizing about what she'd do if she were a normal woman, changing her ideas as trends came and went. Now, it was finally here. She felt beautiful, feminine, like the luckiest female ever.

Runa's cell rang, and she answered it, then returned to Limos. "That was Shade. He said everything's ready. We're supposed to arrive outside where you usually cast a gate."

Limos led them all outside, and even though her hand was shaking, Limos threw a gate, and then she, Runa, and Idess stepped through, coming out in the snowy courtyard in front of the entrance. Someone had erected a long tent and laid out a red carpet, along which a trail of candles lit the way to the front door.

"Wow," she said. "This is amazing." Thanatos and Ares approached, both in tuxes, and both grinning like fools.

"We'll be inside the house," Runa said. "Good luck."

The females hurried inside as Limos's brothers stopped in front of her.

"I've never seen anything so beautiful," Than said, going down on one knee to kiss her hand. He was always so formal.

Ares leaned over to kiss her lightly on the cheek. "You're stunning."

Limos had to choke back sobs. "Thank you." She cleared her throat of the hoarseness. "Who is escorting me?"

"We both are." They each held out their arms, and she took them, walking between her brothers toward the entrance of Than's keep.

When they stepped through, she stopped, momentarily in awe. The great room had been transformed into a true winter wonderland. The floor was strewn with fake snow and glitter. Lit Christmas trees filled the room, and huge bouquets of poinsettias, silver and white flowers, and sparkling baby's breath decorated tables loaded with food and drink. A champagne fountain gurgled near the far wall, and a huge fire roared in the hearth, its flames throwing a mix of colors, from the usual orange to blue, green, and purple.

And upon a makeshift stage in the very center of the room, were Idess and Arik. Limos's gaze locked with Arik's, and her heart fluttered. He was wearing a crisp, formal military uniform that perfectly suited his broad shoulders, deep chest, and slim waist. At his hip he wore a ceremonial black holster, but she doubted there was anything ceremonial about the pistol tucked inside. His long legs were spread slightly, his hands behind his back.

His intense gaze bored into her. Hunger gleamed in the hazel depths of his eyes, taking the breath right out of her lungs. She'd always found him to be handsome, had always seen the soldier in him. But now, as he watched her walk toward him she saw the whole, exquisite package— honorable soldier, powerful warrior, ferocious lover, heart-stoppingly gorgeous male.

"You sure about this?" Thanatos whispered in her ear, and as though Arik heard, he gave a single, slow nod.

If there had been any doubt before, it was gone.

"Yes," she whispered back. "I've never been so sure about anything."

Twenty-six

Regan hated weddings. Seriously hated them. Not only did she despise sitting through the boring-ass ceremony, she didn't understand the point of spending a ton of money, mostly on other people, when the money could be better spent on a down payment for a house or for the honeymoon. Why start off a marriage in debt?

Especially when most marriages ended in divorce anyway. At least if you spent the money on the honeymoon, you'd have several days in a place you probably loved, even if it was with the asshole you ended up divorcing.

People said she was cynical. A pessimist. She wasn't. She was a realist.

But in this case, not a lot of planning had gone into the event, and the Horsemen seemed to have money to burn, and Regan hadn't been required to dress up. Even better, this wasn't your usual wedding ceremony. This was more like a big party, with supernatural beings as guests.

The great hall had been turned into a fantasy, lit with a thousand candles, fir trees draped in lights and tinsel, and confetti splashed on tables and shelves. In the kitchen, Than's vampires and Ares and Limos's servants were preparing hors d'oeuvres for the reception, which really was going to be a liquor-and-food fest.

That was assuming that the ceremony went off without a hitch.

Though the pre-wedding mood had been mostly uplifting, there had been an undercurrent of worry—enough that Sin and Lore had used their contacts to hire an entire den of assassins to act as security, and Cara had enlisted the help of several hellhounds to patrol the grounds. Only one was inside—a floppy-eared drooly pup named Hal that was clumsier than a drunken, three-legged moose. And actually, he might be drunk; Regan had caught him twice with his nose in the champagne fountain.

Then there was Thanatos, who definitely wasn't drunk. The man was a study in grace and control as he stood near the stage where Limos and Arik were facing each other and saying their vows, his silky blond hair framing his angular face, the braids at the temple only adding to his savage handsomeness. His black tux stretched over thick shoulders and hugged his muscular butt and thighs in a fit so perfect it was clear the clothes had been tailored for him.

And with that gorgeous suit...he wore combat boots. Had he been anyone else, she'd have suspected he forgot to change his shoes, but no, not Thanatos. He was too detail-oriented and too careful. This was the man who, for hours prior to the ceremony, had prowled the keep like a tiger patrolling his territory, checking every nook and cranny twice, testing the guards' weapons, and seeming to make a point of ignoring Regan. How the hell was she supposed to seduce a guy who had avoided her since their encounter in the gym, as if she'd given him a disease?

Oh, she'd caught him staring at her, the banked heat in his gaze searing her skin, but a moment later, the cold indifference would return, and he'd turn away with an air of arrogant dismissal.

The man was a puzzle. A dangerous, sexy puzzle. Over the last few days, she'd come upon him reading next to the fire, his fingers caressing a book as if it were a lover. The next time she saw him, he might be armored and bloody, and the very air around him would crackle like a brewing storm. He wouldn't speak, never offered information freely, and his sense of humor was...odd.

Yes, Regan suffered from mild obsessive-compulsive issues, and she had a tendency to make sure all of the notes she took in his library were neatly arranged in stacks of twelve. But Than seemed to delight in moving a single page off one stack to another, just to drive her nuts. And she knew it was him, because the vampires denied touching her work, but the Horseman...he didn't deny it. He'd simply watch her rail, one corner of his made-to-make-women-wet mouth twitching in a half-smile.

Peeling her gaze away from him, she returned her eye to their surroundings, because despite the massive security, Regan didn't feel safe. Not when security was made up of demons, vampires, shapeshifters, and hellhounds. That was like, the *opposite* of safe for a Guardian. Someone tapped her on the shoulder, and she turned to find one of Thanatos's vampires, Atrius, standing there with a bottle of what looked like wine.

"This is very rare mead," he said. "Made by ex-monks

who used their mead-making knowledge and blended it with supernatural magic."

"And you're telling me this...why?"

"It's Thanatos's favorite."

She eyed him suspiciously. "And?"

"It's a gift," the vampire said. "A thank you for improving Thanatos's mood."

She was pretty sure her eyes bugged out. "He's been in a *better* mood since I arrived?" Jesus, what was he like when she *wasn't* around?

"His mood swings have been greater," the vampire admitted wryly, "but he's smiled more lately than he has since he lost Reseph."

"Huh. Okay, I guess."

The guy grinned like she'd opened a vein for him. "I'll put the wine in your bedroom. I would suggest, however, that you take no more than a couple of sips. It's too strong for humans."

"Thanks for the tip." She wasn't planning to drink any. He'd said the stuff was mixed with magic, and that could only be bad. But hey, if Thanatos liked it, he was welcome to it.

The vampire strode away, leaving her alone once again. *Alone* was something she was used to. *Alone* she liked.

Across the room, Thanatos turned, and his gaze drilled into her. All around them, people were laughing, hugging, holding hands. But not Thanatos. And not Regan.

In a room full of people, they were alone.

Good thing, she supposed, that she liked it.

The wedding was everything Limos had dreamed of. The funny thing was, as she stood before Arik in a room full of people and food and beautiful decorations, she didn't notice any of it. Arik was her entire focus, her entire world. She'd repeated the words Idess had prompted her to say, and so had Arik, but the words that filled her with gooey warmth were the ones Arik tacked on to Idess's mandatory, "I shall keep you as my wife, my mate, my desire."

Arik had lowered his voice at the end and added, "My *only* desire."

Idess reached for the athame and chalice on the altar next to her. With the ceremonial dagger, she sliced her thumb and caught the blood in the chalice.

"Hold out your hands." Gently, she repeated the ritual with Arik and Limos, then swiped each of their cuts with some sort of herbal leaf. She held up the chalice. "Your blood will bind you, and by the blood of an angel no more, you will be married. Wet your lips, and then speak true."

"Speak true?" Arik asked.

Idess inclined her head. "You must enter this union on a platform of truth. You will each reveal a secret of importance while your mate's blood is on your lips. The bigger the secret, the stronger the marriage bond. A lie will burn, but a truth will...you'll see. You may ask each other to divulge a specific truth, or you may choose to let the other decide for themselves what they want to reveal."

Oh...God. Anxiety shot through Limos, tendrils of stinging panic that disoriented her and nearly had her armoring up and drawing a sword to combat whatever invisible enemy was attacking her body like this. How could this be part of a wedding ceremony?

Arik took the cup and, without hesitation, put it to his lips, his eyes intense, smoky, like a burning forest. When he brought the chalice away from his mouth, his lips glistened crimson.

"A truth," he mused. "Is there anything you want to know?"

"The women," she blurted. "You haven't told me about them."

"That's because there are more than I'm proud of. And some...I don't even remember." An ache throbbed through her at Arik's words, adding another layer of misery to her anxiety. She shouldn't have asked. "Twenty, for sure, probably more. But I swear to you, there will never be another, and not one of those women could compare to you." His voice went husky with emotion. "So that answers your question, but there's something *I* want to tell you. I would let you take all those women from my memory if you wanted to. And that's the most honest thing I've ever said."

She nearly stopped breathing. That he would allow her to mess with his memories again, given how important *not* invading his mind was, was a huge admission of trust and commitment. Not that she would do it even if she could reach back that far and snip those threads. She would never touch his mind again. Her eyes stung, and emotion clogged her throat. How had she gotten so lucky with this man?

And dear God, how could she possibly ever deserve him?

He handed her the chalice, and her hands shook as she held it. He watched her expectantly. Everyone did. When the trembling grew so severe that she nearly dropped the chalice, Arik took her hands in his and gently guided the rim to her mouth.

"You can do this," he whispered.

Warm wetness touched her lips and tongue, and on her shoulder, both sides of her scales dipped wildly. "Arik," she rasped. "I...I..."

She should lie. Make something up. The compulsion to tell a whopper had her clenching her teeth. She wanted to lay the foundations for a strong bond, but so many people were around, and it was for them that she needed to spin a tale. She'd once stood before a crowd and fired them up with fantastic stories that had led to rebellion against their lord, every word making her drunk with pleasure. Even now, her breaths came faster, her blood flowed like a raging river, and lies swirled through her mind, fighting to be chosen—

"Hey." Arik's deep, soothing voice penetrated her panic, and she realized she'd been looking at everyone but him. "My eyes," he said. "Look at me. I'm right here."

As if she'd grabbed onto a lifeline, she clung to his gaze, letting everyone else fall away. *I can do this. For him, I can do anything.*

Still, nothing came. There were too many secrets to choose from, and all were so horrible and hurtful.

Arik knew...bless him, he knew, and he came to the rescue.

"Since this is our wedding, maybe you can stick it to your ex?" He waggled his brows, dragging a small smile from her. "Do you have a secret about you and him?"

Fear soured her mouth, because yeah, she had a secret she'd never wanted to reveal, but if she was ever going to do it, now was the time, and this was the perfect place.

"I went willingly to my betrothal." She cleared her throat. Her brothers' shocked stares burned holes in her, but she ignored them, keeping her focus on Arik and praying he wouldn't hate her for this admission. "I wanted to be Satan's bride, and if he'd have had me at the time, I'd have done it."

There. She'd said it. Her stomach was churning and her antiperspirant failing, but she'd done it. The silence in the room built as Arik stood there, stoic, his expression neutral.

"If you accept each others' truths," Idess said, "you may kiss."

The wait...oh, dear Lord, the wait. Limos thought her heart might explode, and then, unbelievably, Arik stepped into her and slowly, so slowly, touched his lips to hers. Their blood mingled, their tongues met, and a powerful, intense pleasure washed over them both. She knew he felt it too, because in that moment, it was as if they were one being, merged together in an almost orgasmic ecstasy.

Tingles spread through her feather-light body, and what was that saying...the truth shall set you free? Yes. She felt freer than she ever had, and as Arik's arms came around her, she felt safer too. Safe and wanted and free.

"Congratulations," Idess murmured. "You are married."

Arik never in a million years thought he'd be married. Or, more accurately, mated. Which, in the supernatural world, was a stronger bond than marriage, because generally, it was physical. The Sem brothers, for instance, couldn't get out of their bonds unless their mates died.

According to Idess, the same deal applied here, too. Hopefully, Limos wouldn't want a divorce anytime soon.

His body was on fire with pleasure as they stepped

down from the stage, and he wondered how long the sensation would last. The blood and truth ritual had been powerful on so many levels—uncomfortable, frightening and, in the end, freeing. He hadn't even known how much he trusted Limos until he'd voiced his truth, and when she'd come clean about her willing role in her betrothal, he'd experienced only pride that she'd trusted him with something that must have been a shameful stain on her soul.

People surrounded them, offering congratulations, hugs, and pats on the back. It seemed like everyone from Underworld General had come, and the marked absence of Arik's R-XR and Aegis colleagues gave him a moment of surreal clarity; his world truly had changed.

He did wish Ky and Decker had been able to make it, but they were dealing with yet another attack on an Aegis cell as well as a sudden outbreak of demon attacks on human hospitals. Pestilence was clearly trying to cripple humans' ability to repair the damage he was causing. The bastard.

Eventually, everyone moved off to dive into the food and drink, giving Thanatos and Ares a chance to accost them. Sudden tension rolled off Limos.

"Hey." She squeezed Arik's hand so hard he thought he heard his joints crack. "What I said during the ceremony—"

"It wasn't easy to hear," Than interrupted. "But we all have things in our pasts we aren't proud of. We can't hold something you did thousands of years ago against you."

Ares nodded. "You aren't the person you were in Sheoul. We love you no matter what, Limos."

Ares's words should have comforted Limos, but as her

brothers enveloped her in hugs, Arik caught a glimpse of
worry in her expression, a falter in her smile. But maybe
he imagined it, because by the time they sauntered off,
she was back to her playful self, going up on her toes and
putting her lips to Arik's ear.

"We could slip away to one of Than's empty rooms."

He groaned, and his cock twitched, and he was so on
board with that suggestion. Too bad everyone was watching them. "As much as I'd love to, I think people would
notice."

"So?"

"So...I happen to know how protective brothers
are—" he snared two flutes of champagne from a pass-
ing vamp with a tray "—and I don't want yours to kill me
for making your first time nothing more than a boff in a
closet."

"Boff?" Her laughter rang out, the beautiful sound
suiting her.

He handed her one of the glasses. "Yes, boff. And if
this doesn't work, I don't want everyone in the damned
building to hear me yell when my fingers are chopped
off." The idea settled his errant cock down, right quick.

"It's going to work," she said. "It better. I'm horny."

Arik choked on his champagne, then choked again
when Ares clapped him on the back a few times.

"You okay, man? No dying before you can get Limos
out of her chastity belt."

More choking. When had Ares developed a sense of
humor anyway?

"Agreed," Limos chirped. "I've been looking forward
to losing this hymen for five thousand years."

This time Arik didn't choke. He just stopped breathing.

Ares gripped his shoulder. "Maybe you two should get going."

Jesus. Ares was practically undressing Arik and shoving them toward a bedroom. "I, ah..."

"Until you two consummate your marriage, Limos is still under contract," Ares reminded them gravely.

As much as it was a relief to know Ares wasn't just anxious for his sister to get laid, the reality of the situation sucked. "We'll sneak away in a little while," Arik said. "This is Limos's party, and I want her to enjoy it."

Ares threw his arm around Limos and gave her a brotherly squeeze. "I think you did good with this human."

Limos grinned. "Duh."

Ares strode away, parting the crowd to get to Cara, who was scolding Hal for something. The hell mutt was looking at her with big, sad eyes, his ears drooping, but his tail was thumping on the floor. Arik hoped Cara knew she was being suckered.

"I'll be right back," Limos said, giving him a peck on the cheek. "I need to thank Idess and Runa for everything."

He watched her glide away, his fingers itching to let down the hair piled loosely on top of her head. The style was stunning on her, revealing her slim, shapely neck, but he wanted her hair down and her dress off, and soon. Really, seeing her naked would be worth a severed digit.

"Congrats." Regan sidled up next to him with a bottle of water in her hand. For some reason, she grimaced at his champagne. Maybe she didn't drink.

Maybe she was pregnant.

Oh, damn. Bile bubbled up in his throat. He'd just married Thanatos's sister, and he was sitting on a fucking huge-ass pile of information about him. He got why The Aegis felt they needed to do this, and he might have agreed with their save-the-world thinking not long ago. But what used to be black and white for him was now blended in sickly shades of gray, and his sense of fair play was screaming.

Thanatos deserved more than to be used as a breeding stud. He should have a choice about bringing a child into the world.

He lowered his voice. "Are you pregnant?"

She snorted. "That would require sex."

Thank God. "Don't do this, Regan. Go home, and forget The Aegis's plan for you."

"What's it matter to you?"

"I just married into this family. I can't keep something like this from my wife."

Regan pegged him with a hard stare. "See, this is why I'm never getting married. It takes away your independence and your ability to think for your own damned self."

He wasn't going to argue this, but he was going to make it very clear where he stood. "Leave here tonight, or I go to the Horsemen." Tomorrow he'd pay a visit to The Aegis and convince them that Thanatos needed to be included in this decision.

Regan's eyes blazed. "Fine. But you can explain to the Elders why I failed. And then you can explain to the entire world that the Apocalypse could have been prevented." She glanced at his glass and gave him an evil smile. "Enjoy your champagne." She stalked off, leaving him eyeing his drink and wondering why he felt like the joke was on him.

Whatever. The prickly Guardian wasn't going to fuck up his wedding day. He found Limos, who drained her champagne, tossed the glass into the fire, shattering it, and then let out a loud whoop. All around, the room erupted in cheers and dancing. Limos grabbed his hand and dragged him into a semiprivate alcove.

"You little minx," he said, when he realized what she'd done. "You distracted all of them."

"Yup." She cupped the back of his head and drew him down for a kiss. Her tongue was hot, her mouth wet, and in two heartbeats he was so into it that he had her pushed up against the wall. She purred her approval and wound her arms around his neck. He let his hands drift down her sides to her hips as he licked and nibbled at her lips.

God, she felt good, and when she arched, pressing her breasts into his chest, he was lost to sensation.

Lost to *her*.

"I love you," he whispered, and his heart nearly stopped when she froze.

"What did you say?"

Shit. He'd just ruined everything, hadn't he? Well, there was no backtracking now. "I love you. I'm not sure when it happened, but it did, and I'm not sorry."

She closed her eyes, and when she opened them, they glowed with a liquid purple light. "I never thought I'd hear anyone say that." Her fingers threaded through his hair, clutching tightly. "I love you too, Arik. Also," she said, "I want kids."

"*Now?*"

"Yes." She shook her head. "I mean... my biological clock has been ticking for five thousand years. Human women think *they* have it bad. But it wouldn't be smart.

Not until the threat from Pestilence is over. The worst thing I can imagine is to be pregnant and have my Seal break. But yes, I do want them, so we should practice. Lots."

He swallowed over and over, until he felt like he could speak without sounding like a big sissy. "I think," he breathed, "it's time to go home."

With a wicked grin, she dropped her hand to his crotch to stroke his straining erection through his pants. "Do you think you can make it?"

"Not if you keep that up."

Her hands came back up his shoulders. "I can't wait to make love to you," she murmured. "I've waited so long, and now I'm glad I did. I'm so glad it'll be you, Arik."

She couldn't have said anything better. Taking her hand, he led her out of the cove. They slipped through the crowd and out the front door unseen, but as they exited through the tent, Ares's voice rang out.

"You thought you could sneak away, huh?"

"That was the plan," Arik muttered, and then they were engulfed in Horsemen arms. Thanatos and Ares grabbed them both in a bear hug.

"Come by in the morning," Ares said. "I have a feeling the underworld's going to be buzzing."

"No doubt," Than added. "Stay out of trouble."

"Our sister has never been good at that," a voice called out.

Arik and Limos whirled as Pestilence stepped out of the darkness.

Twenty-seven

Leave it to Pestilence to ruin Limos's wedding night, and as he came closer, gripping a sword in one hand and a hellhound head in another, her stomach dropped to her toes. Arik tugged her close, putting one leg in front of hers in a subtle, protective blocking stance.

Pestilence plopped the severed head into the snow, the blood creating a grotesque slush around it. "Don't worry, your guards aren't all dead. Just drawn off by my minions."

"What are you doing here?" Than growled. He'd armored up, and so had Ares.

"I was hurt that I wasn't invited to the wedding." Pestilence sheathed his sword, the clang of his armor ringing out in the frosty night air. "But I brought a gift anyway."

Limos gripped Arik's hand tight. "We don't want anything from you."

"It's not for you, dear sister." Pestilence's toothy grin

was the very definition of evil. "It's for Arik. Keeping in the theme of the wedding, I brought you the gift of truth."

Limos's vision blurred with alarm as she pulled on Arik and prepared to throw a gate. "Come on. We're leaving."

"You're not going anywhere." Pestilence kicked the hellhound head, and it slammed into Limos's gown, splattering blood all over the beautiful, satiny fabric.

"You bastard." Arik lunged, and Limos, reeling with shock, couldn't stop him.

Thankfully, Thanatos caught Arik around the waist. "Dial it back, bro. He's not worth it."

"Don't worry. I don't plan to kill Arik until he hears what I came here for." Pestilence's fangs glinted like icicles in the darkness. "Limos, tell your new mate and our brothers the truth about your *escape* from Sheoul."

"Reseph, no." Limos swallowed the lump of *oh-shit* in her throat. "Please, don't do this."

She could have sworn she saw something familiar, something regretful, in Pestilence's icy blues, but then it didn't matter, because while Ares didn't lower his blade, he did glance at Limos. "What's he talking about?"

"It doesn't matter." Suddenly chilled, she rubbed her arms and looked between her brothers. "Let this go. Don't listen to him."

"Trust me," Pestilence said. "You want to hear this."

Anxiety spiked, and she put her hands together in desperation. "I'm begging you, brothers. Go back inside and pretend Pestilence was never here." She moved forward, her high heels punching through ice softened by hellhound blood. "You said you love me no matter what, so this isn't important. Please. Go inside."

Silence stretched. Ares and Than exchanged glances,

and then Thanatos released Arik, who was still staring daggers at Pestilence, and Ares sheathed his sword.

"Get the hell out of here, Pestilence." Thanatos strode up to their brother and got so close their armor clanked and their noses almost touched. A breeze whipped their hair until it obscured their faces and mingled strands, pale, warm blond tangling with cold platinum. "Limos is our sister, but you are no longer our brother, and you've fucked with us one too many times."

Another flash of pain sparked in Pestilence's eyes, and he hissed. "I haven't even *begun* to fuck with you." He grabbed the back of Thanatos's head and smashed their foreheads together so hard that the crack of skulls echoed deep into the night air.

Than snarled in outrage, and they went down into the snow and ice, fists flying. Ares and Arik went after Pestilence, but the bastard slashed out with a blade, catching Than in the cheek as he rolled to his feet.

"You know who has fucked with you?" Pestilence snapped. "Your sweet, virginal sister. She didn't *escape* Sheoul. She sent the demons who attacked us in the first place, and then she found us, lied about escaping, and convinced us to start the war."

Thanatos remained sitting on the ground, blood running from his cheek and mouth. "Li? You wanna tell this douchebag he's full of shit?"

"That would make me a colostomy bag, moron," Pestilence chimed in, reminding her so much of Reseph that her eyes stung.

But yes, she did want to tell her brothers that Pestilence was full of shit. The compulsion to lie was so strong that the evil side of her scales dipped low. She slid her gaze to Arik, who was looking at her as if he fully expected her to explain this all away as a big misunderstanding. He moved toward her, but she stepped back, unable to take comfort from him, not when she didn't deserve it.

"Limos?" This time, Than's voice was clipped, threaded with fear. "*Say he's lying.*"

"Can't," she rasped.

Ares let out a nasty snarl. "Who forced you? What were you threatened with?"

"You think she was coerced?" Pestilence laughed. "Of course you would. Limos would never betray us like that on her own." He cocked a blond brow at her. "Go ahead. Explain, little sister. Queen of the Underworld."

"Shut the fuck up." Again, Arik went for Pestilence, and this time, it was she who prevented him from doing something he might not live to regret. When she grabbed his arm, he settled down, though he angled his body so that any move Pestilence made against her would catch him first.

God, she did not deserve him.

"Limos," Ares said quietly. "Explain." The word was no less of a command for the soft tone, and she gulped some air like it was made of courage.

"I was raised to be a demon," she began in a shaky voice. "You know that. But what you don't know is that I was treated like a princess. I...we...were all part of a plan. From the very beginning, maybe from our conception, Lilith and Satan planned to use us to bring destruction upon the human race." Her muscles twitched as she forced out the next bit of information. "So when the time was right, I was sent aboveground to study you. To find your weaknesses."

"You spied on us?" Ares asked.

She nodded. "For a year. You never saw me, never knew I was there."

A dark shadow passed over Ares's face, turning his expression to stone. "And what, exactly, did you learn?"

"That your weakness was your loved ones and your arrogance in thinking you could protect them. Than, yours was your peace-loving nature. Reseph, yours was your inability to focus on anything."

Ares had gone steel-rod taut, and she knew he'd arrived at the end of her story before she'd even gotten through the middle. "Go on." His voice was dead. And to him, she probably was too. But he and Than had said they loved her no matter what, and she had to cling to his words. "What did you do after you learned what you needed to?"

"I went back to Sheoul, and it was decided that it was time to bring you into our fold."

"Jesus." Thanatos jammed his hands through his hair. "What did you do?"

Her throat closed up. The rest of her story only got worse from here.

"She sent demons to attack us." Pestilence filled in the blanks, his voice so thick with loathing that she knew Reseph was in there somewhere, hating her for what she'd done to him. "She sent the demons to wreak havoc on humans. And then, when things were at their worst, she made herself known to us. She pretended she'd escaped from a hellish existence to find us and tell us the truth about what we were."

Ares's eyes became black lasers that lit on her the way they fixed on his enemies. "The demons that tortured and killed my wife... *you* sent them." It wasn't a question. Ares knew. He just wanted her to say it.

She wanted to throw up. "Listen to me, Ares—"

"*Answer me, damn you.*"

Every instinct screamed for her to lie, but if there was any hope of salvaging a relationship with her brothers, she had to make them understand why she'd done what she'd done. To make them realize that if she could take it back, she would. In a heartbeat. No matter what it cost her.

"My job was to encourage you to war against the demons, to bring humans into it in order to destroy them." Hysteria had started to lace her voice, and she fought to keep from losing it. "How I got you to do it didn't matter. The more pain you experienced, the deeper your hatred for demons would be. And once you were corrupted by hate and self-loathing, it would be easy to bring out your demon sides."

"My wife died at *your* order," Ares snarled. "What about my sons? Did you plan to kill them too?"

"You sent them away before that could happen," she croaked. "But I didn't want them dead, Ares. I swear."

Pestilence barked out a laugh. "Only because as Ares's offspring, they were potentially powerful."

True. They could have been useful as they grew. Unfortunately, they became casualties of the demon war, so yes, she was responsible, if indirectly. She risked a glance at Arik, who stared at her in stunned silence. Shame constricted her chest, and when she looked at her brothers, the loathing and disappointment in their eyes constricted everything else.

"The demons slaughtered most of my family," Thanatos said, his voice so icy she shivered. "I watched almost my entire tribe be torn apart by Soulshredders. Do you know how they kill, Limos?" Leaping to his feet, he seized her by the beautiful pearl collar of her ruined dress and got right in her face. "*Do you?*"

Yes, she did, but before she could reply, Arik was there, shoving his muscular arm between her and Than.

"Back off, Horseman."

Than's voice was an avalanche rumble. "This isn't your concern, human."

"It became my concern about an hour ago, when I drank her blood from a cup." Arik said. "So back the fuck off. Now."

No one was more shocked than she was when Thanatos released her. But he wasn't done with her. Not by a long shot.

"That reminds me," Pestilence said casually. "I've released thousands of Soulshredders in the human realm. Things are going to get real fun, real soon."

Ares jabbed a finger at Pestilence. "We'll deal with you later." He turned back to Limos. "But *you*." He practically spat "you" at her. "You're as bad as he is. At least Pestilence has the excuse of a broken Seal."

Her eyes burned with unshed tears. "You said you loved me no matter what. You said you couldn't hold what I did thousands of years ago against me—"

"That was before I knew you are responsible for the deaths of everyone I loved," he roared. Ares's hatred lanced her so fiercely that she stumbled backward, pain radiating through her chest.

"Did you know how Heaven would react?" Thanatos demanded. "Did you know angels would be sent to punish and curse us as Horsemen?"

"No," she rasped. "That wasn't part of the plan. You were to be my wedding gift to Satan." Her fingers flexed at her sides. "Before we were even born, he'd foreseen that we would play a role in the Apocalypse, but he didn't know how. So I was to bring you to him. But I was too slow. Lucifer warned me that Heaven would only tolerate so many human casualties before they took action. I miscalculated, and before I could take you to Sheoul, angels interfered and we were all cursed by them to be Horsemen."

She'd paid for her failure in blood. After two months of torture, she'd been sent back to the human realm to make up for her mistake.

"Tell them the rest." Pestilence folded his arms over his broad chest, the metal clanking loudly in the cold night air. "Tell them how you worked against us for hundreds of years to break my Seal. And tell them how you were responsible for stealing Deliverance from The Aegis, not because you didn't trust The Aegis to keep it safe, but so you could destroy it and prevent Ares or Thanatos from killing me if my Seal broke." Pestilence bared his fangs in a diabolical smile. "The best part of all of this? She killed Sartael to shut him up, isn't that right? You thought he was the one person who could find your *agimortus*, but you were willing to give that up just to protect your piece of shit self. You pissed off the wrong person, Limos. Sartael was Lucifer's pet, and Lucifer's sworn to take out his fury on all of you. So not only did Limos ruin your old lives, she's going to fuck the shit out of your current ones, as well."

"*Limos.*" Ares's big body trembled with the kind of rage she rarely saw—and she'd seen him murderously angry. "You lying, scheming spawn of hell."

Agony fisted her heart, so powerful she cried out. "Ares, please—"

"Please?" Pestilence spat. "You should be Satan's whore. Not the human's. The Dark Lord would give you the pain you deserve—"

Rapidfire gunshots rang out, and the top half of Pestilence's head exploded in a grotesque rain of bone, blood, and brains.

"Christ," Arik said calmly, as he holstered his weapon. "Do you ever shut the fuck up?"

Pestilence fell backward into the blood-soaked snow, but even as he landed, he opened a gate and hurled his destroyed body through it.

Limos looked over at Arik, who stared at her as if he didn't know her at all. Anguish squeezed the blood right out of her heart. "I'm sorry, Arik."

"Oh, Limos," he murmured. "What have you done?"

Twenty-eight

The rumble started first. Then the confused expressions.

"Oh, Jesus," Arik said. "Oh, fuck, I said your name."
*While he hadn't been in misery, exactly, it was fair to say
he was pained by what had gone down.* Damn it to hell,
Limos had gotten him to say her name with a freaking
apology, when some of the nastiest, most vicious demons
in the underworld couldn't do it with torture.

Ares had reminded them that her contract with Satan
wasn't broken until they'd consummated the marriage,
and now they were screwed.

"We gotta go!" Limos opened a Harrowgate just as the
biggest, ugliest beast Arik had ever seen bashed up out of
the ice-covered ground. Chunks of frozen earth and ice
the size of train cars tumbled through the air and crashed
all around them. From inside the keep, the partygoers ran
out, prepared to fight.

"Go!" Than shot Arik a *do it* look, and he nodded, dragging Limos through the portal.

They stepped out in a strange living room decorated like a beach house. "Where are we?"

"My second Hawaiian villa. I wasn't thinking. I just... I had to get us somewhere." She swallowed. "Arik, I'm sorry—"

"*Sorry?* You lied to me, betrayed your brothers, got their families killed, and you're *sorry*?"

The floor shook and bucked as she gripped his shirt collar. "Please, Arik, I swear, I meant to tell you..." It felt as if the entire island was rocking, like a lid on top of a boiling pot.

Arik's adrenaline and sense of self-preservation kicked into high gear. "Doesn't matter. I have to fuck you. Now." Yup, that was *all* kinds of sexy.

Limos didn't hesitate. Reaching up, she tore her bloody gown from the neck to the hem, ripping it in half. Arik's breath caught at the sight he was left with, of her in a white, lacy bra, the pearly belt, and thigh-high white stockings. She wore a white garter, which rimmed the tip of one of the stockings mid-thigh.

If things were different, meaning he wasn't pissed as hell and they didn't have the king of all demons after them, he'd strip everything else off with his teeth.

A horrifying howl rent the air, and the wall behind him exploded inward. Screaming, Limos opened a gate and dragged him through it. They landed in what appeared to be a jungle, damp, dripping, animals screeching. Limos spun toward him.

"Hurry," she breathed.

Man, talk about pressure. He was supposed to get it up

while demon hordes were trying to kill him, and Satan himself was knocking at the door.

But then Limos dropped to the ground and reached up for him to join her.

In the distance, the rumble started up again.

"Arik." Limos's violet eyes were pleading. "He's coming for me."

As pissed as he was, as hurt as he was, he still loved her. He wasn't going to let her be taken. Dropping to his knees, he reached for the chastity pearls, hesitating a centimeter away. "If this doesn't work—"

"It will," she swore.

"If it doesn't..." He inhaled a ragged breath. "If it doesn't, I'm sorry."

A single tear formed in the corner of her eye and dripped down her cheek. "I'm sorry too."

Steeling himself, his ears vibrating at what sounded like a freight train bearing down on them, he wrapped his hand around her chastity belt.

And nothing happened.

"Holy shit," she breathed. "It worked. Break it!"

Adding another hand, he gripped the fine chain, amazed that something so delicate could have been so strong and deadly, and he yanked it apart. Tiny little pearls flew everywhere, raining down on the lush jungle floor.

"Please, Arik. Now."

He looked down and swore. He wasn't hard. This was not going to fucking work. But then Limos sat up and took him in her palm. Before he could suck in a breath, her mouth was on him, her tongue lashing at the head of his cock, and despite the earthquake that was growing more intense all around them, arousal stirred.

He'd always heard that danger was an aphrodisiac, and as it turned out, it was true. Adrenaline surging, his body went safety-off, gunning for action. His blood was hot, and Limos's mouth was silken magic.

A tree only yards away came down with a crash, and a godawful roar rang out. Despite the fact that he wasn't fully erect, he pushed Limos down on the ground and cupped her core, sliding his finger along her slit. Shit. They didn't even have time to get her wet.

A snarl ripped through the air, and he swore he felt warm, rancid breath on his cheek.

"Do it!"

He punched his hips forward and entered her in one stroke. Her barrier gave way, and he sank against her, holding her so tight he doubted she could breathe. They were both shaking, and in his hand was the dagger he'd strapped to his ankle before the wedding. He didn't even remember grabbing it, but he was ready to use it. No one, not even the devil himself, was going to take Limos without a fight.

There was a distant, horrifyingly angry screech, and then the rumble stopped. The jungle went silent, and the only sounds Arik could hear were his panting breaths and the pound of his pulse in his ears.

Carefully, because every muscle in his body had gone rubbery, he pushed off Limos.

She grasped his biceps, her bright pink nails digging into his skin. "Arik, please..."

"I can't." He stood, buttoned his pants, and shrugged out of his uniform jacket. After helping her to her feet, he wrapped her in his coat. Wasn't he just the gentleman. Pissed as he was, he didn't want her to feel exposed.

Fucking idiot.

A trickle of blood ran down the inside of her leg, and she looked down, confused. "Somehow, I didn't think that would happen to me."

The vulnerability in her voice took his fury down a notch, and had this been any other situation, he'd have pulled her into his arms. "Make a gate and get us out of here."

Limos's shoulders slumped. She said nothing, merely opened a gate, and they stepped through, coming out at her primary residence. One of her guards waved and averted his eyes when he noticed that Arik's coat didn't quite cover everything. Silently, they went to her bedroom, where she disappeared into the bathroom. He sank down on the bed next to a pink and white box.

Curious, he pried off the lid and lifted the tissue paper away. Inside was the sexiest lingerie he'd ever seen. A sheer, black babydoll top with half-cups designed to show nipple, blinged-out straps studded with what looked like tiny diamonds, and hot pink lace stitched around the edges. A matching black string bikini sat at the bottom of the box, and with it, a pair of lacy black thigh-highs.

It was every man's wet dream.

"That was for our wedding night," Limos said from behind him. He hadn't even heard her come out of the bathroom.

He didn't look back at her. "Guess it didn't go exactly as planned."

"Yeah. It's silly, but all I wanted was a beautiful human wedding." Her voice held a tremor...barely noticeable, but Arik knew her well enough now to recognize the emotional warble. "You know, like a normal girl. Not some horrible demon."

His fist tightened reflexively on the lingerie, crushing it, just like her dream of a perfect wedding. How could he hurt for her so much, and yet, be so goddamned angry?

"You're neither, Limos." He heard her sniffle, and he finally shifted on the bed to look at her and nearly revised his last statement, because she certainly looked like a normal girl right about now.

She was wearing the fluffy pink robe that wrapped her from head to toe. Her hair was dripping wet, her makeup gone, and her gorgeous eyes were swollen and red-rimmed. What was it with women crying in the shower? He remembered his mom and sister doing the same thing. They'd denied it, but he wasn't stupid, and sometimes he'd hear the sobs over the sound of the water.

He'd been so helpless back then, but never again. It went against his nature to let a female suffer, and he came to his feet to move to her.

He'd only gone two steps when the door burst open and Ares strode inside, his expression a black cloud. He sized the situation up in a heartbeat, knew the threat to Limos had passed.

At least, the threat to her from the underworld had passed. The threat from Ares was still on the table, and Arik moved to intercept.

"Let's give this some time," he began, but Ares cut him off with a snarl.

"Time? She had five thousand years of time to come clean."

"Ares." Limos's voice was desperate. "Listen to me—"

"I've done enough listening!" Ares moved forward, and Arik met the big guy head on.

"Don't, Horseman. Not another step. I suggest you

leave now." He waited, chest to chest with Ares, aggression winging through the two inches of air between their noses.

Arik had no doubt he was going to be beaten to a pulp, but hell if he wouldn't cause some damage before he went down.

Ares bared his teeth, and a low, animal growl rumbled in his chest. "She's my sister. I'll handle this."

"She's my *wife*," Arik shot back. "Husband trumps the brother card. So get the fuck out and don't come back until you have your temper under control."

A tense heartbeat passed. Then two. Then about a million, and just as Arik thought he might as well throw the first punch and get the party started, Ares gave a curt nod.

"I'll go because I respect you, human. What you've done for us can't be repaid." His black gaze shifted to Limos. "But this isn't over."

Ares left, and Arik swore the entire island sighed in relief.

Limos's hand came down on his shoulder. "Do you hate me?"

Closing his eyes, he turned into her. "No." He folded her into his arms, his anger ebbing as his adrenaline crashed. "I hate that you lied to your brothers for so long, but I don't hate you." He pressed a kiss into her hair. "For what it's worth, I don't think your brothers hate you either."

A shudder shook her frame, a reminder that for all the power she carried in that body, she was still vulnerable to pain, and right now, she was as emotionally fragile as she'd probably ever been. The desire to fix this made his heart ache. Give him a disassembled M-16 or a Humvee engine on the fritz, and he knew what to do.

A broken female left him with that awful feeling of helplessness...and a primal desire to kill whoever had hurt her. Unfortunately, her brothers had the immortality thing going for them.

Her arms wound around his waist, and she buried her face against his neck. "Make love to me, Arik. Make all of this go away."

That, he could do. No, nothing could make what had happened tonight go completely away, but he could distract her for a little while.

Finally feeling like he could help her, he let his hands drift down the back of her robe, caressing, easing the tension out of her muscles. Slowly, she began to respond, kissing his throat, pressing her full breasts against his chest.

"Oh, yeah," he murmured, his body coming alive a lot faster than he'd expected. But he should have known better, given that Limos had a way of turning him into a live wire from nothing more than a sultry look.

She gazed up at him, her eyes darkening to a rich, smooth amethyst. "Touch me." Her words were both a command and a plea, and hell, yes, he was going to touch her. And taste her.

He held her with his gaze as he smoothed his hands around to the front of her robe and untied it. The sash fell away, and the fabric parted. Her magnificent body was exposed, ripe, waiting to be plucked and eaten like a juicy peach. His mouth actually watered.

Arousal tested his patience, because as much as he wanted to drop to his knees and use his tongue to make her scream, he was going to do this right. He was going to worship her body and make it last.

Leaning in, he kissed each shoulder as he pushed the robe down. It pooled on the floor, and he kicked it away so nothing was touching her creamy skin except her Seal and *agimortus* pendants.

When he brought his hand down to cup one breast, she gasped his name and threw her head back. He seized the opportunity to ravage her neck with kisses as he stroked her. Her long, lean body was the definition of elegance, the perfect blend of hard and soft, and in moments, he forgot the whole, *make it last*, thing, because he found himself rubbing against her, straining, mating with her even with all his clothes on.

A sudden pounding on the door had him wheeling around in a snarl. "Dammit, Ares, I fucking told you—"

"Limos!" The unhinged voice didn't belong to any of her brothers, and she scrambled to throw on her robe.

"What is it, Kaholo?" She whipped open the door. One of her servants stood there in the doorway, his hands covered in blood.

"It's Hekili," he said roughly. "He's been...butchered. There's a message for you. Lucifer...he said that you took his pet, so he took yours."

Twenty-nine

Ares couldn't remember the last time he'd been this angry or hurt. Oh, he'd been murderously furious at Pestilence when he'd captured Cara and meant to torture her to death, but this was different. Ares didn't want to kill Limos. He wasn't sure what he wanted to do, but right now it was taking every ounce of restraint he had to keep from going on a rampage. There were battles all over the world to join. He wouldn't take sides—he'd just fight. And kill.

He gated himself back to Thanatos's place, and wasn't at all surprised to find that all the wedding guests had gone.

Cara approached him as he crossed the great room toward Than. "Everyone left out of respect for you and Than, but they want you to contact them if you need anything. Are you okay?" Her sea-green eyes were dark with worry, and her concern helped level him out. She didn't deserve to feel the weight of his fury.

But she didn't deserve to be lied to, either. Clearly, there had been way too much of that going on for way too long. "I don't know," he admitted. "What Limos did was—"

"What she'd been raised to do."

He jerked. "You're defending her? She's the reason my family was killed. She stole Deliverance and conspired to break our Seals. She betrayed us all."

"I'm not defending what she did." Cara laid her hand on his chest, which always had a calming effect on him, even through his armor...but then, her very presence turned the hard leather to soft doeskin, so he could feel her touch right through it. "But keep in mind where she grew up and who raised her. She didn't know any better."

"She still should have told us before this."

"I'm sure she's regretting that decision." She went up on her toes and pecked him on the lips. "We should go. It's time for Rath's feeding."

"Give me a second to talk to Than." He pulled her close, needing the brief, full-body contact for just a second. "I'm sorry about the hellhound Pestilence killed."

"I am too," she murmured. "But I'm glad everyone else is safe. Tonight could have gone a whole lot worse."

Ares didn't tell her he had a feeling the "worse" was coming. Maybe not tonight, but soon.

He left her to help Than's vampire staff with cleanup, and joined his brother at the hearth, where he was standing very still, head bowed, doing his best to keep himself under control.

"I'm guessing Arik was successful in freeing Limos?" Than's voice was icy cold and as calm as the ocean before a storm, and Ares's hackles raised.

"It appeared so."

Thanatos peered into the fire, the flames dancing in his eyes. "Losing Reseph was hard. But the things he's done since his Seal broke have been because he isn't himself." Around his feet, the shadows began to swirl. "But with Li...she did what she did with no broken Seal. Because of her, we suffered the curses. And now we could have Lucifer up our asses because she killed Sartael. How the fuck are we supposed to deal with that?"

"I don't know, brother. But for now, we have to stay level."

Now there was hypocrisy at its finest, given how Ares had stormed into Limos's bedroom, hoping she'd arm up and give him a good battle. Fortunately, she'd mated a decent, honorable male who had talked some sense into Ares.

The veins in Than's temples throbbed, and his voice scraped gravel. "I'm not sure I can do that right now."

Shit. That left them with only one option; brace for impact. "Cara said everyone's gone. It's just your vamps, so you don't have to worry if you go nuclear. I'll make sure my Ramreels and Cara's hounds are gone too."

Than nodded, and Ares knew better than to stick around. He found Cara and headed outside to open a gate. It really sucked how their run of good luck had turned to utter disaster. And as he glanced back at Thanatos, he couldn't shake the feeling that the disasters were just beginning.

They found Hekili in the cellar, and Limos, who had seen every atrocity possible, who had grown desensitized to violence, reeled in shock. He truly had been butchered as if he were a cow in a slaughterhouse, and she had no doubt he'd been alive when the cutting began.

She didn't know if she'd have reacted the same way to his gruesome death before she'd let Arik into her life, but it didn't matter. The fact was that she'd liked the warg, had trusted him, and he'd died because of her.

He'd died in part because of her lies...lies she'd tried to protect by killing Sartael. And by killing Sartael, she'd enraged Lucifer, who would stop at nothing to hurt her and everyone around her.

Arik tried to pull her into his arms as they stood in the dark, dank cellar beneath her kitchen, and there was nothing she wanted more.

But she avoided his embrace, certain she'd lose her resolve if he caged her in his strong arms.

"Limos?"

"Don't." She darted up the steps and blew through the kitchen and out the front door. Arik followed, but she wouldn't let him close. "Don't touch me."

He stood in the light of the moon, his dogtags glinting on his bare chest as if beckoning her. They'd been her comfort when he'd been in Sheoul, and now she hoped they'd be his. "Sweetheart, what's going on?"

"I made a huge mistake, Arik." She wrapped her arms around her middle, trying to hold herself together. Funny how she'd calmly dressed in shorts and a tank top after being told about Hekili, but now she was ready to come apart at the seams. "I've let what I *want* to be, a woman, a wife, a mother, overshadow what I *need* to be."

"What are you talking about?" He moved forward, his bare feet sinking in the sand, but she stepped back.

"I've been a fool, hoping for what I can never have. I'm a Horseman of the Apocalypse. Half demon, half angel. All warrior who is meant for nothing but fighting."

The lean angle of his jaw became a knife blade as his expression grew fierce. "You are all of those things and more. You are a beautiful woman, a wife, and we'll make you a mother. Until then, we'll fight together—"

"*No.*" She bit back a cry at what he'd just said. She wanted those things so much, but it was just a fantasy. "We won't. It's over, Arik. Divorce isn't possible for us, but separation is."

His head rocked back as if she'd slapped him. "You don't mean that."

"I do. You're in danger because of me. You'll always be in danger. If not from Pestilence, then from Lucifer. They'll kill you to hurt me. I can't live with that, Arik. I won't."

"Dammit, Limos, it's my choice to be with you. I'm willing to live with the danger."

Of course he was. He was braver than anyone she'd ever met. But he was mortal, and bravery got more men killed than cowardice.

"I'm not."

He ground his teeth so hard she could hear the scrape of enamel. "I don't care. We're married. That means I don't walk away at the first little fight we have. And trust me, this barely counts as a fight. Get drunk, beat the shit out of everyone around you, and tell me you fucked a few neighbors, and then we'll talk."

His father was so lucky he was dead, because at this moment, she'd hunt him down and kill him for planting that kind of memory in Arik's head.

Then it occurred to her that she had to go just as far now, or Arik would never give up on them. She might hate herself for doing this, but at least he'd be alive.

She inhaled deeply, preparing to throw a punch that was going to knock him down. "If you don't accept my decision, I can *make* you accept it. I'll get in your head and do some creative work so you think our breakup is your choice, not mine. Is that what you want?" Her ability wasn't that extensive, but hopefully Arik didn't know that.

He paled, and Limos's chest broke wide open. "You wouldn't. You swore—"

"I lied." Steeling herself against his anger and disappointment, she shrugged. "You should be used to that by now."

"Limos..." His voice cracked, and it dawned on her that he'd avoided saying her name for so long, and now he used it over and over in this conversation, as if using it as a lifeline. "Don't do this. I love you. You love me."

And now for the knockout blow. "That," she said, reaching deep into the Limos she used to be, the Limos who enjoyed being a demon, "was a lie too."

Heart wrenching, she threw a gate and left Arik alone on the beach.

Thirty

Regan hadn't left when everyone else had.

Arik had told her to go, but she wasn't a quitter, and what happened tonight only strengthened her resolve. Some big, bad evil had gone through like a tornado, tearing up the ground outside and completely destroying two outbuildings. A number of the demon guards had been slaughtered, either by Pestilence or by the gargantuan thing, and Regan's mission had been clearer than ever.

The demons had to be stopped, the Apocalypse turned back. And if it took a Horseman's kid to do it, so be it.

While she waited for the last of the wedding guests to leave, she patrolled the grounds. Bundled in her parka, a stang in her gloved hand, she studied footprints and the bloodstains in the snow where demons had died. She'd encountered a lot of demons in her life, but some of the tracks she found were new to her, and some of them, like the Godzilla-sized one thirty yards from the keep, left her shaken. Regular-sized demons were hard enough to fight. How would humans fare against monsters as tall as twenty-story buildings?

Tired and shivering, she finally went back inside, but as she entered the great room, the sensation of being watched froze her mid-stride. Her pulse pounded in her ears as she swiveled her head toward the big warrior standing in front of the fire.

His merciless gaze was trained on her, flickering with cold death. All around him shadows swirled, turning his white bone armor gray and moving faster and faster as she watched. Her dark gift reared up, tapping against her skull as if wanting out.

Stay calm…must…stay…calm.

In horrifying slow motion, the shadows formed mouths and eyes, and then suddenly, one shot toward her.

A scream escaped her as she whirled and sprinted toward her bedroom, but the thing hit her from behind, sending her sprawling on the stone floor. Pain, as if a million tiny needles were being jammed all the way to the bone, became the air she breathed. Something seemed to reach inside her, and she swore she felt an icy hand close around her heart. A tugging sensation joined the pain, and holy shit, now she knew how it felt to be skinned alive, to have an essential part of you peeled away from other essential parts.

The thing was ripping her soul right out of her body.

All her training, all her discipline, went out the window, and she unleashed her gift. Her body vibrated, and light spilled from her, seeping from her very pores, until she was blinded from the white flash. The pain dissolved as a coil of living light extracted the invading shadow from her body.

Thanatos burst around the corner and skidded to a halt, his eyes wide. More shadows tore away from him and attacked the light. The ball of dark and light writhed, tangled in the air, and then, gradually, the shadows swallowed the glow.

Regan didn't wait around to see what would happen next.

On legs so wobbly they could hardly bear her weight, she stumbled into the bedroom and slammed the door. His vamp servants had started a fire in the hearth, but the room was cold, which didn't help the shakes that wracked her body as she collapsed against the dresser, nearly knocking over a bottle of mead and two glasses sitting on a tray.

Mead . . . *yes*. Alcohol sounded like a really good idea. Her trembling fingers knocked over one of the glasses, but somehow she caught it before it hit the floor. The door opened, and she did her best to not shake even harder as Than walked in and gently took the glass from her.

She couldn't look at him, couldn't let him see in her eyes how terrified she was at the close call she'd just had. As a Guardian, she'd been in more life-or-death situations than she could count, but this was the first time she'd actually felt herself dying.

Swallowing over and over, she pointed at the mead. "Open?"

"Damn," he murmured, as he popped the wax seal off the rim. "Where did you find this?"

"V-vampire," she said, hating herself for the stuttering.

A comforting gurgle and splash filled the room as he poured. Taking her hand, he placed the glass in her palm, wrapped her fingers around it, and guided the rim to her mouth.

"Drink," he said softly, tipping the glass as it touched her lips.

The red liquid, spicy and smooth, flooded her mouth like a balm, easing her nerves before she even swallowed. "Those...were your souls, right?"

"Yes." Thanatos stepped back with a glass of his own. He took two large drinks before saying, "When I'm angry, the souls that live inside my armor can break free. They want only one thing, and that's to kill."

"Why?"

"Because if they make a kill, they're freed from me."

She shuddered, remembering the pain as the thing tried to rip her apart from the inside. Was that what her victims experienced when she let loose her ability? Did they feel the living light tear the souls out of their bodies? She took another sip of her wine, and a tingly sensation joined the warmth spreading through her. "How do they get inside your armor?"

"Whenever I make a kill, the dead's soul is sucked into it." His voice was so casual it was chilling. She could barely talk about her own soul-sucking ability, and he might as well have been discussing grocery shopping. "Souls make my armor stronger."

"And they just hang out, waiting for you to get angry?"

"Or to be released. I can release them in battle to do my bidding."

Huh. "Sort of like those ghosts in the third Lord of the Rings movie? *The Return of the King*."

His smile was stunning, but his eyes were sad. "Something like that."

"How come they didn't all come out?"

"I wasn't fully enraged."

She shuddered. "I don't think I'd like to see that."

"No, you wouldn't." His blond brow lifted, the silver piercing glinting in the firelight. "You wanna tell me about your little surprise?"

Her glass froze before it touched her lips. "Not really."

A glistening drop of mead clung to his full lower lip, drawing her gaze and igniting a tiny flame of desire. The liquor, by itself, was bold and exotically spiced, but how much better would it taste if taken from Thanatos's lips? Her breath caught as his tongue swept it up. God, how could he make something so simple and normal seem so sexy?

"Ares would command you to talk," he mused. "Reseph would charm it out of you. Limos..." His voice took on a rough, serrated edge. "She'd annoy the hell out of you until you spilled just to shut her up."

"And you?"

His eyes gleamed. "I excel at torture."

Of course he did. Her hand drifted down to her coat pocket, where she'd tucked her stang. "Are you going to torture me?"

"Are you going to tell me what you are?" He put the glass to his lips and regarded her from over the rim. "And don't think your little Aegis weapon will be effective against me."

Little Aegis weapon? Arrogant ass. "I'm one-hundred percent human."

"A human with empathic abilities, I'd buy. A human who can communicate with the dead, I'd buy. But you have power over souls." He surged closer, no doubt in an attempt to intimidate her with his height and size. It might have worked if she wasn't buzzing from the wine.

As it was, her pulse fluttered madly, and she mentally urged him to come closer. "So I'm not buying the human thing."

"You want a DNA test? I'm human. My parents were both Guardians." Technically, that was true. At the time she'd been conceived, her father had been possessed by a demon, but the Horseman didn't need to know that.

"Is that so," he murmured, and that fast, the aura of anger and menace that had surrounded him shifted into something more pleasant but no less dangerous.

His fingers came up to his throat, and his armor disappeared, leaving him in the clothes he'd worn for the ceremony. The white shirt under the tux jacket was unbuttoned at the neck, and his scorpion tattoo peeked out, its pincers opening and closing.

She blinked, wondering if the wine was affecting her vision. "Your tattoos are special, aren't they?"

"All tattoos are special. People might get one on the spur of the moment, but everyone cares about the design they put on their body."

"No, I mean . . . they do something for you."

She thought he was going to clam up, but instead, he surprised her by shedding his jacket, somehow making the process tantalizing, an unintentional strip tease. He tossed the tux coat to the bed, and those long fingers went to his dress shirt. She couldn't look away as he unbuttoned it and then made the shirt join the jacket.

Man, oh, man. Didn't matter that she'd seen his bare upper body before . . . she didn't think she'd ever grow used to all that magnificent artwork. His Seal, mounted on a fine gold chain, lay flat between his pecs, perfectly outlined by a Celtic knotted tattoo.

"These are scenes taken out of my head and transferred to my skin."

"I knew that, but why?"

"How did you know?" He moved toward her, slowly, his gait rolling, and she got the sense she was being stalked.

The tingly feeling in her limbs spread, both energizing and relaxing her. "I saw it when I touched you before. I can read tattoos the way I can read ink on parchment."

The tingle turned into a pleasant burn unlike anything she'd ever felt. What had the vamp said about the wine? Magic. Right. No more for her.

Thanatos stopped when he was standing so close that she had to look up to see his face. "Can you control your empathic abilities?" His voice was husky, wonderfully deep, and it rumbled through her in a curiously erotic wave.

She put down the glass, feeling disconnected, like she was watching someone else set the glass on the dresser. Then she watched as he took her hand and placed it on his throat, over the scorpion that always appeared to be stinging his jugular when he spoke.

"Yes," she whispered. "I can turn it off and on."

"Are you...turned on?"

Oh, she caught the wordplay, was very aware it was intentional.

"No," she said, and it was both truth and lie. She hadn't switched on her empathic ability, though she could read a faint energy radiating from the scorpion. She was, however, extremely aroused.

Being here now had nothing to do with seducing Thanatos for The Aegis. She wanted him. It was that simple.

The fear that she might let her soul-sucking ability loose during an uncontrolled moment didn't apply here. Thanatos's shadows would protect him, and for the first time in her life, she wanted to unchain her carnal side and let it hunt.

As if sensing her thoughts, Thanatos fastened his hand to the back of her neck and jerked her close, so their bodies were plastered together, and he mashed his lips against hers. His arousal was a brutal, huge presence against her belly, and his tongue was an assault weapon, breaching the barrier of her lips and taking what it wanted. Everything inside her went liquid and hot. Her breasts tightened, her skin burned, and between her legs, her sex ached.

"And now?" he murmured against her mouth.

"God, yes." Her pulse leaped in her throat, in time with the throbbing low in her pelvis.

"You drive me crazy." He rolled his hips against her, and he thought she was the one who was doing the crazy-driving? "I want you, Regan. More than I've wanted anyone, and damn you, I'm about to give in."

"Yes," she breathed. "Do."

His hands dropped to her waistband, and suddenly, it was a frenzy of who-could-strip-fastest. Her mind was fuzzy, her emotions blurry, but she knew nothing but a driving, primal need to get this man on his back.

And *he* would be on his back. She needed to be in control, and she would never, ever be under a man.

When the last item of clothing dropped to the ground, they both stood there, facing each other, their breath sawing in and out, fists clenched. Good God, he was gorgeous. He had a runner's body, sleek and toned. Twin nipple rings decorated his tattooed pecs, his abs rippled with deep, muscular grooves, and his slim hips tapered to powerful legs. And between them, his arousal rose up, thick at the base and ridged with veins all the way to the smooth head.

"I can't," he rasped. "Can't go all the way."

Disappointment sang through her, but hell, she'd take what she could get at this point. Wait... why couldn't he go all the way—?

His powerful arms came around her, caging her against him, and all thought stopped. His kiss was hard, hot, desperate. His cock speared her between the legs, rubbing against her sex as he pumped as though he was inside her.

"Bed." She spun him, clipped his calf with her ankle, and shoved against his chest. Off balance, he hit the mattress on his back. Before he could recover, she leaped on top of him, straddling his thighs.

Surprise registered on his face, but then she started to rock, letting his shaft slide between her folds, and his head fell back, his lips fell open, the very picture of male ecstasy. She ran her hands up his abs, his chest, and over the hard planes of his arms. He responded, lifting his hands to place them on her shoulders...

His fingers dug almost painfully into her skin, and he held her very, very still. His gaze was glassy, drowsy, and his words were slurred. "You want to play, Aegi? I'll play, but keep in mind that I play rough."

"Yeah?" Dropping forward, she slipped out of his grip to take one of his nipple rings between her teeth. She tugged so hard he hissed. "So do I, Horseman. So do I."

Thirty-one

Thanatos was on fire.

A sluggish burn worked its way through his muscles, flames licked at his skin, and smoke clouded his mind. Regan was churning on top of him, her core way too close for comfort, and why the hell had he let it get this far? He'd never, ever, gotten fully undressed with a female. But here he was, on a bed with a woman—another first—and rocking his hips upward to get to her wet heat.

Regan squeezed him between her thighs, and he moaned. Those legs would feel good wrapped around his waist.

"I need to be on top. Driving into you." Somewhere deep in his brain, he knew the words were his, but he couldn't believe he'd spoken them.

"Sorry." She reached between their bodies and stroked his erection. "I only do it this way."

He hissed at the friction of her palm on his hard member. "I can deal with that." Hell, he'd deal with it any way she wanted it. If he was going to lose his virginity...

No.

God, what was he thinking?

"Regan." He groaned, arching into her touch. "Stop."

"No chance of that." Her voice was as soft as her lips as they kissed their way up to his throat, where she nipped the scorpion tattoo before laving it with her tongue.

Thanatos squeezed his eyes shut, enjoying the way she was caressing him, using her entire body like a big cat to rub him all over. Her breasts slid against his chest, her inner thighs brushed softly against his hips, and her hands roved far and wide, stroking, petting. He shouldn't let himself enjoy this, but he was starved for a female's touch. This was something he'd dreamed about his entire life, and he wasn't about to stop it yet.

Maybe he wouldn't stop it at all.

He frowned, wondering where that notion had come from. His body had never overruled his brain, at least, not when it came to sex. Too much rode on his ability to hold onto his virginity. Maybe the mead...

Regan tongued his nipple, and his thoughts fractured into shards of lust. Virginity be damned.

"Ah, yes," he hissed, and hissed again when she trailed her tongue down his body. When she reached his navel, she rimmed it, and he swore nothing had ever felt so good. But would she go lower? Please, please, *please*.

She did. He started panting before her mouth reached his hipbone. Her silky hair cascaded over his skin, and her cheek brushed his erection, and as much as he wanted to look, he couldn't. He was too close to the edge, and the sight would send him right over.

"What do you want me to do, warrior?" she murmured against his inner thigh.

A lump the size of his fist clogged his throat, and he couldn't say anything. He wanted...oh, he knew what he wanted. But this was a new experience, and he'd never been this intimate with a female. No, not even in the seedy back room at the Four Horsemen. Every female he took back there got off, but only because he touched their minds as he touched their bodies, and when he was through, they believed they'd either fucked or sucked him, but nothing could be farther from the truth.

"Hmm," she said, as she teasingly brushed the tips of her fingers over his balls. "I guess you don't want anything..."

"No," he croaked. "I do."

"Tell me." He finally opened his eyes and looked at her. The sight of her crouched over him like that, her mouth so close to his arousal that her warm breath whispered over it, nearly undid him. Hunger glowed in her gorgeous eyes, and a sinful smile curved her lips. "What do you want?"

He swallowed the lump in his throat, but that did nothing to ease the dryness. "Put your mouth on me."

Her smile widened, and she put her lips to the sensitive skin on his hip. "Like this?" She was killing him.

"On...my cock."

"Oh, I see." She dragged her lips down his shaft. "Like this?"

"Yeah, but..."

"But what?" She kept her mouth where it was, and his cock kicked in both protest and pleasure.

"But...suck it."

She winked. "Now we're talking." She dove into her task, taking him into the depths of her wet mouth.

He cried out, a strangled rush of air, and fisted the sheets so hard his hands cramped. Slow, strong pulls met tender, light licks, and all the while, one hand slid up and down his shaft as the other cupped his balls and massaged gently.

He was almost there...his entire body arched, his hips rolled...oh, yeah...

"Touch yourself," he whispered.

Regan moaned around his shaft, and the vibration made him lick the ceiling. Cracking his eyes open, he watched her slip her fingers between her legs. He'd taste her there in a minute. He'd tongue every inch of that battle-scarred body. And that glow on her skin...something about it made the souls in his armor writhe.

Right now they were agitated, but it only increased the sensation inside him. The light on her skin seemed to blanket him as she swiped her tongue over the head of his cock, and just as he thought she was going to take him in her mouth again, she surged up his body. Straddling him, she took his shaft in her hand. Oh...*shit*.

"No!"

The light slammed into his chest, melting over him like shrinkwrap and then disappearing. The souls inside him pushed back in a war that raged just under the surface of his skin, one that pinned him to the bed. He couldn't move, couldn't summon control over his muscles as Regan poised the head of him at her entrance.

"Don't do this. *Regan!*"

Too late, she sank down on him, taking him all the way to the root. Pleasure and terror mixed, and as she started to move, all he could do was try not to hyperventilate. He imagined his Seal breaking, could almost feel the evil tremor begin in his soul.

Regan moaned, grinding on him, the silky slide of her channel around his shaft nothing short of amazing, and he wished he could enjoy it more, but his fucking Seal...

Hadn't broken.

What the hell? And how was she holding him down? Nothing could hold him.

Regan's nails scored his chest, and she threw her head back, eyes closed, mouth open, and against his will, his hips came off the bed to take her deeper. He shouldn't be enjoying this, but she was moving faster now, her breasts lifting and falling with her increasingly rapid breaths. Magnificent... she was breathtaking in her passion. His own passion spiraled out of control, his pleasure searing, intense. His balls felt tight, achy, ready to explode. His shaft swelled, and the first pulses of climax vibrated his nerve endings.

Oh, shit... what if it wasn't the penetration, but the *orgasm* that broke his Seal? *Spilling your seed inside the female will change your life.* The voice of the demon who had whispered in his ear when he'd been cursed clanged in his head, and his throat seized.

"Stop," he rasped, but Regan only moved faster, undulating against him in graceful waves. "Regan, stop *now!*"

"No way... oh, oh, yes." Her body convulsed, and her core grabbed onto him, squeezing, milking, and then it was over. He was done for. The orgasm hit him like a whirlwind, lifting him violently off the bed. Regan yelped as he bucked so hard she had to cling to his shoulders or go flying.

He roared in exquisite ecstasy, in futile anger... and in sheer devastation.

Regan could hardly move. Her body was sated, and yet, she was oddly still...wanting. Beneath her, Thanatos's chest was heaving, the smooth, tattooed skin glistening with a fine sheen of sweat. She wondered if he'd felt her ability raging like an electrical storm. She could have sworn she'd released it at some point, but when she opened her eyes, there'd been no light, no screeching, no telltale sign of the creature that extracted souls like a surgical instrument.

Maybe her fear of losing control during sex had been for nothing.

She listened to Than's heart beating in her ear as she lay plastered against him, one hand petting his silky hair. She loved the braids, and as she wound one around her finger, she sighed in weary resignation.

As much as she'd like to remain like this, maybe go again, she had to leave if The Aegis's plan was going to work.

Weakly, she pushed herself up. The Horseman's yellow eyes were staring at her, his brows locked down in what she'd swear was confusion. Maybe he wasn't used to the woman taking control. Too bad. The twenty-first century was going to suck for him, if that was the case.

She climbed awkwardly off him, her legs stiff, and tugged on her pants. "Well," she said, as she pulled on her sweater, "that was fun, but I have to go."

"You're not leaving." His voice was oddly hollow.

She shoved her feet into her boots. "Yeah, I am. I'm done with my research." She zipped her bag, desperate to get out of there before she changed her mind and stayed. "If The Aegis needs anything else, they'll send someone."

"You aren't leaving," he repeated, this time with a lot more grouchiness. "And you're going to release me."

She cocked an eyebrow. "I'd say I already *released* you."

He stared at her, his brows cranking down in a puzzled scowl. Then, abruptly, something changed. A smoky shadow passed over his expression, and icy glints glittered like shards in his eyes. Even the very air crackled with danger.

"You...*traitor.*" His voice was low, warped with a deep-seated, startling rage. "You released nothing."

Shocked to the core by his sudden mood swing, she stepped back. Clearly, they were not talking about the same kind of release here.

He shot a glare at the mead bottle. "And you *drugged* me."

Drugged him? As if she'd sink to that just to have sex with him? "Look, you need to calm down, and I really have to go."

"Wait." His voice cracked like a whip, and it struck her as odd that as pissed as he was, he hadn't gotten off the mattress. "You came here to seduce me, didn't you?"

She affected her best insulted expression as she pulled on her parka. "I'm sure your ego would like to think so—"

"What did you do to me? How are you holding me like this?" When she blinked, baffled by pretty much every element of this conversation, he bit out a curse. "Your... gift. Your damned light is in my skin. How?"

Oh...oh, shit. It *had* released. "It...is it hurting you?"

"My souls are fighting it," he growled. "They're destroying it, and the second they do, I'm going to wring your neck."

Well, that would be her cue to leave, then. She started for the door.

"Are you working with Pestilence?"

Jaw dropping, she wheeled back around. "You think I wanted sex with you so bad that I'd enlist your evil brother's help? Wow, you really are an egomaniac."

"Sex?" he roared, startling her into taking another step back. "That wasn't sex. You tricked me. You drugged me and defiled me. Do you even know what you did?"

She thought her eyes might have popped out of her head. "*Defiled* you? Are you kidding me?"

"I told you no. I refused." The tendons in his neck strained as he tried to lift his head. "You...violated..." His voice degenerated into a nasty growl. "You *took my virginity*."

She laughed. Virginity. Surely he was joking.

His black expression said he wasn't, but virginity? No way. Ridiculous.

No. Don't do this. Regan! His pleas came back to her, ringing in her ears with deafening clarity. He'd told her to stop, but...no, he hadn't meant it.

He couldn't have meant it.

He lay there, chest still heaving, raw hatred gleaming in his eyes. A trickle of sweat rolled down her temple as she replayed every second of the sex. She'd thought his protests were token, but if he really had been drugged with the wine, and her ability had attacked him, holding him down while she...*oh, God.*

Her stomach rebelled, and she staggered out of the room. She ran blindly for the outside door, Thanatos's furious shouts chasing her. She made it outside just in time, and she lost her dinner next to the snowmobile. Hot tears stung her eyes and freezing wind stung her cheeks as she fumbled in her pocket for her cell phone and keys.

As quickly as she could, she sent an emergency text to Kynan and Val, and then she started up the snow machine with unsteady fingers.

She could still hear Than's angry roar over the sound of the snowmobile's motor. She'd probably hear it for the rest of her life.

"I'm sorry," she whispered. Dear God, she was *so* sorry.

She revved the engine, hoping to drown out his voice, and took off like a shot, holding on for dear life. The ride went on forever, the snowmobile's headlight barely penetrating the early morning darkness. Or maybe it was her watery eyes making it difficult to see. She just wished the cold would numb her out, but all it did was add to the bleak horror of what she'd just done.

Finally, in the distance, she spotted two figures outlined in the glow of flashlights. One would be Kynan, and the other should be one of his demon in-laws... Shade, she thought. Kynan said he could make sure her egg and Thanatos's sperm hooked up and did the baby dance.

That wasn't going to happen.

She spared a glance over her shoulder and immediately wished she hadn't. Against the gray wall of the rising dawn were the outlines of a massive dun horse and armored rider pounding across the barren wasteland.

Thanatos.

Terror tripped through her, and she nearly screamed. If they caught her, she was dead.

She skidded to a stop, and before she could even get off the machine, Shade gripped her wrist. "Let go!" She tried to jerk away, but he held her steady.

"I need to knock you out for the trip through the Harrowgate."

Right. And then, as his arm began to glow and warmth spread from his fingers to her blood, her stomach turned over again. "Just don't—"

A scream rang out, and then another, and she turned to see Pestilence on his stallion come from out of nowhere and broadside Thanatos and Styx. Horseman and horse went down in a massive crash of blood and snow.

"Oh, shit," Kynan said. "We have to get out of here. Hurry, Shade."

"Done." The demon nodded. "Congratulations. You're pregnant."

Pregnant. No. *No, no, no!* God, what had she done?

Weapons clashed and horses whinnied, and Regan cried out when Thanatos was crushed beneath the white stallion's hooves.

More intense warmth bloomed beneath Shade's hand. "Say goodnight, Aegi."

"No, wait—"

Then there was nothing but blackness.

Thirty-two

No amount of pacing and cursing on Limos's bedroom deck could bring Arik down from what she had done. For the first two hours she'd been gone, he'd alternated between being terrified that Limos had gone and done something stupid, like hunt down Lucifer, and being pissed off at her for lying to him.

And no, he didn't believe she'd lied about loving him and not messing with his memories again. She'd been trying to get rid of him for his own safety.

He could handle himself. He'd survived his childhood, the military, a month in hell, and Limos's brothers. He'd survive whatever came after him, and if he didn't...

Pestilence would own his soul.

Okay, so that was a minor glitch, but he couldn't spend what time he had worrying about it. He'd put the R-XR and Aegis on the problem and hope they could find a way out of the whole ownership of his soul crap. In the mean time, he'd be with Limos.

She would have the life she wanted, and he'd give it to her.

He allowed himself the luxury of picturing her fat with his baby as he looked through the sliding glass door at the empty bed. They hadn't even had a chance to make love as a married couple, but he swore that when she came back, he'd have her undressed and he'd be inside her in a matter of minutes. He'd show her what every night with him would be like, would make her crave his touch and forget her crazy idea to get rid of him for his own good.

Goal firmly in place, he strode inside the bedroom just as the door flew open and Limos, fully armored and her eyes red and puffy, walked in. She halted, and her face went ashen before pinking up with indignation.

"Why are you still here?" she snapped.

He folded his arms over his chest. "Well, gee, maybe because I don't have the ability to use Harrowgates, and maybe because we're fucking married."

"Yeah, about that." She tossed her hair over her shoulder in that arrogant way of hers. "I went to Gethel. Funny thing about angels... they can dissolve any marriage that takes place in the human realm." She held up a tiny scroll. "You have an hour to pack. We're officially divorced."

Son of a bitch. Son of a *fucking* bitch!

Pestilence stared down at the steaming lumps of bone and blood that were Thanatos and Styx. The stallion was dying, but Than would be up in a few minutes, good as new. How the hell was his Seal whole? *How?*

Pestilence had gotten a message from the vampire doppelganger he'd stuck inside Than's keep, and the vampire had assured him that the Aegi whore had screwed Thanatos, thanks to a little help from his enhanced mead. So what was going on?

Snarling, he gated himself to Harvester's place. He slammed his way into her home, blew past her, and went straight to the chamber where she kept Reaver. The angel was sitting propped against the wall, covered in blood and dirt, his golden hair hanging in limp ropes around his face and shoulders. Glazed blue eyes watched Pestilence as he stalked in and kicked the angel in the face.

Reaver, blood streaming from his nose and split lip, just smirked. Smug bastard. Pestilence kicked him again. The fucking angel struck out hard enough to knock Pestilence into a wall and split his head open. Blood streamed in a sticky, warm river down the back of his neck and into his armor, which drank it in gurgling sips. If Pestilence wasn't so pissed, he'd be impressed by how strong Reaver still was, despite having his wings removed.

"When will you learn, Reseph?" Reaver said. "You can hurt me, but you will never break me."

"We'll see about that, you fuck."

Pestilence let loose with everything he had. Reaver didn't even fight back as Pestilence kicked and stomped him until the angel was nothing but an unconscious mass of meat in a pile, and gore was dripping from Pestilence's boot. Harvester's hands came down on his shoulders.

"What happened?" she asked, and he rounded on her.

"You know better than to touch me."

He circled her, measuring her level of fear and, deciding he wanted more, he grabbed her by the throat and slammed her into the wall. Inhaling so deeply that he tasted her terror on his tongue, he smiled.

"The Aegi fucked my brother," he whispered into her ear, "so why didn't his Seal break?"

"I don't know," Harvester said, and though he got the feeling she was lying, he also knew that no matter how much he beat her, she wouldn't tell him if it was one of those "rules" she and Reaver had to follow.

"Lying bitch." He was going to fuck her until she broke. Until every bone was shattered and he was slick with her blood. He ripped off her gown, leaving her naked and trembling.

"There's still hope," she gasped, as he thrust his fingers between her legs.

"Leave...her...alone." Reaver's voice, halting but still making the air crackle with power, came from behind him.

Maybe he'd give Reaver a little too. *After* the angel watched him rail Harvester like the whore she was. Smiling, Pestilence looked over his shoulder.

"Don't worry, Reavie-weavie. I'll save a little for you. I'm like the Energizer fucking Bunny. I can keep going and going." He flicked his finger over his throat, and his armor melted away, leaving him as naked as Harvester.

"Bastard," she rasped.

"So true," he agreed.

"*Reseph!*" The thundering voice shook the entire residence, and his marrow became pudding. Very slowly, he turned to Reaver, who stood in his chains, his body glowing and double its normal size. "You will not do this."

There was no reason to fear the angel. None whatsoever, but something so deep inside Pestilence that he couldn't reach it was as terrified as a small child in the face of his angry father.

He raised his chin in defiance and somehow managed

to sound nonplussed as he said, "Now you've gone and ruined the mood." He swiped his fingers over his throat, locking his armor into place again. "Another time, then. The moment the Apocalypse starts, I'm going to use you until your screams no longer amuse me and your skin no longer contains your organs."

With that, he strode out of Harvester's house, hoping like hell no one noticed the trembling in his knees. What the fuck was that? He hadn't been afraid of anything since his Seal had broken. Cursing viciously, he popped a Harrowgate and came out at the black arches that led to his mother's place. She was inside the temple-like structure, lounging on a sofa in the middle of an orgy. As usual. The sight calmed him down, but only a little.

"My son," she purred, crooking a finger for him to come to her. "You look upset."

He kicked at a humanoid male who had sunk to his knees in front of him, and moved through the writhing mass of bodies. "My plan failed."

"The Aegi didn't take Thanatos's virginity?"

"She did. But his Seal didn't break."

Lilith blinked, and her lithe body undulated as she sat up. She wore a thin, filmy skirt, but she was topless except for a necklace with an emerald the size of a duck egg sitting between her ample breasts. "What was it you made The Aegis believe in order for them to send the female to Thanatos?"

"That if she got pregnant, the child would save the world."

She patted the sofa next to her, and he sank down onto the velvety cushion. "And you're certain she slept with him."

"Yes." As he'd been battling his brother, Than had confirmed it.

"You're responsible for this." Thanatos's blade caught Pestilence in the ear, slicing it in half. *"You convinced the Aegi to fuck me."*

Conquest lunged, paying Than back by ripping off a piece of Styx's ear. "Was it good, Than? Was it worth waiting five thousand years for?"

Thanatos's eyes had filled with pain that had nearly given Pestilence an orgasm right there. He loved his siblings' suffering. "Yes."

"Did her womb quicken?" Lilith asked.

He shrugged. "Probably. Harvester says there's still hope, but—" He broke off on a harsh breath. Hope. "The child. The child is our hope. The prophecy isn't about Than's virginity, his *innocence*. It's about his *innocent*. A child." Harvester, that sneaky angel, had known, hadn't she? While she couldn't help directly, she'd done it through the suggestion about the scroll. Now he felt a little bad about everything he'd done to her.

Okay, no, he didn't.

"Brilliant." Lilith palmed his thigh, her eyes, so like Limos's, bright with excitement. "The child is the key to his Seal."

Smiling, Pestilence fell back against the cushions and got rid of his armor. His mind was always clearest when he was naked. Clearer yet when he was coming.

And as mouths and hands covered his body, plans formed. When the first orgasm hit him, he knew what he had to do. He had to get his hands on that child.

That tender, sweet-fleshed child.

Thirty-three

The second Pestilence left her residence, Harvester's knees failed. She hit the floor in a crack of kneecaps, and a heartbeat later, Reaver did the same, falling into a bloody heap. Though she was shaken, her muscles mush, she scrambled over to him.

Leave her alone.

Pestilence had stomped Reaver into hamburger, had caused enough damage that it would take days for him to recover. And yet, Reaver had found the strength to not only speak through the broken bones in his face, but to summon the last of his heavenly reserves, the tiny bit of power left in the stumps that used to be his wings, and he'd become a force to be reckoned with.

He'd protected her for some reason, and the shriveled black lump of coal that used to be her heart cracked. Just a little, no more than a tiny stress fracture, but still.

"Reaver?"

He groaned, a sound of soul-deep misery.

"Whine!" The werewolf hurried inside. "Marrow wine. Hurry."

It wouldn't help Reaver heal, but it would, at least, make his pain tolerable. Especially since, as per orders, she'd forced it down him often, creating an addiction that would render him all but useless as the end of days approached, and now he took it freely, craving it the way an opium addict chased the dragon.

The werewolf brought a bottle to her, and she lifted Reaver's head, cradling it in her palm as she lifted the rim to his lips. "Here," she murmured, wincing when most of the liquid dribbled out the corner of his mouth.

He was too weak to drink, dammit. In this state, this far out of reach of the source of his heavenly powers, he could fall into what would amount to a coma. He would languish in that coma until someone carried him out of Sheoul, which meant he could be stuck here for all eternity if she—or anyone else—wished it.

"Come on, Reaver. Drink, damn you." When he didn't move, she turned to Whine. "Bring me some sugar. Honey if we have it. And a cup and spoon."

Whine brought her back a small pot of honey, and she mixed a spoonful into the cup with the marrow wine. Angels were like hummingbirds, able to manufacture small amounts of life-giving energy from sugar. Taking his head again, she tilted his face upward and poured a little of the mixture into his mouth. This time, as it trickled into his throat, he swallowed.

"Good," she whispered. "A little more."

He drank, and before the full amount was gone, he'd

gained enough energy to raise his head and hold her hand in place as he drank greedily.

"Master," Whine said, and she was so grateful for Reaver's reaction that she didn't snap at her slave for speaking out of turn.

"What?"

"A message came while the Horseman was here." He handed her a scroll—made from human skin.

She broke the seal with her teeth and allowed it to unroll. Reaver could go free. Relief washed over her. She'd hated having him here, hated the scorching glares he gave her, hated how he reminded her of what she'd lost.

His hand tightened on hers, and his eyes, which had been bloodshot, hazy with pain, brightened a little. The sugar was working, and as the aphrodisiac effects of the wine took hold, the blue of his eyes turned sensual, like a warm sea in the moonlight.

She sucked in a shocked breath; this was the first time she'd truly seen him as a sexual being. Oh, she'd appreciated him as a gorgeous male whose presence all but blotted out the sun. But now, whoa. His body hardened as the ecstasy took him, his head fell back, and his body arched. At his hips, a massive erection tented the seam of what remained of his tattered slacks.

Her own body heated as she watched him writhe in the kind of orgasm only the demon wine could deliver. Well, that wasn't true...on the Other Side, in Heaven, the mating of two souls was like that. The Marrow wine had originally been created to simulate what fallen angels had lost when they were booted out of Heaven, and yes, it came close, was the second most incredible thing one could experience.

Her fingers itched to touch him, and she found herself reaching for his thick arousal. She just wanted to stroke it a little. She wanted to trace the outline against the fly of his pants, maybe slide the pad of her thumb over the tip, since it was nearly peeking out from under his waistband.

Liquid lust seeped between her legs, and Whine growled low in his throat, scenting her arousal and sparking his own. He had been there for her when she needed blood, sex, and someone to buffer her anger. At times she treated him harshly, but that was what was expected of her, and if she did any less, both Whine and she would pay dearly.

"Go," she said, and though he hesitated, he obeyed.

His nature wouldn't allow him to go far or to pleasure himself until he'd received her permission, which meant that if she needed him later, he'd be ready and willing.

Reaver moaned, his lips parting, eyes closed as pleasure took him. His hips pushed up and pulled back, a pumping motion controlling his body, and wetness began to spread along the fly of his pants as he came over and over.

He was beautiful.

Leave her alone. He'd saved her. He could have remained silent, let Pestilence violate her, torture her, but Reaver had risked his own safety. The knowledge rippled through her in a wave of gratitude that melded with her lust, and she lunged, prepared to take him in her hand—

His fingers snapped up to snare her wrist just before she touched his arousal. Gasping, she shifted her gaze to his face, where pleasure had etched itself into the set of his parted lips, his drowsy lids, his flushed skin. But behind all that were his sapphire irises, which glowed like hot coals.

"Thank you," she breathed. "Thank you for coming to my aid."

"No female should suffer that." A twisted smile curved his lips. "But I didn't do it for you. I did it for Reseph." His fingers closed so tightly around her arm that she cried out, feeling the bones in her wrist cracking. "You...the first chance I get...I'm going to kill."

Thanatos stepped out of the Harrowgate in front of Ares's house and dialed Limos on his cell. "Be at my Greenland Harrowgate in five minutes. And bring Arik."

He was going to find out if Limos's new husband had any knowledge of what Regan had planned. At this point, he wouldn't be surprised, given Limos's revelations. Maybe she'd married someone as devious as she was.

Except...Thanatos was having a hard time holding onto that anger. He'd been pissed when she'd first admitted her deceptions, but he knew her too well to believe she didn't regret her past. And if he could believe Reseph could be saved, then how could he forsake Limos?

Arik, however, was another story. Thanatos had wanted to believe in the human, but if he was in league with Regan...

Limos's voice buzzed over the airwaves. "Than, I can't. I'm just getting ready to take Arik to the R-XR—"

"*Bring him!*" In a fit of rage, he disconnected by hurling the phone against a stone pillar that rose up like a sentinel at the entrance to Ares's garden. It exploded in a blast of plastic and electronic guts.

Dripping blood and melting snow, he stormed into Ares's house, only to be stopped by Ares's chief Ramreel, Vulgrim. "My lord, you're injured—"

"I know that," he snapped. "Where's Cara?"

"She's . . . busy, sir."

"Where's Ares?"

Vulgrim cleared his throat. "Busy as well."

Right. Than shoved past the demon and stalked to Ares's bedroom, where he pounded on the door, leaving bloody smears on the white paint. "Open up!"

An erotic snarl echoed behind the wood. "Go away, Than." Ares's warning was loud and clear, but Than ignored it and slammed his fist into the door again.

"Styx is dying."

There was a rustle of covers, thumps of feet on the floor, and more rustling. "One minute," Cara called out.

Than paced, his muscles tense and twitching with a combination of worry over his horse, fury at his brother for attacking them, and intense hatred for Regan's betrayal. He wasn't sure which was worse, but they were all blending together in a caustic stew that threatened to release a shitstorm of violence. He wanted to kill. Destroy. Wreak havoc and kill, kill, *kill*. Only his concern for Styx kept him from going into a complete rampage, but he couldn't guarantee that wouldn't happen once the stallion was healed.

If the stallion died . . . he *could* guarantee that nothing would stop him.

Cara and Ares threw open the door and rushed out, Cara in jeans and sweatshirt, and Ares in armor. "What happened?"

"Our brother happened." Than led them out of the house and gated them to the site of the battle.

Though he expected his stomach to turn over at the sight of Styx lying on the ice in a pool of blood like a harpooned whale, he hadn't expected it to hurt so much.

His horse had been injured before, gravely. But Pestilence and his stallion had delighted in making Styx scream, and Than swore he could feel the animal's pain.

Another gate opened, the flash of golden light streaking out over what little snow hadn't been spoiled by battle and blood. Limos and Arik stepped out, and if they were a happily married couple, Than would eat his Seal. They stood apart, Limos in turquoise jeans and a leather jacket, and Arik in military BDUs, a puffy green military-issue coat, and a weapons belt circling his hips.

"Dammit." Cara sank next to the stallion, who was laboring to breathe.

Ares moved in front of Than, blocking his view. "What was the battle about?"

"I don't know." Than closed his eyes. "No, I know. He thought my Seal had broken, and when he realized it hadn't, he went insane. He tried to kill Styx to hurt me."

"Why would he think your Seal had broken?"

Kill. He breathed through the desire to go after every Guardian on the planet. "Because the fucking Aegis betrayed us, and he knew about it."

"You aren't making sense," Ares said.

"Regan." Just the name pissed him off, and he couldn't stop the bloodthirsty growl that condensed in his throat. "She wasn't sent to learn our history. She was sent to seduce me. She betrayed me. They betrayed all of us." Anger singed his control as the caustic sludge that had been brewing spilled into his veins and ran like acid through them.

"Calm down, Than," Limos said. "What are you talking about?"

"Regan." Than started to pace in a futile attempt to

outrun his rage. "That *bitch*!" He spun around to Arik. "What did you know about it, Aegi?" He got up in the human's face. "Tell me!"

Arik's expression shuttered. "I don't know what you're talking about, but I'd appreciate it if you learned the definition of personal space."

"Than." Limos's tone was the one she'd always used when she tried to bring Reseph down from a rare rage, but it wasn't going to work with Thanatos, and he turned on her with a snarl.

"She fucking drugged me." He needed to kill, and the souls in his armor screamed to be let loose. *Soon. Very, very soon*, he promised them.

Ares scowled. "When? With what?"

"After you left." Than seethed at the memory. "She plied me with my favorite mead, spiked with something. Probably orc weed."

"Oh, man." Ares shoved his hand through his hair. "Yeah, I get why you're upset, but obviously, it didn't work—"

"Yes, it did."

Everyone froze. Everyone but Arik, who looked between them all, clearly confused.

Finally, Limos cleared her throat. "It couldn't have."

"I don't get what's going on. What's orc weed?" Arik asked.

"It's an aphrodisiac," Limos replied. "Than, I don't understand what you're saying."

"I'm saying she drugged me. And..." Humiliation shrank his skin. "She took me."

"And I'm still lost." Arik's gaze was wary. "You had sex with a beautiful woman. Why is that a problem? Are you a penis guy?"

Than lunged, but Ares caught him around the waist. "I'm going to kill your man, Limos. I am."

Roughly, Ares dragged Than away from the human. "Let me see your Seal."

Than's hand shook as he reached inside his armor and pulled out the gold coin on the chain. Everyone was still and quiet, the anticipation in the air as thick as fog. The only sound was the ruffle of clothing in the icy wind and the gurgling breaths of his stallion. At least Cara's healing waves were working, and Styx's wounds were closing up with amazing speed.

Ares palmed the Seal, his eyes filled with worry and hard, icy resolve. Ares would do what was necessary to keep Than from heading out into the world as an evil entity, and Than didn't blame him. Still, his gut twisted when Ares's hand dropped to the hilt of his sword.

Thanatos met Ares's gaze. "You have Deliverance." It might not kill Pestilence, but hopefully, if Than's Seal broke, it would kill Death.

"We won't need it," Ares said, his words clipped with the force of his conviction. But truthfully, Than wasn't sure Deliverance would make a difference. If any Seal broke after the first one, they'd all break. But maybe if Ares could nail Than in the heart before his Seal completely cracked in half...

"How long did it take for Reseph's to break?" Limos asked.

"It vibrated for a few seconds, then it cracked," Ares ran his thumb over the scythe on the front of the Seal. "From what Sin said about the timing of the event that caused the breakage, I figure it was almost instantaneous." He shot Than a look. "How long ago did you have sex?"

Than spoke between clenched teeth. "Half hour, maybe."

"Wait." Arik stepped forward. "Are you saying that sex is what will break your Seal?"

"Yeah," Limos said. "At least, we thought that's what it was." She glanced at Than. "Maybe all this time you could have been having sex?"

Five thousand years wasted? No way. There had to be another answer. He snagged Arik by the collar and ignored Limos's snarl.

"Why would The Aegis send someone to break my Seal? It makes no sense."

"Exactly," Arik's voice was pretty damned calm for someone who was in Death's grasp. "It doesn't. Which means they didn't think sex is what would break it. And apparently, they were right. So let go of me and go make up for thousands of years of celibacy, asshole."

A veil of crimson fury slammed down over his vision. Limos and Ares flanked him, moving in slowly, and he prepared to fight. Somewhere in his hate-sodden brain, he knew he was gone, knew he shouldn't be wanting to strangle the human in his grip. But it didn't matter.

"Than?" Cara's voice penetrated the lethal soup clogging his head. "Styx needs you." Dropping Arik, he whirled around to Cara, who was stroking the stallion's blood-caked neck. "He's fine, but he needs to rest—"

"To me." Instantly, the horse dissolved into smoke and shot inside Than's gauntlet.

"Thanatos..." Ares's voice was low, edged with warning. "What are you doing?"

"I'm going to kill the Aegi who betrayed me."

Ares grabbed his shoulder. "We can't start another war between us."

"Then they shouldn't have betrayed us!" The shadow souls spun around him as if in a blender.

"Than," Limos said, a note of desperation in her voice. "You need to calm down. You're getting that crazy look, and we don't need a repeat of Roanoke."

Roanoke...he'd lost his temper after being shot, and...he couldn't remember. A black haze had worked its way into his brain, the death haze, the one that signaled no return and a desire to slaughter.

"Than...we'll figure this out..."

"Than, calm down..."

There was a shimmery flash, and he thought he saw an angel, but his body was vibrating out of control and he couldn't trust anything he saw or heard.

"Reaver...thank God...where did you come from..."

"Ares...do it..."

The words jumbled in his head until he couldn't figure out who was talking or what they were saying. He only wanted to kill. He'd start with Regan, and then he'd work his way through the entire Aegis organization. He'd rend limbs from bodies, rip open throats, kill, kill, kill...

"Limos! Get Arik out of here!"

Too late. With a roar, he let loose, consequences be damned.

Thirty-four

Ares had seen Thanatos in rages, had cleaned up after them and sat with him afterward. But he'd never seen...this.

Reaver had flashed in—dropped off by Harvester— just before Thanatos went off like a nuclear bomb. The power of the blast knocked Ares and Cara off their feet, and both Reaver and Limos, who couldn't get Arik out of there fast enough, leaped on him, shielding him with their bodies.

The shockwave rolled across the land, picking up snow and forming a solid wall of white as it shot in every direction from the epicenter. It would kill every living being in Greenland.

Ares leaped to his feet and tackled his brother. He and Than went down in a heap and crack of armor on ice. Rolling, they fought, but thanks to Cara's presence, Ares was at a serious disadvantage, his weakened armor doing little to protect him from Than's blows.

Frantically, he fumbled for the pouch at his hip and found what he was looking for. Without hesitation, he jammed the small bone barb into Than's neck. Instantly, Than froze up.

The barb, which Cara had convinced him to carry, was coated in hellhound saliva and was just enough to incapacitate for a few minutes. She'd come up with the idea as a weapon against Pestilence...or against any of his siblings, should one of their Seals break. He made a mental note to kiss his wife senseless later.

Unfortunately, time was short.

"Get Hal," Ares said to Cara.

She could call out to the hound with her mind, and the fucking mutt had better hurry. While he waited, he touched the scar on Than's throat, forcing his armor to retreat, and now he was lying naked on the ice.

Hal appeared out of thin air, tongue lolling, slobber flinging everywhere. Cara spoke to him, and he padded over and took a big bite out of Than's arm. The glimmer in his black eyes said he'd enjoyed it, but Ares winced. He knew firsthand that while under the influence of hellhound poison, you felt everything.

"Sorry, bro," Ares murmured. "But this is for your own good."

"Ares." Cara's voice was dripping with alarm, and he leaped to his feet, reaching for his sword.

But it wasn't his sword he needed. His heart nearly stopped when he saw what Cara was looking at.

Arik was writhing on the ground, clutching his head, a silent scream lodged in his throat. Next to him, Reaver and Limos lay motionless.

"What the hell?"

When Reaver had appeared, dressed in a long black robe and looking like he'd lost a fight with a chainsaw, Ares had hoped for help with Thanatos. But this definitely wasn't help, and it wasn't good. Ares kneeled next to Limos and the angel, feeling for a pulse, for breath, for anything.

There was nothing. They were both as cold as the ice around them.

Cara sank down next to him. "What's going on?"

"I don't know."

Fear was a punch to his heart, and for a moment, he thought it might have stopped beating. A tingle made the hairs on the back of his neck stand up, and he spun around, both relieved and worried when Gethel materialized next to Than. As usual, she wore a Greek-style tunic, soft leather boots, and a scabbard at her hip.

She eased to her knees next to Arik. "What happened?"

"Thanatos. He was angry." He didn't need to say more. Gethel had watched over them for hundreds of years. She knew the deal. "How did you know something was wrong?"

"The sudden deaths of thousands of people on this island was a powerful ripple. We were able to stop Thanatos's death wave, but too late. So many people gone." Her voice was leaden with anguish. "More than that, I could hear Reaver's and Limos's souls screaming."

Ares's blood went as cold as the land around them. "What do you mean?"

Gethel stroked Arik's hair, and he calmed, but only a little. He still lay there gasping, like a fish dying on the bank of a river. "Did Reaver and Limos protect Arik from Thanatos's rage?"

"They wrapped themselves around him," Cara said.

Bowing her head, Gethel closed her eyes. "Yes, that makes sense."

"What?" Ares moved forward, not understanding any of this. "*What* makes sense?"

"The shockwave...it knocked Limos and Reaver into Arik. Literally." She looked up at him. "It ripped their souls out of them and cast them into the human. If not for them, he'd be dead. The problem is that he'll die anyway, if I can't retrieve their souls. And if even if I can, it'll be dangerous, and it'll hurt. Greatly."

Cara shivered, and Ares pulled her into his arms. She might be immortal, but she wasn't immune to being cold. "Why will it hurt?"

"Souls are...sticky." Gethel continued to stroke Arik's hair, which lessened his writhing. "They bind themselves to demonic life-forces and make them stronger. Pestilence has been collecting them for that reason. I'll have to peel Reaver and Limos from Arik, and fragments will be left behind or will come off Arik."

Ares had seen and heard a lot in his life, but this was new. And disturbing. "What do you mean...fragments?"

Gethel paused, as if searching for the right words. "Imagine two humans stuck together with...what is that substance called..."

"Superglue?" Cara offered.

"Yes. Superglue." Arik moaned, and Gethel smoothed her palm over his cheek. "If you pull the people apart, bits of skin and hair are torn away. In the case of souls, what is taken or left behind is much more crucial."

Ares digested that for a second, and wished he had some Tums, because this was all going sour. "If Arik dies, his soul belongs to Pestilence."

"I know," Gethel said softly. She looked between Ares and Cara. "Hold him. He's going to struggle."

Cara patted Hal, who lumbered over to Arik and plopped down on his lower legs.

Gethel raised an eyebrow. "Unconventional, but effective."

"Story of my life with Cara," Ares murmured, and pushed down on Arik's broad shoulders while Cara held his head to prevent thrashing.

"Hold tight," Gethel said.

Closing her eyes, she breathed deeply, and her body began to glow. She reached for Arik's chest, and her hand slipped deep inside his body cavity. Arik screamed, arching, veins popping in his temple and throat. He convulsed, and Ares swore he heard a ripping noise as Gethel tugged so hard she fell backward. Even in freefall, she reached behind her and slammed her fist into Limos's sternum.

Limos jerked and came awake with a gasp. "Arik!" She scrambled over and grabbed his arm, looking between Ares and Gethel. "What's wrong? What's happening?"

Gethel splayed her fingers over Arik's heart, as if she was using her force of will to keep it beating. "I'm trying to save him."

A wild sob wracked Limos as she clung to Arik. "I'm sorry, Arik. I take it all back. Just live, okay? *Live.*"

Ares blinked in confusion. Take it all back? What had gone on between them after Ares left her house last night?

Gethel reached inside Arik once more, and Limos muffled a cry with the back of her hand.

Again Arik screamed, a raw, animal sound that made Ares wince despite his years of war and death and destruction that should have made him immune to the sounds of suffering. But this went beyond normal suffering, and suddenly, Ares knew what soul-deep pain really meant.

Finally, Gethel reared back, flinging herself at Reaver. The moment her hand hit his chest, he shot upright, his breath heaving out of his lungs.

"Your souls were knocked into Arik," Gethel murmured, and very, very gently, she pulled the now motionless human into her arms and held him. Gethel, who had never been one to coddle anyone. Ares would have gaped if he wasn't so concerned about the guy.

"Is he . . ."

"He lives, but he's not the same." Gethel looked at Limos. "You'll have to discover his limitations and talents." Her mouth became a grim slash. "And yours. You and Reaver now share bits of Arik, as he shares bits of you." Gethel put a glowing hand to his forehead, and he woke, blinking drowsily.

"I feel like the morning after a bachelor party." Groaning, he sat up. When his gaze lit on Gethel, he barked out a curse. "*You.*" He fisted her tunic as if she couldn't destroy him with her pinky if she wanted to. "How could you dissolve my damned marriage without my fucking permission?"

Gethel narrowed her eyes and peeled his hand away. "I did no such thing. I did, however, save your life."

Ares winced at the not-so-subtle spanking as everyone turned to Limos, who had gone bright red. Glancing down at the snow, she nibbled her lip. "I . . . oh, shit. I might have . . . fibbed a little about the divorce."

"So we're still married?" When Limos nodded, still not looking him in the eyes, Arik let out a long, ragged breath.

"Thank God." He reached out and took Limos's hand. "We'll talk about this later. What the hell happened?"

"You almost died, human." Gethel stood, and to no one in particular, she said, "Take care of him," and then she was gone.

Arik looked over at Ares's motionless brother. "Hellhound?"

Ares nodded. "Yeah. We need to keep him like this for a while."

"How long?" Arik asked, and Ares wished he knew the answer.

"As long as it takes." Ares lifted Than into his arms. "But I suspect that he's going to have a nice, long rest."

Damage control. Shit . . . damage control.

Kynan repeated those words in his head as he sat with Regan, Val, Malik, Decker, and Lance at Aegis Headquarters, where he'd brought Regan immediately after getting the hell away from Thanatos. Just a minute ago, they'd gotten news of a massive disaster in Greenland.

"We're responsible for the deaths of all those people," Decker said numbly, his eyes glued to the laptop on the meeting room's table.

Val shook his head, but he looked just as shell-shocked as Decker. "There's no way we could have predicted how the Horseman would react."

"*Over*react." Lance snorted in disgust. "He went insane over getting laid. What the hell is that about? What kind of asshole freaks out about losing his virginity to a hot chick? Regan, you must have been a shitty lay."

Regan lunged across the table with a snarl. Val and

Kynan caught her before she could hurt herself or the new life she now carried, but they didn't bother stopping Decker, who slammed his fist into Lance's face and knocked the guy out of his chair and into the wall.

Decker planted his big booted foot on Lance's chest as he lay moaning on the carpet. "You ever speak about Regan like that again, and I'll shove this boot so far up your ass you'll be flossing with the laces."

"And don't talk about Thanatos that way." Regan wrenched free of Val and Kynan, but she sat back down instead of going for Lance. "He didn't ask for any of this."

Decker let Lance up, and the guy glared sullenly as he grabbed a paper towel from the coffee counter and held it to his bloody nose.

"So what now?" Malik eyed Regan as if she had an answer, but she just swallowed sickly.

"Damage control," Kynan said. "The Horsemen are going to view this as a betrayal, and rightly so, given the circumstances."

Damn. This should not have been this complicated. Their intel had indicated that the Horsemen, with the exception of Limos, were sexually active, so they'd assumed an easy fling for Regan, a quick and in and out with no complications.

Still, Kynan hadn't been comfortable with the pregnancy thing, and he'd hoped to be able to tell Thanatos about it after they determined how the child would save the world.

Now . . . they were all fucked.

Why the hell had Thanatos been a virgin? Religious beliefs? A personal vow? Shy penis? *Shit!*

"So how do we spin this with them?" Decker asked.

Kynan flopped back in the chair and stared blindly at the huge painting of a demon-angel battle on the far wall. "I'll go talk to them."

"I'll go with you," Decker said.

"No," Regan whispered. "You can't. Thanatos is..." She shuddered. "Just don't."

"She's right," Kynan said. "I'll go alone. It's not going to be fun, but at least they can't kill me."

"We'll stay here and pray," Val said. "Because they might not be able to kill *you*, but I looked up the records of what Limos and Reseph did to the Elders last time we betrayed them, and trust me, they're quite capable of killing the rest of us."

Thirty-five

They all went back to Ares's place. Thanatos was carried, and Arik was propped between Limos and Reaver, though Arik figured Reaver could have used the help more than Arik. He didn't know much about angels, but he kind of doubted they normally looked like they'd been run over by a tank and then shot out of its cannon. Arik had seen a lot of hangovers in his day, and he'd swear Reaver was coming off one hell of a bender.

After they'd settled Thanatos in one of the spare bedrooms with a hellhound guard to nip him if he stirred, they all came back into Ares's great room and stared at each other. No one seemed to know where to start. Not a shock, given that there was the matter of Limos's betrayals, The Aegis's hijinks with Regan, Thanatos's meltdown, and Reaver's...hangover.

For Limos's part, she still hadn't met Arik's gaze as she paced by the cold fireplace.

Ares, who stood next to the chair where Cara sat with Hal at her feet, crossed his arms over his chest and drilled a scowl into Reaver. "So. You going to tell us where you've been and why you haven't responded to any of our summons?"

"It's not your place to question my activities." The angel might look like hell on legs, but his lethal power wasn't diminished, and he still managed to become the centerpiece in an already grand room.

Limos stopped pacing. "Is it my place to question why you didn't come to the most important event of my life?"

Reaver jerked like his holy ass had been goosed. "You found your *agimortus*?"

"Yes, but that's not what I'm talking about."

"Then what?"

Her chin came up. "My wedding."

Reaver's sapphire eyes darkened like a stormy sea. "*To Satan?*"

"No," Arik said. "To me." He finally caught Limos's gaze and he hoped she got his silent message loud and clear. *We're married, and we'll stay that way, no matter what bullshit you pull.*

Him, bitter? Nah.

"I don't understand." Reaver's dull, limp hair brushed his robe as he turned back to Limos. "Marrying Arik won't negate your contract."

"It most certainly did." Limos gave a haughty sniff, as if offended that Reaver would dare question her. "When Arik removed my chastity belt and put his—"

"Okay." Arik cut her off before she could go into detail neither her brother nor an angel should hear. "He gets the picture."

Reaver grimaced. "Too clearly."

Limos looked down at her feet and then back up at Reaver. "I get that you're busy, and you have all those stupid rules to follow, but you know...there aren't many people I care about, and I don't have many friends...and I wanted you to be there."

"I'm sorry, Limos." The regret in Reaver's voice turned it to gravel. "Those responsible for keeping me away will pay. I promise you that."

Arik's phone buzzed in his BDU's leg pocket, and when he palmed it, Kynan's text flashed on the screen: *Will be at Ares's place in two minutes.*

Oh, this ought to be good.

He excused himself, leaving Limos and Ares to question Reaver on his whereabouts, but Arik wished them a silent good luck with that, because the angel didn't seem inclined to answer.

Arik met Kynan in the courtyard, cutting Ky off before the guy could get "hello" out of his mouth. "Do you know what you idiots almost did?"

The other man's expression remained passive, even though Arik had just jumped his shit. "I have no idea, but I'm guessing you're going to fill me in?"

"I'm talking about Than's Seal. Sound familiar? Do you know what was supposed to break it? Sex. His Seal was supposed to be broken by sex, so he's been celibate his entire life."

Kynan paled. "Wait...what? Regan said he was a virgin, but we didn't know why...oh, fuck."

"Yeah. Morons. You told me Regan was going to seduce Thanatos, but—" Arik broke off at the *behind you* gesture from Kynan, and sickly, Arik turned around to see Limos standing in the doorway, flanked by Reaver and Ares, her eyes sparking purple fire.

"You knew? All this time you knew why Regan was at Than's place, and you didn't tell me? Your lie could have caused the freaking Apocalypse!" She advanced, glaring at him with savage contempt that speared him right through the heart. "After all your bullshit about hating liars, you did it to me. You did it *to me*!"

Arik had no defense. Not even a lame, "You're one to talk," because while it might be true, the fact was that he was a hypocrite of epic proportions, and that was what this was about. Not his lie, not his omission. His hypocrisy.

"Well?" she demanded.

He didn't have a chance to answer, not that he knew what to say, because Cara hurried up to them . . . attempted to, anyway, since Hal kept trying to grab her shoelaces. "I just checked on Thanatos. I think you might want to see this."

Ares went bowstring taut. "Is the venom wearing off?"

"No, everything's fine. But . . . you really should come with me."

Ares shot Arik a *you're mine later* look, and Limos did the same. Man, Arik was in a metric fuckton of trouble, and all things considered, he'd really rather go up against Ares than Limos. He had to fix this. Had to fix it *now*.

He started after them, but Kynan grabbed his arm. "A little advice from one married man to another. You have to chase her. Women never forgive you if you don't. But give her a few minutes to calm down first." Kynan smiled wryly. "Trust me on this."

Arik's muscles twitched with the need to go after his woman, to explain the unexplainable and fix all of this shit between them. He wasn't going to feel solid with her until all of their dirty laundry was aired, and until he knew for certain that she would never try to get rid of him for his own good. They had to get past this, and even though he knew Kynan was right, Arik couldn't wait. He was a soldier, and his job was to destroy the enemy.

Right now, the enemy was his own stupidity.

He started forward again, but this time it was Reaver who stopped him. The angel stepped out of the house, seized the back of his neck, and frog-marched him over to Kynan as if Arik was an errant schoolboy.

"We're going to chat first," Reaver said, releasing Arik so both he and Kynan could get the *you've-been-bad-boys* lecture. "When did The Aegis decide to send Regan to Thanatos?"

"A few days ago," Kynan said. "Why? And you look like hell, by the way."

"I live for your opinion," Reaver drawled. "Now, what was the purpose of taking this action?"

"We recently found a scroll written by a Guardian who was an accurate Seer back in his time." Kynan shifted his weight a few times. "He...indicated that in order to save the world from Pestilence, an Aegi had to mate with a Horseman."

Reaver's eyes narrowed. "Where did you find this scroll?"

"An Aegis chamber Limos took me to."

"Ah." Reaver looked out at the sea surrounding the Greek island, his expression troubled, and Arik swore the guy was shaking a little. "Interesting, isn't it, that while I was being held outside of summoning range, Limos took you to a scroll that instructed you to do something every-one thought would break the Horseman's Seal."

"We didn't have any reason not to trust Limos. She said she found the chamber while looking for her *agimortus*. We didn't take action lightly or without researching the items we found in the chamber."

A lump of suspicion the size of a Gargantua demon sank into Arik's gut. Limos hadn't mentioned this chamber, hadn't brought up doing anything to help The Aegis recently. Was this yet another secret? Another attempt to start the Apocalypse?

No. He couldn't think that way. She'd told a lot of lies, but he believed she regretted them all, and if she'd done something to lead The Aegis astray, it hadn't been because she wanted to.

A breeze kicked up, ruffling Reaver's robe, and he tightened the sash before returning his attention to Kynan and Arik. "Since Than's Seal didn't break, no harm done, but the situation leaves a lot of questions."

"Like what will break Than's Seal." Arik blew out a frustrated breath. "Even *he* thought sex would do it."

Kynan's face took on an oddly green cast. "Ah… there's more."

Oh, Jesus. Hoping Kynan wasn't going to say what Arik thought he was going to say, he ground out, "What else is there?"

"It's Regan," Kynan blurted. "She's pregnant."

Absolute silence fell. And then Reaver stumbled backward, eyes burning blue fire. He let out an angry roar, and then he was gone.

Fuming, feeling like a damned fool, Limos followed Ares and Cara to the rear of the mansion. How could Arik have kept something so huge from her? This wasn't a, "Honey, no, that dress doesn't make your ass look fat," kind of thing. He'd known The Aegis had sent someone to betray them all, and he hadn't warned them. How long had he known? Had he been part of the decision?

Maybe, during their wedding ceremony, instead of admitting to how many other women he'd kissed he could have said, "Oh, hey, by the way, Regan is here to fuck your brother and I knew about it."

Yeah, that would have been good. How many people had died in Greenland because of his treachery? And what kind of consequences were yet to come?

And now, because of The Aegis, Thanatos was incapacitated, trapped inside his own head with only his rage as company.

He lay where they'd left him, on a king-sized bed in one of the smaller guest rooms. Someone had put sweat bottoms on him, and a blanket covered his upper body. A hellhound lay on the bed beside him, and judging by the look Cara gave the hound, Limos figured he was supposed to be on the floor. But really, one didn't tell a two-thousand pound, man-eating monster where to sleep.

"If we have to keep Than here long, he'll need an IV to keep him hydrated," Limos said, her voice betraying her anger so clearly that the hellhound bared its teeth as if she were a threat.

"We'll also take shifts to keep him company." Ares wrapped his arm around Cara's waist, and Limos swallowed, wondering if she and Arik would ever find that intimacy again. "What is it you're worried about?"

Cara gestured to Thanatos. "See for yourself."

This couldn't be good. They all eased close to their

brother, who looked as peaceful as if he was sleeping. Except his eyes were open. They stared upward, unmoving but aware. Limos tensed, knowing exactly what he was experiencing and how he felt. At least he was with family, and he knew no one would hurt him. He'd be kept comfortable and safe.

Cara tapped Than's foot. "Watch."

Instantly, Than reacted. Not his body...just his upper lip. And...holy hell...his teeth. His canines elongated into fangs a tiger would be proud of.

Ares stepped back, nearly knocking Limos over. "What the hell is that?" He turned to Limos. "Do you know?"

She couldn't tear her gaze away, even when Than's mouth went back to normal. "I have no idea. Is his Seal intact? Reseph...Pestilence...he grew fangs when his broke."

Ares peeled the blanket away to reveal Than's Seal, which, thankfully, was whole. But that didn't explain the carnivore hardware. Was Thanatos as confused as they were?

"These past few days have been interesting as hell," Ares muttered. "And by interesting, I mean fucked up."

"Yeah, and I'm part of that." Limos took a deep breath, knowing she had to do this and bracing herself for Ares's fury. "I'm so sorry for what I've done and all the lies I've told. I don't expect you to forgive me, and I understand if you hate me—" She choked up at that, because while she might understand it, she couldn't bear it.

And then she didn't have to. Ares hauled her up against him so hard her breath was knocked from her lungs.

"I don't hate you," he said, sounding a little choked

himself. "I hate what you did, and I hate that you lied for so long, but I meant it when I said I loved you no matter what. I was wrong to have taken that away from you and said you were as bad as Pestilence. Can you forgive me?"

Oh, God. *He* was asking for forgiveness? How stupid she'd been for ever doubting him. She'd been raised to believe that everyone was only a single word or a single act from hating and betraying you, and it had never occurred to her that love could truly be unconditional.

But then, no matter how angry she'd been at her brothers, she'd loved them. No matter how angry she was with Arik right now, he still held her heart. Why had she not figured all of this out before? Like, a couple of thousand years before?

"There's nothing to forgive, Ares," she whispered.

He squeezed her tight, and then gently set her aside. Relief made her legs a little wobbly until she looked over at Thanatos. He had so much to deal with on top of *her* lies.

She sank down on the mattress and took Thanatos's hand. "Hey. I know you can hear me. Everything is going to be okay. We can get Kynan to explain about Regan—" She broke off as Than's lip peeled back again, and there went the teeth.

This time, though, crimson spokes flashed in his yellow irises, and a scorching burst of heat came off his body. His tattoos writhed, the scythe on his neck slashing at the scorpion.

Taking a deep breath, she eased off the bed and backed away, but the banked rage in him continued to burn.

Looked like they not only had the mystery of why he was fangy, but it was also apparent that he was still a very, very angry Horseman, and that was never a good thing.

Thirty-six

Reaver stood atop Mount Megiddo and cursed. Cursed until clouds swirled above him in an angry black vortex, and then he cursed some more. He couldn't get to Heaven, not until his wings grew back. This was like being an Unfallen again, stuck between realms and practically powerless.

At least here he could call to his Heavenly brethren... assuming they'd answer. His body was full of marrow wine—but not enough. He craved it so bad he was shaking, and he either needed to score some more or get clean, and right now his brain was too pickled to consider the clean thing.

His scalp grew tight, and he turned as a strike of lightning torched the earth a few yards away. When it was gone, Harvester stood there with a burlap bag in her hand, her eyes glowing, her lips as blood red as the wine she'd forced down his throat.

"Someone's a little pissed."

Pissed didn't cover it, and it took every ounce of restraint Reaver had not to launch himself at her. "What have you done?"

Cocking her head, Harvester smiled at him. "You just found out why I kept you prisoner, I see." Thunder cracked, and rain pelted them with big, stinging drops. With a wave, she cast an invisible umbrella that shielded them both. "We couldn't very well have you telling The Aegis not to send anyone to fuck Thanatos, now could we?"

Some of his fury evaporated, replaced by a sudden suspicion. She didn't seem at all upset that Than's Seal hadn't broken, which told him she'd known it wouldn't. Ending the Horseman's celibacy hadn't been the goal, had it?

"How did you know that his Seal wouldn't break?"

"I don't know what you're talking about. Of course I thought it would break."

She was lying. But why? He looked up at the churning clouds and then back down at the evil fallen angel and realization dawned. "You know what Thanatos's *agimortus* is, don't you?"

"No idea."

"You lie." He lunged for her, but without his wings, she was faster, and his hand closed on empty air.

She stood three yards away, smirking. "I would never lie. I'm outraged that you would think that of me."

"*Outraged*, my holy ass." He ground his teeth. "How is it that you know about Thanatos's *agimortus* and I don't?"

"I'm special. You're an angel with no memory of his past and with especially dirty wings. Oh, wait, you don't have any wings at all, do you?" She reached into the bag she was holding. "Brought you something. Enjoy." She tossed a bottle at him, and he caught it one-handed before realizing he should have let it break apart on the rocks.

Marrow wine. The flask burned his skin, almost as if it were sinking roots into his palm. Rain began to pelt him. Harvester was gone.

The wine…he watched in horror as his body disconnected from his mind, watched as he uncorked the flask and lifted it to his lips.

Stronger than this. I'm stronger than this.

The words penetrated his brain, but not because they were true. It was because he'd said them before, and he'd been wrong. But when? Why? The hazy memory was about as substantial as a phantom and harder to pin down. But the fact that he had any recollection, no matter how fuzzy, was a miracle.

Maybe a touch of Arik's military-honed ability to recall important details was what had clung to Reaver when Gethel had separated his soul from the human's. Interesting.

A thousand bursts of pain shot through his hand, and he looked down to see that he'd squeezed the flask so hard it had shattered. Clay shards were embedded in his palm, wrist, and fingers. Marrow wine mingled with blood and rain and ran down his arm and puddled on the parched ground at his feet.

Part of him wanted to get down on his knees and lick the wine before it seeped into the dirt. Somehow, he resisted.

Harvester was not going to win again.

Harvester flashed back to her place, where Whine was waiting for her, head bowed, eyes downcast. She'd been in a shitty mood when she'd found Reaver at Mount Megiddo, where he'd been cursing up a storm. Literally. She hadn't wanted to see him again so soon after dropping him off, but orders were orders, and only a fool ignored Lucifer.

Feed his addiction, Lucifer had said. *Keep him sodden.* Easier said than done. Although she'd fed Reaver a steady diet of marrow wine while she had him in chains, he'd never asked for it, even when withdrawal tremors and fever set in. She'd stood nearby, wine in hand, waiting for him to beg.

Never once had he done so. She'd been forced to overpower him and dribble it into his mouth. Once he tasted the wine, he took it freely, but he'd possessed the incredible ability to never ask for it.

Such a proud, powerful angel.

She both admired and despised him for that.

Bitterness stung her tongue as she beckoned Whine to her. In a heartbeat he was before her, kneeling and kissing her feet. The scrape of his teeth on her skin infuriated her— the only time he was ever even a little careless in the way he touched her was when the full moon was rising in his native Hungary, which meant that she'd need to release him for three days in order for him to work off his warg energy.

Dammit. This day just kept getting better and better. Eons of planning was coming together and yet . . . it was so close to falling apart.

Arranging for the Aegis girl to get pregnant had been one massive gamble.

In nine months, that gamble would either pay off for Harvester or ruin her.

In nine months, the Apocalypse would either be averted . . . or it would break the world.

Thirty-seven

Arik stared at the empty space where Reaver had been, wondering when and if the world was going to get back to normal. His best guess amounted to *when hell freezes over*, and wasn't that a joke, because if Pestilence got his way, hell was going to be right here on earth.

"Dammit," Kynan said. "This is a mess."

"A mess?" Arik pivoted around. "Understatement of the century, don't you think? The Aegis is fucking lucky they didn't break Than's Seal with that little stunt."

"At least we were trying to do something to stop the Apocalypse," Kynan snapped. "The R-XR is sitting on its damned ass. By the time they act, it'll be too late."

The military had always been reactive rather than pro-active, just like the government, but on the opposite end of the spectrum, The Aegis had always leaped before it looked. But this was old news, not worth arguing about, and ultimately, Arik's anger wasn't directed at Kynan. It wasn't even directed at himself for keeping his knowledge about Regan away from Limos, though he was definitely kicking himself for that.

What it came down to was that Arik knew he had a decision to make, and it was one he never thought he'd have to face.

Kynan, who had always been able to read a situation as if he were two steps ahead of everyone, knew exactly what Arik was thinking. "You coming back to us, or not?"

"You going to make me keep secrets from my family?"

There was a long silence before Kynan sighed. "Man, I know where you're coming from. I'm a Guardian with demons for in-laws. I'm mated to a demon. My loyalties are tested every day."

"But?"

Ky's denim blue eyes drilled into Arik. "But you're in chin-deep with people who could turn on us hard if their Seals break. There are things we have to keep close to the vest."

"I get that, and I know Limos does too." His girl might be pissed right now, but she was far from stupid, and she understood the consequences if she went evil. "She's not going to ask anything she knows will compromise us if her Seal breaks. But the other things...things like tricking the Horseman into getting a Guardian pregnant? Yeah, you just keep that shit to yourself, because here's the deal—I'm not keeping anything from her."

Never again. Secrets and lies had nearly destroyed his relationship with her and her relationship with her brothers. Hell, they could *still* destroy everything. She hadn't come back yet, and he was beginning to wonder if she would.

Kynan cursed. "You know that if you were anyone else, we'd tell you to take a hike."

"I know. But even without all my training, demon-fighting skills, and ability to learn demon languages, I'm too valuable for either the R-XR or The Aegis to lose."

Neither organization would want to lose an intimate insider in the Horsemen's circle. The problem was going to be that as long as Pestilence owned his soul, Arik had to be careful where he went and who he was with. The fucker could sense him, and no way would Arik risk Pest popping in to Aegis Headquarters or some shit.

"I hate it when you're right." Kynan glanced at his watch. "Look, I gotta go. But we need you. We need you now more than ever. Think about it."

Arik didn't really need to think about it. If the pesky little Apocalypse thing hadn't been a concern, Arik might not have considered going back, but the world needed all hands on deck right now, and he wasn't going to turn his back on humanity.

"You're such a dick," Arik called out, as Kynan headed down the path toward the island's Harrowgate. "You know what my answer is."

Kynan didn't turn, merely shot him the finger over his back. "I know."

"Asshole," Arik muttered. He rubbed his temples and braced himself for the next confrontation.

Limos. And Ares. Not only did he get to explain why he'd kept a secret from them, but he got to tell them they were going to be an aunt and uncle. Something told him this wasn't going to be celebration-type news.

As he started for the front door, he wondered how many people would show up for his funeral.

"Hey, Arik."

Stiffening, Arik swung around to the owner of the deep voice. "Tav? What the hell are you doing here?" The blond Sem smiled sadly, and Arik's gut wrenched as he realized just how spot-on his last thought was. "You're here to kill me, aren't you?"

"Yeah."

A chill slithered up Arik's spine. "Why? Limos is out of her contract, so killing me is pointless."

"The Dark Lord is pissed about that, apparently."

"He should be. He lost out." He'd lost big time.

Shrugging, Tavin looked Arik up and down. "You look good. Freedom agrees with you."

"Thanks." Okay, so it was kind of weird to have a friendly chat with the man sent to kill him. "So."

Tavin blew out a long breath. "So."

"How do we do this?"

"Dunno." Tav looked genuinely perplexed, his sandy brows drawn into a deep frown over his blue eyes. "Never had to kill someone I liked before."

"We're quite the pair then, because I've never had anyone I like try to kill me." Arik ran his hand through his hair. "This kind of sucks."

"It's a douche-y situation, for sure."

Tavin reached beneath his jacket and removed a round metal disk, the edges of which looked sharp enough to remove a werewolf's head from its body with no effort. Which was what Arik guessed was going to happen to him.

"I'm sorry about this, Arik."

"I can't talk you out of it, huh?"

"If I fail, bad things happen to me." Tavin's voice had

gone monotone, which signaled a slide from friend into duty-bound soldier.

"And if you succeed, bad things happen to me."

Arik shifted his weight and casually released the holster strap that secured the pistol at his hip. Most demons weren't damaged by regular rounds, but he knew Sems were vulnerable to bullets. Besides, there was his old favorite saying about how firearms brought dignity to what would otherwise be just a vulgar brawl.

He was prepared to be very dignified. Not that he was opposed to vulgarity.

Tavin inclined his head, a sharp, respectful nod, and then it was on. Tavin moved like a phantom, all blur and silver shiny things. The round blade came at Arik with a *whoosh* of air, and he barely got his pistol free in time to use it to deflect the blade—which would have sheared the top of his skull off. As it was, it sliced through the barrel of his Beretta and knocked it from his hand.

Mother. Fuck.

Tavin flew at him, and Arik pivoted to meet the demon, who was a mass of blows and blades he must have pulled out of his ass. A million cuts sliced into Arik at once, as if he'd been tossed into a giant food processor. Hitting the ground in a tight roll, he whipped his stang out of his chest harness and sliced it across Tav's torso.

The demon yelped and reared back, but even as Arik jammed the silver end of the weapon into the Sem's shoulder, Tav shoved a nine-inch, jagged blade into Arik's gut. He heard the slushy sound of blood, felt the gristly resistance of muscle and organs being penetrated. Staggering agony took away his breath.

Somehow, he managed to jam his knee between Tavin's

legs, and the guy barked out a curse and doubled over. Panting, groaning, Arik stabbed the demon in the back with the stang and ripped upward, cutting a seam along his ribs. The demon screamed, spun, his eyes crimson, and sank his blade into Arik's chest.

Dizziness laid Arik flat. A black haze came over him, and damn, he was going to die, wasn't he? He'd lived through a month of torture in Sheoul, survived Pestilence, Satan, Thanatos, and *khnives*.

And this sex demon was going to kill him.

"Dickhead," he rasped.

Tavin's eyes went from crimson to gold, which meant he was only mildly pissed off now. When they returned to their normal blue, the guy would be level, but Arik doubted that would happen any time soon.

"I'm really sorry, human." Tavin shoved the blade home.

Directly into Arik's heart.

Pain. Arik thought he'd known every kind there was.

He'd been wrong.

Heart pain was a unique beast, a sharp, scorching sensation that made it impossible to even writhe in agony.

He lay under Tavin's heavy body, wishing he'd had a chance to make love to Limos before he died. Wishing he could have apologized to her. Wishing he could have made very, very clear that nothing she'd done in the past mattered to him.

The ache in Arik's heart had nothing to do with the knife buried in it. His pain was for Limos.

Tavin wrenched the blade out of Arik's chest and

pushed awkwardly to his feet, his hand slapped over his own gushing injury while Arik bled in the sand.

Or... wait. He wasn't bleeding. Lifting his head, he tested his fingers and toes. They all wiggled. He sat up, looked down, and hey, his injuries were closing up.

"What the—?" Tavin whirled around, launched the dagger, and buried it in Arik's throat.

Hurt like hell, but Arik yanked it out, and a curious zipping sensation went through him as the wound sealed.

"That's so cool." Arik patted himself down, didn't even look up when Tavin brought down a rain of little caltrops that landed on Arik, sticking to him like two dozen burrs.

They burrowed painfully into his skin in a bid to reach his vital organs. They were a nasty demonic weapon, but even as Arik cursed and tried to pry one from his shoulder, his flesh convulsed around them and pushed them out.

"Fuck." Tav stood in front of him. "Why won't you die?"

"No idea." Arik stood, and the little bone spurs dropped to the ground.

Tavin came at him again, this time with a curved blade aimed at Arik's neck. The demon wasn't screwing around anymore. Most things—even immortal things—couldn't survive decapitation. Arik ducked, swung, and managed to knock Tavin off course, but the dude was fast, and when he whirled, the silver blade filled Arik's vision.

He dove to the ground, sweeping up one of the spurs as he rolled. In a quick move, he launched the tiny weapon, catching the demon in the gut. Tavin hissed in pain and dropped the blade. Arik took instant action, grabbing the dagger and doing a replay of his high school football days with a tackle that put Tavin on his back.

Arik jammed the blade against Tav's throat. "You done?"

"Kill me," Tav rasped. "Or I have to keep trying."

The bone spur was going to kill him anyway, but it would be slow and painful as shit. Slitting Tavin's throat would be a mercy. But dammit, the guy had helped Arik at great personal risk by slipping him extra water and giving him an escape route from Sheoul. And then there was the mind thing.

Arik eyed the demon, whose skin had gone ashen and slick with sweat. "You healed my body, but you also healed my mind, didn't you? That's why I'm not a slobbering blob of PTSD."

Tavin's eyes shot wide. For a moment Arik thought he was going to deny it, but a massive shudder shook him, and he gasped, "I have...a limited...ability. Mother... was a...*pruosi*."

Pruosi. A species of demon that possessed off-the-chart mental abilities. So Tav had inherited a Seminus bodily gift from his sire, but also a mental one from his mother. Arik wondered what other gifts the demon was hiding.

And what information he might be hiding with them.

"What do you know about the *khnives* that were sent after me?"

"Nothing." Tav groaned, and a trickle of blood leaked out of the corner of his mouth. "But look...outside Sheoul for the...perpetrator." His pain-glazed eyes met Arik's. "*Khnives* are spies. No demon would...use them as...assassins. Too unpredictable."

Well, that news was disturbing as shit. Who outside of Sheoul wanted him dead?

Pounding footsteps vibrated the ground, and Limos and Ares were there, swords drawn and leveled at Tavin.

"I have it handled," Arik said. "Tavin tried to kill me, but for some reason, I'm not dying."

Ares whistled to one of his Ramreel servants, who was standing nearby. "Prepare the torture chamber."

Jesus. Horsemen definitely didn't mess around. He glanced at Limos, who glared at him, and he wondered if she was imagining Arik in the torture chamber next to Tavin. Arik tossed the blade into the sand and shoved to his feet. No one was going to be tortured, and no one was going to kill Tavin, either.

"Did you hear the part where I'm not dying? I got stabbed in the gut, throat, and heart." Arik rubbed his fingers over the skin on his neck. "Not that you'd know it."

"I'll be damned." Ares shoved his sword into its scabbard. "Gethel said some of Reaver and Limos would be left behind when she ripped their souls out of you. I'd say you got some pieces of immortality."

Tav, still lying on the ground, coughed, and blood sprayed. "I'm...off the hook if..." He sucked in a rattling breath. "...you're immortal."

Arik kneeled next to him and put his hand over the wound in the demon's abdomen. "He needs a doctor." Arik's medic training wasn't going to be worth jack shit in this situation.

"He tried to kill you," Limos snapped. "What he needs is a beheading."

"He helped me get out of Sheoul," Arik said quietly. "And helped me keep my sanity."

Ares swore. "I'll take him to Underworld General. Fucking demons and their fucking demon hospital..."

He gathered Tav in his arms, opened a gate, and was gone, leaving Arik and Limos to stare at each other. Arik was pretty sure she was still mentally fitting him for chains and hot pokers.

"You lied to me." She sheathed her sword, and he let out the breath he hadn't even realized he'd been holding.

"Yeah."

"Why?"

He could tell her it was to protect his colleagues and their relationship with The Aegis, and while that was true, he was going to go with the reason behind the lie in the first place.

"Because The Aegis believed that they could stop the Apocalypse. They did it for the sake of the world. I didn't participate in the decision, but I had to believe they were doing it for the right reasons." He paused, wondering how to break the rest to her. He decided on the bandage-removal method; do it fast. "Regan is pregnant."

Limos inhaled sharply. "Is it... Than's?"

"Yeah." He watched her warily, hoping she didn't blow like Thanatos had. That had been some scary shit, and an experience he never wanted to go through again. "One of the scrolls you led Kynan to indicated that if a Horseman and Guardian made a baby, the kid would save the world."

"Oh, God." Limos squeezed her eyes closed.

"You knew, didn't you?"

"No." Her eyes were bloodshot when she opened them again. "I mean, I didn't know about the scroll. But... I knew the chamber was a set-up."

"I suspected as much," he murmured. "I'm guessing Pestilence forced you?"

"Yes." She looked so miserable he wanted to sweep her

into his arms, but he didn't trust himself to stop there. Oh, he wanted to forget all of this and move on to something much more pleasant, but they had to do this. They had to clear the air between them once and for all.

"All of this is because I wanted to cover up my lies." Limos's voice trembled. "All of this is because of me, Arik. It's never going to end, is it?"

He couldn't stand it anymore. He had to touch her. Stepping close, he gripped her shoulders gently, but firmly. "It'll end, Limos. But tell me, right now . . . is there anything else you've been hiding? Anything at all?"

"No," she whispered. "You and my brothers know everything now. Well, they will, once I tell them about the chamber. And the baby."

Relief nearly turned Arik's muscles to noodles. They'd gotten past the lies and the secrets, and surely her brothers would forgive her, just as Runa—

Shame washed over him, and he nearly doubled over from the power of it. He'd kept so much from Runa. Yes, for her own good, but when Limos had done things for *his* own good, he'd been furious, because *he* could make his own choices.

Once again his hypocrisy became the air he breathed, and for a brief moment, darkness and self-loathing swallowed him.

"Arik?"

"I'm sorry, Limos." Pressure filled his chest cavity until he felt like he might explode. "God, what an ass I've been. All this time I've hated lies, hated people who tell them. But it was okay for me to do it in the name of protecting people like they were too fucking weak to handle the truth." Oh, man, his chest hurt. "My dad used to say

Runa was weak. He said she bruised easily. Cried easily. He called her a little suckling runt."

Limos put her hand on his shoulder, but he wheeled away, unable to bear comfort right now. Not when he didn't deserve it.

"I never thought I treated her like she was weak, but by keeping things from her, that's exactly what I did." He rubbed his sternum, but it didn't relieve the pressure at all. "And then I ran around hating everyone who lied and kept secrets, but shit…I think I didn't hate them. I think I've hated *me* all this time."

This time when Limos touched him and he tried to shake her off, she didn't budge. She clung to him even as he backed away, tried to peel her off. Hell, he even yelled at her to let him go, but she hung on like a cowboy on a bronco.

"Stop it!" she barked. "Arik!" She wrapped herself around him and buried her face in his neck, kissing and nuzzling. "Stop." She petted his hair, stroked his shoulders, and eventually, he fell back against a tree, letting it—and Limos—brace him.

"I'm sorry," he croaked. "I'm so sorry I was such an ass to you. You didn't deserve to be judged like that."

"Yes," she murmured against his skin, "I did. Without you, all of that stuff would still be weighing on me, and Pestilence might have won."

Gently, he pushed her back so he could look at her. "I don't understand."

"He wanted me to lie," she said. "He knows it's an addiction for me. But…you changed that, Arik. I *want* to tell you things. I hate keeping anything from you. You give me what lying and being self-destructive never could. I get an amazing rush from those things, but with you, I get that rush a million times more intense, and without the guilt. I love you so much. Please don't hate the person I love."

Arik's eyes stung. He wrapped his arms around her so tight she "oofed," and then he kissed her senseless. "We're done," he said into her ear. "We're done with the lies and the secrets and the idiotic fake divorce decrees, right?"

She pulled back and grinned. "We're done. You're never getting rid of me, Arik."

He was about to tell her that what she said went both ways when a gate popped open several yards away, and Ares stepped out. "Your assassin friend will be fine." He scowled. "Should have killed him, but whatever."

Limos went up on her toes and kissed Arik. "If he tries to kill you again, I promise he won't make it to the hospital."

"Aren't you all protective and cute." She huffed, and he chuckled as he pressed a kiss into her hair and inhaled her coconut scent. "Hey, Tavin did mention something about the *khnives* that attacked us. He thinks someone outside of Sheoul summoned them."

Limos frowned. "That's . . . not good."

There was a long stretch of silence as Ares caressed the hilt of his sword. "If this new player isn't a demon, then the forces working toward an Apocalypse are growing. We're going to have to start looking at those around us more closely."

A traitor. Ares was implying that there was a traitor in their midst, and as much as Arik wanted to rail against the idea, he couldn't. Not when even The Aegis itself had been compromised by one of its own a couple of years ago.

And hell, the Regan situation only reinforced Ares's words.

"Ares," Arik began, because this needed to be said, "I discussed this with Limos already, but I need to say it to you too. I swear I won't keep information from you again."

A shock of brown hair fell over Ares's forehead as he gave a brisk nod. "I'll hold you to it, human."

That was the thing about Ares; when he wasn't pissed, he was damned reasonable. Unlike Limos's other two brothers. Speaking of which...

"How's Thanatos?"

"Can we talk about it later?" Limos asked. "I want to go home. We haven't had a proper wedding night."

Ares groaned. "That's my cue. I have to do some Christmas shopping anyway."

Arik hugged Limos tight. "It seems weird that you guys celebrate Christmas."

"Reseph loved any excuse to celebrate and buy presents," Limos said. "Breaking the tradition would just make it that much more obvious that he's gone."

"Not to mention the fact that two of us are now married to humans," Ares said, "and you people come with a lot of baggage." A smirk curved his lips, and Arik realized that Ares was reacting to Cara, who had come up behind him with her hands on her hips.

"Are you calling me baggage?" Her tone was huffy, but her eyes glinted with an impish mischief.

In a quick, blur of a move, Ares whirled around, hauled Cara over his shoulder, and strode toward the house. "If the shoe fits."

Arik watched the couple until they were inside with

the door shut, and then he turned back to Limos. "What do you say I haul you off like a sack of potatoes too?"

Limos's smile was so sweet Arik thought he might get struck with diabetes. "You do that, and I'll kill you."

"Can't. I'm immortal now."

She sniffed. "Then I'll...deny you sex."

He laughed. "Now, see, I'd worry about that, except you want it as bad as I do."

"You want it bad?"

He stepped back from her just enough that he could rake his gaze down her body. "Oh, yeah. I want to take you in every way imaginable and keep you so sexed up that when you aren't in bed, all you'll be thinking about is getting back in it." He took in her lush curves, imagining how well they'd buffer his thrusts. "And that's just tonight's itinerary."

Her tongue came out to lick her lips, and he zeroed in on the action, his body hardening already. "Forget everything I said about killing you and denying you...and just take me home."

"What about Ares?" he asked. "We need to tell him about the chamber and the baby."

"Tomorrow," she said. "We've all been through enough hell for the day."

Grinning, he swept her up and tossed her over his shoulder. "Open a gate." When she squirmed in token protest, he spanked her lightly on her firm ass. "Open. Now."

A shiver stole through her, and a gate opened. "There. And Arik?"

"Yeah?"

"Spank me again."

Stepping through the gate, he did exactly that.

Thirty-eight

———

Finally, Limos was going to get what she'd always wanted. Yes, she'd lost her virginity in the technical sense. But not only had there been no finish, it had been done in anger and out of necessity. Now she'd lose her virginity in all the ways that mattered.

She stepped out of her master bathroom, her stomach fluttering madly. The sexy outfit she'd gotten for her wedding night... well, it was on the bathroom floor, where she'd left it after she'd put it on while Arik used the guest bathroom to shower. Of course he suggested that they shower together, but no, her idea of the perfect wedding night had always included her sweeping into the bedroom to greet her new husband and make his tongue roll out at the sight of her skimpy lingerie.

Unfortunately, she didn't sweep. And she wasn't wearing her wedding night outfit. When she'd looked at herself in the mirror, the gorgeous lingerie hugging curves and allowing peekaboo glimpses of skin, she'd realized that she'd never been naked, had always been wrapped in lies and that infernal chastity belt. Yet, here she was, covering herself up again.

She'd stripped, because she was going to her husband as a new woman, completely open to him in a way she'd never been, and in a way she would be only with him.

Arik looked up from lighting a candle, and his mouth dropped open. Awesome. He had a towel wrapped around his waist, but he let it fall, and the effect of his naked body on her was immediate. As she drank in the sight of his hard-cut pecs, rippling abs, and thick, jutting erection, heat flushed her skin, and liquid desire bloomed between her legs.

Limos's effect on him was just as obvious.

He didn't wait. In three strides he was in front of her and was kissing her with a desperation that made her pulse hammer crazily in her veins. His tongue stroked hers, thrusting in a blatant imitation of what they'd soon be doing. One of his hands dropped to cup her butt and haul her up against him, and a warm, sticky wetness smeared her belly as his erection pushed into it.

This was all so new to her, and she reached between them to run her finger over the little slit in the smooth cap. She played a little, exploring, loving how Arik's breath hitched.

Slowly, reverently, Arik lowered her to the bed. "I fantasized about you," he breathed against the shell of her ear as he stretched his big body over her. "When I was in that cell. When I slept, I dreamed about this."

"Yeah?"

His hands glided up her waist and ribs to her breasts. "Yeah."

"Was I good?"

"The best."

A tremor went through her, a tiny shiver of hesitation. "What if I'm terrible at sex—"

He cut her off with a kiss. "Shh," he murmured against her lips. "Let me take care of you. I'll always take care of you."

"Who can argue with that," she sighed, as he blazed a trail of fiery kisses along her jaw and down her throat. Goose bumps fanned out across her skin from every point of contact with his lips.

His hands caressed and massaged, and as he kissed his way lower, his fingers teased her nipple, each stroke sending little electric sparks through her body. Dizzying sensation drew her into a vortex of passion that intensified when one hand slid to her butt to lift her against his erection.

"Now, Arik," she groaned. "Don't tease."

"I'm not teasing, sweetheart." He dipped his head and took her sensitized nipple into his mouth. When she cried out in sheer pleasure, he lifted his head. "I'm making sure your first time is everything you've ever dreamed of."

She arched, trying to take him inside. "It already is."

A lazy smile curved his lips as he pressed his weight down on her. "Not so fast."

"But I'm dying." That was the whiniest thing she'd ever said, but she was so ready for this experience, and she was aching for a release that only two people could have. Too many years of self-gratification had made her impatient.

"Tell you what." He dragged his tongue over her sternum and down to her navel, crawling backward as he went. "I'll take the edge off for you. You good with that?"

"If you mean what I think you mean, I'm very good with that."

He raised his face, his eyes hooded but overflowing with hunger. "And I'm good *at* that."

Before she could tease him about being full of himself, he scooted off the bed to kneel, hooked her thighs with his forearms and dragged her to him so her ass was nearly hanging off the end of the bed. His thumbs spread her wide, leaving her vulnerable and nervous. Instinct kicked in and she automatically tried to close her thighs, but Arik surged forward, blocking her move with his broad shoulders.

"Can't wait," he whispered, and lowered his mouth to her sex.

She groaned as his tongue swept from her core to her clit, and when he reached the top, he paused, leaving the flat of his tongue where it was. He watched her as if she was a treasure, as if every one of her reactions was the world to him, and she swore their eyes were locked for a good sixty seconds before he lowered his head and licked her again. And again.

Eyes closed, she bucked, her body unaccustomed to so much incredible stimulation. Arik gripped her tighter, holding her against him. His breath was hot, his tongue wet, and just as she was about to come, he eased up.

"You...you said no teasing." She spoke through panting breaths, her hands fisted in the sheets.

Arik nuzzled her, planting soft kisses at her center. "This isn't teasing. It's the warm up." He slipped a finger inside her, and she came off the mattress.

"Oh...oh, God." She cried out as he added another finger and began to pump them while his tongue circled her clit. "Yes," she breathed. "Yes...oh, yes, right there..."

Her hips rolled and rotated as she followed the path of his tongue, trying to get it just where she wanted it, but he knew, was teasing out her pleasure, and just as she was about to scream in delicious frustration, he latched onto the swollen knot of nerves and sucked. His fingers thrust deep and did a twisty thing, and her release detonated like a bomb.

She came apart in a blinding explosion, and Arik worked her through it, his touch gentling as her sensitivity heightened. Then, in a delightfully sinful move, he feathered his tongue in super fast strokes back and forth over the slick flesh just above where his fingers were pumping, and she went off again, cresting harder than before.

As she came down, Arik rose up, pressing the blunt tip of his hard cock against her entrance. She arched, wanting him inside her. *Needing* him inside her.

He denied her at first, bending over to kiss his way back up her body as he moved them both more fully onto the mattress. Carefully, he mounted her, settling between her legs.

"You're so beautiful." His words were as whisper soft as his lips as he brushed them over hers.

Deepening the kiss, he slowly pushed inside her. His shaft filled her in one smooth, unrushed stroke, and when he was fully seated, he went still.

"Are you okay?"

"Yes," she murmured. "Oh, yes."

He let out a shuddering breath, closed his eyes, and began to move. "Damn...you feel good."

So did he, but words escaped her. All she could do was cling to him and marvel at the wonderful feeling of two joined bodies. Bearing his weight seemed like an indulgence, one she wanted to experience every day. Twice a day. More, if she had her way.

She ran her hands up and down his back, exploring the hills and valleys of his flexing muscles. Next to her, his arms were taut, his big veins standing out starkly under tan skin. A throaty growl of possession ripped from his chest, and when his nostrils flared, his lips parted, and another guttural sound escaped him, she knew he was close.

Between her legs, sensation built with every thrust. His hips moved faster, stroking her higher, hotter. He reached down to lift her thigh more fully up on his back, and she felt the change in depth as a lightning bolt of pleasure. She reveled in the power of his thrusts, his skill, his ability to know exactly how and where to touch her to wring intense pleasure from her.

His moan joined hers, and then she was coming, her body shuddering, her legs squeezing. Her sex clenched him, each ripple of her climax riding the hard length of his shaft and adding amazing layers to her orgasm.

"Limos." He gasped her name, and his entire body stiffened and jerked. The tendons in his neck stood out in stark ecstasy as hot jets pulsed inside her.

Together they rode the frenzied storm, their straining bodies finding a rhythm with equal give and take, the way she'd always imagined being with a man. When the tempest passed, it was as if Arik's bones had turned to rubber, and he collapsed on top of her. They lay there in the aftermath, panting, sweating, and yes, this had been so worth waiting for.

"Well?" Arik rasped. "Was it all it's cracked up to be?"

She grinned. "If you're asking if it was good, it was." She lost the smile. "You believe me, right?"

He rolled to the side to keep from squishing her, though in truth, she hadn't minded his weight. "Sweetheart, I'll never doubt you again."

"Then I want you to know that I'm glad it was you." She angled herself toward him and cupped his cheek. "I know it wasn't by choice that I had to wait for my first time, but I'm glad it happened that way."

He rubbed his face against her palm like a purring cat. "Well, now you have a lot to make up for."

"Mmm. I can't wait." She smoothed her hand down his chest and over his abs. Lower...lower, and she was pleasantly surprised to discover that he was ready to get started.

He groaned. "I think I've created a monster."

"I think you can handle it." She rubbed his shaft, loving how it was swelling at her touch. "I have faith in your ability to satisfy my every need."

"Is that so."

"It's so." Throwing her leg over him, she pushed up so she was straddling him, and he watched her with half-lidded, curious eyes. "Arik?"

"Yeah."

"Thank you."

His hands slid up her calves to her thighs, leaving tingles in their wake. "For what?"

"For turning my wildest dreams into reality."

One eyebrow raised, and he got a naughty gleam in his eye. "Wildest? Because I can tell you that we haven't even begun to get wild."

She shivered with appreciation. "Then what are we waiting for?"

In a surprisingly quick motion, Arik gripped her waist and flipped her, coming down on her back with his mouth to her ear. "We're not waiting another minute." His teeth clamped down on her earlobe, and she sucked air at the tiny pinch of pain. "You ready?"

"Ready," she breathed. She had, after all, been waiting for this for five thousand years.

And it had been worth every minute.

A Demon-Slayer, a Lethal Rider,
a Prophecy, an Unborn Child—
Can they save the world, or is this
a recipe for disaster?

Please turn this page
for a preview.

Lethal Rider

Available in June 2012

One

Regan Cooper was going to die.

She knew it as sure as she knew the sky was blue. Knew it as sure as she knew the baby inside her was a boy.

Knew it as sure as she knew the baby's father would be the one to end her life.

Screaming, she bolted upright in bed, her eyes focusing on the glow of the nightlight in the bathroom. It took a second to realize she was awake, safe and secure inside The Aegis's Berlin headquarters instead of in the middle of a nightmare.

The dream had come to her again, the one where she saw herself lying on the floor and covered in her own blood. Thanatos, known to much of the human population as Death, Fourth Horseman of the Apocalypse, knelt next to her, blood coating his hands, dripping from his pale hair, and splashed on his bone armor.

She took a deep, calming breath, forcing herself to

relax. Thanatos couldn't touch her. Not here, in the apartment complex deep below the headquarters building that housed the twelve Elders who ran the ancient demon-hunting organization. Most of the Elders used their apartments only when they came to Germany for Aegis business, but Regan had called this spartan apartment home for years, and despite the fact that she was due to give birth in a month, she hadn't done a single thing to prepare for the baby. There would be no decorating, no toys, no cribs.

She'd always hated pastels anyway.

Her hand trembled as she rubbed her belly through the cotton fabric of the maternity nightgown, hoping the baby would stay asleep. He was one hell of a kicker, and her organs were still recovering from his last round of hackeysack.

There was a tap at the door, followed by a softly spoken, "Regan? You okay?" The door pushed open a crack, spilling light inside the room, and Suzi, the Guardian who had been tasked to stay with Regan at night—as a precaution in case some Big Bad somehow made his way inside HQ—peeked in. "You shouted in your sleep again."

Regan offered a shaky smile as she flipped on the bedside lamp. "Just another bad dream."

Her hand fell to the bit of parchment next to the lamp, and she allowed herself a moment to smooth her fingers over the inked lettering. The Latin words were a prayer of sorts, but that wasn't where Regan found comfort. No, as an empath with limited but powerful abilities, she could feel the emotions of the person who put the ink to the skin, and this particular bit of writing had been penned while the author was feeling serene. Regan had kept the page with her for years, and she'd needed it more than ever over these last few months.

Suzi entered, her compact, muscular body moving smoothly to the tiny bureau of drawers on the opposite wall, where a glass and pitcher sat on a tray. "Did you have them before?" Water gurgled as she poured. "You know, before you were pregnant?"

"Yes." The lie slipped easily off Regan's tongue, because while she might not have dreamed of her death before her pregnancy, she'd suffered nightmares that reflected the reality of her daily life.

As a demon slayer, she'd had some really bad days.

Suzi's messy mop of blond hair bounced on her shoulders as she brought Regan the water and sank down on the bed next to her.

"Drink," she said, nudging Regan's hand up, as if she were a toddler. Everyone treated her as if she were made of glass, as if women hadn't been getting pregnant for thousands of years and surviving just fine.

But not everyone got pregnant with a child that could save the world.

Maybe.

She had to remember the *maybe* part, because the thing was, The Aegis had been duped into believing a child born of a Horseman and a Guardian could stop the Apocalypse. Now there was a scramble to discover what role this baby *would* play in the grand scheme of things, especially because they were pretty sure the child was Thanatos's *agimortus*—the key to breaking his Seal.

"Can I get you anything else?" Suzi asked. "Warm milk? A sandwich? Soup?"

This time, Regan's smile was genuine. Suzi was one

of the toughest warriors Regan knew, so it was amusing to see her so attentive and nurturing. Then again, Suzi hadn't always been a demon slayer. Only five years ago, at the age of sixteen, she'd been an Olympic-level gymnast. That was before she'd been introduced to the paranormal world when she'd stumbled upon her coach eating a man outside the gym where she trained. Turned out that her coach had been a demon with a taste for vagrants.

"Thanks, but I'm going to read for a little while." She glanced at the bedside table where her stack of ancient tomes from The Aegis's extensive library sat next to an assortment of snacks. "And I have enough crackers to last me a month if I get hungry."

"I could fetch you more books," Suzi offered. "Or run a bath for you? Put a movie in the DVD player?"

Regan held up her hand. "Okay, what's going on? You're never *this* willing to do nurse work. You're nervous. Why?"

A pink blush crept into Suzi's cheeks. "It's nothing—"

"Tell me."

Suzi looked down at her hands, and when she looked back up, the dim bedside light emphasized dark crescents beneath her hazel eyes. "We just lost contact with two of our Australian cells. The reports from the other two are...grim."

"Dammit," she breathed. "Countries are falling like flies." When Suzi averted her gaze, a dark suspicion rose up in Regan. "What are you not telling me?"

"You know you're not supposed to be worrying about the news—"

"Dammit, Suzi, I'm not an invalid. That little incident was months ago."

The *little* incident hadn't been so little. While watching a news report about the loss of Iceland to demons, Regan had suffered abdominal pain and bleeding so severe that for days there'd been fear she'd lose the baby. Or her life.

Aegis doctors hadn't been able to administer any medications, since oral drugs came back up within seconds, and no needles could penetrate her skin. Apparently, the baby wanted no part of modern medicine.

The physicians and her fellow Elders had decided that bed rest and a complete block of upsetting news was the best thing for Regan and the baby, so Regan had been kept in the dark about the goings-on in the world. Oh, she caught snippets here and there, but for the most part, everyone had been careful to not say much.

"Suzi?" Regan prompted. "The baby could be born today and be fine. I was planning to talk to the Elders in the morning so I can get back into the swing of things. So tell me what's going on."

Suzi nodded. "It's not just Australia. You know about Iceland and New Zealand, but over the last couple of months, the world has lost almost all island nations. Greenland still stands—we figure that's because it's where Thanatos lives. And Great Britain has been repelling demons with help from Europe. But..." She inhaled a shaky breath, and Regan swore her heart stopped beating. "Taiwan is lost. Madagascar, part of Norway, much of Malaysia. And last week, Japan fell under the control of Pestilence's forces."

"Oh, my God," Regan rasped. "What else?"

"Demons are moving across Africa at an alarming rate, and we're getting reports of massive attacks in Canada, Alaska, and dozens of regions in Asia."

Water sloshed onto Regan's hand, and she had to grip her glass with both hands to keep it from shaking. "What do the Elders say about this?"

"According to their calculations, which have been confirmed by the R-XR...the entire planet will be overrun by demons within a month. They think...they think Pestilence is trying to time his takeover with the baby's birth."

The glass in Regan's hand shattered.

The Aegis had been trying to save the world with this baby, but it was looking like instead, they may have doomed it.

Two Weeks Later...

The only thing worse than being paralyzed and trapped inside your own skull, unable to move or speak, was being kept like that by your own brother and sister.

For eight and a half endless, insanity-inducing months, Thanatos, fourth Horseman of the Apocalypse, had been kept in a bed with nothing but a TV for company. Well, he had a hellhound lying next to him twenty-four seven, but only to bite him if the paralyzing hellhound saliva his brother and sister injected him with wore off. And sure, his sister, Limos, third Horseman, and Ares, second Horseman, hung out with him, but Ares wasn't all that talkative.

Limos was a chatterbox, but Than didn't really give a shit about what color nail polish she'd put on that morning or how she and her husband, a human named Arik, were planning a European honeymoon after the threat of Apocalypse was over.

And seriously, a honeymoon? Wasn't it a little late for that? And it wasn't as if Limos didn't live on an island paradise anyway, so every freaking day was a honeymoon for them.

Bitter much, Than-boy?

Yeah, there might be some jealousy there. Because as sick as it sounded, the one thing that had kept Than sane over the thousands of years he'd been alive was the fact that his brothers and sister were as alone as he was. But now Ares and Limos were both married and happy, and he was left paralyzed, miserable, and ripping a massive hatred for the female who'd put him here.

Regan.

Ever since he'd been cursed to be the Horseman who was doomed to become Death when his Seal broke, he'd believed that his Seal was his virginity. He'd guarded his dick like it was the freaking Hope diamond. He might have been an unpinned grenade ready to blow with sexual need, but dammit, he'd kept himself all virginal and shit.

Until Regan came along, with her seductive body, her devious plot, and her drugged wine. She'd managed to get him naked, get him immobilized, and get him off. The why of it still wasn't clear, since not once, in all of Limos's and Ares's ramblings, had they brought up the Aegis Guardian. And the fact that she was a Guardian, one of the human warriors who existed to rid the world of demons, only made her actions more mystifying.

Guardians did not want to start the Apocalypse, so either she hadn't thought that fucking him would break his Seal, or she had known and was secretly working against The Aegis.

So if she hadn't known... why had she gone to

extremes to get him in bed? As a larger-than-life legend, he might have starfucker appeal, and sure, he knew he was handsome, but resorting to drugs and her supernatural ability just to get him in bed?

Fury slithered through him, as hot as the lust he'd felt when he'd been beneath Regan, her wet heat clenching around his cock. God, it had been good. For so long he'd fantasized about being with a female, had imagined all the ways he'd take her. His favorite fantasy had always been with her on all fours and him mounting her from behind, his chest sealed to her back by their sweat, his weight holding her steady for his thrusts.

That position had been his earliest memory of sex, when he'd been a boy living in a pre-Druidic tribal society. He'd witnessed a fertility ritual, a circle of chanting adults surrounding a couple mating the way the village dogs did it. Oh, he'd heard sex before—their single room dwelling allowed for no privacy for his parents—but he'd not witnessed what went on between a man and a woman.

The image had stuck with him after thousands of years, and it had become the mainstay of his fantasies. For these past months, when his mind had drifted to sex, Regan had been that female on her hands and knees.

His cock jerked in response to the direction of his thoughts, pissing him off. His dick had no business getting hard for her, and on his arm, his stallion, Styx, kicked, sensing his master's emotions. The horse, currently in a tattoo-like form, had been stuck on his skin, as paralyzed as Than had been—

Wait. His cock was hard, his horse was stirring... which meant the hellhound venom was wearing off.

Thanatos's heartbeat went double-time as hope shot

through him. Maybe his siblings were finally allowing him to be free. Oh, man, if so...he had serious plans. First, he was going to kick Limos's and Ares's asses. Then he was going to have sex. Lots and lots of sex.

Before, avoiding sex hadn't been difficult. Sure, it hadn't been pleasant, but it had been doable, mainly because he hadn't known what he was missing. But now he knew, and his body craved it almost as much as it craved revenge.

The door creaked open. Ares's heavy footsteps were accompanied by Limos's whisper-light ones and the click of hellhound claws on the floor as the mutt who'd been babysitting him got to his feet to great the newcomers.

"Hey, bro," Limos chirped, as if Thanatos was just hanging out for fun. His hands began to clench, but quickly, he locked up his muscles, forcing himself to stay still.

Ares changed the channel on the TV they'd mounted above his bed. "Sorry about that," he grunted. "The mutt must have stepped on the remote and changed the channel. A cubic zirconia-fest on the Home Shopping Network couldn't have been too exciting."

Oh, no, really. I was just thinking about how great a gold filigree necklace and teardrop earrings would look on me, and at seventy-five ninety-nine plus shipping, it's a goddamned steal. But damn, I missed the deal because, oh, that's right, I'm fucking frozen.

Limos's hand came down on Than's biceps, and he struggled to keep from twitching. "Hey...look...we have to tell you something." Her voice was low and serious, and shit, this couldn't be good. "I know you can probably feel the disruption in the world, and it's gotta be making you crazy."

Crazy? Try ceiling-licking, rabies-frothing, dish-ran-away-with-the-spoon in-fucking-sane. Limos and Ares had been keeping him up on Pestilence's exploits, but they hardly needed to. Thanks to his curse, Than could feel mass casualties around the globe, was drawn to them like a junkie to heroin. Obviously, being paralyzed had put a stop to his ability to travel to them, but the pull was still there, swirling around his insides like smoke from a crematorium.

"It's about to get worse," Ares said. "Pestilence's plagues have caused war and famine and death all over the globe. It's why we haven't been around much. We've been spending way too much time at the sites of the worst of it."

Limos and Ares suffered the same curse as Than; Ares was drawn to scenes of large-scale battles, and Limos was tugged to famines. And yeah, Than had noticed that they hadn't been around all that much to keep him entertained. At least Cara, Ares's wife, had been around. She read to Thanatos a lot, and he didn't think he could ever thank her enough for that.

So why is it about to get worse? He wanted to scream at them, could feel his left hand, which was concealed at his side, begin to curl into a fist.

"The battles and death and famine have poisoned several nations. You knew that before...well, before you were paralyzed."

You mean, before you paralyzed me and left me here to rot?

"Last week, Pestilence claimed Australia in the name of Sheoul."

Oh, shit. Demons who were normally bound to

Sheoul—what humans called hell—could now occupy Australia. A country that size could host millions of demons and would allow for them to set the stage for a massive global attack.

What about the humans?

Limos, who had always been in sync with his thoughts, answered as though she'd heard him. "Any humans who didn't evacuate are . . . lost."

"We got a few out." Ares's voice was grim. "Kynan, Limos, Arik and I got a few."

"It's bad," Limos said. "But the good news is that The Aegis found a way to close the hellmouths. It's temporary . . . the magic they're using is being eaten away by demon countermagic, but it's slowed mass demon movement." She patted his arm. "Be patient, Than. Only a couple of weeks left to go, and we'll release you."

A couple of weeks? Why then?

He heard the sound of shattering glass, and then Cara's shout for Ares, and instantly, his brother and sister swept their fingers over the crescent-shaped scars on their throats, activating their armor. Limos's Samurai armor covered her body as Ares's boiled-leather armor snapped into place. They tore out of the room, the hellhound, Hal, at their heels.

Thirty seconds later, there was the sound of boots, the creak of the bedroom door . . . and then, Hades's ugly mug was in Thanatos's face.

"Hey, bro. You in the mood for a rescue?"

Rescue? Fuck, yeah. And as soon as the paralysis wore off, he had a certain Aegi to visit.

Find out more about Forever Romance!

Visit us at
www.hachettebookgroup.com/publishing_forever.aspx

Find us on Facebook
http://www.facebook.com/ForeverRomance

Follow us on Twitter
http://twitter.com/ForeverRomance

NEW AND UPCOMING TITLES

Each month we feature our new titles
and reader favorites.

CONTESTS AND GIVEAWAYS

We give away galleys, autographed copies,
and all kinds of exclusive items.

AUTHOR INFO

You'll find bios, articles, and links to personal websites
for all your favorite authors—and so much more.

GET SOCIAL

Connect with your favorite authors, editors, and
other Forever fans, and share what's important to you.

THE BUZZ

Sign up for our monthly romance newsletter,
and be the first to read all about it.